$23.95

2008

ALTADENA LIBRARY DISTRICT
3 9270 00293 9456

MAR 1 3 2007

DATE DUE

APR 5 2007 MAY 2 7 2007	
JUN 0 6 2007 JUL - 6 2007	
SEP 2 3 2008	
MAY 2 2009	
2 9 2009	

DEMCO, INC. 38-2931

D1022347

FIC
WAL

MoonPies and Movie Stars

Amy Wallen

70630538

Viking

VIKING
Published by the Penguin Group
Penguin Group (USA) Inc., 375 Hudson Street, New York, New York 10014, U.S.A.
Penguin Group (Canada), 90 Eglinton Avenue East, Suite 700, Toronto, Ontario, Canada M4P 2Y3
(a division of Pearson Penguin Canada Inc.)
Penguin Books Ltd, 80 Strand, London WC2R 0RL, England
Penguin Ireland, 25 St. Stephen's Green, Dublin 2, Ireland (a division of Penguin Books Ltd)
Penguin Books Australia Ltd, 250 Camberwell Road, Camberwell, Victoria 3124, Australia
(a division of Pearson Australia Group Pty Ltd)
Penguin Books India Pvt Ltd, 11 Community Centre, Panchsheel Park, New Delhi – 110 017, India
Penguin Group (NZ), Cnr Airborne and Rosedale Roads, Albany, Auckland, 1310 New Zealand
(a division of Pearson New Zealand Ltd)
Penguin Books (South Africa) (Pty) Ltd, 24 Sturdee Avenue,
Rosebank, Johannesburg 2196, South Africa

Penguin Books Ltd, Registered Offices:
80 Strand, London WC2R 0RL, England

First published in 2006 by Viking Penguin,
a member of Penguin Group (USA) Inc.

10 9 8 7 6 5 4 3 2 1

Copyright © Amy Wallen, 2006
All rights reserved

Publisher's Note:
This is work of fiction. Names, characters, places, and incidents either are the product of the author's imagination or are used fictitiously, and any resemblance to actual persons, living or dead, business establishments, events, or locales is entirely coincidental.

ISBN 978-0-670-03817-6

Printed in the United States of America
Set in Bembo
Designed by Spring Hoteling

Without limiting the rights under copyright reserved above, no part of this publication may be reproduced, stored in or introduced into a retrieval system, or transmitted, in any form or by any means (electronic, mechanical, photocopying, recording or otherwise), without the prior written permission of both the copyright owner and the above publisher of this book.

The scanning, uploading, and distribution of this book via the Internet or via any other means without the permission of the publisher is illegal and punishable by law. Please purchase only authorized electronic editions and do not participate in or encourage electronic piracy of copyrightable materials. Your support of the author's rights is appreciated.

To Mom and Daddy

In memory of
Genevieve Cleo Sims Wallen Freeman Williams Rudman
"Genie"

ACKNOWLEDGMENTS

Ruby would consider it proper to write a good bread-and-butter note to all those folks who helped, and Loralva would invite everyone to the Idyll-On-Up and serve Lone Star on the house.

Much appreciated:

My family: Mom and Daddy, who passed on the song that's in my ear and enough fodder for a rodeo. Suzanne, who gifted books, shared laughter, and believes in magic. Marty, who told me I should read all of Shakespeare before seventh grade (I didn't). Linda, for rolling her eyes at Martin.

Provocateur Judy Reeves who served prompts and nooners on Tuesdays at The Writing Center on Third Street—that old bordello with the stories eking out of the walls. All teachers give, but Judy gives in Maersk shipping container–size amounts.

Janet Fitch, who showed me how to wrestle my writing to the ground until it cried, "Gravitas!"

Meredith Resnick, who started as a writer friend and grew to be the kind of friend who mulls *all* things.

Judi Hendricks, for always showing up, never giving up.

The Journeymen (I preferred the moniker Janetors): Lisa Loop, Beverly Magid. Denise Nicholas, Lavina Blossom (for driving one third of the time), Rita Williams (fellow cowgirl), Judy Reeves (There you are again! You won't stop giving.), Victoria Clayton-Alexander, Steve Tash, and Emil Wilson.

Wednesday Night Writers for sharing your own fabulous stories and for bringing your dogs: Anita Hettena, Donna Marganella (for lending me her keen eye when my own brain had had enough.), Frank DiPalermo (for filling me in on how showbiz works), Eber Lambert, Karma Still (for pointing out that MoonPies are more than a snack), Kelli Ochoa (a Flannery Teammate), Lynda Riese, and Ruth Roberts.

James Spring, whose tattoo changed the rules.

Emil Wilson, again, for making it all a game and listening while I rearranged those bales of hay on the *Titanic*.

Ann Poppe for reading one of those drafts that really would have been better left in the dark soggy basement of a writer's mind. Richard Opper and Ann both for turning tears into wine.

Jill Hall for keeping the Brown Bag fires lit and propping me up in front of them.

My adroit agents, Meg Ruley and Christina Hogrebe at the Jane Rotrosen Agency, for appreciating pink fluff and passing out a Texas-size dose of MoonPies. Moo!

My editor extraordinaire, Katherine Carlson, who tasted MoonPies for the first time and devoured them with gusto.

With special gratitude I want to thank Eber Lambert, who without his wit and love I'd still be trying to finish this book and who for a long time to come I will be laughing, writing, puzzling, and turning many pages with. Thanks for pointing out the twig.

MoonPies and Movie Stars

The Butter Maid

Ruby leaned down, pinched the rattlesnake behind the jaw, flipped it over and milked its venom sacs. Its rattler buttons ticked like a Timex gone haywire. She reached for the deadbolt on the back door. The snake's tail flopped and the rattler buttons shook. The slick scales felt loose between her fingers, so she tightened her grip, enraging the rattlesnake even more. Once she got the door open, she flung the rattler with all her might, hoping it would land in Oklahoma. It flailed and flipped in midair, then hit the ground with a thud and a cloud of dust. Like a shot, it took off in the opposite direction, under the barbed wire fence that divided her property from Earl Glidden's back pasture.

Those damn rattlesnakes snuck into the back pinsetter room of the Devine Bowl every chance they could get. The cool concrete in the hot summer was just too inviting. But Ruby didn't have time for that kind of business this morning. She had gone back to that musty room in the first place to collect the cardboard box with *V&H Wedding* scrawled in purple magic marker on the side in her daughter Violet's curlicue handwriting. She found the box up on the top shelf and by climbing onto the mechanical workings of the bowling alley's pinsetters, she was able to lift it down from the shelf and set it on the concrete floor where the snake had previously lay prone.

The alley's dusty inner workings made her nose twitch. As she opened the cardboard flaps, a wad of tulle spilled out and she brushed it aside. Beneath it sat four rolls of pale purple crepe paper, which wouldn't be nearly enough. Luckily, she'd bought more. Rifling through the rest she found ten white, fold-up honeycomb bells; purple satin ribbon already tied into bows, but now flat as an armadillo crossing Highway 90; and an opened package of paper doilies. Piled on the very bottom of the box, in neat stacks, were lavender paper napkins. Picking one up, she turned it over to see the silver embossing:

Violet & Harley
July 10, 1966
True Love Forever

Biggest lie ever told, Ruby said to herself. She quieted her mind from going down that road and steadied herself with a memory of her dark-haired Violet in the white, high-necked gown instead. Ruby'd been the one who wanted the napkins—she thought it would make the event more sophisticated. She'd had to order a minimum of one thousand from the wedding shop over in Del Agua, even though less than a thousand folks actually lived in Devine, Texas, including the ranchers on the outskirts. The napkin salesgirl had assured her that folks would use two or three napkins apiece. Turned out all the wedding guests thought they looked so pretty they didn't want to waste them. Judy Harper had brought in the roll of paper towels she always kept in the backseat of her Oldsmobile and everyone passed that around instead. So Ruby'd been stuck with more than nine hundred leftover, lavender, lying napkins.

Almost ten years had passed since that day, so Ruby saw no point in letting the napkins sit in the box. Maybe with the wrong names, folks wouldn't feel so bad about using them. Lina and Jason, the soap-opera bride and groom, wouldn't actually be at this wedding reception anyhow. The real nuptial vows would be recited in Hollywood, California, on the set of *Only One Life* at the CBS studios.

Lina and Jason's reuniting had everyone in Devine, at least the womenfolk, so elated that they had decided to hold a wedding reception at Ruby's bowling alley, the Devine Bowl. The ladies even tried to have the actual wedding in Devine. Suddy Wilson wrote a letter to the president of CBS saying that since all this fancy decorating and cake baking would be going on anyway, CBS was welcome to film the wedding episode in Devine—"a town of God-fearing Texans." She'd written "a town of God-fearing Americans" first, but everyone urged her change it to Texans since they really considered themselves to be quite different. In that same letter, Suddy offered up her husband Chester's services. Since he was the minister of the First Methodist Church, all the ladies figured he ought to officiate. They were willing to forego the fact that Lina and Jason practiced Presbyterianism. There was also the issue of their two divorces each, but no one brought that up.

As they waited for a reply, the sheriff assured the ladies that the whole cast and film crew of *Only One Life,* and then some, could come to town. He could handle it, he'd had crowd control training. But the ladies never heard back from CBS.

Ruby hauled the box of decorations from the pinsetter room, up past the bowling lanes whose maple ribbing seemed to echo the crash and bang of bowling balls even when the place sat empty on a quiet morning like this. Ruby wondered if maybe that echo was permanently in her head. When she walked toward the front lobby she caught sight of her sister, Loralva. Ruby hadn't heard the ring of the cowbell tied to the door handle, but Loralva obviously had arrived early and hoisted herself up onto the counter next to a big metal washtub. Loralva held her legs straight out in front of her, admiring the pair of white ostrich-hide cowboy boots on her feet. Today her hair matched the color of the boots. She had a wig for every occasion—soap opera weddings included.

"Don't even think about walking anywhere near my maple lanes in those boots," Ruby said, setting the box of decorations on the other side of Loralva. "And that dress—that the same one you married Shep, then Buck, in? Shorter than is legal in Devine, don't you reckon?"

"Check out my earrings, Ruby honey." Loralva held back thick wisps of platinum curls from her temples to show off the rabbit's feet, ignoring Ruby's put-down as always.

"Your good luck charms already ain't working," Ruby said, pointing toward the glass front doors.

Imogene Davidson marched her heels through the parking lot gravel as she headed toward them, arms loaded down with white tablecloths. Ruby turned her attention back to the decorations, pulling a honeycomb bell from the box to tape to the RENT SHOES HERE sign that hung just above them. Loralva slid off the counter, turned on her boot heels, and said, "Catch you after the party gets going," then took the metal washtub with her as she pushed through the swinging doors of the Idyll-On-Up Saloon, which was next door to the Food Alley snack bar. Loralva would be making what she called Mexican champagne—lemonade-flavored Kool-Aid, fizzy water and tequila. The metal washtub was the closest they could find to a punch bowl.

Loralva dresses bold and talks tough, but she's yellow bellied in the end, Ruby thought, her sister having left her to tend to Violet's mother-in-law all alone.

The lady huffed through the doors, cowbell clanking with her arrival, and dropped the tablecloths on the counter where the washtub had been sitting. "Ruby!" Imogene always shouted as though whatever she had to say was the most dire news. "I got the cake! Come help me bring it inside!" Whenever she got excited she grew even louder.

Ruby followed and together they hoisted the three-tiered wedding cake out of Imogene's El Dorado, lugged it inside the bowling alley, and lifted it onto the shoe rental counter, where Imogene wanted it prominently displayed.

"It's free advertising for Becca Ann's wedding cake business! I'm so proud of her. Becca Ann's practically like a daughter to me. She does everything I tell her to do." Imogene stood back and admired her contribution to the wedding reception.

The icing reminded Ruby of wet cement, not just because it was dirty-dishrag gray, but also because the right side of the layers had begun to cave in. Ruby tilted her head, thinking that if she set it on the back table that only had three legs and leaned to the left, the cake might not look so lopsided.

"It's not just for eating!" Imogene hollered. "It's to make it seem like a real wedding." She patted her hard-sprayed bouffant hairdo, black with thick white stripes on each side that looked pale purple under the fluorescent lighting. Then, in a normal tone of voice—Imogene's version of a whisper even though there was no one else around to hear her—she said, "This wedding ceremony and reception will be a practice run. I've got it all planned, Ruby!" She pulled a small paper sack from her purse. "Becca Ann and my Harley will cut the cake. Hand in hand!"

Ruby felt like a cactus needle had pierced her heart. She knew what Imogene was saying. Violet had run off, Harley should have a new wife. Imogene was shoving Violet's memory to the side.

From the paper sack Imogene pulled two dolls. One was a two-inch plastic bridegroom in a tuxedo and the other a Skipper doll, Barbie's younger sister, dressed in a yellow sleeveless sundress. She stuck them both into the top of the cake.

"Those ain't wedding folk," Ruby said. "They ain't even the same size."

"Becca Ann and I have already talked about it and all I have to do is get Harley to show up here this afternoon." Imogene jabbed the girl doll into the cake down to her rubber knees.

"She looks like she's fourteen," Ruby said.

"Finally, I have found someone perfect for my Harley. Plus, Becca Ann complements my personality."

"And he looks to be forty-five." Ruby cocked her head at the cake.

"He's wearing a tuxedo!" Imogene said as though that explained away any discrepancy in their ages. She stepped back to admire the happy couple.

From the box of decorations, Ruby took the lavender crepe paper and tore off a short strip from the end of the roll. She draped it over Skipper's face and tacked it to her head with a piece of tape. "There. A veil," Ruby said. That way she won't see her mother-in-law coming at her, Ruby figured.

Imogene slapped Ruby's hand away from the cake. "Won't matter. It's just for show!" Hands on her hips, she said under her breath, "The real cake will be store bought for sure."

After Imogene left to spread the tablecloths over the scoring tables, Ruby hung the crepe paper and the bells around the shoe rental counter and cake.

"Did you get the bridge mix and mints?" Imogene shouted from Lane Six.

Bridge mix? Ruby thought. Nope, she'd bought red tamales and spicy peanuts. What didn't get eaten she could sell at the snack bar after the wedding. She looked at the cake. To the girl doll she said, "You'd probably be better suited for Harley than my Violet ever was. But it still ain't right." Becca Ann with her milk-and-water ways made a much more appropriate bride for Harley, but it still violated the idea in Ruby's mind that Violet would return soon. She'd only been missing four years. Ruby still had hope. She still kept a box of Violet's things. Yet most of the hope had flitted away, hadn't it? Until it fit in that one box sitting in the back of the hall closet.

"You know, Ruby," Imogene shouted from Lane Five, "Becca Ann has such a nice smile, and whenever I ask her to do anything she grins like she wouldn't rather do nothing else! What more could you ask for in a daughter-in-law?"

To be home tending my grandkids, Ruby answered in her head. Except for Bubbie's mean streak, which was as wide as old Mrs. Parker who ate nothing but peach cobbler and pork rinds, Ruby couldn't understand why Violet would leave those sweet faces behind.

She wished those kids would run squealing through the bowling alley right this instant so she could give them a big hug, but she had dropped them at the Johnsons' house earlier. Ida Mae Johnson's oldest boys had been assigned babysitting duty so all the women in town could be free to attend their *Only One Life* wedding reception.

"Judy Harper and the extra TVs are here!" Imogene yelled.

Judy Harper's brother-in-law had a TV repair place over in Del Agua and he'd agreed to lend them a few RCA television sets that he'd fixed but hadn't gotten around to calling the owners to come and pick up yet. Ruby hoped he'd sent at least one color set, because a special event like this should be in Technicolor, not just black and white.

At the same time as Imogene's shout Ida Mae Johnson walked through the front glass doors and asked, "Where should I put these ladyfingers, Ruby?" She carried a platter of pink and green rectangular sandwiches covered in Saran Wrap.

"All the food's going on the shoe rental counter," Ruby

said, pointing next to the gray wedding cake. Then she went to help Judy Harper lug in the TVs.

As the two of them set the last of the borrowed TVs up next to the deep fat fryer in the Food Alley, Ruby overheard Imogene say to Ida Mae, who was busy arranging the ladyfingers, "Becca Ann will walk along here to the trellis I saw in a bridal store window in San Antonio. It'll go right between Lanes Three and Four."

Ruby didn't want to know any more and went in the opposite direction toward the shoe rental counter to see what the other ladies brought as they arrived. Peeking under a glass Corning-Ware lid, she saw that her sister, Loralva, had made her signature dish: Vienna sausages in a special secret chili sauce. Loralva called them puppy peters. Besides the cement-colored cake and puppy peters, there were Ida Mae's pink and green ladyfingers, which she brought to every potluck, and Suddy Wilson had fixed up a lime Jell-O and mock pecan salad. It was a cost-cutting *Redbook* recipe that replaced pecans with pretzel pieces.

More and more ladies arrived and asked Ruby where to put their dishes and what they could do to help. She had Judy Harper blowing up balloons and Ida Mae setting out paper doilies and the lavender napkins. Ruby asked her to be sure and turn the napkins upside down so it wasn't obvious right off the bat that they were leftovers. The Devine ladies didn't know what *Only One Life*'s Lina had chosen for her wedding colors, but they assumed that yellow and green balloons would be okay since that's all the Rexall had in stock.

Ruby found Suddy Wilson filling Baggies with rice, then tying them with twist ties.

"Imogene said we could throw the rice at Becca Ann and Harley," Suddy said through a twist tie hanging out of her mouth. "Another wedding." She elbowed Ruby. "Becca Ann and Harley together. Isn't that just glorious?"

Ruby shrugged. "Ain't sure it's legal. Only been four years that Violet's been missing." She picked up a Baggie to help.

"Imogene says all she has to do is file some paper at the court house and Harley's divorced on grounds of 'abandonment,'" Suddy said. "But besides that, Ruby, the Bible says that a man should not have to suffer the loneliness of not having a wife. You must understand."

Ruby didn't know where in the Bible it said that, but she wasn't about to argue with Suddy. "I can't just give up on Violet," she tried to explain. She twisted the twist tie so tight an end snapped off.

"Violet ain't here now," Suddy replied, picking grains of rice off the Formica with her fingertip and dropping them into her Baggie.

Ruby looked at Suddy one too many seconds longer than she should have, and that churchy smile the lady wore for Chester's Methodist congregation slid off and was replaced with a bitter pickle look. "It's time, Ruby," Suddy said, knotting off a Baggie of rice, "that you accept your Violet is never coming back."

With a slam, Ruby folded up the metal folding chair that leaned against the counter next to her, snatched a roll of crepe paper from the decorations box, and turned away from Suddy and her Uncle Ben's rice.

"Ruby, we been praying for her return for four years now. We're all prayed out." Suddy's church smile returned with a syrupy pitch.

Ruby stomped off to hang crepe paper. She knew that's what the whole town thought—that Harley shouldn't have to suffer. He'd suffered enough. That was one of the reasons Ruby had taken Bunny and Bubbie into her home in the first place, so that he wouldn't have more to worry about. His job at the Idyll County Fire Department, where he had four days of twenty-four-hour duty at a time, was inconvenient for child rearing.

Ruby had proven herself good at taking in strays, and since no one in Devine had ever heard of a man raising kids all alone, Ruby volunteered to take over, with Imogene backing her, relieved she wouldn't have to be the one. But besides the concern about Harley, Ruby also knew, and she'd known it all along, that the town had long since given up on Violet. There was something else she knew about Violet's flight; Suddy wasn't saying it, but Ruby knew the whole town thought: *good riddance.*

Ruby stood on tiptoe on the metal folding chair, and reaching for the corner of the ceiling above the Lustre King 300 ball polisher, she attached a twisted yellow streamer of crepe paper to the ceiling with Scotch tape. She liked being across the room from the chitchat. She would rather admire the six shiny maple lanes. Her bowling alley had always been her prized possession, something that she could count on. From the height of the chair, she noticed the stainless steel on the electronic ball retrievers needed polishing. Also, one of the saloon doors hung crooked, but there was no point in fixing that. Loralva always hung over it, talking to all the fellas when she worked nights in the bar. It would sag again in no time.

Across the room, her dead husband Rascal's picture hung over the front doors, beaming at all who passed through. He wore his blue and gold U.S. Champion bowling shirt, holding up his ball engraved with the words, *300 Points. Perfect Game.* That's what he always strove for. "Roll a little off center," he'd say. Yep, Ruby thought, things were definitely off center.

Before climbing down from her perch, Ruby took stock of the rest of the goings-on. Balloons floated all over the floor, getting kicked up into the air as all the Devine ladies milled around, wearing their best dresses, their hair poofed and teased and sprayed. Becca Ann set out bowls of bridge mix over by the scoring table on Lane Six. Apparently Imogene had called and told her to pick some up on her way over. Now Imogene stalked over and whispered something in Becca Ann's ear, probably correcting the girl on her bridge mix serving. The look on Becca Ann's face made Ruby feel a little bad for her, but the white satin headband and small lacy veil over the back half of her dishwater blond hair made Ruby change her mind. She stepped back down to the bowling alley floor.

With the crepe paper hung and Loralva's washtub of Mexican champagne hauled out from the Idyll-On-Up to the shoe rental counter, Ruby had just enough time to run home and change. Fortunately there was only a carport's distance between her house and the bowling alley.

She had picked out the butterfly blue chiffon dress she'd worn to Violet's wedding, thinking it was appropriate for today's wedding too. It'd been hanging inside the plastic bag ever since the first time it was worn. She'd ordered a special pair of red, white and blue patent leather bowling shoes for the upcoming U.S. bicentennial, and she couldn't resist making them part of her outfit today. As she made her way back to the bowling alley, she'd look down at their shininess now and again.

She stopped at the fridge on her way to get her jalapeño pie, which she'd already cut into little squares, each one speared with a colored toothpick. Then she headed back to the wedding reception preparations. As she crossed the bowling alley, going from one TV to another and flipping them to the same channel, Imogene hollered, "Ruby, be sure to give Becca Ann the name of the store where you got the napkins! She wants to order the same. Don't you, Becca Ann?"

Becca Ann nodded and smiled.

Loralva joined the party and stood next to the washtub of Mexican champagne. "Don't worry none, Ruby honey," she said. "Word is that Harley got called out to help untangle a cow from a barbed wire fence. He won't be showing up." She handed Ruby a paper cup. "Here. Jose Cuervo will make you feel better."

As Ruby took a long sip her chest unclenched and her wrinkles smoothed out. "You got a knack, Loralva." Her sister wiggled her drawn-in black eyebrows. Ruby rested against the counter for a moment.

"I was thinking we'd play Patsy Cline's 'Crazy' during the party after the wedding," Loralva said, looking around the room at the crowd. "We don't have nothing else that suits the occasion on the jukebox anyhow."

Ruby ignored her sister, knowing marriage didn't suit her, having just ended her fifth. "We'll leave the wedding march up to CBS," Ruby said, taking another swig of the champagne concoction. "And Hank Williams has some ballads we can play during the reception." Ruby left her sister's side to make certain everyone's paper cup was filled.

Violet's wedding decorations blowing around in the air conditioner's blast had Ruby's stomach churning. The ladies began taking their seats in the rows of metal folding chairs set up in front of each TV. "If you're not wearing bowling shoes, please remember to keep your heels off the maple lanes," she announced over the microphone. She flipped on Rascal's collection of neon beer signs around the alley, which gave the bowling alley a nice, pinkish glow.

"It's time!" Judy Harper hollered from the RCA set over by the Lustre King 300. The theme song from *Only One Life* gushed out into the bowling alley as they turned the volume on each set to full blast. Ruby chose a spot to sit right next to the color TV in the Food Alley.

"Becca Ann, you stand right over here by my side," Imogene said, everyone shushing her. The TV wedding guests filled their pews, settling down just the way the ladies at the Devine Bowl had slipped into their folding chairs. The bride's aunt, who still had amnesia from a car crash just weeks before and now wore an eye patch, sang a solo of "True Love of Mine." Then Lina walked down the aisle as Jason's drug-dealer cousin, who'd been to rehab twice already, played the wedding march on the church organ. Ruby was relieved they hadn't had the real wedding at the Bowl since the train on Lina's dress stretched longer than practically one entire maple bowling lane, and the flower arrangements reached higher than Ruby's carport awning. As the bride and groom stood in front of the preacher at the pulpit, Lina opened her mouth for what Ruby knew would be "I do." Then, with all the Devine ladies' mouths poised to say the words along with her, the station went to commercial.

"Dadgumit!" Suddy said, her hands clasped in prayer.

"I wouldn't be surprised if Jason's already seeing other women again." Loralva brushed off pink bread-crumbs from among the fringe pieces of her white satin minidress. "I'd snatch him away from that Lina if I had the chance."

Ruby hoped it wasn't true, that Jason would be faithful this time, just as she wished her sister could be.

While the gossip and wonderings swirled, Ruby looked down to admire her new red, white and blue bowling shoes one more time, and worried that they might get scuffed before the bicentennial celebration.

"Ruby, where can we find more napkins?" someone behind her asked. Might have been Ida Mae Johnson, she couldn't tell over the TV commercial jingle: *If it's ButterMaid, it's better made.* On the bowling alley floor, a balloon popped a few feet away from the TV stand, making the ladies scream, then laugh.

From her place standing right next to Ruby and the TV set, Suddy gasped. "Why, my Lord, our prayers really did work!"

Across the room where the second TV sat, Ida Mae said, "Wait 'til Imogene gets a load of this!"

Judy Harper whooped, "Oh, I've got to tell—" but with everyone worth telling already at the Bowl, Judy couldn't think of who to share the news with.

"Ain't that your Violet?" Suddy poked at Ruby's arm. Ruby whirled back to the set. Suddy had to be imagining things. It was probably just somebody who looked like her Violet.

"No doubt about it!" Suddy said, this time yanking Ruby by the ear and bringing her face right up to the screen. But she hadn't had to yank too hard, because as soon as Ruby's eyes locked onto that screen she knew what she saw. She mouthed the words, "It can't be." But it was. The reality hit her brain with a big splat.

Four years had gone by, but she still knew the small kink that that wrist made when she walked, the tilt of her head that stayed a little more to the left and the smile that only Ruby knew held something other than happiness in it. The parts of her Violet Ruby didn't recognize were the checkered minidress with the smocking, the two thick braids of hair, and the face all made up with big long eyelashes like Elsie the Cow. Violet wasn't speaking, just smiling, blinking those eyelashes and swinging her milk bucket. In the background of the screen, a black and white Jersey cow grazed while a chorus, sounding like a holy church choir, sang the dairy product's jingle. Sure enough, her Violet was the ButterMaid.

Ruby waved her arms in the air; she wanted to get Loralva's attention, but didn't want to turn her eyes away from the screen and her daughter. Her voice box closed up and she felt like she was drowning. Little John Henry Edelman drowned in thirty seconds one Sunday down at the river—the same amount of time as a TV commercial.

Suddy Wilson screamed in Ruby's ear, "The Lord has returned our lamb to her flock."

Judy Harper bellowed out, "It's Violet Davidson!"

"The ButterMaid!" Ida Mae squealed.

As the ladies screamed, the TV chorus still sang, *If it's ButterMaid, it's better made.*

"Hot damn, Ruby honey! Your Violet's in Hollywood!"

Loralva said, pushing her way through the tight crowd around the TV set. "That's where the game shows are!" She put one long skinny arm around Ruby. "Hollywood here we come!" Then she hugged and squeezed so tight Ruby felt her dress buttons crushing into her skin. Seeing her Violet there in the checkered dress allowed her to finally breathe out and away her old worries that the girl's bones had been stripped clean by a coyote. But, Lordy—Hollywood? Could that be the next worst thing?

Metal folding chairs clanked and crashed as Imogene pushed her way forward, then pretended to faint. Kneeling on the floor next to her, Becca Ann fanned a lying lavender napkin over her.

While everyone crowded around the fallen Imogene, Ruby reached out to touch Violet. But her fingers thumped to a stop at the glass screen and she felt the fuzzy tingle of static electricity instead.

As the jingle tinkled its last note, Violet skipped out the other edge of the screen. The hem of her checkered dress swished just below her bottom.

Devil's Rope

With the TVs still on in case of another ButterMaid commercial, the wedding decorations still up, and the neon beer signs buzzing, a few ladies lingered, pretending to help clean up the Devine Bowl.

After the commercial break, Lina had said "I do," but Ruby'd missed it. Her mind was too bunched up to think about Lina. She sat herself down on the plastic chair at Lane Five's scoring table, not even noticing Judy Harper traipsing down the maple floors in her clickety heels.

"You're related to someone in show business!" Judy said, gathering paper plates and purple napkins wadded up with half-eaten pink and green sandwiches. "Although Hollywood, California, is not exactly a wholesome place."

"Hollywood," Ruby repeated, fiddling with the edge of the scoring pad at Lane Five.

"That's right," Loralva said, straightening her tight dress and pushing up her bra as though she were walking out into the spotlight. "Violet's out there with Bob Barker and all those other game show hosts." She did a little Cotton-eyed Joe in her ostrich boots, her platinum spirals bobbing up and down. With a two-step shimmy across the linoleum, she said, "Ooh, I'd like to meet that Bob Barker."

"You meeting Bob Barker, now that's a hoot!" Imogene said. She sat slumped in the folding chair where Becca Ann continued to fan a napkin over her. "Won't ever happen."

"If we're going to Hollywood, you can parlay your wagers on my getting on a game show." Loralva never missed a beat in her shuffle.

Imogene moved Becca Ann's hand over to redirect the fanning. She couldn't stand Loralva ever having anything she didn't have. "That's one bet," she whispered in her not-so-quiet way, "I won't be making." Then she let out a big sigh as though the possibility of fainting was still in the air.

Ruby couldn't think about game shows. Not now. Not while the TVs blared. Her relief that Violet was alive, not lying dead in a gullywash, overrode everything. But she couldn't help listening to all the chatter ricocheting around the bowling alley.

"The pastor over at Cicada First Baptist says California is a haven for homosexuals," Suddy said. "You don't think your Violet could be a . . . les-bi-an?" She said it all spread out like she was afraid of the word touching her tongue.

"I hear that in Los Angeles they walk around the streets *naked,*" Judy Harper said. "You don't think Violet would ever do a thing like that, do you?" She pulled her suit jacket tighter around her, clumping the collar closed around her neck.

Imogene let out a deep sigh in between each remark.

"Ruby honey, don't pay them no mind," Loralva said. "You just call up Hollywood and ask them how you can get in touch with the ButterMaid."

"She can't just call up Hollywood," Imogene said, acting weak and having a hard time lifting herself to an upright position.

"It's true," Ruby said. "Who would I call?" It wasn't that she didn't want to see Violet. No, in fact, she'd give away her entire collection of Avon bottles to be with her again. But this was going to take more than just a phone call.

"You call them ButterMaid folks, that's who. What's stopping you?" Loralva danced around Ruby's chair, and started to sing, "Bob Barker, I'm coming *on* down!"

Imogene sat up straighter, knocking Becca Ann's fanning hand away. "I got to get home right away. Becca Ann, you have to take me."

"What's the matter?" Loralva said. "Can't handle having two daughters-in-law?"

"I'm feeling poorly, is all," Imogene said, letting Becca Ann hoist her up by her elbow. "And I need to see my Harley."

"Becca Ann, send for Harley to meet me at my house right away. I don't care how many men they need to pry that heifer out of the barbed wire." They made their way out the door, sending the cowbells on the handle clanking. "My nerves rattled over this Violet sighting are so much more dire. Isn't that right, Becca Ann?" The girl nodded.

Ruby didn't want Imogene's opinion floating around in the same pot as all the others anyway. At that moment all she was getting was a mishmash of crazy notions, bad advice and stomach upset, so she had waved a hearty good-bye at Imogene's exit.

The cowbell jangled again just moments after Imogene stepped out. Judy Harper's brother-in-law had arrived to collect the TVs, and Earl Glidden, whose back pasture bordered Ruby's property, came in for his lunchtime beer. Earl hardly ever said a word. Just stood there listening in his boots and hat, one thumb hooked through the belt loop beside his Lone Star belt buckle.

"I bet," Judy Harper said, now on her way out the door, "that Violet is millionairess by now, being on a TV commercial and all." The cowbell clanked as the doors shut, her brother-in-law behind her with the last TV.

"Violet's making it out in Hollywood, Earl," Loralva said, handing him a cold one.

"You must be all wrought up, Miss Ruby," he said, then knocked back his beer. "Can I give you and the kids a lift to California?"

"Ruby, this is a message from God that your Violet has turned to the devil." Suddy Wilson always went a little too far with all her Bible thumping, but everyone in town tolerated it since they didn't know what her connections upstairs might be. Her already high-pitched voice rose with each word. "Something bad is bound to happen if you don't rescue her like you done before."

"How's something bad gonna happen to her on the television, Suddy?" Loralva asked, handing Earl a second beer as he tipped his hat to thank her.

Suddy took a deep breath, obviously impatient with their shortsightedness. "She could hurt herself on the stage, for one thing. And they say those lights are awful on the skin. Makes a person age real fast being under those bright lights all day. Just look at Charlton Heston."

Loralva opened another beer and walked it over to Ruby. "That ain't what Ruby needs to be hearing right now. Listen at Earl wanting to help out and you're just spouting nonsense."

"I am only trying to reach the truth," Suddy continued. "That is all I'm aiming to do."

"The truth I know," Loralva said, "is that Los Angeles is where the game shows are." She sat down on the plastic chair next to her sister. "Ruby honey, did you get a load of how fast that Imogene took off out of here when she realized Violet showing up was going to screw up all her plans?"

"She seemed more upset about your talk about game shows.

You know how competitive she can be—doesn't want you to have what she can't have."

"She's calling in the forces, re-strategizing, is what she's doing. It's hogwash that she wanted to 'be with her Harley.'" She mimicked Imogene on the last part.

Earl laughed quietly and put his empty beer bottle on the counter. "Honestly, Miss Ruby, I wanna help you and the kids any way I know how."

Ruby's breath caught. "The kids!" she almost shouted. That was the most important thing, and all anyone could talk about was the wicked parts of Hollywood.

"They can come to Hollywood with us," Loralva answered without a hitch.

But Ruby was already headed past the scoring tables and out the side door to her car parked under the carport, thinking how not a soul had said, *Oh Ruby, I am just tickled pink you found your Violet*. She hadn't even said it to herself. But Bunny and Bubbie—the two most precious cinnamon-headed kids in all of Texas—the very thought of them made Ruby cry a soft cry, the tears welling up to the surface but not quite spilling over as she started the ignition.

As Ruby turned into one end of Ida Mae Johnson's circular drive, out the other end drove Judy Harper's pickup truck with the gun rack in the back window and a DOLPH BRISCOE FOR GOVERNOR bumper sticker. Bunny must have been watching for Ruby, because she ran out the front door of the red brick house just as the gravel snapped under her tires. The little girl climbed onto the bench seat of the El Camino beside her grandmomma. She held her Mrs. Beasley doll close to her chest. The heat outside the car had seeped in, stealing some of the cool air from the air conditioner blowing on Ruby's face. Both the five-year-old and Mrs. Beasley stared at Ruby.

"Ricky Harper's momma said she'd seen my momma on the TV. Said she was the first one to see her and not to let anyone else say they'd been the first." Her smile said she didn't care who saw her momma first as long as Bunny herself got to see her soon.

"Your momma's not here in Devine, Bunny hon," Ruby said, giving her voice a lilt in an attempt at being heartening. "We just think we know where she might be at."

Bunny's face turned splotchy and tears welled up. "If Momma's not here, why would Mrs. Harper say she'd seen her?" The tiny voice begged Ruby to tell her that her momma would be sitting at home waiting for them.

The car door opened again and this time the car completely filled with heat as Bubbie climbed in. He stared at Ruby for a moment as if checking on the state of things. Then deciding his assumptions were right, he slammed the car door.

"Bubbie called me Rabbit Brain," Bunny spit out. Since Violet disappeared Bubbie hadn't said much of anything that he couldn't communicate by shrugging his shoulders, shaking or nodding his head, or maybe sticking out his tongue. But somehow Bunny talked with him, even though Ruby'd never caught him so much as whispering to her. "He doesn't believe Mrs. Harper."

Ruby put both hands on the steering wheel and stared straight ahead along the pebbled circular drive. "Bunny, like I said, all we know is where your momma might could be."

"Tell him, GranMomma," Bunny said, holding Mrs. Beasley tight to her chest. "Tell Bubbie how now all you have to do is go and get her. That's what you always said: that if you just knew where Momma was you would go and get her for us. He thinks you can't get her off the TV," Bunny whined. "He says it's because she don't want us." The eight-year-old boy thunked his boot toes against the glove compartment at this last statement.

"Don't say such a thing, Bubbie," Ruby said, now digging in her purse at her side. The car engine strained against the air-conditioning and the hot sun outside. Bunny rubbed her eyes with her tiny fists, making more splotches on her pudgy cheeks. "Here, you two split this MoonPie." She pulled out the half-melted, cellophane-wrapped, chocolate and marshmallow pie. It was what she kept in her handbag to stop the fits and fights. It always gave her an extra moment to think. After she broke the MoonPie in half and gave one half to Bubbie and one half to Bunny, she took the car out of park and began to head home.

Bubbie mushed the marshmallow inside of his MoonPie, then pulled the white goo out in globs, flattening it between his fingers, all the while kicking the glove compartment.

"GranMomma?" said Bunny, still small enough to stand beside her in the middle of the bench seat. She looked at Ruby. "We are too gonna see our momma, aren't we?" Bunny now had a ring of chocolate around the outside of her pouty lips.

Ruby swatted Bubbie's kicking leg to make him quit. "Thing is," she sighed, watching the yellow dividing line on the highway, "your momma's all the way out in California, or might could be." This last part she said with a big swallow. "We only just saw her on the TV. We still got so much to figure out."

"Bubbie thinks we won't never see Momma again," Bunny said matter-of-factly through the dollops of marshmallow. It was just like Bubbie himself would have sounded—soaked through with vinegar.

Ruby didn't know what to think or where to begin. She should be happy, but she wasn't sure what to feel. She decided to go to the one other person who could help her with this. She took the next turn down Manzanita Road heading toward the back side of Devine.

"Bubbie thinks I don't remember Momma, but I do," Bunny chirped. Chocolate icing coated the corners of her mouth and she held Mrs. Beasley by the arm. She closed her eyes like she was rustling up all her Violet memories. "Momma drank iced tea from that blue plastic glass, the big one that Daddy puts the change from his pockets in now. She wore a green dress with pink flowers on the sleeves."

Ruby knew which dress she was talking about. It was one of hers that she no longer wore.

"Momma liked to eat MoonPies, like me," Bunny said, looking at Ruby with a smile wider than the grille on a pickup truck.

"She did," Ruby said. "Surprised you remember," because that was the only thing Bunny got right. Violet had a real hankering for MoonPies. Nothing could get in her way when she wanted one.

"I remember because Mrs. Beasley likes MoonPies too." She squirmed against Ruby, her fingertips leaving brown smudges on Ruby's sleeve. Bunny still wore little-girl dresses and loved the frilly socks and patent leather shoes to match. Bunny had only just started to walk when Violet left. She couldn't remember Violet eating a MoonPie, could she?

Ruby drove a little faster than usual, not really paying attention to the road, but more to the ramblings in her head. Loralva had talked about California being the place for game shows, Suddy had said that the very state itself was sin, and Imogene wanted her Harley to marry Becca Ann and just forget Violet altogether. The blue-gray El Camino began to shimmy when Ruby got up to a speed that was more than it could handle, and she came to and pulled her heavy foot off the accelerator. She rounded the corner past Mrs. Duffy's house with all the white poodles in the front yard. That woman raised each litter and never gave a single one away, must have been thirty-some-odd white, curly-haired dogs inside that fence yapping at Ruby's car.

"Aw, hush up now," Ruby said through her closed car window. Bubbie stared out the side window while Bunny and

Mrs. Beasley talked little-girl doll talk: one-sided questions with no answers.

"Do you like MoonPies?" "Me too." "Momma likes MoonPies too."

Ruby turned left, passing the Fowlers' run-down house, the cedar post and devil's rope fence bent over in places. The front porch sagged, and the roof was missing shingles that had blown off ages ago. The front yard had no flower beds and nothing in it but an old rusted Chevy pickup the color of dried blood, which sat hidden by scissoring Johnson grass. No one had rented the place since the Fowlers took off years ago.

"How come you always slow down on this part of the road?" Bunny asked.

"Shush about that," Ruby said quickly. Her tone made it clear not to say another word.

She drove through the gates on the other side of the gully-wash, not even noticing the wrought-iron lettering anymore that read HOLY OATS RESTING PLACE. Buster Sheety, the blacksmith over at Del Agua, had offered to make the gates for free when his daddy was buried there, so no one said a word when the gates showed up with the misspelling of *oaks*.

The gravel road into the graveyard was lined on both sides by another barbed wire fence. This barbed wire was intended to keep the deer out, along with Earl Glidden's pygmy goats and emus. His land extended all the way down from Highway 90, past the cemetery. Nice of him to offer them a ride to California, Ruby thought, wondering if she'd be needing to take him up on it.

Ruby parked on the end of the third row, and as the kids tore out across the grounds she hollered after them, "Watch you don't step on none of the graves." Then sighed as Bubbie tromped across Fred Gilbert's stomach, then Mary Lou Gilbert's head. Bunny tiptoed around the edges trying to keep up with her brother. Ruby murmured an apology to the Whitacres, then hauled over the bucket she kept in the truck bed of the El Camino for just these visits. She made her way over to the fifth gravesite from the road.

Tyler Erastus "Rascal" Kincaid
Born September 19, 1925
Died August 22, 1974
Every thunderclap is a strike.
There are no gutterballs in heaven.

The headstone was laid to face the sky, almost flush with the grass. An old coffee can, left over from her last visit, held dried stems with the flowers missing off the top.

"Looks like the deer ate the roses I brung you last time, Rascal." She sighed a deep heavy lead sigh.

He'd been buried, at Ruby's request, with his feet at the headstone. Suddy had said there was probably some sin in that and it might have something to do with which direction you went in the afterlife, but Ruby wanted him to face the same direction as his La-Z-Boy just in case he could still see the TV from where he was.

"I know you were complaining because I brung you real flowers," Ruby said, as she set the bucket of cleaning supplies down. "I refuse to buy you any of those tacky, ugly, plastic things." She looked his grave up and down, checking out all the weeding that needed to be done. "Rascal," she sighed loud and heavy, "I didn't bring you any flowers today. I brung you news. But you probably knew it before the rest of us. About Violet being the ButterMaid, and all."

Thick green grass had grown to about three inches on the plot. One dandelion had popped up at the foot, or rather at Rascal's head, the yellow flower long since dried, now just a ball of soft white seeds.

"Don't look like Swinger's Mortuary is keeping up your grave," she said as she snapped the dead dandelion off its bed of leaves. Instead of wishing what she had been wishing the last few years—that Violet would show up safe and sound—she now wished there was a damn good reason for why Violet had done what she done. She didn't know if a dandelion would grant two wishes, but she added on that she wished whatever decisions she was about to make were the right ones. She blew hard, scattering the seeds to the spirits. She didn't have a whole lot of faith in a weed granting a wish.

In the distance, she saw Bunny and Bubbie squatting and studying something on the ground. Bubbie liked to pull the wings off of beetles, and there was no shortage of bugs in South Texas. Even in the heat the whirring cicadas seemed to mourn the loss of one of their own.

Ruby turned back to the headstone and took out of the plastic bucket a scrub brush, a spray bottle filled with diluted vinegar and an old toothbrush, the bristles flattened out to the sides. "Rascal," she said, without looking at him, "I ain't feeling like this is a hallelujah moment." Turning to face him, she said, "It may sound strange, but it's made me mad. Madder than Ida Mae's howling, snapping ole bird dog she's kept tied to the backyard clothesline for ten years. And you know I just don't go getting mad over nothing."

There wasn't anyone around for her to wallop, and nothing to tear at except the weeds, so she yanked dirt dobs, roots and all, making the gravesite lumpy like a tiller had just passed over it. "I reckon you're proud of her, ain't you, Rascal?" After a moment she glanced over her shoulder as if to see his expression.

The sun shone through the trees casting shadows here and there. A breeze moving the tree limbs overhead tossed the shadows back and forth. "Violet looked good as the ButterMaid." Ruby smiled her only smile of the day. "Judy Harper jabbered about the length of her dress, but I reckon that's the least of our worries." She looked up at the sky as a cotton ball of cloud floated by. "Violet being on the TV—that's the part that sure as heck has your chest all puffed up, and I'm proud too, but something else is what's got me riled."

She crawled across his chest and yanked another dandelion out by its roots. Then, with the hedge trimmers, she began clipping the grassy mound.

"I'm happier than a pig in slop knowing she's alive," she said, and her voice trembled. "But I also want to . . ." She stabbed at the earth with the pruners. "I want to shake her and ask what the hell was she thinking leaving Bunny and Bubbie behind!" She dropped the pruners and let out half a breath. "Every night when the two of them say their prayers, Bunny always adds, 'Please Mr. Lord, tell my momma I love her and I wish she'd at least drop by for a glass of sweet tea.' "

Feeling a little self-conscious with her carrying on, Ruby glanced around at the other graves. Off in the distance, she saw where Mrs. Theda Johnson, Ida Mae's mother-in-law, was buried, the headstone like a cypress stump, big and thick. The grave was surrounded by a delicate iron fence two feet high. She could have sworn Miss Theda was listening in. All was quiet, save for the wind in the trees and the putt-putt of a tractor far off in the distance in Earl Glidden's pasture. Several rows of graves over, Bunny squealed as her brother stuck something in her face. Then she ran farther into the graveyard, Bubbie behind her.

Ruby whispered to Rascal, putting her hand up to block the sound from traveling to Miss Theda's grave, "I know it's not like me to get so upset, but I can't help myself. I miss her like the dickens, but don't she miss Bunny and Bubbie the same?" She snipped a clump of grass down to the nubbins, then scissored her way around the rectangular plot. Her hair began to come loose from the bobby pins she'd used to pull it back. Her frosted brown hair carried the sticky sweet smell of Aqua Net.

Going back to the headstone, she scrubbed the crevices of the *E* in *Erastus* with the toothbrush.

"Right now, Violet's probably sitting in her big mansion drinking martinis or sweet grape wine." She raised the bottle of vinegar, as though imitating Violet making a toast. "Not even caring in the least about her two kids that came straight from her very own belly." Ruby plunked down on her behind. She felt plumb awful saying these things about her daughter. "Oh, listen at me. Of course she cares about her own kids. She must have realized by now she made a big mistake. It'd be so hard to come back, what with all the folks in town being as gossipy as they are.

"You'd say I was just making excuses for her, but everyone around town has been talking too. Can't you just hear Judy Harper's tongue wagging?" Ruby imitated the scratchy cigarette voice, saying, " 'Maybe Violet's been having sex with one of them movie producers.' " She cleared her throat. "Course, I know she wouldn't be doing that, Rascal." She took care, especially in the corners of the engraved letters, poking the bristles around, to get out any dust that had accumulated since her last visit.

She stood up to walk around, put her hands on her hips, and looked out at Earl's pasture next door, not hearing the tractor anymore. She paced back and forth across Rascal's stomach, shaking her head, running her hands through her hair. The smell of vinegar on her fingers and the Aqua Net hairspray stirred together and overpowered the fresh-cut grass. Her fingers met up with mats and tangles as if the thoughts in her mind had twisted the locks of hair into knots.

"Burns my chest like Vicks VapoRub, her leaving them like that." The wedding ring she still wore got caught and she had to yank it free, painfully tearing out a small clump of hair at the temple. She winced and tears came to her eyes, but she didn't feel like crying right then. She stopped her pacing.

"I'm more confused than all the fellas after a whiskey-drinking Saturday night." She bent to pull one last weed. "What am I supposed to do now, Rascal?"

She must have put a little extra pressure on the gas pedal as she pulled out of that gullywash, but the pinging of gravel hitting her back bumper and the zing of rocks flying out from under the rubber tires didn't faze her as she turned left back onto Manzanita Road. The two lanes of asphalt led them back toward town. She had talked to Rascal about the Violet sighting, but he hadn't given her any answers.

Her blouse clung to her skin and the vinyl seats stuck to the backs of her legs. The air conditioner blew warm on her arms and face, not having had a chance to cool off in the distance from the cemetery. Both kids stared at her.

"Your hair's stuck out all over," Bunny said, "like a crazy lady's." Then she asked, "Were you looking for Momma in the cemetery?"

Bubbie humphed and rolled his eyes.

"Tell him to stop, GranMomma."

As she passed the old Fowler house again, Ruby slowed down. Surprising herself, she pulled off onto the lane that ran down toward the condemned house.

"Why we going down here?" the little girl asked.

Ruby couldn't drive very far with all the tall weeds taking over the lane just like they had the yard. The house sat sallow and yielding, giving in to the weight of its roof and looking like an old woman who sags in the bosom with cheeks sunken and shriveled to the bone. "Y'all hush up for a minute. I'm listening in my head." She could almost hear the house creak. Like she's moaning a loss, Ruby thought. She focused on that front porch railing. She could still see where a piece had been sawed out of the middle by Angel Vasquez. Her mind went back to a memory she had hoped to stay away from.

One day, almost some twenty years ago now, Ruby had been to visit her momma's grave. Rascal was still among the living then. It was way before they owned an air-conditioned car; Ruby had the windows open and drove slowly to keep the dust down, since Manzanita Road wasn't paved then. She remembered that when she'd come up out of that gully at the cemetery gates the sun had shone behind her, casting shadows on the Fowler house.

Just a couple of days before, she'd seen the Fowlers packing up their beat-up station wagon. She knew they were hightailing it out of there, and she meant to call Perlesta and Lester Clyde as soon as she got home to tell them their tenants were taking off, but she'd completely forgotten. That had been the day Rascal had bought the Devine Bowl from old lady Pudge Rose and surprised Ruby when she got home. She was still reeling from the news and learning all about how to run a bowling alley and never did call the Clydes.

But then, a few days later, Ruby saw that the Fowlers had left something on the front porch. She parked her car all cattywompus and made her way down the lane toward the falling-down house, climbing over the flattened trash and broken toys strewn about the front yard. No sounds of children anymore.

The rugged gravel poked at her feet through the soles of her pumps. Burrs stuck to her ankles and weeds grabbed at her skirt hem. She was within about ten feet of the house when she saw what the Fowlers had left on that front porch.

"Jumping Jehoshaphat" was all Ruby could think to say. A young girl left to bake in the sun as if she wasn't more than a mud pie, her skin dry and cracked like a jack-hammered sidewalk. Her long, dark hair was sunburned to a reddish brown from sitting on that porch for what Ruby figured must have been three days, counting back to the last time she'd driven by.

Stepping closer, Ruby pushed matted hair away from the tiny face to get a better look. The little girl gazed up at her with drained eyes. She had dirtied herself and the smell burned Ruby's nose. Her right arm was caught in between two posts of the railing. The elbow now swollen like a cantaloupe, more than likely a spider bite irritated by her yank and pull, while mosquito bites dotted her face and arms. A person could get bit by worse than that sitting outside on a hot Texas night, Ruby thought. She wore what at one time had been a pink and white dotted-Swiss dress, smocked around the collar. Now it was soiled a gray-brown and the little puffy sleeves had deflated. Ruby wanted to find Arlene Fowler and slap her face raw, going off and leaving her own daughter like this. Probably got halfway to Del Agua before she realized it, what with all the other kids she had. She must have been too lily-livered to make her way back here. She had half a mind to tell Rascal to get out his hunting rifle.

"I'm taking you home with me." Ruby's voice cracked. "Right now." She tugged at the arm, but between the swelling and the filthy little girl contorting sideways as she scooched away from Ruby, she couldn't untangle her from the railing. The urchin had wide-open eyes the blue-purple of storm clouds, which just stared off down Manzanita Road. It gave Ruby the heebie-jeebies, so she sat herself down next to the girl and wrapped her arms around the little shoulders.

"It's a wonder a rattlesnake or coyote didn't get you," Ruby said. The girl twitched at those words, and Ruby's mind rushed around trying to figure out what to do next. The girl's lips were split and cracked, sealed tight but hoping for water or something wet. "You got a name?" Ruby asked. The girl didn't answer, just blinked. "Maybe something sweet to suit a pretty girl like you?" But not a word passed those chapped lips. "I'd guess you're no more than three and probably never even heard a lullaby." Ruby started humming, "Hush little baby, don't you cry." It was the only line she could remember of the song, so she sang it over and over.

The skin around the elbow was rubbed red-raw like the inside of a prickly pear, so Ruby didn't want to force the arm out from between the railings. "We'll get you out real soon," she said, passing her hand down the little girl's cheek and realizing the eyes were dry. All cried out. Ruby rocked a little more. "You're mine now," she whispered, still rocking. She and Rascal hadn't had any kids of their own, but now they had a gift left for them and Ruby wouldn't ever let go. "How about I call you Violet like your eyes?" She kissed the grimy little forehead, tasting something bitter.

"I gotta go get someone." Ruby started to raise herself back to standing. "We gotta get you outta here somehow." The little sack of bones tried to wiggle, then that dirt gray face just stared up the lane like she was still watching her momma and daddy's car drive off, and the eyes darkened. "Hush little baby, don't you cry." Ruby rocked harder. Little Violet turned back to her and rested her matted head on Ruby's chest. She hesitated to get up again because she didn't want the child to see her leave, even to get help. Then Angel Vasquez came through the weeds around the side of the house.

Ruby cut her hair first thing. "Full of mats and straw with a bunch of living creatures you don't even want to know about," she'd told Loralva. "I'm thinking, maybe they left her as back rent. Worth more than just that six months Perlesta said the Fowlers never paid." She beamed at her new daughter like she was Miss America—that's what she had decided Violet was—her daughter. All Ruby knew about the Fowlers was that they'd left a girl behind. All anybody really knew. Ruby liked it that way. She wasn't about to give the girl back to folks who would do something like that. She could take the girl in and raise her herself.

After washing her up they found bruises. Yellow spots from bruises past the tender stage, bruises gone on into the dead, yellow-brown bloodstream of memory.

They'd set up a play area in the bowling alley behind the counter, but not too close to the rental shoes. "Don't want her breathing in those fumes," Rascal had said. He'd been the one to tease her and finally get a giggle out of her and eventually she was talking like all the other folks in Devine.

Sitting in her El Camino, air-conditioning straining against the idling engine, Ruby looked at that house, the porch rail still sawed in half. How could Violet go and do to her kids what Arlene had done to her? Ruby still remembered that empty gaze in Violet's dark eyes. Even years after the day she was found on the porch Ruby'd still seen that emptiness. Now looking at the front porch, Ruby wondered if Violet had that look in her eyes today. Somehow Ruby knew she still did and always would. It was her real momma she wanted to have love her. She'd always be missing that. But what about the deep love, the true love, Ruby and Rascal had given her, didn't that make them more of a momma and daddy to her? Ruby looked again at the cutout in the porch railing. Just a small piece of a whole house, but enough to cause it to collapse.

And then the one thing she couldn't let go of: *How could any momma leave her baby like that?*

Bunny had reminded Ruby of what she'd promised them. *If we just knew where she was at, we'd go and get her.*

Bunny now sat silently next to Ruby, holding tight to Mrs. Beasley. Bubbie looked out the side window, his bottom lip stuck out. Ruby spoke to the ceiling of her car. "Violet went through a lot to get to us, Rascal, sitting on that porch baking." Both kids stared at her now. "I'm willing to go through a lot too. Even going all the way to California."

Star-in-Law

After backing out of the Fowlers' lot, Ruby had pulled off Manzanita Road and turned onto Highway 90, which took them home to the Devine Bowl.

As Ruby put her purse under the counter, the kids ran back outside. "Mind you stay out of the road," she hollered after them.

"Yes, ma'am," Bunny said, and waved her little hand while Bubbie just kept running.

Taking out a tube of lipstick from her pocket, Loralva said, "Where you been, Ruby honey? Started to worry about you."

"Had to go tell Rascal," she told her sister. "He hadn't bothered to let me in on Violet being safe and sound, so I had to make sure he knew all sides."

"Things got a little bit exciting around here as well," Loralva said. "Harley told Imogene he didn't want to be married to a movie star."

They both took a moment to swallow, then Earl said, "Surprised she didn't run over him in her El Dorado."

"Better than that!" Loralva leaned over to look in the stainless-steel side of the deep fat fryer and rubbed on a new coat of Revlon Red lipstick. "This morning Beaufort, the Orkin man from Del Agua, had gone over to do her roaches. He was still there when Becca Ann took her home. First thing she did was get on the phone to Harley before he could leave the fire station. Imogene took her phone with the long cord out onto the patio and called Harley while Beaufort squirted away in her living room."

"How do you know all this?" Ruby asked, opening a beer for Earl.

"Beaufort hisself," Loralva said, matter-of-factly. "He came straight over here after. His heart was still pounding he'd had such a scare." She leaned against the counter watching Ruby. "Imogene had left the sliding door open for the phone cord, so he heard her entire side of the conversation. He didn't know what Harley was saying to her, but she started in on how his being married to a movie star would change their status."

"TV star," Ruby said, folding up the giveaway bicentennial bowling towels that were to be used the next day at the tournament.

"Anyhow, Harley said something back and Beaufort said her eyes got big around and she told him she didn't know what she'd done wrong in raising him."

Ruby could have told her what she'd done wrong.

"And then," Loralva kept on, "Imogene ran into the house and fainted right in Beaufort's arms."

"Fainted?" Ruby didn't believe it, and started to roll her eyes. "You mean just her usual pretend faint."

"No." Loralva shook her head, very serious now. "Beaufort, he thought it was the poison that got to her and figured her for dead. He laid her out on the sofa and called Swinger's Mortuary. You know Beaufort's not all there."

"It's the chemicals," Earl said in his defense.

Ruby pictured Imogene laid out dead on the sofa with the

clear plastic slipcovers. The sound of a semi truck's horn blaring came from outside, but it stayed in the back of Ruby's head because she knew the kids in the yard would all the time be making the chain-pull signal with their arms when a truck went by, and how the driver would oblige them and honk his horn. They'd have to cover their ears with their little hands to keep the loud sound from hurting, but they still did it every chance they got.

"You know how that Elwood Swinger has always had the biggest crush on Imogene," Loralva said. "Must be that pasty face of hers. So he goes rushing over there in his limousine." Ruby folded the last giveaway towel and turned to let Loralva finish the story. "Turns out Imogene had come to before Elwood got there, causing Beaufort to just about keel over hisself, thinking she'd come back from the dead."

"Poor Beaufort."

"Poor Beaufort? It's poor Harley. Imogene's madder than a Hereford with a twisted gut." Loralva spoke with her lips held open as she smeared the red lipstick across her bottom lip.

Earl shook his head and downed his beer. Setting the bottle on the counter, he said, "Better stay out of Imogene's way for a few days."

Then the glass front doors swung open. "GranMomma!" Bunny wailed, "Bubbie's done something bad."

"Bunny hon," she said, wiping her hands on a dish towel. "I am very busy for the moment. You go on back outside and tell Bubbie I said to stop whatever it is he's doing."

"No GranMomma," she cried, "you said if there was blood it was an emergency. So this is one."

"Well, damn," Loralva said.

"Want me to go check on him?" Earl asked, rising from his stool.

"Thank you anyway," she replied. Ruby eyed Bunny all over and saw no blood on her, but then the semi tractor-trailer glided past in her head. "Didn't I tell you kids to stay away from the highway?" It came out shrill and more accusing than it would have normally, Ruby hollering over her shoulder as she ran out the doors, Bunny right behind her.

"I told him he was gonna get in trouble," the little girl said, pleased with her tattling.

Ruby could tell she wasn't worried about a roadkill brother, so she breathed a little easier.

Bunny continued, "He took the smushed 'dillo from the highway. And I told him, 'GranMomma's gonna yell.' You are too, aren't you? It ain't even got a behind no more. And its head looks like that devil's food cake Miss Suddy makes with the red icing."

Ruby and Bunny hiked around the house, scooting and scraping between the honeysuckle bushes that had taken over the side yard. The sugary blooms twisted her senses like Imogene's presence when she sprayed on a gallon of White Chantilly eau du toilette.

Around the corner, Bubbie squatted under the window-unit air conditioner. The warm, metallic smell of an open animal broke the honeysuckle scent. Dead deer hanging in the garage during hunting season had the same odor of something wild, wet and cloying. The dead armadillo lay in a puddle of blood soaking into the thirsty, gray Texas dirt, its tail end pinched off. His fist wrapped tight around the knife handle, Bubbie whacked at the chest casing of the body armor, which made a tough cracking sound, like pounding a nail into dried bone. Another line of armadillo blood, now smeared, streaked diagonally across the little boy's round face. In his deep concentration, and in that child's way of getting rid of something sticky, his tongue reached out and licked as far as it could around the edge of his mouth, swiping off a patch of the red smear.

"See, GranMomma," Bunny said, giving Bubbie notice they were there, "that 'dillo is smushed flat dead."

Bubbie's hands went behind his back and while she couldn't

see exactly where it landed in the scrub brush, she heard his pocketknife hit the ground after an awkward throw.

"Whatcha got there?" Ruby asked him.

The air conditioner rumbled over his head, condensation dripping into a small crater the drops had created in the dirt. Squatting by his prize, he turned his head sideways and away from her, his cheek resting on his knee. Then, staring at the gray and tan dirt beside him, he picked at a half-buried stone with his fingertip, trying to lift it from its place in the earth, where it had sunk during some long-ago rain and now was lodged.

"Dead armadillo," Bunny said. Then after a second, "Kilt by a tractor-trailer. Half of him's still up on the road. Need a shovel to get it up."

"Not again," Ruby said to Bubbie.

The animal's long rat ears lay flat. A nine-banded armadillo with only about six bands of the bony armor left intact. The rest was still up on the asphalt of Highway 90, she guessed.

"What's got into you?" Ruby wiped her hands on her shirttail, feeling a need to clean them even though she hadn't touched anything. "Carrying off roadkill like that. You part turkey buzzard?"

That made Bunny laugh. "Bubbie Buzzard." She tried the words out quietly, but he still heard and glared at his little sister until she was safely hidden behind her grandmomma's legs. He looked down at the rock he was picking at.

"You know you ain't supposed to go up on the highway. What if that truck had rolled right on over you instead?"

Bubbie's eyes got suspicious, then turned angry again. "He wanted the 'dillo," Bunny said.

"What were you about to do with your pocketknife? Doesn't look to me like you were burying it this time."

He looked at Bunny accusingly, then back in the direction the knife fell. He shrugged, and for a second Ruby thought she heard him mumble something.

"Nuh-uh." Bunny clung to Ruby's leg, as if she knew that if she gave away her brother's secret she'd need protection. "You said you was gonna cut it open. Pyoo-ee."

Bubbie picked at the stone some more. Ruby sensed something was eating away at the little boy, something bigger than he was. Something even his pocketknife wasn't going to protect him from. The armadillo picked that moment to have a fit of rigor mortis. Its pointy head lifted, twitched and jerked to the side, then plunked back in the dirt while one clawed foot reached out like it was waving up at Ruby. Bubbie's eyes got big as throwing washers and he shot up off the ground, taking off for Earl Glidden's pasture behind the Bowl. One of the animal's long rat ears still fluttered and its mouth opened, showing its peg teeth.

"Bunny, you get yourself back inside," Ruby said.

Bunny whipped around. "Yes, ma'am! 'Fore it comes back alive!" The girl took off toward the Bowl doors, her Keds tapping the dry ground as she ran on her tiptoes. She had a round dirt imprint on her backside. Ruby traipsed after Bubbie, tall grass and burrs scratching her legs beneath her blue culottes.

She had half a mind to wallop that boy's bottom for not doing what she told him and now acting up like his momma. When she saw him bending over to climb through the barbed wire fence, his half-scared, half-squall face turned toward her one last time. "Whatcha doing cutting up a fresh-dead armadillo, Bubbie?" she hollered, trying to climb through the weeds to get to him before he took off on the other side. But she didn't make it in time and the last she saw was a streak heading down into the gully of the back pasture.

Ruby stood at the fence with her hands on her hips. She sensed a shadow pass by and looked up to see a black buzzard already swooping in for the armadillo.

Back inside the Bowl, she washed her hands first thing. Bunny sat up on a stool next to Earl, and Loralva had started microwaving burritos for their lunch. "Bubbie took off for the north side of your pasture," Ruby said to Earl. "He's like a roadrunner, that kid."

"I'll head back that way in my pickup. Take a look-see." Earl pushed his half-empty beer bottle toward the kitchen side of the counter.

As he swaggered out the glass doors, Ruby walked around to the stools at the front of the counter. "Dadblasted kids," she said. "They're gonna end up being as ornery as Violet if they don't mind me."

"And look where ornery got Violet," Loralva said.

"I mind you," Bunny said. But no one paid her any attention.

"Ruby honey," Loralva said, turning the burritos over after the microwave beeped. "Both Violet and Bubbie been through a lot, cut 'em some slack."

Ruby turned around to her sister and said through her teeth, "What the hell do you know about raising kids? You can't even stay married long enough to have any of your own." At that, Bunny spilled her root beer all down the front of her jumper, crying at the icy dampness. Ruby hoisted the little girl off her stool and used the dish towel to swab the root beer off her as she whimpered.

Loralva studied Ruby. "You're reaching a boiling point. Don't happen too often, but this is gonna be a big one."

"It's not right, Loralva. Her leaving these kids," Ruby said, pulling the jumper over Bunny's head, then sending her off to get something dry. "But I reckon that isn't going to stop me from trying to set it straight."

"Well, I'm already working on getting those game show tickets, Ruby honey," Loralva said, heading back toward the Idyll-On-Up. "I'm going with you, no doubt about it." Loralva often knew what Ruby was going to do before Ruby herself had completely decided.

Later, Earl found Bubbie up a live oak throwing a pocketful

of pecans at a stump. Earl said the boy hadn't given him any trouble, but Ruby knew that his dungarees weren't torn to shreds just from climbing a tree. "I owe you, Earl. I owe you more than you know."

"Just doing what neighbors do," he said, tipping his hat. He was all the time doing for her, she thought, more than most neighbors.

She sent Bubbie to bed early, but didn't have the heart to send him without supper.

Early the next morning, before the sun was even up, Ruby sat in her new blue velour Barcalounger while the kids still slept in their beds. After Rascal died she'd bought the recliner for herself to replace his Naugahyde La-Z-Boy. She'd grown tired of the cracked outline of his body always staring at her.

She had the TV on, nothing but the test pattern since it was too early for any shows. The room so quiet that Ruby could hear only the fuzzy electricity of the muted TV. She looked over at the black phone hanging on the wall between the dining area and kitchen. The stretched-out cord hung nearly to the floor. Could she really call up Hollywood and talk to the ButterMaid folks like Loralva had said? A flicker went through her mind as she folded up the Barcalounger and walked to the phone.

Devine's phone book wasn't any bigger than a *Reader's Digest,* and it included Cicada, Del Agua, Devine and the yellow pages for all three towns. She flipped a few of the onion-skin pages in front until she got to a map of the entire United States. From Devine's area code, she trailed her finger directly west to the bottom of California. Two area codes for Los Angeles—213 and 818—not a one indicating Hollywood. Two area codes for just one single city. You could put all those Los Angeles people inside Texas and they'd have a lot more room than they did trying to live inside one crowded city, Ruby thought. Violet was smack-dab in the middle of that stampede.

Her perspiration made the phone slip in her fingers. She tried 213 first. It rang twice and Ruby considered hanging up, but someone picked up and asked, "Listing, please?"

She swallowed the biggest horse apple in her throat. "Violet Davidson, please."

Didn't take her but a second and the operator came back with, "Sorry, no listing." Ruby asked again, this time for Violet Kincaid in case she might be using her maiden name. Then the operator gave Ruby one last chance to ask for something else, so she asked for the ButterMaid company, but as she heard, "Sorry, no listing," again, Ruby hung up. What would she say to Violet anyway? She couldn't imagine having a decent conversation with someone in California. Sure, Violet was her daughter, but it had been four years, and she certainly hadn't gone out of her way to contact them. That, Ruby knew, was why there were no well wishes, and why she couldn't sleep at four a.m. If Rascal were around, would it be any easier? At first she thought so, but since he'd been gone she'd handled everything just fine on her own. She ran the bowling alley, let Loralva take over running the saloon and even got the wasps' nest out of the shed last summer and took care of that other rattler that climbed into the pinsetter and dropped down with Jimmy Ray's pins in the 7–10 split at the tourney last spring. But nothing like this had ever come up before.

With the phone snug in its cradle, the national anthem replaced the test pattern. She would go over and start preparing the Bowl for that day's bicentennial bowling tournament, and her upcoming absence.

The early morning quiet of the bowling alley always made her feel a little off kilter. Without the echo of pins and balls crashing, it didn't feel quite right. But this morning the chirp of a cricket wrangled her nerves even more.

At first she only heard it. She tried putting it out of her mind.

She started a list of supplies that would have to be stocked. Two jars the size of Jimmy Ray Johnson's bird dogs sat on the end of the Food Alley counter. One filled with pink liquid, the other yellow-green. Only about four or five pigs' feet rested on the bottom of the pink one and a half dozen pickled eggs were piled on the bottom of the other. Ruby was kicking herself for not picking up some more when she was last in Del Agua at the restaurant supply. Now it was a purchase that would have to wait until she got back from California. That made her sigh. She got out the stack of red, white and blue napkins she'd bought for this event and put them out on the counter. A pile of lavender wedding napkins was still left over and she put them at the bottom of the stack. That made her sigh again. She looked out the glass front doors, but the sun had only eked up and the gravel parking lot sat empty.

The chirping got her all riled again, so she followed the sound until she spotted the brown house cricket jumping and sliding in one of Lane Five's gutters. For the last three years they'd been having a drought so bad that even the wind snapped and cracked when it blew. So when Ruby heard the cricket inside the Bowl, she knew that was a sign that rain was coming. Maybe it was a sign of other good things to come. She took a used paper cup from one of the scoring tables and scooped him up carefully. She held her hand over the top of the cup, feeling the little insect hop up against her palm, and she whispered, "It's all right. I'm just gonna put you outside where you belong." She reckoned he was as nervous as she felt right that moment about her own life.

As she walked toward the front doors with the cricket in the paper cup, Earl Glidden waved at her through the glass. She hadn't heard his pickup pull in and his face in the window startled her, but she was glad to have some company. She smiled back, not wanting to take her hand from the top of the cup. But trying to hurry up and unlock the front doors and hold on to the cricket at the same time posed a problem, and in the process she dropped her keys and the cricket spilled out. Ruby unlocked the door and quickly tried to put the paper cup back over the insect, but she snapped off the cricket's hind leg in the process, and her heart snapped along with it. The edge of the cup had caught the leg, severing it at the base of what would be the cricket thigh.

Earl opened the door and knelt down to help.

"Now, look what I've done," Ruby said, watching the cricket struggle to turn over. She flicked him right side up with her finger. "I only wanted to put it outside where it could chirp on its own." Rascal would have made a joke about how now it could only jump in circles, but what occurred to Ruby was how it would no longer be able to sing—to rub one hind leg against the other and call for its mate. The cricket would spend the rest of its life alone.

As if he'd known what she was thinking, Earl said, "Aw, Miss Ruby, maybe there's another one-legged cricket out there, and they'll find each other and spend the rest of their cricket lives making music together."

But Ruby worried that even more than a sign of rain, this cricket was an omen.

She scooted the cricket out the doors just as Loralva's rattling Buick Skylark truck crunched in the gravel parking lot. She could hear a muffled Chet Atkins singing from her AM radio. Ruby waited at the door to make sure her sister didn't squash the cricket with her high heels as she came in.

"Howdy, Earl," Loralva said. "Sorry I'm late, Ruby honey, but you won't believe how close I am to getting us tickets to *The Price Is Right*!" Today Loralva wore a short black wig and a red polka-dot dress like Daisy Mae and carried a shopping bag from Landers' Dry Goods. Ruby followed her and Earl inside. It must be later than she thought if Loralva was showing up. She reckoned she must have spent more time sighing than she ought to have. Earl sat himself down at the Food Alley counter and Ruby opened him a beer, knowing Loralva would have to check her lipstick before she could start work.

"Just six to eight weeks is all it's supposed to take," Loralva said, unpacking the bag.

Earl whistled his surprise.

"Can't you speed it up?" Ruby said. Now that she knew she was going, she wanted to hurry up and leave. "You're welcome to start practice on Lane Four," Ruby said to Earl, who just smiled and watched her. He was always doing that. She went across the foyer to the shoe rental counter. "We can't wait that long, Loralva."

"Oh Ruby honey, it'll go by fast. You'll see." She followed Ruby and plopped her bag on the counter. She dug around in the bag and pulled out a shoebox. "My special-order bowling shoes finally arrived over at Landers'."

"Maybe you could get some tickets after we get out there?" Ruby asked.

"I'm going to be the sexiest bowler alive," Loralva commented, ignoring Ruby's plea.

"I think you may have already accomplished the sexiest bowler bit," Ruby said, trying not to sound too judgmental. She heard Earl chuckle across the way.

Loralva opened the shoebox lid and set out the sequined red and green pumps. They had a slight heel of about two inches, but thick enough to not cause nicks on the wood floors. Cutouts dotted the sides and the tops of the toes. "Toe cleavage. Very important," Loralva said, pointing to the tops.

Ruby inspected the soles to make sure they would be okay for the wood floors.

"Look what else I got." Loralva began pulling clothes from the other bags. "Just a few new things for California. They just got these in over at Landers' and I'd say it's perfect for a pool party. What do you think?" She held up a purple bikini top with fuchsia flowers.

Ruby nodded. Loralva laid the bikini on the counter, then pulled out a red leather miniskirt with metal studs outlining the pockets. "I thought this would be perfect for the game show."

"A game show?" Imogene's pinkish lips made a small O the way they did when things weren't going her way and she wasn't sure what to do about it. "Just how do you expect to manage that?"

"Oh, hello, Imogene," Ruby said, a little embarrassed that she was holding a bikini top at that moment. The mother-in-law and Harley had just walked in the doors. She waved at Harley as he walked off with his bowling bag toward his favorite lane. Everyone was starting to show up for the tournament.

"I'm getting on a game show by writing a letter to that address that scrolls up the screen at the end of *The Price Is Right,*" Loralva told her, holding the miniskirt up to her hips.

Imogene humphed, rolled her eyes and blocked her view of Loralva with her shoulder. Loralva turned to continue showing off her new outfits to Earl, who gave her the okay sign. He always seemed to be the one fella that never really flirted back with Loralva.

"Rooby!" Imogene sang.

After dredging up all those feelings about Violet, Ruby still had some nettles in her behind and didn't want to have to deal with Imogene right then. She looked at the zebra-striped head, the mauve lips, and the blue-eye-shadowed lids. The lady's shoulders that sloped down like two ramps on a horse trailer, making her neck look longer than it actually was. Ruby just knew Imogene would try to talk her out of her decision to go to California to search for Violet, so she wouldn't say anything until she was practically in the car with the hood pointing toward Hollywood. Loralva kept on admiring her purchases.

"Ruby, can you believe all this is happening?" Imogene said. "I mean becoming famous overnight. Who would have figured?"

Taking a tube of lipstick out of her purse Imogene reapplied the mauve she always wore. "I'll never ever be the same again," she said, checking her lips in the tiny mirror attached to the tube. "Never ever."

Loralva held a twisted smile on her face, obviously holding back her laughter.

"I mean, after all," Imogene continued, "being famous is a big responsibility."

"How do you figure you're famous?" Ruby asked. She looked around for the can of shoe deodorizer—it had gone missing again and she had a sneaking suspicion Suddy was taking the stuff home to use in Chester's shoes. He did have a foot-odor problem.

"Isn't it obvious?" Imogene said, her hands on her waist and her hips thrust forward like she was trying to stand like a movie star. "Violet is famous by making those TV commercials and I am her mother-in-law. That makes me famous by marriage."

"I don't think you get to be famous unless you do something yourself," Ruby said, then wished she hadn't.

"Ruby"—she sighed big and heavy—"you are obviously very much a neophyte at this."

Ruby didn't know what a neophyte was unless it was one of those long, thin fish with the narrow snout that Oboe Wilson caught in the Pedernales River. She didn't want to be called one of those, nor any other animal that Imogene might be referring to, so she got her bowling-shoe laces all in a knot over it and turned her back on Imogene.

"Think of what this will do for us." Imogene tapped Ruby on the shoulder. But Ruby had already spotted the can of deodorizer and she crossed over to get it.

"Ruby, are you listening to what I'm telling you?" Imogene said. "It's like you can't handle having good things. Which I suppose could be true since you aren't so used to them like I am."

Ruby turned around to face her now. "Good things," she

said, the words snapping off the end of her tongue, "good things are not circular driveways and formal dining rooms, or whatever it is famous people have."

Imogene looked at her like she might be thinking of that funny-named fish again. "What could be better than having a movie star for a daughter-in-law?"

"TV star," Ruby muttered under her breath, then bit her tongue so hard her eyes watered. She kept having flashes of her Violet as the ButterMaid cross her mind's eye.

"Well, never mind that. I have told Harley about the Violet sighting so you wouldn't have to. Let me tell you, my son is *so* excited."

"Excited?" Ruby and Loralva both said it at the same time.

"Of course," Imogene said. "We talked about it until late in the night. I was so distraught and he just took the sweetest care of me. He loves Violet the same way."

Ruby recalled when Violet and Harley were married just a few years: Bubbie a toddler and Bunny just a rolled-up ball of baby blanket and spit-up, Violet ignoring Harley and just about everyone else, acting like she deserved so much more than this. More than what? Ruby had thought, never thinking outside Devine herself. She looked over to where Harley stood polishing his ball at the Lustre King 300. His belt buckle as big as a goose egg, shiny silver like aluminum foil, with gold inlay letters spelling out ICFD, for Idyll County Fire Department. His belly sat right on top of the egg-shaped buckle. The bottom snap on his fireman-blue workshirt tugged at the placket.

Loralva began packing her things back into the bag, casting sidelong glances at Ruby.

"Harley, come here a sec, sugar," Imogene hollered. Then to Ruby, "I want him to tell you himself."

Ruby flicked the switch under the counter that lit up the neon beer signs at both ends of the room, casting a blue and red glow from Lane One to Lane Six. The hum from the Lustre King 300 joined the buzz from the neon. Harley left the ball in the polisher and headed toward the three women.

Ruby was resistant to adding one more piece to the confusion. She came from behind the rental counter and headed toward the Food Alley. Harley and Imogene followed behind her.

The Food Alley was no bigger than a small kitchen, with a few stools set in front of the green Formica counter that faced the lanes. Rascal had even installed a window between the Idyll-On-Up saloon and the kitchen so Loralva could get food orders and Ruby could order beers to go with the fried foods. Short racks of chips and nuts sat at both ends of the counter. The back wall had the sink, deep fat fryer, grill for burgers, reach-in freezer, and sandwich prep deck. The shelf above held industrial-sized cans of jalapeños, nacho cheese sauce and Ro-Tel tomatoes. Loralva made her way around them and stood inside the Idyll-On-Up right by the cutout window so she could hear.

"Tell Ruby what you said to me when I told you about Violet," Imogene said to Harley. "Go on, tell her." They both climbed onto the stools in front of the counter. She gave his shoulder a little nudge with a manicured mauve fingernail. "Tell her."

Harley still smelled like fresh-tanned hide from the previous day's work. To Ruby, he could be a little better at his hygiene. His brown hair had turned black with sweat, a wave around the circumference of his head where his cowboy hat had sat. He'd grabbed a bag of pork rinds off the chip holder at the end of the counter and had already stuffed one puffed-up pinkish beige rind into his mouth.

"Well," he started out slowly, like chocolate syrup on ice cream, the way he always talked. Imogene gave him another poke. "I figure . . . it's a nice thang . . . to know that . . . Violet ain't . . . dead."

"See," Imogene said, "you and Violet can be back together and I'll have a movie star as a daughter-in-law."

"Ye-ah," Harley said, in two syllables. His face was brown from being on the outside most of his life, with red under his eyes at the tops of his cheeks from being outside all the day before yanking on that cow. "I mean, it's a good thing for the kids to know where their momma is now." Ruby didn't think he sounded too convinced.

He looked at his hands covered in pork rind dust, then up at Ruby with sorrow in his eyes. "It's good news for you too, Miss Ruby. You being her momma and all."

Poking Harley with her pointy nail, Imogene said, "What do you mean 'good for Ruby'? It's good for *us*." Ruby knew *us* meant exclusively Imogene.

"What about Becca Ann?" Ruby asked. "What about the wedding plans, the trellis and rose petals?" Ruby pointed toward Lane Three. "And that cake?" She glanced at the shoe rental counter where it still sat, the yellow innards cut into and spilling out. Imogene walked right over to it, hoisted the leaning mess on her own and carried it over to the supersize trash can in the Food Alley, where she dumped the remains of the concrete-colored pastry.

"I think my Brunswick is done," Harley mumbled, sliding off his stool.

"Ruby," Imogene shouted, "it has become very clear to me that Becca Ann is not right for my Harley."

Ruby watched Harley's shoulders rise and fall as he walked toward the Lustre King 300.

"In fact," Imogene kept on, "just yesterday after she drove me home, she came to light for me as being a lady with no sparkle like my Harley deserves." She paused, waiting for Ruby to agree with her. "What I mean to say is Harley could easily handle Becca Ann, but Violet is much more his"—she paused again as though thinking of the right word—"style, yes, his style. Harley's more the type to be married to someone with pizzazz. Wouldn't you agree?" Imogene fluffed her hair and looked at her reflection in the door of the microwave at the end of the counter. Then as an afterthought she looked over at Harley standing just out of earshot at the ball polisher. "Stand up straight, sugar," Imogene hollered.

Harley instead bent over to lift his ball out of the polisher. She looked like she was about to tell him again, but then sat back on her stool, gazing at Ruby as if to say, *Surely you see it my way?*

Ruby turned on the fire under the deep fat fryer. "I see," she said, only she didn't see, and her voice gave it away.

Harley had returned and stood next to Imogene holding his black shiny Brunswick between them. Imogene reached up to brush the pork-rind crumbs off his chest.

"You don't seem to understand the importance of *our* Violet being on the TV." Imogene directed "our Violet" to Harley as though pressing it into his brain. "Everyone in town is now aware. She's famous. That makes *us* famous, Harley baby." She poked him again in the shoulder with that sharp mauve nail. Harley stepped back just out of fingernail reach. "The best part is," Imogene said, so smartly, "Harley is going to California." She smiled like she was doing her own Colgate toothpaste commercial.

The clanking of Loralva dropping a bottle opener into the stainless sink could be heard from the saloon.

"California?" Ruby looked from Imogene to Harley. His blank face made Ruby all the more certain she herself was going. Imogene's big smile just turned her stomach.

Ruby came out from behind the Food Alley counter and headed toward the lanes. Imogene hopped off her stool and followed. As her thick thighs rubbed together, her panty hose made a fshht-fshht sound. "With Violet now a movie star—"

"TV star," Ruby corrected, tearing the used score sheets off the top of the pads on Lanes One and Two.

"She won't be coming back to Devine," Imogene continued. Ruby closed her eyes tight on that one, but kept walking straight ahead. "So, Harley will move out there."

Ruby wanted her to leave. Wanted her and her pile of skunk hair out in the middle of Highway 90.

"I figure"—Imogene rushed alongside Ruby, trying to look her in the face—"it's best, and I'm certain you agree"—Imogene grabbed Ruby's arm—"that Harley, as her husband, should go to Hollywood and find Violet." They now stood at Harley's lane. "What man doesn't want to be married to a movie star?" Ruby turned in Harley's direction. He opened his mouth to say something, then shut it. His eyes darted, then focused on the shiny wood floor of the lanes.

Imogene poofed and poked at her streaked hair. Ruby picked up stacks of the paper plates and napkins piled high from the day before. Dumping them into the trash, more visions of her Violet in that checkered dress crossed her mind. She wanted to tell Imogene right then that she would be going to California with another intention and it had nothing to do with TV or fame.

"I figure I'll wait until I know her exact whereabouts, then join Harley," Imogene rattled on. "Harley baby!" she shouted across the foyer. "We need to start making our plans. Violet is going to be *so* excited to see you." She winked at Ruby as he picked up his ball from the return. "You are going to forget all about that Becca Ann." And he threw the ball down the lane so fast that Ruby wondered if there wouldn't now be a dent in her maple floor.

"Obviously, no one is taking this as seriously as I am." The black and white hair sat ridged as Imogene shook her head. "You may be her mother, Ruby, but Violet's got different needs now that she's famous, and I'm the one that can handle stardom best.

You must stay behind and mind those kids." Then she hoisted her purse back onto her shoulder and hollered at Harley, "You come by my place when you're done, you hear?"

"Yes, ma'am," he answered, watching his ball spiral down the lane.

Imogene hadn't noticed Harley's lack of interest, or if she had she didn't let on to Ruby.

Imogene marched out the double glass doors, which swished back and forth on their hinges, sounding just like her thighs. Harley rolled a strike scattering pins up the lane. Imogene hollered over her shoulder, "I bet Violet even has a pool!"

"Deadwood on Lane Five," Ruby announced, but before she went off to retrieve it she said to Loralva through the little window, "Can you believe Imogene's sending Harley to California? And she don't even think for one minute about her grandkids."

Loralva had slipped on the new bowling shoes. She now held her foot out in front of her, the sequins glittering with the twist of fluorescent light. "He don't have a chance in hell on *The Price Is Right*."

After the leaguers began to arrive, Harley came up to the counter, rubbing his ball with the freebie Budweiser bowling towel Ruby'd given him.

"Can I do something for you, Harley?" Ruby asked, standing the cowboy boots that were too big for the shoe rental cubbies up against the wall.

He stepped right up. "I ain't going to California, Miss Ruby."

Loralva and Ruby looked at each other and then at Harley.

"I loved Violet. Really I did. So it ain't that. I don't want you to think I never did." He let out a big long breath. "But she's been gone a long time. Left me like a two-bit loser, which I ain't." His eyes looked her straight on. "Not to mention she left our Bunny and Bubbie. Even the worst mommas shouldn't do that."

The two women nodded. Loralva added, "And if there's one

thing I've learned, they lied when they said absence makes the heart grow fonder. It's been my experience that absence makes the heart go wander."

Harley looked down at his ball like he wanted to hug it. Loralva had said it exactly.

"Becca Ann?" Ruby asked.

"Yes, ma'am," Harley whispered, not looking up.

No one said anything for a moment. The thunder of balls rolling rang in their heads. Ruby wondered how Imogene was ever going to deal with this.

"My heart been broke once," Harley said. "Don't want it broke again. Even if it is by a movie star."

"Oh honey." Loralva wrapped her arm around his big, soft shoulders. "Don't you let that momma of yours trample on your heart any more than you can help."

Oh, Ruby thought, Imogene's gonna trample on more than your heart when she hears.

Suddy walked in the doors then, swiftly and with a take-charge attitude. She stood just at the edge of the rise to the loaner-ball shelves. She pulled a whistle out of her purse and tweeted twice, her signal that the leagues had begun. She ran the leagues as part of her deal with Ruby. If Ruby let her run the leagues, she'd only institute one church team. She could run the Bowl while I'm gone just fine, Ruby figured.

"Time to get busy," she said, handing a size ten pair of shoes to Joe Dean Williams, and taking his Tony Lamas. The air brakes on the beer delivery truck out front got Loralva going and everyone took their places: Ruby at the register and shoe rental, Loralva in the saloon, and Harley back at Lane Five with the rest of the Fire Balls, ready to get through the Bicentennial Bowl-a-thon. Now the only thing out of place was Ruby's heart. It had been thrown a little off center. But Rascal would say that was a good thing.

Psychedelic Hearts

After Harley told Ruby about not wanting to go to California, Suddy got the leagues under way and had the Tournament for Jesus going. Six-year-old bowlers were competing to play Baby Jesus, five-year-olds to be angels and four-and-unders to be lambs in the Christmas pageant. Suddy said she figured that to God, America's birthday was the perfect occasion for picking the actors to play the parts in a pageant about Jesus' birthday. Loralva reminded Suddy that the whole thing could be considered gambling in the eyes of the Lord, and therefore she was getting six-year-olds to sin in order to play Baby Jesus. But Suddy, who considered bowling to be the best sport ever invented by man or God, said there was no way that God would consider something as beautiful as bowling to be gambling.

By noon, the news that Ruby was going to California to search for Violet had gotten out, and as the day rolled on the Bowl buzzed louder than the neon beer signs, as no one in Devine kept their opinions to themselves much. Ida Mae Johnson's husband, Jimmy Ray, told Ruby how she'd end up in a ditch somewhere in

Los Angeles with transvestites licking her ear and stealing her dresses. They did that sort of thing, really they did. A big rancher, Jimmy Ray stood at the rental counter holding his paper boat filled with fried cheese, using his giveaway bowling towel as a napkin. Ruby wished he'd use it to wipe the ketchup off his belly before it left a stain right on top of the outboard motor on his boat racer T-shirt. It would leave a stain just like the things he was telling her would leave a big stain on her brain. But she didn't say a word. Instead she lined up the unrented shoes on the counter, pulled out the tongues to stick straight up, and as Jimmy Ray kept on rambling, she doused the inside of each shoe with deodorizer and antifungal spray.

"That's right, Ruby." Judy Harper had joined Jimmy Ray now and told Ruby she was talking crazy if she thought she could go to California. Judy wore the same sundress she'd worn for the past three summers and every year it got another size smaller. By now the armholes cut into the flab around her upper arms. Judy talked with the straw from her cup stuck in the corner of her mouth, her pink lipstick leaving a gummy ring around the top. "Better keep a good eye on those kids. They could get kidnapped out there," Judy continued. Ruby scouted around for Bunny and Bubbie, who stood in line for the Gutterballs for Gideon competition, the last chance at a part in the pageant.

"Just last year April Root from over at the Piggly Wiggly in Del Agua," Judy kept on, "she took her three kids to SeaWorld in San Diego, not even Los Angeles, and her little boy, Reed, went missing for a good hour. No telling what happened to him in that amount of time. April's scared to death her little boy's gonna show up in some porn movie. I told Clyde Gordon—you know he goes to Del Agua and watches them movies every Friday night—to watch for a little brown-headed kid with a mole on his upper lip." She sucked the liquid off the bottom of the cup, making the ice crackle, and Ruby shuddered and pinched her eyes tight at the thought.

As she reopened her lids she saw Judy and Jimmy Ray still yakking. Her stomach lurched and that raw feeling on her nerves came back to haunt her. Stop! Ruby wanted to shout. But she turned away and placed each freshly sprayed shoe in the cubbyholes marked W5 to M14.

"Ruby!" Imogene had walked up to the counter. "Have you seen Loralva?"

"Said she had to go to Del Agua for something. Probably a date." Ruby continued spraying the shoes, relieved for the interruption, but wishing it was someone else.

Imogene acted edgy. "Is she gonna be back this evening? Before the tournament's over?"

"Dunno," Ruby said. "She left her friend Verdee Whitacre in charge of the Idyll-On-Up, so I suspect not."

"Dang it." Imogene looked around the bowling alley like maybe Ruby was wrong. "I'll just have to catch up to her at her house then," she said as she walked off. Ruby thought she sounded way too nice to not be up to something. "Don't tell her I was looking for her."

"Why Jesus and St. Job, we haven't even mentioned earthquakes," Jimmy Ray said to Judy Harper, as though it was a conspiracy gone wrong. They hadn't budged from their soapboxes. Ruby clenched her mouth shut, but screamed inside her head that if she wanted transvestites to lick her ears then so be it. And she wanted to tell Judy Harper to buy a new first-of-the-summer outfit, something at least three sizes bigger. She knew those were mean things to think, so she felt a little bad. But just a little.

A whooping and hollering came from Lane Six, where someone had bowled a strike, so Ruby flipped the neon-light switch on and off a few times to keep the crowd's excitement going.

"Hope you don't plan on driving while you're there," Jimmy Ray said, scraping one last cheese stick on the bottom of the paper boat to get the remaining ketchup.

"Course they're driving," Judy Harper twirped. "You don't think she'd be going in no jet plane, do you? Scary enough she's going at all."

Contemplating this, Judy and Jimmy Ray just stared at each other in relative silence as Judy slurped and Jimmy Ray chewed with his mouth open.

"Loralva's doing all the driving," Ruby said in her own defense.

The two of them nodded their heads as though they had mutually determined that Ruby had gone and lost her mind.

The next day, as she cleaned up the bicentennial bowling tournament debris of wads of red, white, and blue, and lavender (she'd used up the rest of the wedding napkins), spilled beer, and fried food smudges on the loaner balls, she still had the ramblings of the night before stuck in her head. Transvestites struggling for her Samsonite, Bunny and Bubbie getting hoisted up under the arms of a hairy man wearing Judy Harper's white sundress, bulging in the same places. She had opened the Bowl late that morning, something she didn't ever do. But after a big tournament like yesterday's she knew most folks wouldn't be arriving too early. She did find out she'd missed Earl for his morning beer when he showed up again after she'd arrived and seemed a little hurt that she wasn't there sooner.

"Sorry about that, Earl," she told him as he tossed back the first beer. "Getcha another?" Ruby asked.

"That'd be fine," he nodded. Quiet fella. Ruby liked that. They didn't say much during these times alone. They'd gotten used to each other, she reckoned. Their only other opportunity for conversation was when his livestock got out the back fence, which they did quite often. She'd call him up and he'd be right over to help get them back through.

"Earl," she said as she pulled the bottle cap through the iron Coca-Cola bottle opener nailed to her side of the counter, "how's that fence out back holding up?"

"Not too badly," he told her, taking the beer. "Looks like the barbed wire's hanging a little loose in a couple of places, but I'll get to it right away."

Ruby knew he wouldn't, knew he'd wait until the goats started eating the little grassy area she'd set up for barbecues. They walked side by side over to the shoe rental counter, knowing that after the second beer, he'd be ready to bowl. She looked up at him, and right then he looked so kind and sweet hearted, she thought she oughta give him a little warning.

"You might want to fix those spots sooner than usual this time. I won't be around to give you a call, you know." She handed him the best pair of 11D rental shoes she had. The tongues hadn't even started to curl yet.

"Miss Ruby," Earl said, looking a little pouty, "you always said my goats and emus were welcome at your place anytime. I took that to mean—" But he stopped himself, and looked at her with a crosshatched brow. "How long you reckon you'll be gone?"

"Long as it takes," she said, although she worried how long that would be. She'd raised enough money at the Bicentennial Bowl-a-thon to pay for a few nights' stay in a motel room. She wasn't sure what she'd do when the money ran out, but she wasn't going to add that to her worries right now.

Earl's gray eyes got a little watery. Silence hung in between his nods. He looped one thumb through the belt loop by his Lone Star belt buckle. "Reckon it's best to follow the trail until you can't follow it no more."

"I reckon," Ruby said, not quite understanding, but watching the water in his eyes start to spill over a smidgen.

He pulled out his handkerchief and wiped at his temples like it was just sweat and not tears. "Reckon you'll be gone a while," and his eyes welled up again, but this time he looked away, bending down to pull his boots off.

"Not too long," she said. "I got the Devine Bowl to run."

"That's right," he said, pulling off his other boot. "And emus to chase out of your parking lot."

Ruby laughed, then asked him, "What do you mean 'follow the trail until you can't no more'?"

He zipped up his bowling bag and dabbed at his temples one more time. "Nothing," he said, "just that you gotta go see. Just take care of yourself, is all."

Ruby figured he meant to be careful of all the hippie, drug-dealing transvestites like everyone else had warned her about. She watched him walk toward Lane One somewhat slower than usual. She flipped the switch under the counter to turn the lane on for him. Sweet fella, she thought.

She called Suddy after a while and talked to her about running the bowling alley while she was in California. Suddy was all for it, but wanted to close down the saloon. "You can't expect me to be pouring no whiskey, now can you?" she said, sounding sour.

Ruby told Suddy she'd ask Verdee Whitacre if she could cover the bar since she'd done a fine job last night. So, it was settled.

When it became time for the Idyll-On-Up to start some whiskey pouring, Loralva still hadn't shown up yet. But just as Ruby thought she'd give her sister a call to see where she'd gone off to, Loralva showed up.

"Yoo-hoo, Ruby honey," Loralva sang as she entered the bowling alley through the Idyll-On-Up's swinging doors. In one hand she carried a Piggly Wiggly sack, the top half rolled down. The nearest Piggly Wiggly was over in Del Agua. Ruby hardly ever shopped there, and Loralva never did.

"I'm over here polishing the loaner balls," Ruby said.

Setting the sack down on the shoe rental counter, she stood across the Lustre King 300 from Ruby. Today she wore her rattlesnake rattler earrings, which dangled below her salt-and-pepper shag cut. Loralva scratched underneath the wig with one of her long nails. Ruby wondered why Loralva chose to wear wigs when she could always be found scratching the itch.

"What'd you get at the Piggly Wiggly?"

"Nothing. It's just the bag that Burt's Iron-ons gave me my purchase in." She pulled out three red T-shirts, laying them out on the counter next to Rascal's trophies. All three had a psychedelic iron-on heart. Above the heart was a rounded iron-on *I* and below the heart *Bob Barker.* Ruby studied them for a second, then said, "I heart Bob Barker?"

"I *love* Bob Barker." Loralva closed her eyes as the words swirled across her frosted lipstick.

"You got game show tickets!" Ruby was so excited for her sister, this being Loralva's biggest dream, next to meeting John Wayne, and she'd done that already. Ruby hoped it was a good sign for their trip.

"Imogene got the tickets." Loralva held a T-shirt up to her full chest. This T-shirt had a V-neck, unlike the others, and was the smallest. The other two were a medium and a large. "She's got this cousin or somebody living out there somewhere and they can get us tickets. She said it's all set."

"Imogene?" Ruby rubbed her finger over a plastic shimmering heart, then stopped. "She's pulling something over on you."

"No, she promised," Loralva said. "She said she'd already called and made the necessary arrangements. We just have to pick them up."

Ruby let her mind calculate all this information. Then looking into Loralva's green eyes, she said, "And that's why there's three shirts?"

"Well, I reckon I should have asked you first, but I just got so thrilled that I couldn't help myself. You know how you can't take back anything you say to Imogene. I couldn't very well—"

"You ain't trying to tell me Imogene is going with us?" She heard her own voice climb louder, and Oboe Wilson, practicing way over on Lane One, looked over to see if she was all right. So she toned it down. Loralva was talkin' crazy. Imogene must be stringing Loralva along.

"Ruby honey, maybe she can help. One more person to do the looking, another set of eyes."

Ruby shook her head no. "What are you trying to do? Scare Violet off?"

"I couldn't help it! She called me up, said she had tickets to the game show," Loralva burst out, switching back and forth on her high heels, her tiny ankles looking like they could snap. "*The Price Is Right,* my all-time, very most favorite. Ooh, that Bob Barker." Loralva rolled her eyes into the back of her head as if she were making love to him right there on the Devine Bowl's shoe rental counter. Her navel twitched as her tummy shuddered. Ruby looked away, ashamed her sister would be so flagrant.

Ruby opened the porthole door on the Lustre King 300 and put another of the loaner balls inside. "Imogene?" she said again.

"But we'll all get to be on *The Price Is Right,*" Loralva said. "That's why I got you a T-shirt as well."

"I can't be on no game show." Ruby looked at her sister, the ball polisher rumbling between them. There'll be no one to watch the kids, and besides, I gotta spend all my time hunting for Violet." What she hoped was that all her time would be spent *with* Violet. "But *Imogene*?" She had to ask again. "I ain't just worried about me being in a car with her for however long it takes, but you can't even make it from the Idyll-On-Up to the shoe rental counter without having a brawl with her yourself."

Loralva nodded in agreement, but twisted her mouth up in a

tangle, her frosted hot-pink lipstick darkening in the cracks of her taut lips. She was wearing seamless blue jean hip-huggers stretched snug and flat against her abdomen and an ordinary white blouse with the shirttail tied in a half knot just below her breast bone; her belly button, usually open and accepting, was scrunched and fretful.

The machine stopped and Ruby put the polished ball on the loaner shelf and replaced it with a black AMF with two thumb-holes drilled in it etched with the initials J.R.J. Her hands trembled even though she hadn't flipped the Lustre King 300 on switch. Loralva stood in front of her with pleading eyes and pouty lips. She tried to ignore Loralva's face.

"Just tell her no. Say we don't have room. That's more or less true." The machine coughed like a small child before it started up.

"Well . . ." Loralva looked at her nails. "There ain't actually a question to be answered with a no," she said, picking at a possible hangnail. "She didn't *ask* if she could come with us. *I* asked *her* along." Ruby looked at Loralva, whose small round eyes opened wide, her pink lips pulled into a pleading smile and her belly button in an O. Loralva's voice turned high in pitch and speed. "She was telling me about *The Price Is Right,* and how her second cousin's brother-in-law told her how to get the tickets the fastest. Then she called him and put him on the phone and when I heard him say, 'You're as good as in,' I just couldn't help myself. I blurted out, 'Imogene, how about riding with us?' and she said yes right away, as though she'd already given it plenty of thought." Loralva's curled lashes blinked slowly and flirtatiously, the same way she got a man to do what she wanted with a swoosh of those lashes.

"No," Ruby said. "Anyway, I'm not so sure I can afford this trip." She just couldn't bring herself to point out that Imogene had to be yanking Loralva's chain. Under normal circumstances,

Loralva would never fall for one of Imogene's tricks. Ruby knew Loralva wanted to be on a game show so badly she'd believe even the most two-faced skunk. "I can't have any delays," Ruby said.

"That's where it gets even better." Loralva straightened up, her hips even, the skintight jeans flexing, her belly button now straightening into a smile. "Imogene said she'd pay. If I drive her Winnebago, she'll pay for our motel in Hollywood. It won't cost you hardly anything. Just meals."

"The sitting bull Winnebago?" Ruby asked, thinking she might even laugh at this.

While Imogene was married, her husband had bought the Winnebago as a surprise. But Imogene refused to go camping, saying that was for cedar choppers who couldn't afford motels like decent folk. So ever since, the motor home had just sat on the special concrete pad they'd had poured on the side of their house. Then when Imogene's husband ran off with that heavyset breakfast waitress over in Cicada, he left Imogene with everything: the house, the drilling business, and both pickups. All he'd wanted was the Winnebago. But Imogene refused to let him have the vehicle in the divorce, and so there it still sat. Everyone it town called it the sitting bull.

Imogene liked to flaunt her money, but she wasn't always generous with it. Ruby knew Imogene intended to pay for the trip so Ruby would be forced to agree to her going with them. And if Imogene knew that Harley wasn't going, and obviously she must, then she'd want to hone in on their trip so she could get her way. She may think Ruby wasn't the right one to go even though she was the momma, but the fact was Imogene didn't have the gumption to go by herself. Ruby realized Imogene had plotted all this out very thoroughly. Ruby had to admit there'd also be plenty of room for the three of them and the kids in that camper. Ruby'd been inside it when it was first purchased, and it was dadgum nice with a bunk above the front seats, a double bed in back and the dinette made into another bed with the table folding down and seat cushions on top. "You got me between the devil and the deep blue sea," Ruby said to Loralva. "When you scheduled to be on the show?"

"I don't know yet," Loralva said. "Imogene said we'd know more when we got there."

Baptisms and Bagos

Purple and orange weren't two colors Ruby would ever put together and she couldn't for the life of her understand how this Lord God of theirs could have come up with the combination, but He had, and there they were in the sky outside the Winnebago's windshield. Ruby watched the colors darkening and felt them coming closer. She noticed how when the sun set the world became quiet, especially inside the 'bago.

A day and a half on the road, somewhere inside Arizona, which didn't look much different than Texas yet. Same cactus, dirt and sky. Made Ruby feel safer. She hoped it might even stay this way, and in that case she wouldn't be out of place in Hollywood. But she knew from the TV and magazine pictures that it would be different. She'd seen the palm trees and long lawns thick with grass and flowering plants in colors like the sky up ahead.

The vehicle creaked as it made its way down Interstate 10. Imogene dozed, head bobbing over her chest, making snortling noises like a skunk digging for grubs.

That's how she got that crick in her neck, Ruby thought as she watched the head bounce and Imogene's mouth gape a bit, her lips dangling.

Loralva sat up high in the driver's seat, today wearing a pile of black curls that made her even taller, as her body swayed with the road. With a long nail she scratched just behind her right ear.

Ruby sat in the dinette booth that also folded down and served as her and Loralva's bed at night. Bunny had fallen asleep in Ruby's lap, and her long skinny legs like Violet's hung over the end of booth. Now Ruby faced west, looking toward Violet's new home. From where she sat she could see out the windshield between Loralva and Imogene's heads. While Ruby'd ventured several times to wonder what lay ahead, right now she could only think about what she'd left behind.

She'd left behind her bowling ball. She'd left it sitting in its turquoise vinyl bag at the foot of her bed. She wasn't even sure they had bowling alleys in California. She figured they probably did in some parts, but just couldn't picture an alley in Hollywood. Besides, she wouldn't have time. She had to keep her nose to the trail like Earl Glidden's bird dog, Betty.

Ruby'd also left behind the picture of Rascal after he'd won the American Bowling Congress championship in Oklahoma City. She kept the photo in the side zipper pocket of the turquoise bowling bag. She wished she had remembered that; she would have liked to have him by her side right about now.

Imogene's head popped up, one half of her black and white basketball of hair mushed flat. "Good Lord," she said, looking straight ahead. "They got sunsets bigger than the Del Agua Drive-in Theater."

Bunny squirmed in Ruby's lap, but didn't wake up completely, just stirring up that little-girl smell of strawberry candy. Bubbie peeked over the edge of his bunk, but quickly slunk away.

All that could be seen of him was the saggy sock on his foot, with a cellophane MoonPie wrapper clinging to the bottom.

"What's the next town?" Ruby asked.

"Phoenix," Loralva said, catching her sister's eye in the rear-view mirror. "We'll pass through, then stop on the other side for the night."

"Looky there!" Imogene's voice brought Ruby back around. "Two hundred miles to the California border!" She pointed out the big, green highway sign that came closer, then disappeared behind them.

Two hundred miles seemed too short, too close. It was only five hundred miles ago that Bubbie turned over the potato chip stand at the Park and Eat truck stop. Only a thousand miles ago that Bunny had spilled a Dr. Pepper in her Mimaw Imogene's lap. Only 1,500 miles ago that Bubbie had started scratching his head like a swarm of mosquitoes had wined and dined just above his right ear. Then the spot, about the size of a drop cookie, had started oozing and Ruby had dabbed his crew-cut prickly head with Merthiolate, leaving a big, bright orange circle the color of a Halloween cookie. By the time they reached Midland/Odessa, too far to turn back, Ruby knew what that oozing, itchy spot was all about. "Loralva, we gotta pull off at the next exit. Find a drugstore, maybe they have a Rexall out this far. I need to buy some ointment," she'd said.

"Can't go chopping up armadillos from the middle of the road and not get the mange," Imogene had said in her oh-so-sensitive way. And that's exactly what he had too.

Bunny wouldn't look at the spot or even in Bubbie's direction. "Ooh, ick," she had said. Bubbie now stayed hidden in the bunk. Ruby had scrubbed down the inside of the 'bago, scared to death they'd all catch the mange. Bubbie, he sulked and looked like he wished the whole lot of them would contract it.

But before that, two thousand miles ago, Ruby was waiting

at her house for Loralva and Imogene to arrive in the Winnebago. She didn't anticipate the tantrums, the confessions or the mange, but she had the bugaboos bigger than Dallas. Trying to keep her mind off where they were going, she concentrated on what she had packed, going over her list and making sure she'd included everything they would need. She reviewed the contents of the Idyll County Fire Department duffel bag, the pink Barbie suitcase and her own Hardside Samsonite that had been Rascal's for his bowling tours: short sets for Bunny, T-shirts and jeans for Bubbie, new culottes from Landers' Dry Goods for herself, along with the toys she'd told the kids to pick out. Bubbie brought along his G.I. Joe.

Bunny picked only her Mrs. Beasley doll. She claimed it smelled like her momma. "Like mayonnaise and the dirty clothes hamper when it's full."

They had filled two eight-quart Tupperware containers with fried chicken and a third with potato salad. A case each of root beer and Coca-Cola had been stacked by the front door. When Imogene arrived with Loralva and noticed there was no Dr. Pepper she insisted they'd have to make a stop before leaving town. Said she'd get constipated if she didn't drink it every day, so there was half a case of that too. "It's the prune juice they put in it," Imogene said.

"They quit putting prune juice in Dr. Pepper years ago," Loralva told her. "It's your way of living that causes constipation."

Imogene said under her breath, but intended for all to hear, "It would behoove you to watch how you talk to me." Finishing up with how she was financing the trip and therefore they were already taking advantage of her too much anyhow.

"We can stop once we get outside of Idyll County," Loralva said.

"We can only stop in respectable places and that may mean only Devine and Hollywood," Imogene said. "Judy Harper's cousin, Rosellen, stopped at one of those roadside places that sells pecan rolls and she found a thumb inside one. Swear to God."

"How'd she know it was a thumb and not a finger?" Loralva asked. But Ruby hadn't wanted to hear any more, so she went outside to check on Earl Glidden's back fence one more time before she left.

She kept rosebushes growing behind the bowling alley. No one would be taking care of them while she was gone, and there would be no roses to take to Rascal when she got back. She paused to think what she would bring back for Rascal, but that was something she didn't have an answer for yet, and she wasn't even sure what to hope for.

As she reminded herself to get out extra rolls of toilet paper to take with them, her thoughts were interrupted by the squeak of the back screen door and Bunny running right up to Ruby's leg. "Aunt Loralva says let's get a move on—Hollywood, California, here we come!" Ruby's heart stopped somewhere between Hollywood and California. It snagged on the comma.

Now, here in the 'bago, she sat only two hundred miles away from that sticky comma, her heart still stopping its beat every so often. Imogene, wide awake now, ranted about the movie stars' flaws. She almost knew theirs better than she knew the ones that belonged to the town of Devine. Most certainly she knew them better than her own. Sean Connery had oversized adenoids, Olivia Newton-John had to have ingrown toenail surgery. "Far more embarrassing than Suddy's toes when she wears sandals," she'd said. Even before the mange incident Ruby had begun to get frustrated with Imogene and her ranting, gossipy ways. Loralva, she just reached over and turned up Johnny Cash on the cassette player.

The light outside the camper was gone now, making the inside glow brighter. Bubbie played with G.I. Joe and a tiny hand grenade, making exploding noises every few minutes, blowing up the mounds of rumpled sheets. As she watched the MoonPie wrapper on Bubbie's foot slip loose and float to the floor, she worried about his anger and his acting up, chopping at a roadkill armadillo.

For years, she'd done nearly everything she could think of to get him to talk again. At first she'd try to get him to say please or thank you. Then she'd threatened not to let him have his MoonPie if he didn't ask for it, so he'd just sit at the kitchen table in silence until she finally felt so bad she'd unwrap one and put it on a plate in front of him. After all, the hurt from his momma's leaving was still in the razor-sharp stage and Ruby herself didn't have the heart to withhold anything from the kids. But as time went by she tried other tactics. She'd even gone so far as to pin him down on the floor in a half nelson, holding tight, not letting go, hoping he'd finally yell, "Stop it!" like a normal kid. But he'd just stare at her, round face and hair sheared down to the nubbins, making him look like Harley, so she couldn't hold on very long. She also tried talking to him about it like the ladies' magazines suggested in articles on child rearing, but she might as well have been trying to explain Texas history to a Yankee, he couldn't care in the least. His teachers complained about his silence and sent bad report cards home. But somehow, he and Bunny still had their sibling secrets and rivalries. They'd fight and he'd pick on his little sister, but Ruby heard nary a word of it except the names Bunny claimed he called her.

Ruby had thought that maybe when he heard they were going to California to look for his momma, the hope would pull him out of it. But she somehow sensed the trip was like a drawstring pulling him further inside.

The sky had darkened to navy blue and the Winnebago swayed back and forth down Interstate 10.

Imogene's voice brought her thoughts back to the inside of

the camper. "Ain't that right, Ruby? Didn't Violet look like Elizabeth Taylor on that ButterMaid commercial?"

"Violet's prettier than even Liz," Loralva said, turning the big steering wheel slightly to change lanes. Phoenix's city lights were visible up ahead.

"Of course she's prettier, she don't have that tendency to put on weight like Miss Taylor," Imogene said.

"Looked like a milkmaid to me. A pretty one," Ruby said. She'd only been half listening to their argument about Violet's stardom while her mind wandered.

"I just know she's trying to become the next Liz Taylor. And she will be," Imogene said.

"If you have anything to do with it," Loralva finished the sentence for her. "I agree with Liz and her view on marriage—gotta keep trying 'til she gets it right."

"Violet and my Harley will be married for all eternity," Imogene said.

Just like the lying napkins, Ruby thought, and she pictured the lopsided plastic couple on top of the gray cake that Imogene had brought to Lina and Jason's wedding reception. The cake that had been thrown out the next day.

They hit a chuckhole in the road and the back-and-forth motion of the motor home swayed inside Ruby. Imogene went on to talk about Violet's body parts that were the same as Elizabeth Taylor's in *Giant.* She might look like Liz, violet eyes and coal black hair, but Arlene was where she got the dark hair and light complexion. Ruby'd never been close enough to see Arlene's eyes, so there was no way of knowing if hers were violet. Maybe there was something she didn't get from her.

Violet's light complexion and dark hair contrasted with Ruby and Rascal's blond and light brown hair, and skin like freckled khaki canvas. Ruby and Rascal weren't big nor small, just in between. Medium in height and width. When she first brought

Violet home Ruby thought she wasn't eating enough, thought she'd never grow, but Violet was just small in stature and delicate. Once in a while Ruby thought she could see a resemblance to herself or Rascal. Violet's ears had that small fold at the tops like Rascal's, and her chin, when she was thinking hard, crumpled right at the bottom—Ruby had that same crumple. She liked to think Violet got those ingredients from them.

Imogene must not have been able to stand having Ruby off on her own thinking because she kept interrupting. "Ruby, Violet never had no boyfriend besides Harley, did she." She said it more as a statement, more than likely an attempt at proving Loralva wrong.

"How about Petey Carlyle?" Ruby answered.

"Oh pooh. He doesn't count." Imogene tossed her hand back as though volleying Ruby's wasted response back to her.

"Don't count?" Loralva said. "Bet she lost her cherry with him."

Imogene gasped at the word *cherry* as though Suddy were in the vehicle with them and would be checking to see how they were behaving. "Why must you take everything in that direction?" Violet's mother-in-law turned to Loralva with a cross face—vertical wrinkles creasing the space between her black eyebrows and making the stripes in her hair more prominent, or maybe that was from the way she leaned her head forward and glared up with her eyes.

"You afraid of the word *cherry*?" Loralva said across the console to Imogene. "Cherry, cherry, cherry," she repeated, making it ring in Imogene's ears as long as possible.

"I'm not afraid of it," Imogene said, looking out the passenger window, turning away from the word.

Ruby, a little embarrassed to be thinking of her daughter with a boy in that way, didn't think either one of them was right. "Her best beau was that Zeb Walker," Ruby said. "Remember him? That cute boy with the red ears. I liked him." She'd wanted Violet to marry him, even though they weren't more than fifteen when they went out. But Zeb's family had moved. Where was it they moved to? Alabama? Arkansas? Arizona?

"Violet," Imogene announced loudly and authoritatively, the way she did when she wanted to make certain she had the last word on everything. "Violet was pure when she married my Harley."

That's that. That's the way it was. Amen, Ruby almost said out loud.

But Loralva didn't like letting someone else have the last word any more than Imogene did. "What'd you do?" she said. "Take Violet into Dr. Peterson, have her hymen examined before allowing Harley to propose?"

And so it was, Loralva got the last word on that subject. Imogene looked out the passenger window and in the darkness Ruby could see the bitter woman's reflection, her scrunched-up mouth, and she could hear her suck in her breath and hold it for what seemed to Ruby long enough to make a person light headed.

Ruby gazed outside at the darkness passing by. Her own reflection looked back from the glass. The outline of her hair a little mussed, her face looking sallow. But she told herself the black night made the shadows dark and the black circles under her eyes were not quite so deep. Through the reflection she looked outside at the dark landscape of Arizona.

Even God wasn't able to tame Violet, and she reckoned it had to do with being christened with goat piss.

Suddy and Chester had always been on Ruby and Rascal about baptizing Violet. "She's well past the proper age," they'd say. "She won't get into heaven if she ain't baptized," Suddy always added. As far as Ruby was concerned you got into heaven based on merits. But by the time Violet was ten years old, she had so few merits and such a stockpile of demerits that Ruby figured it couldn't do the girl any harm and would get Suddy off her back. "What's a little water dabbed on here and there to keep the girl from rotting in hell," Suddy said, smiling sweetly.

Ruby found a yellow dress with blue cuffs for herself. Rascal got gussied up in his seersucker suit. White wasn't very practical in the dust of Devine, so Ruby hadn't gone to all the trouble of buying matching white shoes for either herself or Rascal. She just used a bottle of white shoe polish over a pair of each of their bowling shoes. But Violet, she wore a white lace dress and got new shoes. Patent leather.

Violet never acted too sure about this baptism. Her friend, that delinquent Claudia Whitcomb, who belonged to the Southern Baptist over in Hondo, had been baptized and she'd had to be dunked full body in the Nueces River during a drought year. The water level sat so low that when that Baptist preacher dunked Claudia's head back, he'd knocked her clean out on a rock at the bottom of the river. Reverend Alabaster said it didn't count if you were unconscious during the baptism. So the next weekend, when they were out of the worry of a concussion, Claudia had to do it again. This time they found a sandy spot.

When Violet's time came she was scared as a chicken on Sunday after church. Ruby shushed her, telling her that Methodists don't go all out like the Baptists. Reverend Wilson would just dip a yellow rose into holy water and then dab it on her forehead. She looked relieved until they got inside the sanctuary.

When Chester grabbed her around the shoulders to lean her back over the christening bowl, her face went to gray. She went crazy mad and turned over the birdbath that Suddy and Chester used for holding the holy water, causing all of them to be baptized over and over with holy water sprinkles. Ruby didn't reckon a single drop landed on Violet, though, because she was already out the door. She screamed and tore and turned over and upset and yanked all the way out of that sanctuary. Suddy said they wouldn't charge them for the scratched and nicked pews. Ruby and Rascal thanked them and left.

When Earl Glidden found the girl in his barn with all the pygmy goats and brought her back to the Bowl, those white patent leather shoes had turned ochre from the goat piddle. Earl had a scratch as long as a baby rattler down his arm, pointy tooth-marks in his hand and a grimy Mary-Jane print on his Wranglers. He'd told Rascal that she'd fought him the whole way home. Ruby reckoned that was the streak Bubbie had inherited from Violet.

Mustard and Mustangs

Loralva found a spot to park the Winnebago in the back lot of a place called Plooker's Pitstop in a town called New Hope, Arizona. It was just a few miles before the California border, and Ruby said she wanted to wait until daylight to cross so she could see California from one side to the other clearly.

"With the curtains closed you won't know no difference between this place and a KOA campground," Loralva had said. Other than the rumble of the sleeping semi-truck engines all night, she was right, Ruby thought. Even that drone eventually disappeared into the background. Still, Ruby didn't get much sleeping done, but got plenty of worrying done instead. Mainly she worried about how the next day by noon, they'd be in California, which was farther from Texas than she ever imagined she'd go.

The next morning, from the moment the sun rose over Phoenix, it started off as a harum-scarum day. Getting the kids up and dressed was the first vexation. Bubbie turned himself into a boy of lead and wouldn't budge. Bunny rubbed the sleep from her eyes with her fists and said, "He don't want to go to California, so he ain't gonna get dressed."

Ruby sighed. "It's too late to take you back now," she told him, pulling herself onto her tiptoes to see him up on the bunk. "And, I ain't about to leave you here in Arizona all by your lonesome." That didn't seem to matter to him either way. Though he didn't appear to be about to change his mind, she went ahead and laid out his nice blue trousers with a tiny check, his yellow western dress shirt with cream piping, a clean pair of Fruit of the Looms and dress socks, hoping this wouldn't set off a tantrum inside this tight drum of a 'bago. But he wouldn't climb down from the bunk. He'd scrunched himself up into the far corner by the narrow window that looked out the front of the Winnebago. Finally, Ruby decided to bribe him with a MoonPie. He thought about it for a moment, then thrashed and kicked the covers off his feet before climbing down off the bunk.

While Ruby continued to feed and dress the kids, Loralva shaved her legs over the tiny kitchen sink and got herself dolled up for their entry into Hollywood. She slipped into her shimmery, bright orange satin minidress with stockings and carrottop fall, while Ruby shoved Bubbie's arms into shirtsleeves and Bunny sang "Jesus Loves Me, This I Know" over and over. Nearly drove Ruby crazy.

"How about you sing something else today?" Ruby asked the little girl. Hoping she had another song that she knew more than one line of.

"Okay," Bunny said, her words always full of sugar. She appeared to be flipping through the repertoire of songs in her head. "How about 'You Are My Sunshine'?"

Imogene leaned against the counter drinking a Dr. Pepper. "How about you don't sing when you're around your Mimaw

Imogene?" she said, giving the little girl a fake smile, then recovered from a carbonated burp.

Violet's mother-in-law was dressed to the hilt. Along with her costume jewelry of pearls and bauble rings she wore panty hose and a black and white suit that matched her hair. "I save money buying a suit that's black *and* white," she had said. "Can wear it to both funerals and weddings." She'd finished off the outfit with a pair of spectator pumps.

They bumped into one another as they each dressed themselves and tried to ignore their nervousness about entering California that day. But it wasn't long before Imogene peeled off her panty hose and then changed into a pair of culottes. Loralva dabbed the sweat off her cleavage with a paper towel and Ruby herself rolled a cold can of Coke across her forehead. Each of the kids had on their nice new California outfits, but they both pulled and shifted in their clothes, wanting something lighter. "But I only just put you in those clothes," Ruby said, thinking she sounded like a whiner herself.

"It's too dang hot in here," Loralva said. She started the engine of the Winnebago, turning the knobs to get the air conditioner to work harder. After a few minutes and several exasperated sighs from Imogene, Loralva said, "Looks like the air conditioner on your Winnebago quit sometime during the night, Imogene." Ruby wished Loralva wouldn't have put it like that because Imogene's fuming just caused the inside to get hotter. The sun was rising higher and the metal motor home had quickly become an Easy-Bake Oven. Ruby opened the door. Now in the daylight she saw the landscape of the truck stop they'd pulled into late last night. Rows of semi trucks parked between the extra-long diagonal lines indicating parking spaces on the tarmac just for the rigs. A gas station with row after row of pumps, mostly diesel, and a mini-mart sat not too far off in the distance. A big-lettered sign on the side of the building read NEW HOPE, AZ—HOME TO SWINGERS OF AMERICA.

"Wonder if them Swingers of New Hope are related to the Swinger's Mortuary family over in Cicada, Texas?" Ruby said. "Wouldn't that be the dangest coincidence?"

Loralva looked out the door to the sign Ruby pointed at and said, "Ruby honey, those ain't the same swingers. That much I know."

"Well, okay," Ruby said, thinking Loralva could sure be obstinate when she wanted to.

They all agreed they certainly couldn't continue across the desert without AC. Loralva said not to worry, she'd walk over across the big parking lot and sweet-talk the Plooker's Pitstop mechanics into looking into making the necessary repairs.

With stalls and parking spaces made for the big rigs, the place teemed with vehicles five times the size of the 'bago. Written in big block letters across the rooftop of the station a sign advertised GOOD FOOD. There was a mini-mart inside the main building and picnic tables outside. Ruby and Imogene lugged the ice chest over to set up for lunch at the concrete tables in the grassy area just past the gas pumps.

While they waited for Loralva to get back, they bought a supersize package of baloney and a loaf of white bread. Bubbie riffled through the T-shirts on the rack by the cashier. MENUDO, THE BREAKFAST OF CHAMPIONS excited the boy the most, but Ruby wouldn't buy it for him. "You don't even wear the nice clothes I buy you." She took his hand and led him and Bunny back outside to the picnic area. Bubbie pouted and Bunny drug Mrs. Beasley along in the dirt beside her. Bubbie tried to quietly pull his hand from Ruby's but she held ever-so-slightly tighter. She didn't want any more cut-up roadkill or a run-over Bubbie.

At the table, Ruby sat facing a round thermometer hung in what little shade came from the eaves of the main building. As they set out sandwich fixings she kept glancing at that thermometer hoping for a break in the heat, but the temperature never dropped below 100 degrees the whole time.

Eventually Loralva came striding across the tarmac. As she approached she said, "They put the 'bago right up to the front of the line, thanks to my sweet-talkin'."

Ruby shook her head as she smeared French's mustard on her bread slice. "You are always flitting your body parts in men's faces."

"Would you like that I go back and ask them to treat us regular and we can sit here sweating for two days?" Loralva cocked a hip in her sister's direction. Ruby didn't think Loralva had to be so snitty, but they did have to get back on the road, so she didn't say any more.

"I am not sitting here one minute longer than I have to," Imogene said, fanning herself with a paper plate. "You can offer up any part of yourself you want today. We don't need any more delays." Ruby busied herself making sandwiches for the kids as though she wasn't listening. She wouldn't dwell on it, but a teensy part of her was glad there was a delay.

After they finished eating, they all sat waiting and sweating. Bunny tugged on Ruby's arm. "Can we go to the shops, GranMomma?" she asked, pointing directly across the parking lot to the row of wooden shacks. There was an Indian Trading Post that advertised moccasins and arrowheads on a sign out front, a Crystal Emporium, and a store called Sweet Shoppe. Next to the shops was a building with six doors all facing the stoop, each door a different color. Ruby thought it looked like *Let's Make a Deal,* but figured it was a small motel instead.

"Not right now," Ruby said, not wanting to get up. "Play with your Mrs. Beasley doll and G.I. Joe."

"It's too hot," whined Bunny. Bubbie slumped his head and arms on the table. The air was hotter than grease in a deep fat fryer and with the gravel snapping and popping from the semis passing by Ruby felt like she was sitting right in the middle of that grease. Imogene pumped her paper plate fan and Ruby cleaned the mustard off Bunny's white shorts.

Ruby got to thinking: What kind of momma was she that she didn't want to rush out to Hollywood to get her daughter? Was California really scaring her? Maybe it was just the heat that had her all twisted up on the inside. She considered asking Loralva to do some more of her kind of talking to the mechanics and hurry them up when a big bus with white Mustangs painted on the side pulled into Plooker's. The pshoo of the air brakes made Loralva turn around and watch as five men in white jeans climbed down the steps of the bus. One man stepped down and stood off to the side, looking in the direction of their picnic table, while the rest of them headed toward the mini-mart.

Bubbie tapped Bunny on the shoulder, then pointed for her to look. "It's a band!" Bunny shouted. "Can we go over, GranMomma?"

"You can't be talking to strangers," Ruby told them. "You ain't in Texas anymore."

She wondered if it would just be celebrities from here on out and would they be getting in her way.

The man kept standing there looking in their direction. Imogene stopped fanning herself. "Oh my, he's looking my way," she said.

"Why's he standing directly in the sun when he could go inside like the others?" Ruby said.

"He may be admiring what pretty ladies we are." Loralva

unbuttoned the top button of her sundress real subtle-like and with her other hand she pulled a small piece of red hair from around her temple, spit on her forefinger and thumb and then twisted that piece of hair into a ringlet. "I knew I should have brought my other wig," she said.

He caught sight of Loralva in her orange sherbet dress sitting cross legged with one foot sticking out from under the table waving up and down as if to say "come here, come here," and he obeyed her, paying not one bit of attention to the rest of them. That day Loralva wore her new "glass slippers," as she called them, clear plastic uppers on clear Lucite high-heeled wedges. "Better than toe cleavage," Loralva had said while shopping with Ruby. "Showing the whole thing is always better than being a tease."

The man finally came up to their table, but not before Ruby thought Loralva was going to waggle her foot off.

"Howdy, pretty ladies," he said, tipping his white cowboy hat. His voice rang in Ruby's ears like the low hum of a bass guitar. He looked so sharp in his eelskin boots with the silver tips, and buckskin vest with turquoise buttons. The silver tips on his collar matched the ones on his boots. This fella looked so respectful and clean they all sat a little taller and straighter, even the kids.

Loralva latched on to his long-lashed eyes and wouldn't let go. "Well, hello to you too." She darn near sang it like a song.

"I'm Duke." He stuck his big strong hand out to Loralva first, like the rest of them had become part of the dust of the parking lot. Loralva took his big thick hand in hers, then put her other hand on top, holding on tight. Her foot pumped up and down like a Chihuahua's hind leg when he's being scratched behind the ears.

Imogene cleared her throat and waited to be recognized. Duke didn't even try to remove his hand from Loralva's. But with his left hand he tipped his hat again briefly, giving Imogene and Ruby a nod. Ruby didn't want to be rude even though he wasn't looking in her direction anymore, so she said hello and told him her name too.

"Have a seat, Duke." Loralva gestured for him to sit between her and Mrs. Beasley on the cement bench. "Can I get you a baloney sandwich? We have plenty."

They chatted with Duke for a while and found out he was in a country-and-western band, Duke and the Skirt-Tailers. Imogene claimed she'd heard of them and even said she thought she had one of their record albums until Duke said they didn't have one released yet, but were getting ready to. Loralva said she would buy it right away.

"Don't you want to hear what we sound like first?" he asked. That made sense to Ruby.

"Why certainly," Loralva said, "but I can just tell you'd be *good*." She said the *good* like she wasn't talking about music.

"Which way you headed? East or west?" he asked.

"To California!" Imogene said like she was already on a game show. "My daughter-in-law is a movie star."

"TV star," Ruby corrected under her breath as Bunny shouted, "She's my momma!" and Bubbie yanked one of the arms off his G.I. Joe.

"That so?" Duke said, not in any way particularly impressed, which Ruby took to mean famous folks would be everywhere you looked the closer you got to California.

"We're stuck here for the time being," Loralva said. "Our Winnebago broke down and we're having to wait here while they fix it."

"Well then, you can come hear us play over at the Hootin' Annie Lounge right here in New Hope. It's a respectable joint that would welcome a bunch of fine ladies like yourselves," he said, as he continued to stare in Loralva's direction.

"We'll already be on the road by then," Imogene said. "On our way to see my movie star daughter-in-law." She said the last part louder in case she hadn't been heard the first time.

Ruby tried to refrain from saying "TV star" but just couldn't help herself.

"That's a shame," Duke said, "because I was gonna have guest passes left at the door for you."

"You were?" Loralva said, slipping her arm around his elbow.

"But if you're heading to Hollywood, me and the boys will be playing at the Giddyup. It's a small place off of Vine, but we can pack 'em in." Duke and Loralva smiled at each other as though getting packed in a tight place together sounded like a fine idea.

"Do you go to Hollywood often?" Ruby asked, thinking he might have some connection with TV folk.

Imogene must have been thinking along the same lines, because she followed Ruby with, "Maybe you already know my daughter-in-law, Violet Davidson?"

"No ma'am," Duke answered, "can't say that I do."

Imogene humphed and crossed her arms. Duke was not ever going to pay Imogene enough attention.

"Wish we could stop in tonight," Loralva said. "But we'd be happy to come and see y'all play in Hollywood."

"You just out this way visiting?" Duke asked.

"We're looking for Violet Davidson!" Imogene never did like having to repeat herself.

"We're gonna be on a game show too," Loralva said. "All my life I been wanting to be on *The Price Is Right* and Imogene's getting us tickets. So now's my chance!" She smiled at Duke and her eyes lit up. Ruby noticed Imogene fidgeted in her seat.

"I've been on *The Price Is Right,*" Duke said.

"You have!" Loralva nearly squeezed his arm off.

"Don't you think you oughta go check on the Winnebago?" Imogene said.

"You have gotta tell me everything you know," Loralva said. She ran her long-nailed hand up and down his bicep.

"You just have to know the prices of everything you can think of. Best bet is to study up first."

"Study up!" Imogene laughed. "You can't study for a game show!"

Loralva and Ruby both gave her shut-up looks.

"You got a Sears catalog handy?" he asked. "Or a Montgomery Ward's will do, but Sears is the best. The thick one. This season's."

"We'll get one," Loralva said without a hitch.

"Where we gonna get one of those?" Ruby said. The closest Sears & Roebuck she knew of was back in San Antonio. As much as she let little thoughts of turning back flutter through her mind, she knew in her heart of hearts she wasn't going back now. Not 'til she got to Violet.

"Why don't I go check on the Winnebago?" Loralva said, standing up from the picnic table, Duke's arm still looped through hers.

"Fine idea!" Imogene said. She started fanning herself with the paper plate again.

"Wanna walk me to the pit to check on my vehicle?" Loralva asked. Ruby knew she just wanted to get more *Price Is Right* instruction from him without interference from Imogene. Hopefully, the 'bago would be ready to go.

Then one of the other white-jean-wearing band members came out of the mini-mart and waved a yellow T-shirt that Ruby recognized from the pile by the cashier. WILLIE NELSON FOR PRESIDENT was emblazoned on the chest. The fella walked over to the White Mustang bus and held it up to one of the tinted windows. Ruby could make out someone giving the thumbs-up sign in the window.

"Who's inside that bus?" Imogene shouted, and then she got all sweet and buttery. "Is Willie Nelson himself in there?"

Duke didn't answer her directly, but said, "Let's just say we got a great opportunity to play backup for his Outlaws is all." He winked at Loralva as he said it.

Willie Nelson? Ruby didn't want this trip to be focusing on anything other than the search for Violet, and the thrumming in her chest made her worry that as they got closer to Hollywood they could all get distracted too easily.

It was times like this that Bubbie seemed to know he had a good chance to take off. He scooched himself off the end of the concrete picnic bench and started to run, but Ruby grabbed his wrist in the nick of time. He tried to yank his hand free again, but Ruby was quicker.

"I'll walk with you," Duke said to Loralva, "but then I better be getting back to the bus. The other guys will be wondering where I got off to. And I don't mind saying, I got off to a darn fine place." Then he turned to the rest of them. "Been nice meeting all y'all."

Ruby worked on settling the kids down while Loralva walked off with Duke. Imogene watched their every move like she might get to see a glimpse of Willie Nelson if she didn't let Duke out of her sight. Ruby couldn't pay the adults no mind when she had Bunny squirming and flailing her Mrs. Beasley around while Bubbie tried to yank his arm free. With one hand holding the boy and the other trying to put away the lunch mess, Ruby wished Imogene could just once take a moment to be a grandmother and help out but she knew it was useless to even ask. It would only put everyone in worse moods because that was the last thing Bubbie and Bunny wanted—they were glad Mimaw Imogene wasn't a hand holder.

"Would you just look at those two," Imogene said. "She don't even know him yet."

Ruby didn't look because she knew Loralva didn't have to know much more than the color of his boots to become friendly with a fella.

Imogene kept watching as Loralva talked to the mechanic. She gave the blow by blow. "Don't look good, everybody's shaking their heads no."

Now Ruby really didn't care to look. This town of New Hope was not panning out too well.

"What in heaven's name is she doing now?" Imogene kept on. "She and Duke walked off from the mechanic, but she's not heading back here."

"She's not going to leave us, Imogene," Ruby said. She sat Mrs. Beasley up straight from her prone position on the picnic bench. Bunny poked at her half-eaten sandwich bread. She didn't want to give the kids a MoonPie when she'd just given them one for breakfast and she needed the treats to last until they got to Los Angeles.

"Rooby! That is your sister. Would you just look at them!" Imogene shouted and even Bubbie stopped his yanking to see what all the commotion was about.

Loralva and Duke had crossed the tarmac all the way to the big bus Duke had arrived in. Now Loralva stood on her tiptoes to reach up and give Duke a big kiss good-bye at the bus doors. Ruby found herself wondering if she'd ever get to kiss a man again. But before she could even imagine who it would be, Duke climbed aboard and the bus doors whooshed closed as the bus engine rumbled.

Loralva sauntered back toward them, looking over her shoulder and waving as the bus drove out of sight. Ruby's eyes teared up and she wasn't sure why. "Did you find out about the Winnebago?" she hollered to her sister.

"They had to send someone to Phoenix for a part. Won't be ready 'til—" She waved as the tail end of the White Mustang bus pulled out onto the highway.

" 'Til when?" Imogene shouted.

Bunny whined, "It's hot, GranMomma."

Ruby closed her eyes. Then a fingernail pricked her palm and she opened her eyes as she dropped hold of Bubbie's little hand.

"Tomorrow sometime," Loralva said. "I tried my darnedest to make them deliver it earlier." She didn't sound entirely sincere on the last part.

"Damn." Imogene slammed her foot down on the tarmac.

Bunny wrapped her arms tight around her Mrs. Beasley doll, which had accumulated a new layer of dust waiting in this desert parking lot. "Will we see Momma *then*?"

"Not tomorrow," Imogene replied for Ruby. "But very, very soon. And she will be so happy to see us. That's why you have to start behaving." She wagged a mauve-painted fingernail in the girl's face.

Ruby checked on the sore, pinched spot on her palm and made a note to trim Bubbie's nails when they got the 'bago back. They weren't but a few hours away now, and another day wouldn't make a difference when it had been four whole years since Violet ran away. Ruby wondered if Violet counted the days like she had. *Look 'til you can't look no more,* or something like that—wasn't that what Earl Glidden had said to her? *Follow that trail,* that was it. Ruby looked out at I-10 that sat just a couple of semi tractor-trailer lengths away from her, and knew she still had a good stretch of trail left ahead of her.

Motel à Trois

Loralva came traipsing back across the lot with two young fellas behind her carrying the luggage from the 'bago. The mechanic had told Loralva to check with the cashier in the mini-mart to rent one of the colored door rooms in the building over by the Crystal Emporium for the night.

Bunny was happy because they got the room with the purple door—her favorite color. Loralva put the key in the lock and let them in, but once inside, all but Loralva stood and stared at their new surroundings.

Ruby'd only been in two motels in her life: the Devine Motor Lodge at the opposite end of town from the Bowl, where she'd worked cleaning rooms two hunting seasons when she was a teenager, and the one at Big Bend National Park with Rascal on their honeymoon, but the rooms there had been more like cabins. Even from her minimal experience she figured most motel rooms didn't look anything like this one.

There were two four-poster, double beds covered in purple chenille spreads that matched the door, with organza draped from post to post in an attempt to make the place look ritzy. On a nightstand in between the beds sat a lamp with a pink lightbulb and no shade. Ruby switched on the light switch by the door. The overhead light hung on a chain that draped across to a golden globe between the beds and gave the room an amber glow.

The television blared in the next room. It sounded like *Only One Life* and Ruby was dying to see if Lina had got out of the hospital yet. A possible brain tumor had been detected before they'd left Devine.

Imogene didn't like the place one bit, and you could see it in her scrunched-up nose and tightened lips. "Bet some sinning goes on in this place. What would the dear Lord above have to say?"

"God's not paying," Loralva said and hauled her suitcases inside the purple door.

Imogene put her hands on her squatty wide hips while Ruby and the kids helped Loralva bring in their things.

Loralva hefted one of her suitcases up on the bed. "I don't know if I brought anything at all appropriate for this evening's outing." She yanked a few blouses from the pile in her bag and draped them across the chenille bedspread. Turned out they were walking distance from the Hootin' Annie Lounge. The proprietress of Plooker's Pitstop had given Loralva directions to walk along the back of their property to the main road in New Hope—this would take her right to the Lounge. Loralva began her preparations on what to wear and how to do her hair, and as she did so she whistled "Blue Eyes Cryin' in the Rain."

Imogene wouldn't be letting Loralva go off and have a good time without her, which Ruby could tell Loralva was none too happy about. Still, she didn't argue, and made Imogene leave with more than enough time to be at the Hootin' Annie Lounge for the first show. "We'll just be sitting there twiddling our thumbs," Imogene said, teasing her pile of hair.

"But we'll be twiddling our thumbs in the front row when those Skirt-Tailers walk onstage," Loralva said. "I plan on taking my time to find out everything I need to know about being on *The Price Is Right* tonight." Loralva waggled her hips back and forth with the thought of the game show. "Ruby honey, first thing tomorrow we got to get a Sears catalog."

"It'll have to wait until we get settled in Los Angeles," Ruby said, worried this was going to be another distraction.

"Come on, Imogene. I got research to do." Loralva stood in the threshold of the open door. "We'll talk about the catalog tomorrow, Ruby honey."

Imogene snatched her big pink leatherette purse off the bed and off they went.

Once they were out the door, Ruby let out a big sigh. As the night wore on, the kids watched TV while Ruby played solitaire. The headboard on the bed next door banged against her wall well into the night and she got terribly confused when the sounds of two men and one woman came through the wall, until she realized the Swinger family in Cicada, Texas, really wasn't related to the swingers of New Hope, Arizona.

Loralva and Imogene got back close to one a.m. Imogene was madder than a rabid dog. Loralva, Ruby swore, had a hickey on her neck.

"Ruby honey," Loralva said with whiskey breath, "You ain't gonna believe who was there."

"Willie Nelson?"

"How'd you know? Did you see him?"

"We guessed when we saw him wave from the bus, remember?" Imogene snapped. Ruby assumed they didn't come home as soon as Imogene had wanted to.

"He's going out to Hollywood to talk to some producers about doing a movie," Loralva continued, as she sat on the bed and took off her red pumps. "It's gonna be called *The Electric*

Horseman or something like that. With Robert Redford. So Willie had to ride incognito. And, he doesn't like to fly."

"Maybe Violet will be in the same movie. She'd be so good opposite Robert Redford," Ruby said, propping herself up on her elbows.

"See, I told you she had the makings of another Liz Taylor." Imogene slipped onto her pillow a satin pillowcase she'd brought with her to protect her hair. "Oh my, I didn't remember to tell Mr. Nelson that my daughter-in-law is also a movie star."

"TV star," Ruby corrected. She'd sat up from her prone position. "Did you get an autograph, Loralva? I could frame it and hang it at the Bowl."

"Course, Ruby honey," her sister said through the bathroom door.

"Did Duke at least buy you a beer for coming to see him?" Ruby asked, as her sister came back and sat on the bed opposite Ruby.

"Oh Ruby honey, you have no idea," Loralva said. "Duke was the perfect gentleman, wasn't he, Imogene?" Ruby could see Imogene smirk even though her back was turned to them. "Duke didn't just buy me a beer, he dedicated a song to me." Loralva sighed. "Then when they took their breaks, the entire band came and sat at our table. You should have seen the rest of the women in that place. They was so jealous."

Imogene grunted like she was one of the jealous ones.

"We all got up to dance, but no one asked Imogene," Loralva said as though explaining the grouchiness.

"It wasn't that," Imogene said. "I just didn't care to dance in that filthy place. Folks of all sorts in there. All sorts."

Loralva and Ruby exchanged a glance, each one knowing what the other was thinking. Ruby thought she ought to change the subject before it got ugly.

"You got a hickey, Loralva Jean?" Ruby whispered, not wanting to wake the kids next to her in bed.

Loralva and Imogene both climbed in the same bed and the plastic liner on their mattress crunched and crackled. But Ruby could see Loralva's smile through the dark.

"Just doing everything to ensure I do the best I can on the game show, Ruby honey."

The room was dark, except for the parking lot lights creeping in through the crack in the heavy curtains.

"Can he sing any good?" Ruby asked.

"Can he sing good? Ruby honey, he sings like he was straight out of Nashville. Remember them fellas that came to the Longhorn Club and had that lady tambourine player? Remember how good they sang?" Ruby nodded her head. "Well, let me tell you something, Duke and the Skirt-Tailers is better. Don't you think so, Imogene?"

Imogene had turned to the edge of the bed. She made a noise that sounded somewhere close to "mm-hmm."

"Loralva," Ruby said, more than ready to go back to sleep, "You be careful. Remember, Duke's in show business and probably treats all the ladies like he did you." Still, she figured that more than likely, even though Duke was the one in show business, he'd end up being the one with his heart broke. Not one man yet had broken Loralva's heart.

"Ruby honey," Loralva said, "I'm going to have all the fun I can, while I still have all my parts working."

"What do you suppose Judy Harper is saying about us right now?" Imogene asked. "She told Ida Mae that we wouldn't even make it as far as the Texas state line before we'd turn back, so she'll be eating her words now that we just crossed into California."

That's when it dawned on Ruby that she hadn't thought about home all day, but had been thinking about what was ahead. Right now, she was just so relieved to have the 'bago back and be on the road again.

It was late afternoon, and Imogene was in better spirits than she had been the night before, although she hadn't quit rattling on since she climbed into the Winnebago's passenger seat that morning. Ruby reckoned Imogene's nerves were just as edgy as her own.

"I don't know why they lay these highways down so that they head right into the sun. Can't see a thing!" Imogene said. "Loralva, watch out for that piece of tire up ahead. I don't understand how those tire treads come flying off and those truckers can just keep going. Don't understand it at all!"

Loralva turned up the stereo and Ruby dealt out another hand of solitaire on the dinette table. Waylon Jennings sang, "Mammas Don't Let Your Babies Grow Up To Be Cowboys."

"Oh geez, Loralva! You almost ran that car off the road, don't veer so close!"

"They came across to my lane," Loralva said back and Ruby wished she'd just keep quiet and not add fuel to Imogene's fire. "I ain't letting nobody get in front of me, not when they got a whole lane of their own." She turned the music up a notch higher. Waylon sang about picking guitars and driving old trucks.

"It don't matter!" Imogene said, her right hand holding on tight to the dashboard and the other hand to her armrest. "You're going to wreck my expensive vehicle!"

Loralva didn't say anything back, but that just got Imogene more riled. Ruby set her cards down to watch, while Waylon said mammas should make their babies be doctors and lawyers.

"You have no idea how much this Winnebago costs!" Imogene wailed.

Loralva swayed to the music and Mr. Jennings explained how cowboys never stay home and are always alone.

"This is not the cheap version like some folks have!" Imogene raged on. Mixed in with her description of the 'bago she'd shout out a warning about a car about to change lanes or the oncoming traffic that was clear across the median ("they could cross over if you don't pay attention!"). "My Winnebago has the bath-and-shower combo! Don't think that didn't cost a pretty penny!"

Steel guitars twanged, and Waylon sang about cowboys and smoky pool rooms.

"I had to pay extra for a full-sized toilet! Watch out for that fancy import car! They never use their blinkers."

"Imogene," Ruby finally said, "it's not like Loralva hasn't been driving us all the way out here from Texas for two whole days." She thought somebody ought to stand up for her sister. Not to mention she was getting dang tired of hearing it, and with Imogene and Waylon Jennings competing for volume she was finding herself wanting to do a little screaming of her own.

"Ruby!" Imogene turned clear around in her seat. "You are not sitting up here where you can see how crazy she drives. I have bit my tongue ever since we pulled out onto Highway 90 back in Devine!"

"Don't worry, Ruby honey," Loralva said, looking at her through the rearview mirror. "I got earplugs in."

Oh geez. Now Imogene blew a gasket and Ruby was surprised the steam coming out Imogene's ears didn't melt the inside of the 'bago. Never mind that the woman had never wanted to own a Winnebago in the first place, suddenly it was her prized possession.

"I cannot believe," the skunk-headed lady bellowed, "that I volunteer my motor home at your most desperate time, and I am not appreciated in the least. From Loralva I expected it, but from you Ruby, I thought better. It's becoming quite clear to me now that you are not as sweet as you put on airs to be at the Bowl."

She turned back around to face the windshield again.

"I could have taken my El Camino," Ruby said, not sure

why she was willing to step into an argument, especially one she knew she'd never win, but the Winnebago was the only reason Ruby had agreed Imogene could come along on the trip in the first place, and she thought maybe Imogene could be paying a little respect to the rest of them. Like by being a grandma to the kids who now played with G.I. Joe and Mrs. Beasley on the upper bunk.

"Your El Camino, humph." Imogene tossed her head in that way she had that showed her disgust.

"I don't need—" Ruby started, but swallowed her words.

Imogene whipped around and glared at Ruby. "You don't need what?"

"Nothing," Ruby said, catching Loralva's eyes in the rearview mirror. "I don't need to discuss it anymore. You have a nice rig here."

"Loralva, if you are going to change lanes you need to turn on the blinker much sooner than that," Imogene said, not changing her tone one bit.

Ruby had started to say she didn't need Imogene's help, but here they were all the way out west and the 'bago was their home. She knew if you pushed Imogene far enough, she might just take the motor home and go back, although Ruby doubted Imogene would give up on looking for Violet. Still, she couldn't chance it and while she boiled on the inside and wanted to let Imogene have it, she shut her trap for now. She should probably be just as mad at Loralva for letting Imogene horn in on this trip, but she understood how much her sister wanted to be on *The Price Is Right*. Still, they'd only been gone three days now—how much longer could they all be cooped up together?

Waylon wailed about how cowboys were hard to love and hold, and Loralva chimed in on how those cowboys would rather give you a song than diamonds and gold.

★ ★ ★

Loralva turned the music way down. "Y'all don't mind if we stop at a Sears store so I can start studying for *The Price Is Right,* do you?"

Duke had given Loralva all sorts of advice on how to get the best chances of winning on *The Price Is Right.* "Gotta get a Sears catalog right away," she told Ruby. "So we can study all the prices."

"A detour?" Ruby said. "How you gonna find a Sears store in these parts?" Oh, it seemed there were too many delays already.

"You'll have more than enough time to study for that game show," Imogene said. She turned her head to look out her side passenger window.

Ruby looked outside, hoping she'd see something that showed they'd made progress, but the same hot, dry tan dirt and spiny cactus rushed by the window, making her feel like she'd never left Texas.

"What day are our tickets for?" Loralva asked Imogene.

"We need to get looking for Violet first," Ruby added.

"We'll know when we get there," Imogene snapped.

"Do we even have tickets?" Loralva asked, turning the radio down even further. The 'bago got real quiet as they waited for the answer. "You better have tickets," she said between her teeth while watching the road with sidelong glances.

Ruby shuddered, and she wasn't sure if it was because she was afraid Imogene had deceived Loralva or because no one was paying attention to the road.

"We'll get them when we get there. We go to that fancy Chinese theater they have there. I can't remember the name."

"You don't have tickets!" Loralva swerved back into their lane after veering too far to the left and suddenly realizing.

"My cousin's friend guaranteed it," Imogene said.

Loralva sighed and Ruby held her breath. "Duke did say something about getting tickets at someplace like that." She went deep into thought and Ruby worried the 'bago would explode from the tension building up. "We'll still go to Palm Springs and get a catalog. I'm getting on *The Price Is Right* no matter what."

"Palm Springs?" Imogene asked, her tone softened.

Loralva spied Ruby in the rearview mirror. "It's only about another hundred miles and it's not that far out of our way. It could mean the difference between knowing the prices of the Kenmore washers and the Maytags."

Ruby didn't like the idea of veering off their set route. They were to be in Hollywood that day. She'd already got her nerves in order for it.

"All the movie stars vacation in Palm Springs," Imogene said. "Maybe we'll spot a few. Maybe have dinner at a table across from Barbra Streisand. Course I don't know if I'll be able to digest if I have to look at those god-awful long nails. You'd think she could afford to have someone keep them trimmed. Tacky, tacky, tacky." Then she sucked in her breath. "Ruby, if movie stars vacation there, we have to go. Violet could be there."

Ruby knew, deep down in her gut, that Violet was in Hollywood and not Palm Springs. But she agreed to go, mostly because she just wanted everyone to hush up for a moment.

Waylon Jennings still sang of lone star belt buckles, which took Ruby back to Devine and she wondered how well Earl was keeping his pygmy goats and emus on his side of the fence.

Loralva looked sideways at Imogene. "You had better hope we can get tickets."

Imogene looked out her window.

Venus Enters Aries

"I told you there were movie stars here," Imogene said, pointing out her passenger side window as they pulled into Palm Springs. "Look, there's Frank Sinatra Drive. And just back there was Gene Autry Trail." She pointed at green and white street signs as the Winnebago crept along.

"Any old town can name their streets after famous people," Loralva said. "Even in Devine we have Washington Street. That don't mean George Washington ever stepped foot in Devine, Texas." Ruby sat at the booth looking out the side window as they passed Frank Sinatra Drive. She looked down its length, but didn't even see so much as a Sammy Davis, Jr., just palm trees and rows of one-story houses.

"There's Bob Hope's house!" Imogene waved her arms in the air. Loralva slowed down even more and they all looked up toward where she pointed.

"I've seen it in a magazine before and I think you're right, Imogene," Ruby said, her eyes squinted. The sun hot and bright, the sky blue like in a photo. The traffic was thin but constant as the two lanes heading west through town wove their way past one-story shops and restaurants. On top of a hill that spread out above the shops to their left sat a house with sliding glass doors wrapped around it and what looked like a big bonnet for the roof.

"I know I'm right," Imogene said. The house was on the driver's side of the Winnebago. Ruby stood behind the driver's seat and Imogene practically leaned into Loralva's face. "Look, I think someone's standing outside on the patio."

Ruby squinted to see better.

"Loralva, you watch the road. We'll tell you what we see," Imogene said as the camper veered toward the oncoming traffic. Ruby could make out images on the deck and her breath caught.

"Wave!" Imogene said. They all waved as hard as they could. Loralva even rolled down the driver's side window and stuck her arm out to wave. Ruby eyed Bubbie in the rearview mirror leaning down from his hideout in the top bunk to look out the windshield. Bunny had come down from the bunk and knelt in the dinette bench seat, waving her little arm like a spring broke loose. "Is it the funny Mr. Bob Hope?" she asked.

"They're waving back!" Imogene yelled. The house was so high on the hill it was hard to see what Imogene thought might be someone, but to think Bob or Mrs. Hope might be waving at them was thrilling. Even if it was just the maid, that would be all right too.

Bubbie practiced the rat-a-tat-tat of machine-gun fire and Bunny warbled "You Are My Sunshine," or at least that first line, over and over as they pulled into the mall housing Sears and other smaller stores. Now that they were in Palm Springs, the cactus had started to turn into palm trees. Texas had disappeared, Ruby reckoned.

The Sears parking lot loomed bigger than a football field, with just as many cars parked in the spaces as a Friday-night homecoming game between Cicada and Devine. Loralva drove up and down the rows of cars and found no vacant spots available. Finally, way in the back she located a spot, but Imogene wouldn't allow her to park there because of the bank of motorcycles lined up. "Hoodlum bikes," she said, pointing out the leather satchels hanging from the sides, the low-riding seats and extended front wheels. "We'd come back to our vehicle to find nothing left but the toilet seat."

"It won't be for that long." Ruby wanted to just park, get the catalog and then get back on the road. But Loralva drove around a bit longer until they found a place to park on the opposite corner, quite a hike from the front doors of the Sears, but across from a drugstore where Ruby figured she'd pick up some more mange salve for Bubbie before they got back on the road.

"Imogene," Ruby asked, "you don't mind staying here with the kids while I run inside with Loralva, do you?" She desperately needed a moment of quiet.

"I am not waiting out here while you and Loralva go and visit with all the movie stars!" the skunk-headed lady shouted at Ruby.

"I'll only be a moment," Ruby said. Her gut twisted with the vexation of one grandmother taking on more of the responsibility than the other. For once, couldn't Imogene share some of the obligation? But she didn't say anything more, because she'd always shouldered it.

"No, I have to go in too," Imogene said. "Sears is the only store that carries my size underwear."

"This ain't gonna take long. I'm going in for a catalog only," Loralva said. "I need every moment of practice."

"Can we look at the toys?" Bunny asked.

"See, they all want to go in," Imogene said. "We can stretch our legs one last time before getting to Los Angeles, where we won't be able to stop until we get to our motel."

Ruby pointed Bubbie in the direction of his shoes so they could all go in. "Why can't we get out nowhere else in Los Angeles but our motel?" Ruby asked.

"You are so naïve!" Imogene said. "It is not a safe place!"

Why did everyone keep throwing that in her face, Ruby wondered, and took Bunny by the hand. They stepped down the 'bago steps behind Imogene and Loralva into the California desert heat.

"Remember, we're only gonna be a moment," Ruby said, figuring they'd never get to Violet if they kept taking these side trips.

"Hurry it up, y'all," Loralva said. She traipsed several feet ahead of them in her spiked heels, anxious to get a catalog and learn all those prices. Ruby was impressed by her sister's dedication, but she didn't really think it would make a difference.

Inside they each headed off to different departments. Bunny, led by her nose, knew right where the toy department would be. She tugged on Ruby's arm to head that way, and whined, "Please, oh please, GranMomma, just for a bit?" So, while Loralva headed off to the Customer Service booth for catalogs and Imogene went toward Women's World, Ruby let the kids wander the aisles of games and tops and costumes.

Before too long, Loralva showed up in the toy department hauling the heavy Sears catalog on her hip like a baby. "I'm all set, Ruby honey," she said to her sister. "I'm on my way down that *Price Is Right* aisle." She wiggled her hips.

"You have to memorize that whole thing?" Ruby asked, taking the slick book from her and flipping the thin pages.

"Duke said I gotta have all them prices in my head. I gotta learn grocery store items as well. Shake 'N Bake and the like." Loralva seemed worried. "You gotta help me study, Ruby honey."

"I'll do what I can," Ruby said. Right that instant though,

she had to slap Bubbie's hand away from pulling down the entire shelf of Milton Bradley games.

"I saw Imogene over by the TVs," Loralva said.

"Let's go on over, get her and then get back on the road," Ruby said, and she led them all toward the electronics department.

They found Imogene watching *General Hospital,* which was playing on multiple televisions around the room. Ruby didn't care too much about the show because it always came on when she had to get the deep fat fryer heated up and the hot dog rotisserie started.

"We gotta get going," Ruby said, the kids running every which way.

Loralva stood with the catalog open, running her long-nailed finger down the columns. "Gas-powered lawn mower, with edge trimmer attachment, fifty-three dollars," she muttered.

"Just wait 'til commercial," Imogene said.

Loralva hoisted herself up on one of the Zenith consoles, but Ruby didn't want to get fingerprints or any scratches on the new television sets, so she stood in between two on the floor and stared at the screen straight ahead.

Bubbie, clothes already mussed, but his hair still slicked back, ran around between the TVs with a paper airplane, making it dive-bomb and crash over and over.

When the show broke for commercial it went to a newsbreak first. Walter Cronkite's face spoke all over the room, from twelve-inch to eighty-four-inch screens. "It's the Hundred Year Flood," Mr. Cronkite reported. "Torrential rainfall throughout the southern half of Texas."

Ruby knew the rains would be bad, because they had a Hundred Year Flood every four or five years in South Texas.

"Wet weather heading up through the Gulf," the meteorologist on eight of the big Sears televisions predicted. Rain in South

Texas meant creeks rising and passes flooding—a deluge and never a sprinkle. Ruby pictured the parking lot of the Bowl turning into the lake it became when the rains came. Pickup tires leaving gullies in their wake. Suddy would probably let all the folks trample across the maple floors with muddy boots. "Come on, Imogene," Ruby said, "we can't be dillydallying any longer."

"Let me finish watching my show," Imogene said. She shifted her mauve leatherette purse up on her shoulder. "It won't hurt you to let me have my way once in a while."

"Yard hoe with wooden handle, six dollars," Loralva mumbled next to Ruby.

Then, Bunny screamed, "There's Momma!" as they heard the trill of "If it's ButterMaid, it's better made." The blond Violet with pigtails and smocked dress skipped across the TV screens stacked floor to ceiling on all sides of the room. Ruby couldn't blink without Violet's perky smile and swinging milk bucket blazing in front of her. She thought she might feel physically closer to Violet being so near to Hollywood now, but that glass screen felt just as thick in Palm Springs as it had in Devine.

Bubbie started to dash out of the department, but Ruby stepped up and grabbed him by the hand. The kids had seen the commercial several times in between the first sighting and when they got on the road. Each time the little boy got poutier and more fitful—like the fits couldn't hold themselves inside.

"Oh my heavens," Imogene said, "it's my movie star daughter-in-law!" She screamed it loud enough for all the Sears employees to be aware who she was related to. Made Ruby's ears itch.

"TV star," she corrected.

Bunny started singing, "If it's ButterMaid, it's better made" and added the milk-bucket arm swing to her routine, using Mrs. Beasley as the bucket and skipping in between the console TVs. Bubbie yanked on Ruby's arm, nearly pulling it out of the socket.

Ruby wanted to get the kids and herself out of the Sears as quickly as possible to stop any damage thirty-two concurrent visions of their momma might do. A Lifebuoy commercial was next, but Ruby wanted to get the heck out of there.

"Ruby honey, I almost forgot," Loralva said, barely taking her eyes off the catalog, "Duke told me I gotta talk to the manager of the appliance department about the retail prices on those new microwave ovens."

"We gotta get," Ruby said. Even she could hear the anxiety in her voice.

"Why don't you go on out and wait in the 'bago," Imogene said. "We'll be out soon enough." Ruby knew the black-and-white-haired mother-in-law was just punishing her for making them hurry, but she didn't want to stay there with the chance of Violet's perky smile throwing the kids for another loop, so she took their hands and left Imogene staring at the wall of TVs and Loralva reciting prices and product details.

Back in the 'bago, Ruby pulled out her Bicycle playing cards to wait until they could get on the road for that last leg to California. Already one half of the daylight hours gone and instead of being on the road to Hollywood, just a couple of hours away, they baked in the desert watching soap operas and collecting catalogs for *The Price Is Right*.

Bunny had added on an extra stanza to her singing: If it's ButterMaid, *"it's better made. So don't be afraid!"* She sang it loud, drawn out and off key, until Bubbie shouted from the top bunk, "SHUT UP!" making Ruby's cards scatter out of her hands and all about the dinette area.

"What in tarnation?" she said to the boy, who hung over the edge of the bunk and stared bug-eyed at his little sister, who now bawled, both children with faces the shade of pickled beets.

"Bubbie!" Ruby jumped up with the news that he had spoken.

But he quickly scrambled to the far side of the bunk. "You saved up all that time not talking just to holler 'Shut up'?" Ruby said over the edge of the upper level, but he was curled up in the way back. She knew that'd be the last he'd say for a long time.

"Why can't I sing my momma's song?!" Bunny bellowed. Ruby'd done all she could to stay calm till she got to Hollywood and now here she had everybody else exploding around her. "It's bet-ter ma-de," Bunny warbled, trying to spit the words out at Bubbie. She tried to reach up into the bunk and swat his mange-infested head, but he grabbed her little wrist instead and then Ruby latched on to both of them and clenched her fist around their arms.

"This place ain't big enough for carrying on like this! Both of you, stop it!" Ruby yelled, and her own echo bounced around inside the tin vehicle along with the kids' wailing. Bubbie yanked his hand out of Ruby's and Bunny pounded her feet on the floor. Ruby felt the 'bago rock slightly with the churn. She pictured it rocking so hard that it fell on its side and cracked open.

The little boy had scooched himself back into the far corner of the upper bunk. Ruby took Bunny by the tiny shoulders. "Bunny hon," she said, her voice still ridged. "You've got to stop this crying. You'll be all puffy eyed by the time we get to Hollywood. How will that look?"

But Bunny just let loose another wail. Then G.I. Joe came flailing off the top bunk and grazed the girl's arm, at which Bunny reared back Mrs. Beasley and let her fly right into Ruby's gut.

"That's it!" Ruby screamed at the ceiling, her body taut, her neck strained like her head wanted to leave the scene. "Bunny, you sit. Now!" She pointed at the dinette booth. Sniffling, the girl crawled up onto the seat, taking Mrs. Beasley with her. "Bubbie, no more throwing." Ruby picked up G.I. Joe and set him down hard on the washbasin with a clank. "I know you're mad about all that's happened with your momma." She wanted to add that she was too. "But we still got a long way to go. We have to take it easy."

Ruby opened the cabinet door above the kitchen sink where she kept the box of MoonPies. She took two saucers from the dish drainer and ripped open the two cellophane-wrapped chocolate and marshmallow pies, then set them on the dinette table. With her back to the kids for a moment, she tried to get her breathing started again. She had to step outside for a minute to get fresh air.

"I'm going out," she said. "Eat your MoonPies and think about how you're acting. You better not be whining when I come back." With that she took her purse and stepped back out the door to the hot asphalt Sears parking lot.

She continued to stand there, just at the bottom of the Winnebago's steps. She stared across the parking lot wondering how much longer Imogene and Loralva would be. All the sunshine coming down on the parking lot made a person squinty-eyed. They had sunshine in Devine, but not such brightness as they had in Palm Springs. Ruby reckoned she knew why they said movie *stars.* It was because everything seemed to sparkle here in California. The windshields on the pickups, the chrome bumpers, the glass on the phone booth next door at the drugstore, the little pieces of metal in the asphalt, even the gas tanks on those motorcycles way in the back of the lot caught Ruby's eye with their glinting. Would Violet have a sparkle to her now?

Maybe she would take a short walk. She wouldn't be gone long, she thought. She'd only be gone a second. She'd just cross the street and get Bubbie some more ointment for his mange. But as she'd spotted the phone booth out front, she figured that maybe calling home and putting a little bit of Texas back in her system would calm her down some.

After about the eighth ring, Ruby started worrying that it was so busy at the Devine Bowl that Suddy was having a hard time handling it. Was Loralva's friend, Verdee Whitacre, reliable enough to take over the saloon? On the tenth ring someone finally picked up. At first all she could hear were background noises of folks' voices sounding like a big amen. Then a whisper, "Hello?"

"Suddy, is that you?"

"Ruby, Chester is in the middle of his sermon."

"Sermon?"

"We're praying for y'all, Ruby. Praying you'll find Violet right away.

"Thank you for that, but how's the Bowl?"

"I'm fixing the place up fine. Took down all those gosh-awful neon beer signs on the walls."

"But those provided lighting at Lane One and Lane Six! Not too bright, not too dark. Just right. A pain in the rumpus to dust, but pretty light." Ruby got a sick feeling.

"I just replaced them is all. Ordered some special ones. And don't you worry, won't cost you a dime. It came out of the church coffer."

Ruby was afraid to ask. "What do you mean, 'special'?

"They flash the Lord's Prayer on each line as the congregation recites them." Suddy's voice got excited. "Jesus sent the neon man right to the door of the Devine Bowl. I was just minding my own business, reorganizing the pro shop into a Sunday school for the kids, when this fella came in and showed me his brochures."

"Are folks still coming in for bowling?" Ruby asked, a lump the size of a ten commandment tablet stuck in her throat.

"Sure!" Suddy said. "But they complain that it's not the same without you. They all miss you and ask about you."

Ruby missed them too. She knew Luke Jessup was not one bit happy with the Lord's Prayer hanging over him. He'd given up on the whole Jesus bit while sitting in his prison cell. Said he'd figured it hadn't done him any good to ask the Lord to help him win that barroom brawl when all He did was cause the other fella to pop a blood vessel in his brain, sending Luke away fifteen years for manslaughter.

"Earl Glidden's keeping the beers cold for you," Suddy said, "so the place is running fine. But I can't talk now. Chester's sermon's coming to a close and I gotta pass out the collection plate."

"Sermon? At the Bowl?" Ruby's rage had fallen into a puddle.

"Here, Earl wants to say hello."

Church? At the Devine Bowl? Suddy was more than taking over, she was converting her bowling alley. Ruby pictured the Big Bob's Tire Team in their orange shirts, and Purdy's Pig Pins in their black and white sow shirts, all with their heads bowed toward their red and green rental shoes, saying the Lord's Prayer as it flashed in pink neon.

"Hey there, Ruby," Earl's voice talked into her ear now. "I got the fence out back fixed. The livestock's staying on my side of the property line while you're gone."

Ruby smiled at having someone do something nice for her for a change. " 'Preciate that, Earl," she said. She realized she missed that early morning visit from him at the Bowl even though neither one of them ever said much.

"How are things out in California?"

"California?" Ruby didn't want to go into how busy she was with tantrums, but she was still wound up. "Well, the kids are driving me crazy with their whining and whatnot and we're all locked up inside this tackle box of a vehicle. Don't know if I can make it all the way there without—"

"Oh Rube, you wouldn't know what to do without someone to take care of. You're always taking in those left behind." He cleared his throat and Ruby used the moment to say she better go. She hated to cut Earl off, but this phone call wasn't making her feel better like she had intended.

Turning to face the doors of the phone booth she looked out the scratched glass and wondered about what Earl said. She'd only taken in kids whose mommas had left them. That got her all wrangled up in a knot again. The things folks did. Her thinking made her sigh. She could see the Winnebago in the distance.

She had to get the salve for Bubbie's head, so she headed inside the drugstore with her heart still racing. As she stood in front of the eczema creams and dandruff shampoos, she tried to gather herself. Tried to think about what lay ahead, about how finding Violet was more important than a worse-than-usual tantrum or a Methodist bowling alley. That's when she overheard the two women next to her and realized that maybe Judy Harper and Jimmy Ray Johnson hadn't been too far off in their speculations about Californians and their ways.

"It's all because Venus entered Aries." Two blond women, one in a purple flowy dress and the other with a scar around her neck like her head had been removed and soldered back on, stood just down from the foot powders. As Ruby stood in front of the ointments looking to replace the flattened-out-empty tube for Bubbie's mange, she resisted staring and felt a little ashamed that she was listening in.

"Whenever Venus enters my sign, it's like an out-of-body experience," the woman in purple said. Ruby scooted a little closer to the foot powders and picked up a bottle of Wart-Away to pretend she was looking at something. She'd never heard anything like this in her life. "I can't keep my feet on the ground. My car keys go missing, my hair goes frizzy."

"It's only going to get worse. Jupiter is in reversal and Mercury is in retrograde," the woman with the scar said. "I'm afraid to drive."

"Don't you have a Capricorn moon?" the flowy dress lady asked.

"No, Libra. And Gemini is my rising sign."

Ruby knew Capricorn and Libra. She knew her own sign was Cancer and hated it because she couldn't get past the fact that that's what her own momma had died of. She'd read her horoscope in the Sunday comic section of the *Idyll County Courier* until Suddy and her whole Methodist congregation had gotten together a petition requesting the horoscopes be removed from the newspaper because it was Satan's folly.

"Aries with a Libra moon, well that explains it." The woman in purple put two Dr. Scholl's insoles in her basket.

Explains what? Ruby thought, putting the Wart-Away back on the shelf where she'd found it. These two ladies were talkin' crazy. She already wasn't feeling quite right. California was going all wrong. So strange. It was what they said next that hit the big Violet nerve in her and then curled itself around her heart.

"Looks like real trouble ahead," the scarred woman repeated. "Mercury going into retrograde. And with my own Scorpio moon—nothing's going to go right for a while."

"I don't know if I can handle any more craziness in my life." The lady in the flowy dress shook her head.

Jesus Christ and all of Suddy's congregation, I know just how you feel, Ruby wanted to say out loud.

The lady with the removable head patted her friend's arm. "Remember, if your will is strong enough, you can change the course."

Oh, Ruby hoped and prayed that wasn't just some weird California mumbo jumbo, because her will was strong, but was it strong enough? She grabbed the tube of mange salve and headed to the checkout and back to the kids. She hoped they hadn't gotten into anything what with the planets wavering out of alignment too.

⋆ ⋆ ⋆

Stepping inside the Winnebago, Ruby spotted the uneaten MoonPies first thing. Imogene stood at one end of the vehicle sorting out all her Sears purchases on her big comfy bed that she got all to herself.

"Hey Ruby! Loralva said she'd be here in a bit. Wait 'til you see what all I bought!"

"Where are the kids?" Ruby asked her, closing the door behind her to keep the heat outside.

"What kids?" Imogene said, holding up a flowered jumper. "I thought they were with you."

Ruby glanced around the inside of the camper quickly, thinking they might be hiding in any of the alcoves, but the place wasn't big enough to not see a foot or an elbow sticking out somewhere. "Oh . . . dear . . . Lord," Ruby said, wondering again about her will and just how much it could withstand. "They must have gone outside. Did you see them when you were walking back?"

"What are you talking about?" Imogene said. "They were with you in the Sears. Did you lose them between here and there?"

Ruby didn't wait around to argue with the skunk-haired mother-in-law and stepped back out into the roasting parking lot. She stared at the lot full of cars and pickups. The desert air, dry and scorching, made Ruby's air-conditioned skin feel cold to the touch. The RV sat behind her now in this field of cars, and Imogene puffed up behind her trying to keep up with Ruby's anxious pace as she headed toward the first row of automobiles.

"You get yourself too darn worried about them kids," she hollered at Ruby.

"They can't be far," Ruby said. "They ain't got but tiny legs." Trying to make herself feel better. Trying not to let such a wide swath of cars and pickups make her feel the situation was hopeless. She kept going down one row of cars and then shimmied between two others to the next row, heading toward the far end of the lot.

Her mind rushed to a picture of Bubbie and Bunny out in the middle of the highway, with the big rigs roaring by.

"Them kids never do mind." Imogene said, as Ruby sidled between a Ford F-150 and a Buick.

"Probably just hiding," Imogene rattled on. "Playing tricks on us. Shouldn't let them get to you."

Ruby took a moment to stand on her tiptoes to scan the huge parking lot. Sears was just five rows away from her now. Would they have gone back inside? Then she saw Loralva coming out the doors of the store carrying the Sears catalog.

"What'd you go and leave them for anyhow?" Imogene said. "You don't even know where to look."

Ruby wanted to tell her to go look for her common sense, but how could she when she herself had deserted the kids? The heat from the asphalt came through her soles as she strained her ears for Bunny's singing. It would sound so sweet right now.

"Well, you got one thing on your side," Imogene said, still trailing. "Ain't no way any soul, good or bad, is going to have the gumption to swipe that Bubbie in the mood he's always in."

"Bunny! Bubbie!" Ruby hollered into the blistering afternoon. The piping hot metal cars radiating. The kids' names rolled along getting lost in the distorted wavy air that settled over them. All she heard in response was the gunning of engines from the other end of the lot. Neither kid was taller than a trunk lid so Ruby began run-walking up each aisle of cars, bending down to look under and between for little feet and then lifting up to look into the truck beds and all the while calling out their names.

"My Harley always behaved when he was a child," Imogene said. She'd caught up with Ruby.

"Bubbie!" Ruby called, her heart pulling its way up her throat. "Bunny!"

Loralva met up with Ruby and Imogene now. "What's up?" She thumbed through the catalog as she walked.

"The kids," Ruby said. "They've gone missing." Her throat catching on something thick and prickly, as she thought she shouldn't have to say something like this. "Run off, I reckon."

"You'd better hope you have enough soap and water in my Winnebago to scrub them hard, if they've been over there," Imogene said, pointing toward the motorcycle gang lined up at the back end of the parking lot. Ruby'd been avoiding that section, scared of what they might do.

"Maybe they've seen the kids." Loralva headed right that way, marking her place in the catalog with a finger. "Let's go ask them."

"Oh Lord, I don't know if I want them to know anything," Ruby said.

"Oh, come on," Loralva said. "They don't bite and if they've been watching this parking lot since before we went inside, they've probably seen the kids. And maybe they'll have some good advice on prices that might not be in the catalog."

Ruby didn't think it was the time to be arguing, but she knew from the motorcycle gangs that passed through Devine and stopped in the Bowl, they did not smell pretty and they never said please. And once they'd spilt a beer right down the center of Lane Two.

As the three of them approached the line of motorcycles off to the side of the building, they could see shiny chrome blazing in the sun. About ten black-leather-clad men and half that many scantily clad ladies stood around or sat on Harley-Davidsons. Ruby headed straight toward them, though she figured those tough fellas wouldn't have noticed any small children as any more than a nuisance. But as she stepped up to the lineup of bikes she spotted Bunny bouncing up and down on the seat of a low-rider chopper, her bare feet dangling, toes wiggling, her arms not able to reach the handlebars.

"Vroom, vroom!" the little girl said, ignoring her approaching grandmothers and great-aunt. Bubbie straddled another bike on the seat in front of a biker, nearly on the gas tank.

Ruby stepped up, then hesitated for only a second before lunging straight for Bunny, who called, "GranMomma!" with her arms reaching out. Ruby ran as fast as her bowling shoes would carry her toward Bunny. As she neared, she couldn't see where it came from, but she heard it—the kachink of chain being thrashed in the air. A warning. It rippled inside her bones as Imogene gripped her arm to stop her from moving any farther into the circle of bikers.

"Ruby, don't get too close. They could kill the lot of us," the mother-in-law whispered.

"This your kid?" a big biker in grease-covered jeans asked. His mottled beard as long as Ruby's right arm, a fine mess of curly hair matted and mussed, his black motorcycle jacket worn with creases like wrinkled skin sloughing off, a bandana tied around his head like Aunt Jemima on the pancake syrup bottle. *Burl* was embroidered in script over his heart, and around his wrist was a black leather band covered in silver studs, like a watchband without the watch.

Loralva walked right up to him and pointed toward Bunny. "Burl honey, this here's my grandniece."

"Ain't a good idea to be leaving kids alone these days," he said, looking down at Loralva. He gave Ruby a fright, but she walked around that fright and stepped toward Bunny. Burl put his arm out to stop her. Ruby could smell motor oil and stale sweat from his hairy arm just under her nose.

"Where'd you find her?" Ruby asked him. Both stupid and

scared feelings were crawling on her skin, but her wanting to get to Bunny was the biggest feeling overall.

"She found *us,*" he said.

"The heck she did!" Imogene jumped in. "You were trying to kidnap them!"

Thurump! went the chain again.

"Kidnappers!" Imogene tried to yell in his face, only the top of her striped football-helmet hair reached no higher than the top of his belly. The fella who had the chain was whomping it against the calf of his boot, making Ruby's heart bounce. She considered it might not be safe to reach for Bunny. The little girl stared up at her with big eyes and poochy lips. Imogene's voice became high and screeching, and the thick hairy arms of the fellas seemed to puff up like tires, getting bigger with each chain whomp.

"Vroom, vroooom!" Bubbie said, as though he was taking off for parts unknown, riding off into some western sunset, away from all these troubles he'd seen in his nine years. He kicked at the side of the motorcycle like it was a horse and he wore spurs.

A lady Hell's Angel stepped up to the other side of the bikes the kids sat on. She wore the tiniest pair of cutoffs, so short Ruby figured it was possible to see things that a person wouldn't even get to see in the movies. Her halter top and tattoos made Loralva look like a churchgoer. "How do we know they belong to you?" the lady said.

Ruby stared at the inky blue row of scorpions that wound its way up her shoulder and neck. "These here are my grandkids," she said as stern as she could, trying to look at the whole crowd of them. She wanted to show them she wasn't afraid, but she couldn't even convince herself. She reached out to Bubbie's hand on the handlebars, but he was too quick and snatched it away.

"We have half a mind to call the police." Imogene stuck her pointy nose out further.

"Imogene!" Ruby hissed. "Let's just take Bunny and Bubbie

and go." She tried to sound calm, but it didn't come out that way.

"Look lady," Burl said, "we could call the cops on you. Child abandonment. It's against the law." He wrapped his thick, grimy fingers around Imogene's upper arm and Ruby watched her wince, but Imogene wrangled free.

"You oughta know what's against the law," she said, stepping back toward Ruby in response to Burl's big chest pushing out. The chain thurumped against the Hell's Angel's boot. Only this time the fella wasn't sitting on his bike any longer. He stood up heading toward Burl as backup.

"These are my grandkids," Ruby said. "I only left them to go run a quick errand." Her eyes scanned from the biker lady to the crowd in the shadows to Burl. "Thought they'd be safe for just a moment." But in her head she knew it was a stupid thing to have done. Maybe in a place like Devine you could leave your kids for a short spell and they'd be safe, but not here on Interstate 10.

Burl took another step closer to Ruby so that his belly knocked up against her. "Found the boy ripping into the chest cavity of a dead coyote down in the gully over there." He pointed toward the ditch just behind their lineup of bikes. Ruby could see the red-brown crud around the edges of Bubbie's fingernails. "He likes to play with dead animals, I guess." Burl placed his thick hand on his heart. "Seemed intent on finding something."

"He's just like any little boy," Ruby heard herself lie. "He probably only wanted to see what all the parts were." She put on a fake smile, knowing Bubbie's fascination with roadkill wasn't right. "He can't wait for his hunting days."

The lady biker asked, "Where's their mom?" Ruby forgot all about the tattoos that wrapped around her body. No one had ever asked that question before, since everyone in Devine knew. Bubbie stopped his vroom, vrooming to look up at Ruby. Bunny clung to the lady biker.

"Their momma," Imogene shook a finger at Burl, "is in

Hollywood being a famous movie actress." She got only a stare from the tiny round eyes on his thick face. "You should show some respect."

Bubbie slid one leg over the gas tank and sat sidesaddle for a moment, looking at how far down it was to jump.

"Help the little cowboy down, Carly," Burl said to the biker lady, but before she could Bubbie jumped out of her arms, landing right at Ruby's feet on his hands and knees. Ruby leaned over as far as she was able and grabbed his arms to help him up. He latched on to her hips. She suddenly felt so tired. Wouldn't these folks just let them go without any trouble?

"Where's their ma?" she heard Burl ask this time. Then the truth burned its way up from her stomach like acid after a bean burrito with jalapeños.

"I told you already—" Imogene started in.

But Ruby interrupted, "She took off some years back." She looked right up into Burl's face, the top of her head reaching no higher than his bottom lip, red and thick, sticking out of his beard like Santa's. "We're hoping she's in California." She checked the expressions on the kids' faces. Bubbie's was turned down, looking at the asphalt. Bunny's was wide eyed, waiting for more. Ruby tweaked her teensy little nose. She listened for the chain whacking, but it had stopped. So she lifted the girl to her hip opposite Bubbie.

"My ma did the same." Burl spoke slower and softer than anything else he'd said before. "Took off, left me with a lousy drunk of a daddy."

"Now see there," Imogene said, "that's where we differ because their daddy is a respectable member of Devine society." The chain splayed out in the air as though it was a musical instrument playing a flat note with each link.

Burl looked right at Ruby. "My granny took me in. Loved me like nobody has since." Ruby thought she saw a little puddling in the small eyes above his cheeks. "Don't know if I'd have turned out so good otherwise."

Ruby sensed a little puddling of her own. "I thank you for watching over them. I'm real sorry for the bother." She began to lead the kids a step away, feeling safer now.

Burl patted Bubbie on the head. To Ruby, he said, "You want a piece of advice? Don't bother looking for their ma." Bubbie looked up, twisting his head under the thick hand. "It'll only be trouble."

As they walked away, Loralva asked if they minded giving her the current retail price on their Harleys. Ruby thanked them and then pulled Loralva along. They hadn't gone more than ten feet across the parking lot when Imogene started up again. "Hateful bunch. No respect for relatives of a famous person. And, did you smell that rancid odor? Worse than burnt pigskin."

Ruby looked straight ahead, aiming for the 'bago across the asphalt lot filled with cars and pickup trucks. Bubbie slipped his hand out of Ruby's and ran ahead, his little feet splat, splatting on the pavement. She let him go. He wouldn't run too far as long as she had him in her sight. Bunny sat on her hip, Mrs. Beasley on the girl's in the same manner.

"And," Imogene said, raising her voice even more, "it's amazing I got us out of that fix at all. Those kids could have been swiped if it weren't for—"

Ruby's ears and mind couldn't take it anymore. She stopped in her tracks, faced the skunk-headed woman and said, "Imogene, shut up!" her voice deep and strong. "And one more thing—quit saying 'movie star!' "

Imogene tilted her head, taken aback. "I can't believe after all I've done for you, you speak to me that way."

Ruby couldn't believe she'd said that to Imogene either. But she couldn't help herself. The heat inside her was churning like gas on top of an oil well. It could spew at any moment.

Ruby and Loralva took a few more steps in the direction of the 'bago. With Imogene trotting to get back in step with them, Loralva said to Ruby, "The price of those bikes were a whole lot more than I would have expected. Goes to show how much I need to practice for the game show."

"You'll do fine, Loralva," Ruby said, still seething about Imogene. "You always do."

"I'll be needing your help though, Ruby honey."

"Whatever you need," Ruby said, realizing Loralva had gotten her this far, and the least she could do was see to it her sister got as far as she could on *The Price Is Right*.

"Good. Let's start with the patio furniture at the back of the catalog."

Back at the 'bago, Ruby stood on her tiptoes talking to Bunny and Bubbie snug in their bunk. Imogene had gone straight to her private room, slamming the door, making the walls of the motor home shiver. Loralva sat at the dinette restyling the black wig she would wear the next day, while she flipped the pages of the catalog reading out loud. "Package of three lady's polyester underpanties, two dollars and fifteen cents; one beige girdle sizes twenty-five through forty-eight, six dollars and fifty cents."

Wrapping the blue blanket around the kids' black-stained feet, Ruby talked to them about not going out like that again. "Don't know what I'd do without you two. Your GranMomma Ruby was so scared. Thought I'd lost you for sure."

"We had fun on the motorsicles," Bunny said. Bubbie kicked his feet in the air, tangling the blanket.

"In a couple of hours we'll be in Hollywood. Most folks from Devine don't never get to go to Hollywood." She tried to sound like it was an adventure, something to look forward to. Bubbie rolled over facing the wall and his G.I. Joe.

"Aw, Bubbie." Ruby reached over the edge of the bunk toward

him, but he shoved her hand away. This part, the not wanting Ruby to touch him, had only started since she'd said they were going to California. Since she'd caught him chopping roadkill.

"We'll see Momma tomorrow, won't we?" Bunny asked.

Bubbie threw his G.I. Joe off the bunk, just missing Ruby by inches. He hit the side of the tiny half-sink in the kitchenette, making the plastic head break off.

"He's mean, GranMomma. Make him stop," Bunny cried. She drummed her feet on the bed and tears spilled out of her eyes.

Here we go again, she thought. Ruby's mind twisted up, but she knew he was acting up because his heart was caught in a prickly pear bush. She breathed out air that had sat on her belly since she'd spotted Violet on that ButterMaid commercial. "It's not likely we'll see your momma tomorrow." With one thumb she wiped the wet stain from the side of Bunny's face. "But we'll see after that. Now rest. Big day coming up."

Ruby scooted into the dinette booth across from Loralva. She could hear Bunny talking to her Mrs. Beasley doll, vroom, vrooming like they were riding around on a motorcycle.

As she watched Loralva make spit curls on the temples of the black shag with one finger and with the other hand run a finger down the page of the catalog filled with pictures of undergarments, she thought again about that Burl fella going looking for his ma. Maybe he'd even found her. Ruby wanted to sneak back outside to the Hell's Angels and ask him what he meant by "it would be trouble." Had his momma turned him away? Her head filled full to the brim with these thoughts and she wished she'd never let them in. She squeezed her eyes tight like the kids did when they pretended sleep.

"You look like you're wincing in pain," Loralva said. She scooted the Sears catalog across the table. "Here, start quizzing me on this page of Playtex Living bras."

City Limits

The way Ruby saw it, maybe it would be safer to back into Hollywood. She sat in the dinette booth facing the rear of the 'bago. From this position she couldn't see it coming at her so fast. The smell of the coffee grounds from earlier that morning eked up from the trash container, but at least there were no windows to have to look out of.

Just a few moments before, she'd been up front, calling out household furnishings and their prices to Loralva from the Sears catalog. She had stood between the other two women, Loralva in the driver's seat, Imogene in the bucket passenger seat. Through the stereo cassette player Patsy Cline twanged about feeling so lonely. That was all there was between Ruby and the big wide, bug-splattered windshield, which was the only thing between her and Los Angeles because they had just passed the green highway sign saying LOS ANGELES CITY LIMITS.

When you drove into the Devine city limits, past the sign saying DEVINE, POP. 894, heading west on Highway 90, the only road into town, you got sagebrush on the left, blue sky up above, and Jack's Gas-Up on the right. Then you passed the trailer park and Ida Mae Johnson's rental duplexes and a turnoff between the trailer houses that would take you back into town to Manzanita Road. But if you kept heading west on 90 you'd see the big neon sign Rascal ordered up special from San Antone. DEVINE BOWL it said in red letters, with the O made to look like a bowling ball with three finger holes and the L shaped like a bowling pin. The ball repeated in neon three times, each O flashing on consecutively, so it looked like the ball was rolling toward you. If it was Saturday or Wednesday league night then the parking lot was full up with Ford and Chevrolet pickups, mostly two-ton duallies, and probably a few Cadillac Coupe de Villes. Keep on heading west and the only thing from there until Cicada, another twenty miles away, was a brown, one-foot-square sign on a metal post that read LEAVING DEVINE. At the bottom, Ida Mae's juvenile delinquent son had carved "Fuckoff" with his pocketknife. Rascal had later carved over it, changing the letters to say, "ByebuYY."

When they drove past the LOS ANGELES CITY LIMITS, POPULATION 8,223,894, Ruby realized Devine would fit right inside those last three digits of the population. The other eight million and some odd made her mouth go dry.

"Test me some more on the dining room sets," Loralva said. The closer they got the more anxious Loralva seemed about the game show. Ruby knew it was her big dream, so she'd been helping her practice, quizzing her on Kenmore washers and dryers and power drills and riding lawn mowers. Ruby stood up and faced Los Angeles again. She caught her sister's blue-eyeshadowed gaze in the rearview mirror.

From inside the rubber-sealed RV the outside view looked rackety. What seemed the strangest of all to Ruby was the sky. Here they were in a place with eight million people all jampacked into one carton and the sky wasn't nearly as big as the one in Texas. The color of a dirty dishrag, it hung heavy like the back of Earl Glidden's pickup when he took a load to the dump. In Devine, while it wasn't always blue, in fact sometimes, when the thunderboomers rolled in, it was blacker than the underside of a diesel pump. The sky was always high and wide and out of reach, rising heavenward. Here it was low and thick and the horizon was just right there, in front of her face. Like when someone got too close and made you want to back up a step or two. Right then, as the city got bigger and the lanes on the highway multiplied and the concrete walls on either side climbed higher to hide the houses packed like cattle in a livestock auction hold, right then she decided to look the other way.

"Flip to the furniture section," Loralva kept on, turning Patsy Cline down just a tad, piano keys tinkling.

"Watch the road, please," Imogene said, double-checking the push-down lock on her door for the umpteenth time.

"Oh hell, I've driven through Houston during rush hour with one hand undoing the snaps on a fella's shirt while he nibbled on my earlobe. Think I can handle this."

Fearless Loralva, Ruby thought. Wished she could rub up against her and get some of what was in her blood. "Gonna sit down for this last bit of the ride," she said, holding the catalog in her left hand like a hymnal, and as she spoke she closed it up.

In the rearview mirror, Loralva's eyebrows, drawn in with a rust tone pencil, dove into a V. She wouldn't ask Ruby what was wrong in front of Imogene since it would just make whatever it was bigger, and Ruby knew this, so she just smiled back at her sister and turned toward the dinette. The glare from the windshield reflected off the countertop she should have scrubbed down earlier, but otherwise the room was dim. She peeked over the bunk edge to make sure Bubbie hadn't done anything too dangerous. He lay on his stomach drawing monster pictures on a pad of paper and Bunny lay on her back holding up Mrs. Beasley, who sat on the little girl's tummy. She was telling Mrs. Beasley a story she made up. "She's a movie star who eats MoonPies and takes us to the swimming pool in the summertime."

"You won't even quiz me on the Broyhill bedroom suites?" Loralva asked.

"Not now," Ruby said.

"Broyhill is not a very valuable brand anyhow," Imogene said.

Loralva turned up Patsy Cline.

Now Ruby had three women carrying on as Loralva read the signs they passed. BALDY VIEW MOTEL. HOUSE OF MEAT SMORGASBORD. STARDUST MOTEL. All the while Imogene told her that *The Price Is Right* was not worth all this trouble considering she probably wouldn't even get to see Bob Barker but from the back of the audience.

"Stars are respectable folk and they will only want to mingle with the sophisticates." Imogene meant herself, Ruby knew. "Violet will be getting us better connections. I'd like to meet that Sally Field. Maybe find out who does her hair."

"Or Clint Eastwood," Loralva said. "I could mess his hair."

And all the while Patsy wailed, *Worry!* And on and on about why did she let herself worry so.

Ruby slid into the booth seat, pulled the side window curtains to. The smell of the coffee grounds made her look at the trash can by the counter—full to overflowing. Above Bunny talked softly to her doll. "She will love you and make you her princess and you'll wear a crown."

What am I doing here? Ruby thought. How am I ever gonna find Violet in this big circus of a city? She wanted to cry, felt it down in her belly, those tears sloshing around, wanting to come out. Her head whined: I don't have the slightest idea how to go about finding our Violet.

"What'd you say?" Imogene asked from up front.

Ruby hadn't meant to say it out loud. "Nothing," she replied. "Talking to myself."

"Almost there. Sign we just passed said, 'Hollywood, next eight exits.'"

Ruby's head went swirly.

"Quiz me some more, Ruby honey," Loralva said, "maybe the toaster ovens?"

"Ask Imogene," Ruby snapped. She didn't mean to, but this just wasn't the time.

Loralva didn't ask Imogene, she just turned up the volume on the stereo even louder. Patsy Cline sang on about how crazy she was for even trying.

Yeah, Ruby went on to herself. *Crazy,* that's what I am. She looked at the Formica tabletop. Put her finger on a fuzzy sticky spot, probably melted MoonPie icing. She tapped her finger up and down on it. Tack, tack, tack. Thinking she should wipe it up, but didn't budge.

"GranMomma?" Bunny's chestnut head swung down from the bunk overhead. "We almost to Momma's house?"

"Almost to Hollywood, that's all," Ruby told the little girl.

Mrs. Beasley hung over the edge of the bunk alongside her. Upside down, Bunny's face looked contorted, but the doll's plastic face stayed wide eyed and grinning. "I'd give Momma my Mrs. Beasley doll, if she wanted her," Bunny said.

Ruby didn't answer. She wished she had something to offer Violet, but come to think of it offering up Bunny and Bubbie was almost the same.

"You look sad, GranMomma." She pooched her bottom lip out. Upside down she looked silly to Ruby. Then Bubbie's head came over the edge of the bunk. His eyes looked his grandmother over.

God, maybe I shouldn't have brought the kids, Ruby worried, panic rising from her breastbone.

"Maybe you want my Mrs. Beasley doll?" she asked her grandmomma.

"There it is! Sunset Boulevard. Then Hollywood Boulevard." Imogene's voice had that movie-star-watch quality that came out when she forgot that she was hiding her true mission for this trip.

"Bob Barker, here I come," Loralva said, steering the RV toward the ramp.

Bubbie quickly disappeared from Ruby's sight, feet thumping on the bunk.

"Goody, we're here!" Bunny said, and followed her brother, yanking the doll with her.

"Watch for the Hollywood sign on the hillside," Imogene said over her shoulder.

"Too much smog," Loralva said.

Ruby peered through the brown-gray haze that sat on the hills in the distance, but she couldn't see anything but concrete and guard rails. Then she heard the tink-tink of the 'bago's blinker, as they swayed with the curve of the highway exit.

"Ruby honey, come help us watch for a motel," Loralva yelled back.

"I already have the motel picked out and the directions from my Triple-A guide," Imogene corrected her.

"Come help anyway, Ruby honey."

Ruby rose to go to her sister, and Bunny hung her head back over the edge and sang along with Patsy, "crazyyy!" Then she giggled and rolled back over to the upper bunk window to look out for her momma.

MAPS OF THE STARS' HOMES $2.00 was handwritten on a cardboard sign propped up against the post of a stop sign. The patch of grass between the sidewalk and the road looked uncared-for, like the thin, patchy fur of a mangy old dog. Loralva kept the 'bago going at a steady pace. They all had a dazed look about them, like it was a long, slow dream with all eyes on the view out the big windshield.

"Ooh, one of those maps would be perfect," Imogene said. She nearly twisted 180 degrees just looking back over her shoulder at the scrawled sign.

Hollywood Boulevard was lined with crowded storefronts needing a paint job. She couldn't see inside, but Ruby could just tell that the whole row of businesses needed a dusting, a vacuuming and a general straightening up. They looked like someone's old wore-out barn used to store broken furniture and equipment. Nothing new, just junk no one cared enough about to repair nor to throw out. Even the air and sky at late afternoon were the color of a horseshoe pit. But mostly Ruby looked at the faces that passed on the street. The crowded sidewalk made it hard for her to scan each one, but she still did her best to watch for that long, silky, coal-black hair and those big, mirrorlike eyes of Violet's. She hoped Bunny and Bubbie watched for the same thing, that maybe between the three of them they'd spot her. Loralva and Imogene, she knew, were keeping their eyes on other things. Loralva, always looking at the men, and Imogene might have Violet in the back of her mind, but she really wanted to see the big stars. If she was looking for any violet eyes at all they were Miss Elizabeth Taylor's.

"Both that man and the lady are wearing high heels," Bunny pointed out the side passenger window at a psychedelic couple. Ruby'd seen these getups in magazine pictures, but never in person.

What would California do to these kids, Ruby wondered, looking at the long-haired man in thick-soled high-heeled patent leather shoes, hip-huggers and a red, brown and green checkerboard shirt, only it looked more like a blouse with its balloon sleeves.

"I'm gonna get me a pair of them platform shoes," Loralva said, staring as though she was memorizing their outfits.

"Good heavens," Imogene said. "Why in tarnation would you want to put us through that? You'll fall off and bust your head open for sure."

For Ruby, all she could think about was how they'd dent her maple lanes if folks started wearing them to the Bowl.

They'd just passed another sign for Maps of the Stars' Homes plastered on the front of a souvenir shop called Hollywood or Bust, although it looked like it could be a strip joint. "Maybe Violet's listed on that map," Imogene said.

"Oh Imogene," Ruby said. "She's not even been mentioned in *People* magazine yet."

Imogene checked her lipstick in the sun-visor mirror one more time. "Doesn't mean she's not on that map," she said, her voice skittery with excitement.

Ruby wondered if folks acted as friendly here as they did in Texas. Everybody would wave at oncoming drivers or nod at folks walking in the street, even if they were a stranger. Here, there were so many strangers. Strange strangers.

"Probably we should get one of them maps anyhow," Imogene said, applying her lipstick with wide strokes. "It could help us locate Violet."

"You just gonna walk right on up to Clint Eastwood's door and ask him where Violet lives?" Loralva sat up straight in the driver's seat, slowing down so much that the cars behind her honked. "There's Frederick's of Hollywood! I can save myself a mail order!" She rolled down her window and waved for the honkers to go around her. The mannequins in the window wore see-through negligees and feather-trimmed baby doll pajamas. "What a good find when Duke is going to be in town in just a few days," she said.

"Loralva, the kids!" Ruby said.

"I reckon I won't need to know those prices for the game show," Loralva continued as she let off the brake. With the bumper-to-bumper traffic they barely moved. They tailgated the car in front of them, which was on the rear end of the car in front of it, which sat on the bumper of a tour bus, all of them just inching along. The line was as far ahead as Ruby could see.

Imogene checked the AAA guide in her lap, then lifted the visor to see in front of her. "Turn right just up a ways, Loralva." Ruby hoped this motel Imogene had picked out was decent. While Imogene probably wouldn't put up with a grungy place, she could sure be a tightwad and Ruby was certain this was going to be expensive.

"Hey, there's a palm reader," Loralva said, looking across the street.

"Good thing Suddy ain't with us." Ruby leaned over the console to get a closer look.

Shaking her head disapprovingly, Imogene said, "I'm not saying I believe in palm reading and séances being devil worship like Suddy believes, but remember when Jessica Parker told fortunes at the Oktoberfest we had last year in Devine? Jessica and Elwin have had an awful lot of bad luck since then."

"Right," Loralva said, rolling her eyes. "She got that bad perm and Elwin had the pinkeye."

"And their hot water heater busted and flooded their basement. You never know. Could be from conjuring up the devil."

"Could be," Ruby repeated, wondering about the strength of her will being able to change the course like those ladies back at the drugstore in Palm Springs talked about. Did Satan have a part in this whole Violet situation?

"I got my palm read at that Oktoberfest," Loralva said.

"Jessica told me I'd be meeting a man in a sapphire jacket who'd give me a gift. Hasn't happened yet, but I'm still watching for him."

Ruby tried to remember what Jessica had told her. Something about being near water. She stared out the glass windshield at the strangers with afro hairdos, wearing those low-cut, belly-button-showing, hip-hugger blue jeans, girls with hair longer than their cutoffs, or were those boys? Then right next to them passed a family who could have been mistaken for Ida Mae Johnson's brood—looking like they stepped right out of Texas. Must be visitors like themselves, Ruby thought.

At the same time, Imogene pointed to the other side of the street. "Is that the Mod Squad?" Everyone shifted their gaze to the left-hand side. "That boy's afro is the size of the back tires on Jack Gordon's tow truck." Both he and she wore matching loud orange and hot pink paisley blouses, sleeves puckered.

"Bubbie says it ain't them," Bunny said. Sitting behind the kids, Ruby had seen him give a little shake of his head before she spoke. He watched TV faithfully every night, so he'd know.

"Folks would be gathered around asking for autographs if it was them," Ruby said.

"Maybe everyone around here is so used to seeing movie stars they hardly even notice anymore." Imogene checked her lipstick in the sun-visor mirror again, as though she was wishing she'd be mistaken for a star. She flipped the visor back up, and they all stared out the windshield in silence for a moment, not sure whether to absorb what they saw or spit it back out.

To think that in order to hunt for her daughter, she'd have to get out and walk among these psychedelic folks made Ruby's nerves crawl. "They ain't all hippies," she said. "Why just back there I saw some families in nice short sets and culottes walking along ordinary like."

"Don't matter none if they are hippies or freaks or any other longhairs. But let me tell you," Loralva sighed, "so far I am plainly disappointed in these California fellas. They all look a bit starved to me."

"You? Disappointed in fellas?" Ruby asked. After what she'd seen in California so far and all these psychedelic folk wandering about the streets, she kept having to look down to make sure her own skin and clothes and even toes were the same as she remembered. And Violet was supposed to be here—that's what Ruby couldn't quite untangle from her judgment—Violet was not going to be any Violet she knew.

"All these high heels and satin pants," Loralva went on. "Not that I mind tight pants that tell all, and satin can be real smooth against the skin, I just don't want my fellas wearing my clothes. Just look at that one." Everyone turned their heads to where she motioned out the glass front. "His shirt's cut lower than mine and he ain't even come close to my cleavage."

The hairy-chested guy stood leaning against a light post, smoking a cigarette, wearing gold chains to his belly button, shiny black shoes with thick four-inch heels and two-inch platform soles. His pants flared wide below the knee, and the waistband sat down around his lower hips—with no belt, how did they stay up, Ruby wondered.

"Turn here, turn here," Imogene shouted. "Our motel should be just a couple more blocks."

"So close to this?" Ruby asked.

"Oh good," Loralva said. "I need to get settled somewhere and get that catalog memorized. Ruby honey, more prices please!"

And Ruby agreed that looking at the Sears & Roebuck Craftsman tools section at that moment would probably help calm her stomach more than looking out the window any longer. Even Patsy Cline had moved on to "I Fall To Pieces."

Kidney-Shaped Pool

Hollywood wasn't blinking lights and movie stars in glittery gowns and limousines. To Ruby, it was hippie freaks and winos. She wanted to put her hands over her ears to stop all the voices of the folks back in Devine reminding her of dress-stealing transvestites and devil-worshipping heroin dealers.

Imogene pointed out the 'bago window. "That must be the place." A three-foot-high pink neon 7 rose from a salmon-colored oleander bush. Across the middle of the numeral was the word PINK and sitting on the flat top of the tall 7 was a marquee that read MOT3L on the first line, "Ktchnets, C0lor TV, Phon s, Po01" on the second and third lines. "It's not at all what I had expected," Imogene said, and she didn't sound pleased. But Ruby was. A kitchenette, TV, and phone were all they needed to fix themselves something to eat, watch *Only One Life,* and call Violet. Her mind was reeling. There was so much to get done, and she wanted out of the motor home as soon as possible.

"Color TV!" Bunny shouted. She couldn't read yet, but she knew those words. "Only the Johnsons have color TV." She followed behind her brother as they climbed down from the bunk.

Behind the neon sign a two-story motel sat back from the road in a squared-off horseshoe shape. There were several more motels on the same street, and this one looked the best in comparison, but not exactly what you'd call a luxury motel. The Pink 7 at least appeared as though someone had come along and knocked the dust off.

"This reminds me a little of that place over on the north side of Cicada next to the drive-thru striptease joint." Loralva slowed the 'bago and finagled her way in between the parked cars on the narrow side street.

"Well, pull in." Imogene sounded agitated, probably not wanting anyone to second-guess her choice. She sniffed the air.

They drove in one end of the horseshoe, under a pink and white metal awning in front of the glass doors where a sign read OFFICE. The two-story building, a gray–brown stucco that Ruby could imagine had once been pink, did have, freshly applied right over the previous dirt-covered layer, a pink trim around the eaves and each door. Pale pink, not a Loralva hot pink. Rosy doors faced the parking lot where right smack-dab in the middle, surrounded by a chain-link fence, sat the kidney-shaped swimming pool. Ruby'd seen pools like that on the TV and in magazines about movie stars, but never in real life. The only people who even had a pool in Devine were the Johnsons, and it was one of those round, above-ground types. All the kids in town hung out there all summer, or sometimes they'd drive over to the public pool in Del Agua, but even that was just a rectangular pool, smelling of chlorine so strong it reminded Ruby of the formaldehyde odor in the hospital when her momma died. She stared out the windshield, keeping her eyes on that pool, tuning out everyone else.

"What do you think, Ruby honey?" Loralva broke the spell, but not completely.

"It has a kidney-shaped pool," she said, feeling giddy, wanting to take off her bowling shoes right then and there and dunk her big toe in that water.

"Looks more liver shaped to me," Imogene said. The RV barely cleared the pink and white aluminum awning over the motel entrance, and came to a stop.

"Can we go swimmin', GranMomma?" Bunny asked, staring at the same blue pool.

"You all just wait right here while I go in," Imogene instructed them.

As the mother-in-law clambered out, dropping to the asphalt, Loralva said to her, "This ain't so bad. Better than the place across the street." They'd all seen the women in miniskirts and white go-go boots standing outside some of the doors of the other motels.

"It is important we stay in a respectable place," Imogene said, "not only for the children, but for our own sakes"—she cleared her throat—"and my reputation." She closed the door with a rubber-sealed, muffled slam. The inside of the 'bago became quiet. A patch of the warm outside air had snuck in from the open door before it closed, and Ruby could smell grit and something like burned hot dogs. Reminded her of when the rotisserie at the Bowl got set too high with the foot-longs going round and round inside it. They watched Imogene walk inside the glass doors, her mauve vinyl purse clutched tight against her chest. As Loralva leaned over and slid on her strappy high-heeled sandals that she'd taken off for the drive, Ruby took another glance at the kidney-shaped pool. On the other side a tanned girl, brown as a leather strap, lay flat on her stomach on a chaise lounge. She wore one of those teensy bikinis that barely covered her at all and the spaghetti straps were untied and spread out to sides, dangling over the edge of the chair. Ruby worried that if something scared the young woman and made her sit up too fast she'd be showing all to the world. Then she wondered if Violet now sunbathed like that.

Loralva kicked her two sandaled feet in the air. "Loralva Jefferson . . . Come . . . on . . . down!" Planting her feet again, she said to Ruby through Bunny and Bubbie's giggles, "I even sound like Rod Roddy, don't I?"

"Finest imitation I ever heard."

"I'm gonna watch you on the TV," Bunny said, getting just as thrilled as her great-aunt.

Loralva sat up straight. "Imogene must have got a sweet deal. She's charging out here like Rod Roddy just called her down to the stage."

They all watched as Imogene's black and white, well-coiffed 'do bounced out the office doors and toward them. She was smiling.

"You'll never guess who owns this motel," she said before she even had the 'bago's door open all the way. "You'll never guess." Big gulp of air.

Violet, was the first person Ruby thought of, but she stopped herself from saying it because she knew it was just a hope that this would all be over and done with that quickly.

"If we'll never guess, then tell us who the hell it is," Loralva said.

"No need to cuss," Imogene smarted back. "Remember Sugar Robbins from over in Cicada? She married that Leroy Jake Hines? Well, his sister-in-law is the owner of this motel! Is that not the craziest thing?"

Ruby and Loralva waited for more. The only one of those folks who Ruby knew was Sugar Robbins, and she only knew her from one of Rascal's family reunions. Sugar was Rascal's momma's second cousin twice removed, and she always carried a peanut can filled with gin-soaked raisins. "For my achy arthritis, child. And it keeps the mosquitoes away besides," she'd say.

"Well?" Imogene said, throwing her arms out. "Aren't you going to thank me for picking a motel that happens to be run by a fellow Texan?"

"Depends," Loralva said. "There's two kinds of Texans. Is she a beer-drinking Texan or Bible-preaching one? 'Cause if there's Bible sayings pasted on her walls then I'd just as soon stay across the street."

"Listen at you," Imogene laughed and waved Loralva off as if she was joking. Ruby knew it was no joke and was worried they'd lose their opportunity to stay at the motel with a kidney-shaped pool. Imogene kept on, "She said to come on inside right now, she wants to meet y'all. She's gone to fetch her husband who's painting the place."

"Do you know her from back home?" Ruby asked as she patted the kids, indicating that they should head toward the side door of the vehicle.

"Never met her in my life," Imogene said, "but I was scared to death this place would end up being run by some of those hippie freaks we just passed. I've heard what goes on in their places." She put her hand up to her mouth, cupping it so the kids couldn't hear, and mouthed, "Orgies."

"That might not have been so bad," Loralva said as she climbed out the driver's side.

Ruby and the kids made their way to the side door and down the step to the asphalt, wrapped in more warm, burned air. The heavy sky seemed only to be kept off her back by the aluminum carport awning.

Inside the office, Penny the Texan wasn't back from locating her husband yet. No Bible sayings were pasted on the pink walls, only typical motel art and one dangling spiderweb so heavy with dirt that even the spider had moved on. The air conditioner ran full blast, pumping the room with the smell of chilled cigarette smoke. For a Texan, the motel owner hadn't decked the place out much in a way that reminded Ruby of back home. There were no western scene paintings, and no neon beer signs like the ones Ruby had collected from her vendors. At least the Lord's Prayer wasn't blinking on and off at her like Ruby envisioned must be happening at the Devine Bowl. In fact, the only neon sign was the one in the window saying NO VACANCY with the NO turned off.

"Said she'd be right back," Imogene announced, peeking through the doorway behind the counter.

Loralva tapped her foot and drummed her long raspberry-tart-colored nails on the counter. "Don't know, Imogene. I've stayed in places nicer than this and they only charged by the hour."

"Are you questioning my choice of motels, Loralva Jean?" Imogene's white stripes looked lavender under the fluorescent lights. "This establishment is run by a Texan. A Texan—meaning one of us. We will be surrounded by enough strangeness, and you should be appreciating that I'm protecting us from folks that don't do things normal." The mother-in-law sighed with impatience. "Besides, Penny tells me they are in the process of remodeling it all themselves. That's why we got a special deal."

"I knew it," Loralva said. "How many rooms we got?"

"Penny said the rooms are more like suites, but we got a special Texan discount."

Loralva, don't argue, Ruby wanted to say, afraid she might not get to enjoy the kidney-shaped pool like in the magazine pictures.

Voices came through the door behind the counter and they all turned to greet the motel owner they'd heard so much about.

"Howdy, howdy," the little lady said. She stood no more than the height Bubbie'd be in about two years, and she was wearing a orange and purple paisley double-knit jumpsuit with a wide elastic belt cinched in the middle. Her long hair was silver gray with white streaks, and tied back in a braid with ribbon that matched the fabric of her jumpsuit. A thickly crumpled face held a Texas-friendly, hospitality smile. Ruby reckoned she was at least seventy-five, but she exuded the energy of a twenty-year-old. Probably the way Loralva'd be in thirty years, only Loralva wouldn't be caught dead in that jumpsuit. Through the doorway behind Penny walked a man so tall he had to duck at the threshold. Ruby felt the wrinkles around her eyes stretch wide open. Other than the pink paint spot on the side of his nose, his skin was the color of Sugar Robbins's gin-soaked raisins.

"Looks like it's more than just the TV that's colored around here," Imogene muttered under her breath, but still loud enough that Ruby worried that the innkeepers heard.

"Howdy," Ruby said back, filling in the silence.

Her sister too stuck out her hand. "Loralva Jefferson."

"This here's Warren"—the tiny woman thumbed behind her—"and I'm Penny. We're the Lipscombs."

Imogene had maintained a safe distance, looking down her raised nose, not coming forward to shake hands, then she said, as though she was just pointing out a mistake, "I take it you ain't Leroy Jake's brother."

Penny looked up at her tall husband, then back to Imogene, a satisfied smile on her face. Answering for him, she said, "I left that son of a bitch fifteen years ago." She took Ruby's outstretched hand in both her tiny crinkled ones and rubbed them like a mothering soul.

"How 'bout a cold beer?" Warren said to the lot of them, his voice rocky like the Nueces River. "No Lone Star this far west, but got some cold Schlitz."

"That'll do it," Loralva answered first, holding her hand out, fingers in a circle ready to be filled with a can.

"I'll take one of those too," Ruby said.

Penny hadn't let go of her hand yet, and patted it in approval. "Imogene?" she asked. Ruby pleaded silently that she not say anything too embarrassing, for the look on her face was still a lemon-drop pucker.

"Awful early in the day for me." Imogene poked at her pile of black and white hair, not sure where to put her eyes, but letting them flicker on Warren quickly. "That's just not my way."

"Well, we better get to our rooms. I gotta get back to my studying for *The Price Is Right,*" Loralva said.

"Penny's been on *The Price Is Right,*" Warren said.

"First thing you have to do is get yourself a Sears catalog," Penny said.

Loralva smiled. "Done that! What I need is tickets." She glanced in Imogene's direction.

"That's easy," Warren said. "The hard part is getting on."

"Tell me everything," Loralva said, learning in closer to Warren and Penny.

Imogene wandered toward the door of the motel office. She looked relieved. "We gotta unload my Winnebago," she said. "You can come back over later and talk about the game show."

Ruby was ready to settle in too. She liked this place and its proprietors. She knew she could stay here as long as it took to find Violet. She remembered what Earl had said about following the trail until she couldn't anymore. Right now, the trail was wide open.

Black, White and Colored

Ruby was relieved the motel suite fit the four of them just fine. Imogene got her own private room on the other side of a connecting door. She hadn't opened it yet, and she warned that she'd be the one to use it. Said it like a command. Loralva told her she didn't have to use it at all, that she could just stay on the other side, which caused a scary moment like when two rattlers spot each other in the goat pen.

When they'd first come in, Ruby'd felt homesickness wallop her in the belly. Dull light came through one lamp shade stained a yellow-orange, making the room glow like a nightclub lounge, like the Idyll-On-Up saloon after-hours on a Saturday night when Loralva had promised she'd close up. The only thing missing was the cigarette smoke, but the fried ham smell made up for that. An air conditioner hung halfway in and halfway out of the window by the front door. It choked, not quite coming on, but not quite going off either.

"It has trouble clicking on," Penny said. "Nudging it with your boot toe helps."

Loralva used the pointy heel on her strappy sandals, causing the machine to go off. Ruby wondered if it'd come back on and looked around for windows to open just in case. Another smaller window over the kitchenette sink was all she could see. The kitchenette was really just a wall with the makings of a kitchen stuck in it—a miniature stove, sink and fridge only slightly bigger than the 'bago's. To her left sat the TV set, no bigger than a case of beer, on a tray with casters. Bubbie'd already turned it on and flipped the channel knob. Crowded next to it and shoved against the same wall sat a table and four chairs. She'd have to figure out a way to get a fifth chair up to that table.

To her right, to one side of the boxy, brown sleeper sofa, was a short hallway with two doors, one leading to the bedroom where she and Loralva would sleep, and one to the bathroom. She'd only peeked in the bathroom and got just enough of an eyeful to know she didn't want Bunny and Bubbie touching the aqua tile and the yellowed shower curtain with the black moldy bottom half. Most definitely no one was to sit on that toilet seat, at least not before she cleaned in there.

After showing them around and demonstrating how the electric massager on the bed worked, Penny headed back to the office, but not before saying, "By the way, that toilet don't work so well. Warren'll have to come by later to unclog it." Then she left them to their unloading and unpacking.

"Seems nice," Ruby said.

"It would be better if I had my own room," Loralva said.

"No, I meant Penny," Ruby said.

"Yeah." Loralva looked at her sister. "She's a beer-drinking Texan. And she not only told me how to get *Price Is Right* tickets, they've been to the show, so I can get even more advice."

Ruby wiggled and maneuvered the TV antenna trying to get a clear picture. "How you gonna get the tickets at this late date?"

"Tomorrow morning I'll go down the street just a couple of blocks and get them at that Chinese theater everybody's been talking about. Can you believe it? Just a couple of blocks away."

"That's Hollywood for ya," Ruby said.

Loralva sat down on the boxy couch facing the TV. "Do you mind working with me some more on these catalog items?"

"Reckon that'll kill the time for now." The kids sat themselves down in front of the screen. Walter Cronkite announced that the weather would be next, while the station went to commercial. Ruby kept one eye out for a ButterMaid advertisement, but for some reason couldn't bring herself to sit down.

A Dial soap commercial came on. Ruby took the catalog from Loralva. "You got awful quiet, Ruby honey. What kind of cat got your tongue? Am I pestering you too much about studying for the game show?"

"Not at all," Ruby said. "I'm happy to do it. Just feeling like I don't have my land legs after setting foot in California. Didn't picture myself ever staying in a Hollywood motel."

"Well, you're here and everything's working in our favor."

Loralva always did look at the bright side, and after a few more moments of shifting from one foot to the other, Ruby decided that she would try hanging out on the bright side too.

After the Dial commercial came a SpaghettiOs spot and Bunny sang along, "Uh-oh, SpaghettiOs!!" Then Walter Cronkite came back and Ruby breathed a sigh of relief for no ButterMaid commercials. The weatherman in the background showed pictures of the rains coming down in Texas. Over the top of Bubbie's bobbing head Ruby watched the scenes of folks making their way across the towns in motorboats, or scarier shots of pickups that stalled out in low crossings and were now floating off down a river. The TV camera focused on an elderly lady watching the water rise above the sandbags at her front door.

"Heavy rains are expected to continue throughout the week," Mr. Cronkite reported.

Ruby knew if she were home there'd be as big of a mess to clean up as what lay ahead here in California.

"Free Spirit three-speed bicycle," Ruby called out from the catalog as she sat on the couch next to her sister. She'd make fried baloney for dinner, she thought. That would make it seem even more like home. Then she'd stay up an extra hour longer to quiz Loralva on garden tools from the Sears & Roebuck catalog.

"Twenty dollars for the three-speed and thirty-five dollars for the ten-speed," Loralva answered within seconds.

Ruby turned to her. "You are even faster at this than you are at picking up fellas at the Idyll-On-Up."

"Ruby honey," Loralva said, putting her strappy sandaled feet up on the coffee table. "Duke said timing is everything. I have to be quick on the draw. I figure if I can be fast in one thing, I can be fast in other things as well."

The sisters smiled.

The next morning, Loralva got up before any of the rest of them and just like Penny had said she got tickets from a young man right outside of Grauman's Chinese Theatre.

"He walked right up and stuck them in my hands, Ruby honey." Loralva waved the tickets in her face. "For free. I told him I'd pay, but he refused."

Ruby could see that there were three tickets that Loralva waved around. "How come he didn't want you to pay for them?"

"He said it's the way it works. No charge. We just show up tomorrow bright and early."

"Tomorrow? We? That's right away."

"Thought that was what you wanted, Ruby honey, so that then you could spend the rest of your time on the Violet trail." Loralva laid the three yellow tickets on the table. They didn't seem near fancy enough for what she thought game show tickets should look like. "And you get to be on the show with me. You're my coach. My price coach."

"Oh Loralva," Ruby said as she set the table for breakfast. "I can't be on no game show." The kids stretched and yawned over on the sleeper sofa. Ruby indicated with a nod of her head in their direction that she couldn't be on because there'd be no one to watch the kids.

"If it weren't for that, then could you go with me?" Loralva pleaded.

"Where we gonna find a babysitter in these parts? I ain't leaving the kids with no go-go-boot-wearing girl from the motel across the way."

"We'll work it out," Loralva said and Ruby knew her tone meant she was determined to figure out a solution. She had to admit, the thought of being on a game show did sound pretty exciting. But the tickets sure looked flimsy. And to get something like that for free, it just didn't make any sense to Ruby.

Right after breakfast, Ruby got the little ones ready to go down to the pool. Both in their little suits, Bubbie in blue Superman boxer shorts, Bunny in her pink gingham suit with its frilly lace skirt that stuck out ninety degrees over her tummy and tiny round behind. Ruby herself didn't feel so good about putting on a bathing suit in front of all these California bathing beauties like the one she saw down at the pool yesterday. Besides, she was chomping at the bit to begin her search for Violet's whereabouts, and wanted to start by making some phone calls, so Ruby had Loralva take the kids on down to the pool.

"Mind you stay away from the deep end," she hollered after the kids. They swam like little carp after all those summers spent down by the Pedernales River, so she didn't worry. They ran ahead of their great-aunt Loralva in her zebra print bikini and clear plastic slides, Sears catalog resting on her hip. Ruby thought she noticed a bit more of a swing than usual in her sister's sway, probably just from the thrill of getting on a game show soon.

All settled in now and alone in the motel room, Ruby went to the fridge and got out the carton of ButterMaid half-and-half that she used in her coffee. On the back of the pint was listed the address of the ButterMaid corporate headquarters in Lincoln, Nebraska, and a phone number: 1-800-BM-DAIRY. Ruby hadn't planned what she should say, so when the ringing stopped and a voice came on, the skitters ran through her chest. When she realized it was just a recording she almost hung up, but it said her call was very important to them, so she figured it wouldn't hurt to wait, all the while listening to the ButterMaid jingle. *If it's ButterMaid, it's better made . . .*

She stood in the kitchenette underneath the tiny window that faced the rundown motel next door, humming along with the tune. She felt brave, telling herself she'd just ask to talk to the ButterMaid. She imagined explaining that she was the ButterMaid's momma and that made her feel proud. But when the lady finally came on the other end of the line, Ruby didn't feel brave so much as ashamed that she was the ButterMaid's momma and yet didn't know how to get in touch with her. "I need to talk to the ButterMaid," Ruby warbled.

The woman on the other end of the phone laughed a little, in a nice way. "We have several ButterMaids. If you'd like to correspond with them we have an address you can write to."

She pictured the streets of Hollywood filled with ButterMaids and all of them looking like Violet. Or would they be wandering around Lincoln, Nebraska, where the corporate headquarters were? "Oh no," Ruby said, then hesitated. "I suppose I could—" Then she tried to explain, "You see, my daughter, Violet, she—"

"Your daughter's a ButterMaid fan?" the customer service lady said. "We have twelve-inch exact replica dolls you can order for nineteen ninety-five. Have you seen the ad? Is it for a special occasion, maybe her birthday?"

They celebrated Violet's birthday November second, the day she was found. Angel Vasquez had told Ruby that it was also the day Mexicans around town celebrated the Day of the Dead, when all the spirits rise from their graves. Ruby liked knowing what they deemed as Violet's birthday was a special day.

"No," Ruby said. "It's just *one* ButterMaid I need to get a hold of. I recognized her on the commercial during *Only One Life*. She's my—" She backed up. She didn't want to identify herself as a mother who didn't know her own daughter's whereabouts. "She's someone I know and I want to get ahold of her. Urgently." That sounded too pushy, she reckoned.

"An ad agency does the commercials and hires the actresses through a talent agency."

Of course, Violet would have an agent. She'd seen something like that on *Bewitched* with Darrin Stephens.

"Hold, please."

She listened again to the ButterMaid jingle. *If it's ButterMaid, it's better made* . . . Irritating, she thought, but then decided she should like it no matter what, for Violet's sake. Violet had probably worked hard for that job. But Ruby couldn't get past the fact that no matter how hard she'd worked to become the ButterMaid, she'd left Bunny and Bubbie behind. She'd left all of them behind. She felt her insides start to heat up and her jaw tighten. For a moment Ruby considered hanging up the phone, but she spotted the lavender Bugs Bunny plate smeared with chocolate MoonPie icing and she couldn't.

Sunbeams thick with gray dust came through the soured eyelet-lace curtain above the sink. Ruby waved her hand through the sunbeams, watching the dust motes bounce and swirl in the air. Then a knock at the hollow door made her jump, causing the sunbeams to dance around nervously.

"Just a sec," she hollered out, the phone cord too short to reach all the way to the door. Then the lady on the phone was back. "Whyte & Simon Advertising in Los Angeles, California, is the advertising agency." Ruby wrote it down on the pad by the phone, and even had the woman spell it out twice. She got the phone number too, but didn't call after they hung up because the knocking persisted. She sensed this was a good start and folded up the scrap of paper with the number and stuck it down the front of her paisley blouse and into her bra. It was a Loralva thing to do, but she reckoned that way she wouldn't lose or forget the information. In fact, she couldn't forget about it, not with the sharp edges poking at the soft skin of her left breast.

She knew it wasn't Imogene at the door, because she wouldn't have knocked first, she would have just come on through the connecting door. Ruby wiped her hands on a tea towel and made her way across the room, nearly tripping over a chair from the green and chrome dinette set.

When she opened the door, Warren stood so tall his forehead was hidden behind the door frame. He smiled at Ruby and she noticed the edges of his gums were brown, not pink like hers. He told her he was there to unplug the toilet. The sweat poured from his temples like a sprinkler head set on low pressure. She thought maybe he needed something to cool himself off and she needed something to say. "Can I fix you an icy cold Coca-Cola?" She'd heard that on a commercial and liked the ring of it.

"No thank you, ma'am," he said in that low sweet Karo syrup voice. "Been meaning to fix that toilet for some time and since y'all are staying here now, Penny figured I better do it right away." Ruby knew she should say, "Come right on in." But she worried her words would come out funny, like last night when she was getting change in the office for the pop machine on the landing. She'd handed Warren a dollar bill from her billfold and asked for "four quarters black." She stammered to correct herself, which just made it worse. His smooth face hadn't changed, like he'd heard it before, but she'd felt her own creased face turn pink and then red hot.

"Mind if I come in?"

Ruby knew he'd had to ask twice now. He held a plunger in one hand and a long metal rod in the other. "Fine by me," she said.

It wasn't like his skin was really black, but she'd heard on the TV that's what she should say now. Weren't supposed to say "coloreds" or "Negroes" anymore. Some folks griped about it, but she figured she'd call anybody anything they preferred. Black didn't seem right either, though. Just like Ruby didn't consider her own skin to be white, but more the color of a load of off-whites and beiges that had a red sock thrown in by mistake. It wasn't that she'd never seen a colored man before. She had, once or twice in Del Agua when they drove through town coming from Cicada, they drove right through the section where all the colored folks lived. While there weren't any living in Devine, that was only, she supposed, because none had ever had the inclination to move there. Course, none had ever come to bowl either. That made her feel bad. Made her feel like she'd forgotten to invite someone to a party and only just remembered them after all the other guests had gone home. She followed him to the bathroom.

"Saw the others at the pool. Why aren't you down there?" he asked her as she watched him kneel on the splotchy gray linoleum of the bathroom.

"Making some phone calls." She didn't tell him the details of her call, but wondered if he could know something about Violet's whereabouts.

"First time in Hollywood?"

"First time in California even," she said.

"Finding things different, I bet."

Was he referring to him and Penny being married, she wondered. As he flushed the toilet, she watched the water rise too high, and it made Ruby skittery that it would spill over the rim of the bowl.

"You're gonna see some things you've never seen before in your life out here," he said.

"You ain't a kidding." Ruby thought she already had, just on the I-10.

Warren went back to roto-rootering. The metal rooter scraping on ceramic made her molars twinge.

"Your sister told me what brought y'all out here. If you need any help searching for your daughter, Penny and me will do all we can." He smiled at her again. "Whatever we can to make it easier on you. Gotta be a tough time." He shook his head as Ruby nodded. Maybe he would know something, but she didn't know what to ask him, or maybe she was more afraid of what would come out.

Rascal used to tease Ruby that she had a crush on Flip Wilson, she laughed so hard at his program, made sure the TV was on every Wednesday night to watch even the reruns. But Warren was a bit more like Nat King Cole. Sharp shoulders, tight-skin face, only his was skin five shades lighter than Mr. Cole's.

"Appreciate that offer of help," Ruby said, as he bent back over the commode. "Seems folks all along the way have been real helpful." Although she couldn't say the same for the folks back in Devine, even Burl of the Hell's Angels had passed on some advice. Not the sweetest kind of help, like Warren was offering, but he'd made her feel like she'd done right by taking in the kids.

"Penny and me, we like helping folks out," Warren said. "Most people that come to California have a hard time finding their way at first. We know that from our own experience."

"Folks from Texas are neighborly," Ruby said. "You from Texas too, like Penny?"

He pulled the rooter out the rest of the way. Then he wound the metal spring back inside its coil and gathered the rest of his tools. "I'm from Colorado, but Penny's Texas friendly way is what I like most about her. Bet you're the same." He thwucked the plunger one last time, then flushed to see if all was clear. "Aren't ya?"

"I'm neighborly, I reckon," Ruby said, "but I'm more in the situation right now where I just might take you up on your offer to help. I don't know the first thing about California. Right this minute, my daughter Violet's somewhere in this mess of a city, and Loralva's wanting to get on a game show and she got some flimsy tickets that look like they were mimeographed at Idyll County public schools, and I don't know what to make of any of it."

He stood up, straight and high as a barn door, holding the plunger in one hand. He chuckled a little. "Those tickets that Loralva has are all they give out. They get you a place in line, but don't guarantee you'll get on."

"Oh," Ruby said. She reckoned it might be better if Loralva at least had Imogene to blame.

"The best bet to get on the show is to get there very early tomorrow morning," Warren said. "I reckon you sassy Texas ladies will get just about anything you come to California for."

"Oh you," she said, feeling a pink frosting coming back over her face.

"Everyone comes to California because they want something bad enough."

Ruby waited a moment to ask, thinking maybe she better not, but she had to. "Think we'll get what we came for?"

"I'll tell Penny to give Loralva the scoop on how to get on the show. And I'll even drive you there myself."

Scoop. Ruby didn't know what he meant by that and knew her face was scrunching up with her confused look. She also noticed that he said nothing about Violet. "Don't know if I can be taking the time to be on a game show," Ruby said, hoping that would be a hint to him that she came for another reason. She'd come because there was something she wanted bad enough.

"Looks like your pipes are cleared. I felt something give," he said. "Let me know if you have any more trouble."

Ruby followed him toward the motel room door. As he leaned his head down to go under the door frame, she said slowly, "You come back now." She was real careful to make sure it came out "back" and not "black."

After she closed the door behind Warren, the piece of paper in her bra poked her again. She pulled it out and read the name of the agency and the phone number out loud. But instead of calling, she set it on the nightstand in the back bedroom.

Ruby knew she wanted it bad enough to call. She wanted it as bad as Loralva wanted to be on *The Price Is Right*. But she had started thinking, what was it Violet wanted bad enough and how could it ever be worth leaving her kids?

Red Feather Boas

Ruby wanted to keep making headway. She'd had good luck with her phone calls so far, so she should keep calling. But what Warren had said about the game show and Loralva's tickets being for real after all, it had Ruby all in a tizzy. She wanted not only to share her own good news about getting the phone number for the advertising agency, but also help Loralva study so she'd be ready first thing tomorrow. She dug her bathing suit out of her suitcase. Her mind had gone around in a big circle and come back to what Warren had said as he left. "You sassy Texas ladies will get just about anything you come to California for." Ruby let her shoulders do a little jig, testing out how sassy she might be. She knew he didn't mention anything specific, but she was excited for Loralva too, and she wasn't going to let anything get in the way of their finding Violet.

She tugged her suit down around her thighs, thinking maybe she should have bought one just a bit more revealing. Looking in the full-length mirror hung on the back of the bedroom door, she did a Loralva move and adjusted her breasts to sit up higher in the cups of her suit. Then watched as they deflated back into the foam rubber of the suit. Now dressed and ready to go, she didn't have any high-heeled slides like Loralva's to wear, not even any rubber flip-flops like Bunny's, so she put on her soft-worn, red and green bowling shoes because she didn't mind if they got wet, and they could easily be slipped on and off without her having to untie the laces. Taking deep breaths the whole way, she went down to the poolside.

Looking at the reflection of the pool, it hit Ruby that she really was in California. When she got to the pool gate, she hesitated a bit rather than going straight for putting her toes in because it seemed too precious yet. She'd only seen pictures of pools like this in magazines. For the teensiest moment she imagined herself laid out curvaceously on a chaise lounge by a pool like this one. Her plaid bathing suit more of a sleek purple and a pair of Loralva's slides on her feet, maybe even one shoe dangling from her toes. A certain calm to the silver blue water had her thoughts straying a long way from the ordinary. But then, like a hurricane wind from the Gulf, Bubbie swooped by, shaking her from her daydream.

"Walk!" she hollered although his body was already splayed out midair and he was headed for a big belly flop, which got the splashing and waves going. Ruby applauded him as he bobbed to the surface, a wide little-boy smile on his face, drops of water shining on his prickly haircut.

"Me too!" Bunny said, running to the edge, then squatting down on the rim, her legs like chicken wings as she slowly rolled into the still-churning water.

Ruby applauded again as she came to the top, her pigtails floating out behind her. Every summer in Devine, all the kids in town spent every hot minute in water somewhere. The pond over by Earl Glidden's back pasture, the creek, the Johnsons' pool, the back-and-forth sprinklers in the front yard.

"This is better than the Johnsons' 'bove ground pool," Bunny said. "My toes don't scrape the bottom. They don't even touch. Ever!" Her arms and legs doing the dog paddle.

Ruby regarded this as a good moment. Things were going well. And if she tried real hard she could imagine it staying that way.

From the corner of her eye she saw Loralva sitting across the pool. She wanted to run over and tell her all the good news, but her sister was sitting next to that same girl who had been there the day before when the 'bago had pulled under the awning of the Pink 7 Motel. Ruby felt a little uneasy about her, but then told herself she was being silly, she didn't even know her. Penny hung over the chain-link fence between the office and the pool, in her double-knit zippered jumpsuit and matching espadrilles, chatting with the bathing beauties. Ruby made her way toward them. The pool was trimmed in concrete, but over the rest of the deck Penny and Warren had installed green turf carpet that had worn down in a few places where the chairs had been scooched around. Ruby knew from quizzing Loralva out of the Sears catalog that this was no low-class outdoor pool. Tables with aluminum framed chairs and chaise lounges with plastic webbing sat in two corners. Aluminum pagoda umbrellas stuck up from the middle of the tables with yellowed fringe dangling along the edges like Judy Harper's husband's teeth. Ruby knew Penny had spent good money on this pool furniture. With seven bands of tangerine and honey webbing in those chairs, that could run a person fifteen bucks each. Those umbrella tables were somewhere close to a hundred dollars. Some of the webbing was shredded and ripped, but Ruby'd tell Penny about the webbing kits she'd seen advertised in the Sears catalog.

"Hey, Ruby honey!" Loralva waved from under a big floppy straw hat that Ruby didn't even know she owned. The Sears catalog sat open on her lap. "Whatcha doing down here already?"

"I got news," Ruby said.

"About Violet?" Loralva asked.

"About Violet and *The Price Is Right*," Ruby said. She relayed the details of what happened that morning after Loralva had left the motel room, and as she talked she found herself staring at the young lady lying next to Loralva. She must have spent all her days lying by this pool, because she was the color of dates. Her skin was darker than the barely there gold lamé bikini she wore. Her body laid out long, but rounded off in all the right places. Ruby's own breasts deflated even further into the foam rubber of her suit as she looked at the cantaloupe shapes of this girl's chest. Around her narrow waist she wore a silver bikini chain with a tiny red jeweled dagger for the clasp, which stuck to an oily hip-bone. Her body cocked at all the sexy angles. Her hair was the color of butter pecan ice cream, and from her forehead down, all her brown skin was greased in what smelled like ambrosia fruit salad.

"And Warren said we had to get there very early," Ruby said.

Penny must have noticed Ruby's staring because once Ruby stopped to catch her breath, she said, "Don't think you've met Barbi."

"Get this, Ruby honey," Loralva sat up in her chaise lounge. "She works just over on the next block as a stripper."

"Dancer," Barbi said, correcting Loralva. "I work temporarily over on Hollywood Boulevard."

Ruby's eyes went looking for the kids to see if they were in earshot. Their little heads bobbed up and down in the water across the way. "That so," she said, looking again at the slick, oiled body, trying not to appear as though she was staring.

Barbi raised her big, round, white-rimmed sunglasses and looked Ruby up and down. "In a higher-class joint than most." She had a voice like toenails on a screen door. Ruby felt a little self-conscious in her plaid extra-coverage swimsuit when Loralva and Barbi had on next to nothing, although gold lamé would not be in Ruby's wardrobe either. Maybe she should have bought the yellow suit with the sides cut out that she'd considered.

"Nice to meet you." Ruby'd known a couple of strippers before—there was Loralva's friend Verdee Whitacre who had worked in the drive-thru strip joint in Del Agua, and she reckoned you could count Randi Nightingale who sang country over at the Longhorn Club and sometimes took her shirt off after midnight. But she'd never met one that looked quite like Barbi.

Then Ruby turned back to Loralva. "Aren't you interested in what Warren passed on about the game show?"

"He stopped by after he fixed the toilet," Loralva said. "I know just how to work it. Penny and me, we'd already been discussing about how to get to the CBS studios too. It's all arranged."

"Warren can take you over in the morning," Penny said. "He knows right where to go."

Ruby laid out her tiny white motel-room towel on the chaise lounge on the other side of Loralva, still looking in Barbi's direction. "I can't be going to no game show when I got so much to do and the kids to mind." She watched Barbi's concave belly glisten in the sunlight, the red dagger pointing down to her unmentionables.

"The kids can stay with me," Penny said.

"Oh, that's nice of you to offer," Ruby said, "but I just got the number for the ButterMaid advertising agency and I have to call them tomorrow. I think this may be the way I get to my Violet." She closed her eyes with hope for just a moment.

"That's great news about the advertising agency," Loralva said. "You should celebrate!" She held up a plastic tumbler.

"Margarita?" Penny asked, holding up another glass and pointing to the church-potluck-sized thermos. Ruby noticed she held an empty ivory-colored cigarette holder in her mouth.

"Tequila makes me burp," Ruby said, shaking her head no. Then, thinking she should celebrate the small steps along the way, and that she'd soon be circulating her toes in the pool water, so she said, "Maybe just a little one." She put her finger and thumb together to show how little.

"Help me study up some more," Loralva said, handing over the catalog to Ruby.

Barbi put her sunglasses back on her face. Her long butter-pecan hair stuck to her oiled shoulders and chest. She rolled over onto her stomach, and reaching up her back she untied her bathing-suit straps. Ruby didn't want to stare, but was startled and worried that she might be starting her dance routine right there and then. Barbi laid the spaghetti straps to the side and coiled her hair around on top of her head. "Do I have any tan lines?" she asked Loralva. "I'll get in big trouble if I have tan lines." That had Ruby worrying she'd be taking off her bikini bottoms next.

"I thought about being a stripper once," Loralva said, as Penny handed Ruby a tumbler full of margarita.

"Loralva!" Ruby whispered, looking over at the kids diving. "You did not."

"Heard you can make a hundred bucks a night easy. Ain't that right, Barbi?"

"Mm-hmm," Barbi said. She turned back to her magazine and flipped the pages. *Variety*, it said in ritzy letters on the front.

Ruby took a sip of her drink. Her cheeks turned inside out with the tequila bite—it was about the strength of the ones Loralva made back at the Devine Bowl on league nights when the games started to get boring. Ruby smacked her lips.

Then the pool gate clinked as Imogene came into the pool area waving at them. She wore a chevron-striped polyester dress with kick pleats. "There's a beauty parlor just a few blocks away," she announced, "The Hairem, it's called. The ad in the yellow pages said, 'Styles from fairy-tale books to movie star looks.'" She stopped talking and looked Barbi up and down. They locked gazes and each appeared to be disgusted by the other's outfit. Imogene put on her churchy look she got from Suddy and turned away.

"Margarita?" Penny asked, the empty cigarette holder waggling between her teeth.

"Oooh." Imogene liked a nice salty margarita. "Maybe later."

She looked back at Ruby. "Why aren't you looking for Violet?" Imogene asked her.

"I made some calls," Ruby said, but she didn't feel like repeating her story to the mother-in-law and she didn't like the fact that Imogene had obviously placed all the responsibility on her.

"When can the salon take us?" Loralva interrupted.

"Right now, they said." Imogene's gaze studied all the women. Then to Ruby, "Well? Do you think you can find Violet by sitting by the pool?"

"Come on, Imogene," Loralva said, "I'll tell you all about it on the way to the beauty parlor." She looked back to Ruby. "Ruby honey. Wanna go?" Loralva asked as she pulled her white short shorts over her bathing suit bottom and fastened the snaps on her western vest over her bathing suit top. "I'm gonna get my hair done. Don't want to take a chance on my wig falling off in the game show excitement."

"Somebody's gotta stay with the kids," Ruby said, sipping more of the tangy drink, noticing her toes warm up.

"Bet Barbi and Penny'll watch out for them," Loralva suggested, slipping into her clear plastic slides.

"It'd be a pleasure," Penny said.

Now Barbi looked up. "As long as they don't drown or nothing. I'll be here anyhow." She poured more margarita from the thermos into her glass.

Ruby scrambled for a polite way to decline. She pictured Barbi taking all her clothes off and going for a swim, polluting the same water Bunny and Bubbie were in with her nakedness and banana-flavored oil. Penny smiled at her, holding the empty cigarette holder between her teeth. She seemed to understand. "Thanks anyway," Ruby finally said. "Gave myself a trim before we left Devine. Y'all go on without me." She shook the ice in her glass and took a bigger swig. She'd rather stay by the kidney-shaped pool anyhow. That's what she planned on doing all day the next day while Loralva and Imogene went to the game show. Right now, she liked the way her body felt all swirly on the inside. She never minded a good drink now and again, but usually she was just too busy at the Bowl to stand around drinking and socializing. Seemed to Ruby at that moment that with the magazine-picture pool here and margaritas available, Hollywood was a place where anything could happen.

As the others walked out the pool gate, Penny picked up the thermos and said she'd be right back with a refill. When she'd gotten out of earshot, Ruby said to Barbi, "Where's Penny's cigarette?"

Barbi's ice crackled as she took a swig of margarita. Through a piece of ice she held between her teeth she said, "She's trying to quit." Never looking up from her magazine.

"Smoking?"

"No, being a rock star." Barbi lowered her white-rimmed shades and looked over them at her. Ruby started to laugh, but something about the girl, maybe the oiled-down slickness that looked like toughness, made Ruby feel a little nervous being alone with her. Like she could get arrested as an accomplice just sitting there sunning herself in the next chair. She was a stripper after all.

She looked out at the kids in the pool, swimming and dunking each other. Bunny seemed to bob best with her little bottom in the air, her head toward the bottom of the pool. Bubbie just sank. She was glad to be watching them be little kids for a while.

Barbi flipped her magazine pages. As Ruby readjusted her

tiny white motel towel behind her back, she figured she should start some sort of conversation. It seemed impolite not to. Both of them sitting right next to each other and neither one saying a word.

"Any good recipes in that issue?" Ruby asked, with a howdy-do smile. Her eyes felt somewhat loose in their sockets. She sipped her margarita, wanting it to last until Penny returned with more.

Barbi looked over at her without taking her glasses off, so Ruby was unable to see her eyes to know what her expression was.

"Some of my best dishes come from magazine recipes." Ruby cocked one of her legs in a sexier pose, kicking off her bowling shoes.

"I don't cook," Barbi answered, licking her finger and turning the page. She turned back to the article in front of her.

Well, Ruby thought, I didn't mean nothing by it. So she tried again, "Is that like one of them *People* magazines? Because Imogene, the black-and-white-headed lady that just left with my sister, she reads that all the time. Knows everything about everybody." Now she felt like she might be going off at the mouth, but that's what happened when her nerves got to her and she'd never sat beside a Hollywood stripper before, and one almost naked at that. She waved at Bunny and Bubbie even though they weren't looking in her direction.

Barbi shook her head, but never once looked up from the magazine.

"What kind of dancing you do?" Ruby asked. "Sometimes I go square-dancing over at the Longhorn Club on Mondays when the bowling alley's closed, but only if they got Mr. Murphy as the caller, otherwise it's no good."

Barbi stared at her again with those big, round, white-rimmed sunglasses, flat as vinyl records.

"Don't reckon you square-dance."

"I have my own routine," Barbi said, "with red feather boas." She raised up and twirled one arm up over head, exposing one big, smooth, round breast as she rolled to the side. Sitting up on one elbow, Barbi suddenly found something she wanted to talk about.

Ruby tried to figure out, without staring, how that breast could be so round and full like a balloon full of Jell-O. She shifted herself to block the view from the kids.

"I'm not going to being doing this for long, though." Barbi's voice scratched. "I'm really an actress."

Ruby's focus came off the breast. An actress. Like Violet. Had Violet done striptease? She tried to picture this girl next to her as Violet. But it was all wrong with the bleached hair and gold lamé. "Actress?" Ruby asked, her tongue thicker and her head feeling a little swimmy.

"I've already done a TV spot. The Waterbed Warehouse. Those are my legs on the waveless bed. Recognize them?" She stretched one long brown leg toward the top of the pool fence. Every time Barbi moved, a whiff of the pineapple upside-down cake passed Ruby's nose.

She checked to see how close the kids were. Both were at the opposite end of the pool trying to see who could make the bigger squirt between their hands on the top edge of the water, making little fart noises. Their squirt noises became louder as Ruby and Barbi's conversation had gone quiet. Ruby scooted up a little higher in her chaise lounge, her shoulder blades flat against the plastic webbing and her legs stretched out. Hers weren't so curvaceous, but had some shape to them, although somewhat stickish. Rascal'd always said her legs were her best feature. She giggled a little in her head as she recalled Earl admiring them too.

As she downed another swallow of margarita, the tequila wrapped itself around her windpipe and forced a deep breath.

With this last gulp she felt a little more gumption and not so jittery about sitting next to Barbi. So she asked, "Maybe you know my daughter?"

Looking at the greasy page in front of her, Barbi responded sharply, "Is she a dancer?"

My Violet, a striptease dancer, Ruby thought. That went the way of all the Devine ladies' suggestions and she shoved it into the way back of her head. "No, she's the ButterMaid," Ruby said, proud and puffed up when she announced it.

Barbi took a new interest. "Oh yeah?" she asked, sounding much friendlier than she had. "What's her name?"

"Violet Davidson." Ruby said it strong and tequila certain.

"Never heard of her." Barbi turned her tone back a notch. Then switching to friendly again, "ButterMaid? A *national* TV spot? Is she using a stage name?"

"Stage name?" Ruby knew what that meant—like Marilyn Monroe's momma named her Norma Jean and John Wayne's momma named him Marion. But Ruby had to depend on the name she'd given Violet that day on the porch. "Don't know," she answered truthfully, but it came out her throat like a pyracantha branch. "Do you know any ButterMaids?" Ruby asked, hoping beyond the smoggy hope of California that Barbi might know Violet.

"So you're not in touch?" Barbi asked.

"Not right now." Ruby looked out toward the kids. They'd climbed out and squatted beside a puddle on the other end of the pool.

"Oh," Barbi said, flattening the *Variety* magazine out in front of her on the chaise. "Thought it might be—well, like you knew *somebody*." Her scratchy voice made the *somebody* sound like a pickup spinning out on gravel. "But never mind." She flipped a hand at Ruby, insinuating she couldn't be bothered.

Ruby saw a little bit of Violet in that move. She thought it was just plain rude. But Ruby also knew how to handle a rattlesnake, and she figured that particular talent came in handy in Los Angeles.

"Look, Grans, maybe your daughter doesn't want to see you. Know what I mean?"

Ruby's heart went rubbery with the not-so-new thought. "Why do you say that?"

Barbi looked around the pool area. "She hasn't let you in on where she is, has she?"

"She don't know we're here yet." She heard it and felt it catch in her own throat.

Barbi looked over those annoying white-rimmed glasses again, making Ruby's tequila heart pump scalding blood through her chest. "We're all running from something out here."

That wasn't what Warren had said. Ruby had tequila swirling all around inside. "Folks also come here because they want something too," Ruby said.

"Yeah, they want to get away!" Barbi snapped another page over.

"That's just being hurtful for hurtful sake," Ruby said back.

Barbi snickered and then toned down her voice. "Don't take it personal, Grans."

Take it personal? Of course she was taking it personally. It was her own daughter. "You don't know the situation," Ruby said, trying to smooth things out.

"I know that if your daughter wanted you to know where she was, she would have told you." The stripper licked a finger and flipped a page.

"And that's just plain wrong!" Ruby didn't want this slicked-down girl telling her she shouldn't be here.

Barbi scratched the back of her knee. "Wrong for you, maybe."

Ruby had herself in mind, sure, but she was also thinking of the kids and maybe even Harley and Imogene. They'd all been hurt by Violet. Right and wrong here were clear cut.

"You saying it's right for Violet? That she can just *not* take any of the rest of us into account, and that's okay?"

"I don't know what's right for her. Doesn't sound like you know either." She reached for her bottle of suntan oil but her fingers couldn't quite get hold of it. "Could you hand me that?"

"I do know what's right for her. I'm her mo—" Ruby winced. "Just trying to set things straight." She handed over the brown bottle, then wiped the greasy residue off her fingers.

"Straight you won't find in Hollywood. That's your first mistake." The practically naked girl looked at Ruby with a smirk. "People come here to find themselves, to leave behind who they used to be, to get discovered."

Ruby had discovered Violet all alone on the front porch, wasn't that enough discovery? "What about how the rest of us feel?" She couldn't seem to get the grease off her fingers and rubbed them harder on her towel.

"You're not hearing me, Grans," Barbi said. "People here are looking out for themselves."

That's just not true, Ruby thought. Why, Penny and Warren were a fine example of folks doing for others just like they did back home.

"GranMomma! He's gonna drown!" Bunny screamed from the other side of the pool. "GranMoooooommmmma!"

The two kids knelt on the concrete edge of the pool. As Ruby ran barefoot across the prickly turf she saw Bubbie pushing his little sister to the side with one arm as he shoved his other fist into the deep end.

Arriving at their side, Ruby could see it was a tiny sparrow he was reaching for. Ruby tried swiping it out of the pool as it drifted away, but she missed. The poor thing just floated with one crippled wing dangling toward the bottom.

"What were you doing with that bird?" Ruby asked, somewhat afraid of the answer.

"He was washing it off," Bunny said, bouncing from foot to foot, making the ruffles on the skirt of her swimsuit flutter. Her face was one of disgust and fear. "Then he changed his mind."

"Washing it off?" Ruby heard the question come from deep inside her in a bubble of anger, not in a calm space from her heart.

"You always tell us that momma birds won't take their babies back if we touch them."

"So you were gonna rinse it off in the pool?" Ruby thought that, while it was a bit deranged, the boy was trying to do a sweet thing.

"Then he said he was gonna pluck it like Miss Ida Mae does with the Sunday chickens," Bunny screamed.

"Oh, Bubbie!" Ruby said. "It's just a little bird."

"He got mad," Bunny said. "Couldn't help it."

"What's got into you?" Holding his wrist tight, Ruby shook his hand and tried to make eye contact. With her other hand she held his chin and made him look at her, but he averted his eyes. "Playing with roadkill ain't bad enough?" She tried again to get him to look at her. "I don't understand," she said to the boy with a wavery voice. "Tell me why you are doing this. I know you're mad. But I don't know what else to do. I'm trying to find your momma." When their grandmomma's eyes got watery both kids looked down at the fake grass surrounding the pool.

Bubbie yanked himself from Ruby's hold, then leaned over the edge of the pool to look. He quickly sat back, his body quivering, his chin tucked under.

"He wanted to save it so its momma would love it again," Bunny whispered. "But he didn't know how."

Bubbie glanced at her for just a moment—she thought he

was about to say something, but he didn't. This was going too far. This wasn't just a boy who likes to be dirty.

"We can't have this," Ruby said with a gentle rub on Bubbie's nubby head. "We can't let you go on doing this kind of thing—poking at half-dead animals. What should we do?" She looked at both kids and really did hope they might give her the answer.

Penny's crepe-soled espadrilles treaded quietly across the black tar parking lot, so they hadn't heard her come up behind them until the thermos clanked on the chain link as she lifted it over to hand it off. "Save me some, Ruby. I'm on my way to Room 218. The massager's out because the last couple jammed a Canadian quarter in it." She put the empty cigarette holder up to her lips.

"Oh Penny," Ruby said, not sure what to say next.

Her tone must have registered with Penny because she became instantly concerned for these motel guests she hardly knew. "Is there a problem? One of the kids fall in the deep end? Anybody got pool ear? I've got drops for that."

"We . . . one of the kids . . . well, something got dropped in the water. Do you have a pool scooper?" Ruby wanted to keep it their own business. Figured it would not be such a fine how-do-you-do for Penny's generosity to drown a bird in her pool. Maybe she could just scoop it out herself and Penny would never have to know.

"Bubbie drowned a bird," Bunny said.

"Got ya." Penny nodded. "I'll get Warren to help us out." She set the thermos down on Ruby's side of the fence. "Help yourself. I'll be right back."

Penny padded off across the parking lot for Warren, and Ruby told the kids that under no circumstances were they allowed back in the pool until that baby bird was fished out. Then she went back over to the chaise lounge next to Barbi to get her glass and leave the replenished margaritas for her.

The greased girl rolled over enough to look up at Ruby. "Those the ButterMaid's kids?"

Ruby nodded as she poured the lime-green liquid and crushed ice into her plastic cup.

Barbi had an annoying smacking noise she made when she talked. Ruby didn't look at her, just screwed the lid back on the thermos, picked up the Sears catalog Loralva had left behind, and started to head back over to Bunny and Bubbie, when Barbi added, "I'll let you know if I hear her name around."

Ruby looked at Barbi over the rim of her glass. She'd filled it to the brim and she took a long swig and gave Barbi a hard glare. "I appreciate that. I do intend to find her. Whether she wants me to or not." The icy drink froze her chest and she walked away.

Penny returned as Ruby wrapped towels around the kids. Warren came along not too far behind with the pool scooper.

"Sorry about dirtying your pool and we haven't even been here but a day." Her embarrassment made her not know where to look.

"Don't worry," Penny said. Her lime-green jumpsuit matched Ruby's margarita.

"You probably don't want folks causing trouble in your place of business, and this isn't exactly the nicest thing." Ruby let her tongue hold the crushed ice so she talked with a wobble. "We're not such bad people under normal circumstances."

Warren stood at the pool corner trying to manipulate the tall pool equipment.

Ruby looked from Warren to Penny. The little lady in double-knit smiled. Bubbie had started to lean over the edge of the pool to see what he could of the bird that floated around the bottom of the pool. Bunny had Mrs. Beasley laid out in the sun and she tried dabbing the wetness out of the doll's blue skirt with her towel. Ruby looked over in Barbi's direction to see if she might be listening in.

"Don't mind Barbi. She's—" Penny held her hand up to her face to block the words from floating in the bronze girl's direction. "Did she give you any hassle?" Ruby shook her head, but only because she wasn't sure what their connection was.

Warren finally ladled out the bird and laid it on the concrete next to the pool, sopping wet, flat feathers and the marble of a head flopping off the edge of the blue plastic rim of the pool scoop.

"I'm real sorry," Ruby whispered, wanting to explain the dead-bird-in-the-pool incident. "At first he was just poking sticks at roadkill. Now he's taken it too far."

Penny took a long drag off her cigarette holder. "My oldest, gotta be fifty-two now, he used to bite people." She took another drag as Warren picked up the drenched bird and tossed it into a Glad bag he'd brought with him. Bubbie tried to touch it, but Warren already had the twist tie around it. "He'd not want to share his toys with a grabby friend and so he'd just sink his teeth in instead," Penny continued. "He had to have been about the same age. What is your little boy, about seven?"

"Almost eight," Ruby said, wondering what would make a boy bite.

"Yep, he bit down like he was a rabid dog himself. I tried spanking, I tried talking to him, I tried bargaining with him. But nothing worked. All his friends' mothers were calling me complaining about the black-and-blue marks on their kids."

"Is he still doing it?" Ruby asked, because she had started to wonder if Bubbie'd keep this up until he ended up in jail, or worse.

Penny pretended to blow smoke out of her mouth. Ruby wanted to help Penny in whatever way she could to stop her cigarette habit, so she watched what would have been white swirls rise about the little lady's head. "Gosh no," Penny said, "but I've never been so embarrassed in all my life."

"What made him do it?"

"Mad at me for leaving his daddy I figured."

"What finally stopped your boy?" Ruby asked, hoping for a cure.

"He grew out of it." She shrugged and sucked hard on the empty cigarette holder.

"I don't know," Ruby said, looking over at the boy, who was now stepping on a line of ants one by one with his big toe. Ruby figured a rage bigger than Texas sat on his chest. He'd have to grow into a giant to outgrow that. She didn't like it one bit, but she couldn't blame him either. All she could do was keep an eye on him.

"I think we should go upstairs and have ourselves a MoonPie," Ruby said to the kids.

Hairdos and Howdy-dos

"What do you think?" Loralva said. She twirled around in front of Ruby on the carpet by the coffee table, blocking the view of *Dinah Shore*. "I'm expecting Duke will really like it when I see him next." Loralva's hair was naturally the same shade of brown as the Texas nutria rat, and she normally kept it pinned up under her red, black and blond wigs, but it now rolled down around her shoulders in big waves and layers of Golden Umber and Copper Shine, with a slight bit of Burnt Sienna sweeping off the sides and feathered back from her forehead.

"How you gonna hook up with him again?" Ruby asked.

"I know where his next gig is here in Los Angeles. He told me to come on by and he'll sing me another song." She raised and lowered her eyebrows, and Ruby knew there'd be more than singing going on.

Ruby had thought it was best she and the kids came inside from the pool. She could keep a better watch on them in the motel room. No animals, dead or alive, within reach. The kids had planted themselves Indian-style in front of the television and Ruby sat behind them on the couch feeling sulky. Barbi's words had gotten in the way of her remembering how things had been going well just an hour or so earlier. Her worries had been interrupted when Imogene and Loralva returned from the hairdresser.

"She's supposed to be Farrah Fawcett," Imogene said, rolling her eyes.

"Only a different color." Loralva ran a long cognac-colored nail through the big curls along the bottom. "Wouldn't be surprised if Farrah Fawcett herself doesn't change to my color."

Ruby figured there might be a good chance of that. But seeing as how Hollywood wasn't Devine, she'd wait and see. "Gotta hand it to you, Loralva, Hollywood suits you mighty fine." Loralva cocked her head with an expression that said she might have an inkling that her sister's mood sat crooked.

"You didn't even notice mine," Imogene said. Her hair still the same skunk black with the white streaks, only much shorter and pushed behind her ears—more of a Florence Henderson or Shirley Jones shag. A brown mole the size and shape of a chocolate chip had been revealed in front of her left ear.

Ruby offered the mother-in-law the appropriate niceties about her hair, but didn't feel up to much more when there were other things to fret over at this moment. And Ruby thought Imogene should be sharing in some of this fretting.

"What're you doing holed up inside instead of out by the pool?" Loralva asked, setting her red leatherette purse down on the coffee table, then coming around to sit next to her sister.

"Bubbie drowned a baby bird," Bunny shouted out for everyone to hear.

Ruby exchanged glances with the little boy as he looked over his shoulder at her. "I figured we needed to spend some time inside thinking about not doing it again." He turned back to the TV. Dinah had Burt Bacharach on and he now played the piano and sang. Ruby hadn't seen a ButterMaid commercial in a while. This bothered her too.

"Nasty children. Just nasty," Imogene said, glaring down at both of them. They both continued to stare at Mr. Bacharach.

"Hush up, Imogene," Ruby snapped. "We gotta figure out what to do about it. It doesn't do no good to stand around saying mean things."

"A bird?" Loralva patted Ruby's knee, then said, "A little helpless bird? Bubbie, you always struck me as a gentle fella. What's got into you?" He shrugged but kept his back to them.

Bunny tried to help. "GranMomma says he's mad."

"Mad?" Imogene shouted. "You ain't a kidding. He's gone mad all right. He'll grow up to be like that Edgar Grimes, the sin-eater over in Cicada who would show up at funeral parlors waiting for handouts in return for taking on the sins of the deceased." They all knew the fella, and he was strange in more ways than one.

Imogene stood by the connecting door to her own room, and Ruby could almost feel her hot breath from where she sat. Bubbie'd hung his head and a sexy note swirled out of Burt on the TV. Bunny's eyes took in all the adults, while she rocked Mrs. Beasley and appeared muzzy.

"I don't see you doing nothing to help," Ruby said it under her breath, because when it came right down to it, she feared Imogene somewhat. The skunk-headed mother-in-law's shouting made Ruby want to back up.

"Oh, nothing so terrible's gonna happen," Loralva said, standing up and coming in between the two ladies. "Edgar Grimes is just hungry is all. And Bubbie's a sweet boy all confused about why his momma left him. So now he's gotta get used to all the other ladies fighting over him. Ain't that right, Bubbieboo?" She bent down and shook his sunken shoulders.

"Not doing anything?" Imogene said to Ruby, ignoring Loralva. "I'm paying for this trip!" she shouted.

"Uh-oh," Loralva said to the two kids. "How about you come with me to visit Miss Penny." Their great-aunt Loralva could always find an escape route, so Bunny took Mrs. Beasley by the hand and then she took Bubbie's and all three, plus the doll, traipsed right on out the door. Ruby had scooted to the edge of the couch.

Imogene didn't stop for one second while the kids, still in their wet suits, trailed out. "You've been raising him these last years. You're the one that got him into this mess. Just took over like you always do!" The nubby sofa upholstery collected under Ruby's scrunching fingers. "I'm beginning to think," Imogene said, "that you kept Violet from her dream of being a movie star and that's why she had to sneak off from me. The boy wants loose of your stranglehold too. But you have to blame me!"

"How could I blame you when you've done nothing? As far as this trip, you only want to pay for a movie star daughter-in-law. But the fact is, you got a heartbroke grandson. I had to take the kids," Ruby continued. "Who else could have? Your shaved-headed son with the personality of gumbo who didn't know a fire truck from a potted plant?" Not long after Violet had left Harley had been found in a daze hosing down a fire engine with the truck's hose until he'd run the tank dry.

Ruby sat back down too hard, and one of the springs poked her behind. She pretended not to notice and faced the TV. A newsbreak was on, but the volume too low.

"I'm just glad," Imogene said, "I will be spending the day away from you tomorrow." Imogene huffed like she wanted to say more, but couldn't think of anything hurtful enough. "You can spend the day with those mixed-up brats and when I find Violet we will decide what to do with *our* new life. She'll tell me the truth." And with that, she slammed the connecting door shut behind her.

The truth, Ruby thought, the truth was Imogene would never change. It didn't stop Ruby from feeling frustrated, but she told herself that if she was going to get through this ordeal, find Violet and return home with all her parts, she'd have to not let Imogene get her so riled.

She fixed her look on the TV. The caption at the bottom of the screen read *Record Rainfall South Texas, Louisiana, Mississippi, Alabama*.

The motel room door opened and Loralva rushed in. "Imogene gone?" Ruby nodded. "Good riddance." She came and plopped back on the couch beside Ruby, putting the Sears catalog in her lap. "I took the kids down to the pool where Penny and Warren said they'd watch them for a sec. Didn't want to leave you too long with the Dark Side of Texas."

"I've done so damn much, Loralva," Ruby said, studying her nails, now full of brown fuzz from gripping the couch. "I'm getting too tired of it. I don't know what to do with Bubbie. I don't know how to go about locating Violet in this city so big it could eat us both as crumbs. I don't know for certain what I'm even doing here, because when I see Violet, knowing that her running away has got Bubbie digging at the hearts of roadkill and plucking and drowning that bird, I don't know as I can give her such a kindly howdy-do."

"Don't you worry none about that," Loralva said. "When you get to her, and you will, you'll figure out what to say."

Ruby smirked at her sister. "It's so easy for you. You don't worry about a thing."

Handing Ruby the Sears catalog, she replied, "It's not so easy, I just don't want to get wrinkles, so I pretend it is."

"Oh come on." Ruby took the catalog. "I've known you your whole life and you don't pretend nothing."

"Not true." Loralva pointed at the catalog, indicating Ruby should open it up. "Take this game show. Don't you know how nervous I am to be on *The Price Is Right*? Don't you see me practicing these prices and asking everyone I meet what they know about the show? Oh! By the way, Penny gave me more details today."

"About being on the show?" Ruby asked, flipping the pages at random.

"About *getting* on. It ain't so easy as just having tickets. And you know, Ruby honey, I gotta have you there by my side."

Ruby laughed, looked down at the small appliances page and held the catalog up so Loralva couldn't see.

"No, really," Loralva said, "you have to be there."

"I got the kids to look after and I was gonna make that phone call to the ButterMaid advertising agency tomorrow." She pictured the folded paper by the bed in the other room.

"Come on. You're like my good luck charm. And Penny'll watch the kids."

Ruby regarded her sister and recalled the rabbit's feet earrings. "I'm not lucky."

"Not just anyone can know all these prices. Look how thick this catalog is!"

Ruby agreed there was a lot to know to be on *The Price Is Right,* but to be on a game show took a lot of smarts and she told her sister as much.

"Ruby! Honey!" Loralva leaned back on the sofa, shaking her head. "Look at you, you run your own bowling alley, you look after two rambunctious grandkids after raising a wild hair of a daughter, and you took that ole coot Rascal to task whenever he decided beer drinking tasted better than professional bowling. I wish I had half your smarts."

"Oh go on." Ruby knew Loralva only wanted to flatter her.

"Rube, please oh please say you'll go with me and Imogene tomorrow."

She just didn't know if it was right to ask Penny and Warren to watch the kids.

"Earl Glidden may be watching the TV," Loralva said, elbowing her. All the time she tried to convince Ruby that Earl was sweet on her, but Ruby took it for nonsense. "Listen, Penny says we have to be down to the television studio by four a.m. to get in line ahead of everyone else. These tickets we have aren't guaranteed seats, it turns out."

"That's not long from now," Ruby said, looking up at Loralva and then quickly thumbing through the catalog. "Sunbeam Mixmaster hand mixer." Ruby wished she could help her sister be the big winner, just like Loralva had boosted Ruby toward finding Violet.

Ruby crisscrossed her legs and faced Loralva. "Hamilton Beach blender, five-speed with glass pitcher."

"Fourteen ninety-five."

Ruby thumbed through to the back of the catalog. "Riding lawn mower—"

She stopped because of the knock at the door. But they didn't have to answer since Bunny and Bubbie came flying in.

"GranMomma, Miss Penny fed us root beer floats and said we could spend all day tomorrow with her at the pool." In the doorway stood Penny and Warren both.

"Come on in," Loralva waved to them.

"Can we GranMomma? Pleeeaaase!" Bunny wailed.

Warren bent down to come through the door following Penny. His big lit-up smile made Ruby smile back.

"Listen, Ruby, Warren and me been talking," Penny said, as Loralva glanced back and forth between all of them, almost as bouncy as the kids. "You had better get those washer and dryer prices in your head, because I am not gonna let you miss out tomorrow." She pointed her empty cigarette holder toward Ruby. "I'm gonna babysit. You hear?"

Ruby liked Penny. She had right away. Texas friendly even if she had lived in California for years.

"Between Warren, me and Barbi, we can keep those kids entertained all day." She sucked long and hard on the tip of that cigarette holder, resting her other hand on her hip.

"We ain't taking no for an answer now," Warren continued.

"That's mighty nice of you to offer, Penny, but I can't be asking you—"

"Maybe you're not so sure because you don't know us too well." She flapped her free hand at Ruby. "But I got the whole thing already figured out." She leaned on the television set, the wrinkles in her face like a jillion smiles. She never took a breath, but sucked on her holder in between words instead. "You gotta get to Burbank well before the sun is up, so Warren can take you. I'll stay here with the kids."

Ruby had been nodding yes the whole time Penny carried on. It did sound tempting to get to go to *The Price Is Right*. Penny had been so hospitable already. Ruby reckoned that was the Texan in her, then thought maybe it was just the way she was. Like giving them the extra-fancy suite without charging any extra.

Penny sucked on her cigarette holder and Warren squeezed her shoulder. "So what do you say? Will you go have fun tomorrow?"

"Ruby, don't make me spend my lifelong dream with Imogene," Loralva said.

Ruby asked the kids, "If I go with Aunt Loralva tomorrow, will you two behave with Miss Penny and Mr. Warren?"

"Better than having Mimaw Imogene stay with us," Bunny said and Bubbie shrugged.

California was delivering to Ruby a whole lot more than she'd expected. For the rest of the afternoon and well past bedtime she called out prices to Loralva. They even called a nearby travel agency and worked on putting together the prices of package deals. Considering Penny and Duke's advice, there was so much Loralva needed to know before the show.

At three a.m. "package of a hundred linoleum tiles?" and "case of Pennzoil motor oil?" could be heard coming from their room.

High-Heeled Fantasy

By three-thirty a.m., Ruby finally set the catalog aside. Loralva'd been in the bathroom for almost half an hour, primping, coiffing and spraying so much out of that aerosol can of Aqua Net it had started to waft across the hallway and into the tiny bedroom. Ruby waved her hand in front of her face. Imogene could be heard humming to herself in the adjacent room, so Ruby knew she was up. This morning she'd chosen Frank Sinatra. Just one line, "I did it my way," hummed over and over, as though that was the only line she knew.

Loralva hollered from the bathroom, "Quiz me on the blenders!" Loralva was never panicky, but today she was on the verge. Ruby had felt a little nervous at first when Penny insisted she go too, but after quizzing Loralva so much over the last couple of days, she'd found she'd memorized lots of the prices in her own head. Even so, she really didn't want to be on the TV to do any more than wave at the folks back home in Devine. Loralva, she was dead set on being the star. Ruby picked up the catalog and hollered back to her, "Ten-speed Osterizer with pulse button."

"Twenty-five dollars and eighty-nine cents." Loralva knew without so much as a stumble.

"Hamilton Beach in curry yellow."

"Seven-speed twenty-one forty-nine, fourteen-speed twenty-four ninety-nine."

Wearing only her underwear and bra, Ruby laid out her clothes on the bed: she had a pool-tile-blue skirt with cherries in clumps of three scattered around the fabric, and the red in the fruit matched the red of her "I ♥ Bob Barker" T-shirt.

Loralva stepped into the bedroom for a second to ask Ruby's opinion on which shoes she ought to wear. "These rhinestone ones with the sexy heel, or these green patent-leather ones with a lower heel, but a little more toe cleavage," she asked, standing in the doorway wearing the short fuchsia kimono a Vietnam soldier had brought her back from overseas. Ruby told her the rhinestone pair made her legs look even longer, so Loralva tossed them on the floor and put the others back in her suitcase, then went back to the bathroom. On top of the yellow chenille bedspread, Ruby smoothed the pieces of clothing out, wondering if the skirt needed ironing. Hard to tell in the dimness of the overhead light. Seemed as though Penny kept only forty-watt bulbs in all the fixtures.

Ruby'd decided this was another perfect opportunity to wear her red, white and blue patent leather bowling shoes, so she set them out next to the bed. Loralva's high-heeled sandals, strappy things with rhinestones the colors of tutti-frutti gum, lay on their sides tossed apart where she'd dumped them. Ruby started to set them neatly by the door, but as she picked them up she thought they were awful glamorous and how she liked the sparkle of the plastic stones. Maybe she'd try them on. No one was around to see. She sat on the edge of the bed, careful not to crumple the skirt she'd laid out so neatly. She slid her left foot into one of the strappy slides, not bothering with the teensy buckle at the side.

She pictured herself in one of those glitter gowns the Miss Americas wear, the ones with a long slit up the side. She imagined herself arm in arm with Warren or maybe Harry Belafonte as her toes stretched across the bottom of the shoe.

"Another one," Loralva said from the bathroom. "Ask me the toaster ovens."

"General Foods, pop-up," Ruby said more to herself than to Loralva, her mind and eyes admiring the shoe as she crossed her legs and turned her pointed foot this way and that way. Maybe Violet would like a more up-to-date momma. Someone with more style, like Imogene would say.

"What?" Loralva hollered, and Ruby could tell from the closer movement of her voice she had leaned out of the bathroom door. "General Foods makes raisin bran, not toasters."

Ruby sat up straighter, putting both feet flat on the floor in case Loralva came in. Mr. Belafonte stepped out for a second. "General Electric, then," she hollered back, watching the door. Mr. B came back and Frank Sinatra snuck in her brain too, since that's what Imogene could be heard humming through the walls. He grabbed hold of her other arm to walk her down the runway as she began to slip the right foot into the second shoe. Her ankles were thinner than she remembered, or at least than they appeared in her flat-heeled bowling shoes. Her calves cut in about halfway down, making a nice muscle curve. Must be all that force she put behind the roll of her bowling ball, she reckoned, building those muscles. She also didn't have those ping-pong balls of flab on the sides of her knees like she'd seen other women get.

"General Electric pop-up goes for fourteen bucks. Give me a harder one." Ruby knew Loralva had returned to the mirror in the bathroom because she could hear the hairspray going again.

"Electric can-opener with knife sharpener included." Ruby stood up. The heels being close to four inches, Ruby felt slender and extra long in the torso. She could see why Violet would want to be a movie star. Then her balance went off and she flailed a bit.

"Nine dollars and seventy-six cents without the sharpener and eleven forty-five with," Loralva said, as Frank Sinatra slipped an arm around Ruby's waist to keep her from falling and helped her sit back down on the bed.

Nobody'd seen her pretending, but she got embarrassed just knowing it herself. She sat on the edge of the bed in only her white panties and the beige bra she'd bought to go under her white things so it didn't show too much through the fabric, yelling blender brands to her sister.

Loralva now stood in the doorway. She had a curling wand and was trying to achieve the Farrah Fawcett look again after a night of studying prices; neither Ruby nor Loralva had slept what with all the anxiety over the game show. "Ruby honey!"—her voice got high pitched and her arms went down, leaving a clump of rolled-up hair falling over to the side—"you ain't even dressed!"

"I know, I know." Ruby'd already tossed both shoes to the side, so it wasn't obvious to anyone what a silly thing she'd been doing. She picked up a pair of panty hose from the bed to show Loralva she wasn't dillydallying.

"Reckon you can quiz me some more in the car," Loralva said, and she raised her arms back to curling her hair, then disappeared back to the bathroom. When she was gone from sight, Ruby scrunched up one leg of the hose to slip her toes into. Today, she would have fun. Tomorrow she'd go back to worrying about Violet.

The connecting door always clunked when it opened, like it wasn't set right on its hinges. Imogene clomped past the pulled-out sleeper sofa where the kids slept, past the bathroom where Loralva turned up the Aqua Net spray, and straight on back to the bedroom. Ruby sat up straighter. She didn't want to be in her underwear in front of Imogene and started pulling the "I ♥ Bob Barker" T-shirt over her head. She had to guide it carefully to not mess up her hair since she'd already sprayed and combed.

"We're gonna be late," Imogene hollered. They had told her when she came back over for supper what the day's plan would be. As Ruby's head popped out of the T-shirt's neck, she saw Imogene smack-dab in front of her, dressed and ready to go. Imogene had on a white pleated skirt with her T-shirt, and across her size-D chest all Ruby could read was

I
♥
ob Bark

with the heart rippling in the middle. Imogene had included a small, red bow on the side of her hair like Sally on *The Dick Van Dyke Show.* It looked a little silly to Ruby but she wasn't about to say anything.

"Warren's downstairs warming up the Gran Torino right now. Better get a move on." Her wrinkles tugged at her face as it pulled into a grin.

"We're moving as fast as we can, Imogene. Maybe you could get the kids up and take them downstairs with their pillows to Penny's apartment?"

"Can't we just leave them here and have her come by later when they wake up? They are so difficult in the mornings. That's why I don't have them spending the night at my place anymore. And I told them so." Imogene pushed the red bow deeper into her pile of striped hair. She had been acting like the argument between them had never happened, but Ruby had noticed the skunk-headed mother-in-law wouldn't look her in the eye.

Ruby stepped into her cherry skirt and fastened it at the waist. She doubled the waistband over once to raise the hem a tad. She didn't even consider getting into it with Imogene right then. For the first time in a long while she felt giddiness in her hips and she wasn't about to let go of it.

A cloud of Aqua Net followed Loralva into the room. "Bathroom's all yours, Ruby honey. Try some of my new lipsticks if you want." And Ruby wondered if maybe her sister had seen her trying on the shoes after all.

Down at the car, Ruby headed toward the passenger door to sit up front with Warren, but Loralva got there seconds before her and as Ruby reached for the door handle, Loralva looked at her. The front had always been Loralva's spot—next to the man. Ruby gave in and opened the back door and climbed in next to Imogene, who'd come in from the other side.

"So, you ladies feeling lucky today?" Warren made a cluck-cluck noise from the side of his mouth.

"You betcha," Loralva said. "I got all the prices in my head and Ruby's gonna keep quizzing me until the very last minute."

Imogene continued her attempted smile while she looked out the side window. Penny waved from the motel office, the kids with their pillows leaning against her. Ruby waved back as they pulled out of the parking lot of the Pink 7 Motel.

Parking Lot Preamble

"Sunset Boulevard," Warren said. "If we kept going straight ahead we'd hit the Pacific Ocean." He'd been pointing out sights all along the way in the dark.

That reminded Ruby of what Jessica Parker had told her during her Oktoberfest palm reading, that she'd be near water. She tried to wrestle up the rest of the reading in her head to see if it foretold of good fortune. Maybe she could link it to finding Violet. But she put those thoughts away because, while she didn't believe that palm reading and tarot cards conjured up the devil like Suddy said, she still didn't want to take any chances of passing along bad luck on this day. When no one said anything in response to Warren, Ruby wanted to fill the silence.

"Kenmore gas dryer and top-loading washer in avocado green," she said off the top of her head.

"I am going to have a Guernsey cow, right here and in this car, if I have to listen to one more appliance and its respective price," Imogene said, licking her thumb and forefinger to wet them, then slicking down the curl beside her ear as she tried to cover the mole that had been revealed with her new haircut.

"Five hundred forty—no," Loralva said. "If it's avocado green then five hundred sixty-six."

"Excuse me," Imogene said, "did you not hear what I just said?" She looked back and forth between Loralva and Ruby. Her show of being pleasant had disintegrated faster than pork rinds into crumbs.

"Same for harvest gold," Loralva continued.

"No," Ruby corrected her, "avocado is the super premium, gold is the second highest."

"Damn!" Loralva said, her fingernails a blur of orange, clattering out the Lone Ranger theme song on her armrest.

"Does it really matter?" Imogene asked, poking at her red bow.

"Only if I want to win the Appliance Round-up." Loralva looked at her like she was dumber than a goat roper who'd lost to the billy one too many times. "We're almost there, Imogene. If I can't get these prices down now, then I won't have a chance on the stage."

"You ain't gonna get up there. It's all rigged. I told you already. They only let actors and actresses up there."

Loralva didn't believe this. She had her own information from Duke and from Penny.

"Frostless Coldspot top-freezer refrigerator in avocado." Ruby fiddled with the hinged chrome ashtray lid, wangling it back and forth, not letting it snap shut.

"Five hundred eighty-nine," Loralva said.

"Side by side," Ruby said quickly.

Loralva whistled. "That's a biggie. Seven hundred eighty-nine. Now try some of them trips we put together."

"Skiing in the Swiss Alps."

Imogene snorted. "That would be a good one for you to

win, Loralva. I could see you skiing down the slopes in those high heels of yours."

"Who says I'd be doing any skiing on my trip?" Loralva said. "I'd say three thousand, Ruby honey."

"I'd say higher," Ruby said, closing the lid of the ashtray, which was stuffed full of red and white Dentyne wrappers. "It's got golf clubs and airfare and a stay at a castle."

Loralva looked over her shoulder at Ruby, as though thinking for a moment. "Nope, can't overbid or I'm out."

Loralva was right, it was better to bid low than high. Ruby looked out her side window at the houses that had grown bigger and fancier. Lawns like magazine pictures. Ruby could see them well in the dark through the headlights on the Torino and because of the smartest little post lights stuck in and around the hedges. Would Violet live around here? Was she sleeping soundly inside one of these houses? Some even had three stories. Not even the Johnsons' house had three stories.

"Oh my stars," Imogene said, "lookee there. The Hollywood Bowl it says." With both hands at the same time she straightened each side of her hair, as though checking every curl on her black and white head of hair.

Ruby looked in the direction Imogene pointed. She was looking for a big neon bowling pin or other indication of a bowling alley nearby. All she saw was a marquee bigger than the side of Earl Glidden's barn, and it said, BARBRA STREISAND JUNE 11–12.

"Gotta admit," Ruby said, "their entertainment's better than that little Johnny Rodriguez and Freddy Fender who pick those guitars in my place."

A few more appliance prices later and they arrived at the CBS studios. A cluster of whitish buildings, not so tall, but long and wide, stood just to the side of the black tar parking lot. Looked to Ruby like they might already be too late to get a good spot in line. Must have been a hundred times longer than the line at the snow-cone booth at the Idyll County Fair every July. Loralva was turning red in the face from not breathing, she was so excited.

"Jesus, Mary and Hank Williams, look at the competition," Loralva said, adjusting her cleavage up.

Warren had hardly pulled the car up to the curb before Loralva began running toward the line's tail end, tutti-frutti high heels click-clacking. Imogene hoisted her purse onto her shoulder and trotted behind. Ruby turned around one last time to wave good-bye to Warren, who waved back with his big hand as he pulled away. He said he'd be back that afternoon to pick them up, and it occurred to Ruby that between now and then the most exciting time of her life might happen.

The sun still not up yet, the parking lot buzzed with all the talk. The three of them got in line and soon found out they were behind a church handbell choir who'd come all the way from Arkansas. Ruby started up a conversation right away with the lady directly in front of her. Linda, she said her name was, had traveled with the First Southern Baptist of Bentonville. Then she asked Ruby, "Where's your church home?"

Ruby wasn't really into religiosity, but was used to it with Suddy. "First Methodist of Devine." The sun had just started putting a pink tinge in the sky, making Linda's white hair look like cotton candy.

"How big your congregation?" She sounded like she was competing and Ruby didn't care to partake, even though Suddy and Chester managed to bring in quite a crowd. Sunday mornings at the Bowl were the biggest cleanup time, so she didn't really attend that often, preferring to pray while she vacuumed. Ruby just answered, "Big enough."

"I'm sure tain't as big as ours," Linda said.

While she went on to explain to Ruby that the handbell choir would be having a prayer meeting in a while, in hopes of getting God on their side for the game show, Ruby watched Loralva standing among a crowd of young boys wearing UCLA T-shirts. Looked like she was teaching them how to do high kicks. "I'm gonna study my own Bible," Ruby said, holding up the Sears catalog.

"The Lord will be watching and will see to it only His children win," were Linda's departing words. Ruby wasn't so sure God watched *The Price Is Right*. She figured Him more for the *Truth or Consequences* type.

The lady turned back to her group as Imogene, who'd been talking to the people behind them in line, turned to Ruby. Pointing over her shoulder, she said, "That fella and his momma handed me a list and wanted to know if I would back them on appliance prices by hollering them out to them."

"What'd you tell them?" Ruby asked.

"I told them they should have practiced like we did." She threw her little nose in the air and her red bow clung to the hair as it tossed. "There is some mighty fine competition here."

"Thought you didn't think we could get on the stage," Ruby said to the mother-in-law.

"I been thinking, that just in case, it wouldn't hurt to be prepared." She said this to Ruby as if it was her suggestion and Ruby might want to take heed. "Loralva ain't the only one who could end up there, you know."

"Where's Loralva now?" Ruby'd lost sight of her. The UCLA boys were over there whooping it up on their own.

Imogene pointed toward two men in dark glasses carrying clipboards. Loralva stood in front of them shifting her weight from one hip to the other, back and forth, as she talked to them in a most convincing fashion. They laughed along with her. Nodded their heads a lot.

"Flirting. Always flirting," Imogene said, in complete disapproval.

Ruby sensed Loralva was up to something. What, she didn't know for certain, but most of the folks in this parking lot were up to something. While they acted friendly enough, she sensed winning was first and foremost in their minds. It was no different with Loralva.

"How much is a frost-free refrigerator?" Imogene asked, sounding a little panicked, not looking at Ruby but in the direction of the fella who was studying his appliance list.

"Depends on the cubic feet."

"Self-cleaning range?"

"Five hundred nine dollars with cooktop." Ruby fanned herself with the catalog. She liked knowing things Imogene didn't know. And now she might even get to be on the TV. She and Violet would have that in common. She wondered if Violet watched *The Price Is Right*. She used to when she lived in Devine.

The sun coming over the roofs of the white warehouse buildings started to burn through the morning cool. A long line stretched out ahead of them. Only eight a.m. and they wouldn't be let in until two o'clock. They'd now been given their numbers for the order they would go into the studio and they had their price-tag-shaped name tags with their first names written in black magic marker. Imogene kept sticking and unsticking hers, causing the corners to start to curl up. While they waited, sitting lined up on long benches, Imogene began brushing up on the prices of sewing machines and living room furniture, having borrowed Ruby's catalog.

"I think it's best if Loralva came back over here and stood in line like the rest of us. We should practice like a team," Imogene said. She set the Sears catalog next to Ruby before walking off. "I'll go get her."

A married couple looking to be about ten years older than Ruby came and sat on the bench next to her after Imogene stepped away. "It sure is a hot one," the man said.

"Sure enough," Ruby said back, pinching the neck of her T-shirt, fluttering the shirt to create a small personal breeze.

"We're gonna get on the Showcase Showdown. One of us is, that's for sure," the lady said. To Ruby it didn't just sound like bragging, but a threat.

"I'm just here to watch my sister." And Ruby pointed toward Loralva, who now had a big crowd surrounding her.

"You're *her* sister?" the man asked. Ruby only nodded, a little worried that Loralva might be getting herself in some sort of trouble. The couple looked at each other. Then the man leaned over his wife, getting right up to Ruby's face. "We are experts at the Big Spin."

"That's right," his wife said smartly.

"Been on the show before?" Ruby asked, wondering where the hell Imogene was and what Loralva was up to.

"No," the lady answered, "but Frank here, he built us a Big Spin wheel replica in our garage to practice on. His cousin has a sister-in-law who's roommates with one of Bob Barker's Beauties." She leaned in closer to Ruby. "You know, that Janice Pennington."

Ruby knew of that Beauty because Janice always made the news, and she knew the Big Spin wheel. Prices from five cents to one dollar in huge block letters were pasted on the rim of the wheel. Contestants who'd won in the first round spun the giant wheel to see if they got to participate in the Showcase Showdown—the real biggie.

"We got all the right dimensions from my cousin and that's exactly how I built it so the weight was the same. Then we trained," Frank said. They sounded a bit like Imogene when she got highfalutin.

"Trained?" Ruby asked, blowing down the front of her T-shirt, feeling rude, but in another way hoping to fend off these folks.

"To spin with skill," he said to Ruby as though she was the greenest *Price Is Right* contestant he'd ever come across. She supposed she was, although she doubted he knew the price difference between Shake 'N Bake's cajun chicken and regular chicken, and you had to have this knowledge to ever get to the Big Spin.

"You gonna use that catalog?" Frank's wife asked, pointing to where Imogene had set it next to Ruby on the bench.

"Yes," Ruby said, picking it up, "I am." And she fanned herself fast and furious.

Rod Roddy and John Wayne

At two o'clock sharp, the doors of the CBS *Price Is Right* studio opened. Now all the folks they'd stood in line with outside started acting like cows at the Fat Stock Show trundling to get through the entrance and down the aisle. All that pent-up frustration from waiting in line had them wound up tight, pushing, shoving and shouting. Ruby experienced elbows in her ribs, shoe heels smashing her toes, and one woman even dug her fingernails in the back of Ruby's arm in an attempt to pull ahead.

"Heading down close!" Imogene shouted. She pushed her shoulders back and headed on through the crowd. Ruby surmised it had been Imogene's fingernails she'd felt in her arm.

Loralva's hand squeezed Ruby's tighter than a bullrider's handshake, and she leaned over and whispered in Ruby's ear, "I'm so close to that Showcase Showdown I can taste it." Then she ambled on down the aisle through all the double-knit-wearing participants to the row where Imogene stood waving them to join her.

When Ruby first walked inside, the air-conditioning slapped her, giving her a shiver after the sun and the heat of the asphalt outside. Their aim, she figured, must be to cool the studio colder than the freezer section at the Piggly Wiggly. She envisioned them all turning into Mrs. Paul's fish sticks before it was over. But she got too engrossed in glancing around the room to think about the cold for long. Cameras hung from the ceiling along with microphones dangling from long black wires, the stage lit with lights as big as up-close stars. But the orange and purple prize doors that appeared so gigantic on the TV stood no bigger than a single garage door. From the outside, the studio looked the size of the rodeo arenas back home. But once inside you could see the place wouldn't have even held a two-lane bowling alley.

Still, there were two hundred other people in that studio audience and only three got called down each day. Ruby had misgivings about Loralva's chances. Course she could say the same thing to herself about trying to find Violet. Maybe that's why they'd come to California—to try their luck. If she was her sister's lucky charm, then maybe Loralva would be hers. Ruby followed the other two to their seats. Thing was, when Loralva wanted something, no matter how big, she got it. Like that time John Wayne came through Devine and Loralva got him and herself conveniently locked in the Devine Bowl storage shed out back. Took the whole town and all of the original Duke's entourage most of the day to find them. In spite of it, Mr. Wayne was in good spirits when they came out, and said he'd appreciated the mighty fine welcome he'd received. Even gave Loralva a nonspeaking part in *Rio Bravo* where she ran up to his horse just before he rode off. That same skill Loralva had, Ruby would need for finding Violet. But she couldn't think about it now.

Ruby pushed on through *The Price Is Right* crowd, waving her hands over her head, feeling the thrill of the other folks seep into her skin. Crossing over the legs of five other folks, Ruby scooched through behind Imogene. Loralva chatted everybody up, coming around behind Ruby. "Howdy, howdy," she'd say, shaking hands, introducing herself. Then folks started quieting down and men in suit jackets were going around asking everyone to take a seat and settle down.

Relieved to finally be sitting, Ruby still had Imogene and Loralva talking at her in both ears. Imogene pointed everything out, twisting around in her seat. "This place is jam-packed. Rod Roddy looks bigger on the TV in my house," she went on. "Think those cameras are directed at me?"

Ruby tried to take it all in. Rod Roddy sat in a big glass box, his sapphire, sequined jacket sparkling like a million jewels inside a case. Rod Roddy—the man who announced the next contestant and answered Bob Barker's questions. Every weekday morning from ten to eleven, it would go something like this:

"What have we got for these folks to bid on today, Rod?"

"How about . . ." Rod Roddy would say, and the onstage doors would slide back as one of Bob Barker's Beauties, usually Janice Pennington, would step to the side. "A BEAUTIFUL Broyhill dining room set!" And the audience would ooh, then ahh, as a table and chairs swiveled and Miss Pennington ran her shapely hands over the surface of an oak veneer table.

Now, Ruby was flabbergasted to see that very same Rod Roddy sitting no more than fifty feet from her, in person and not through a TV screen.

Just beneath the front of the stage sat Contestants' Row—four narrow cubicles, like horse stalls for people. The folks left over from the last week's show took up three of the cubbies. One spot was vacant for whoever got called down today by Rod Roddy.

Loralva whispered to Ruby about how she'd taken care of things while they'd been outside standing in the heat. She'd found out from Penny how sweet-talking the gentlemen in the suits increased the chances of getting called as a contestant. "Those gentlemen are the producers," Loralva said, matter-of-factly. She blew a kiss toward one. He grinned back at her.

Imogene carried on in the seat on Ruby's other side, saying, "You'd think they'd figure out a more orderly fashion to get us in here. I darn near started to perspire." She opened the Sears catalog back up to where she'd been saving her place with her thumb and returned to studying prices. Ruby glanced over Imogene's shoulder. She knew the prices right off. Hair removal cream and applicator, $5.95. Package of five hairnets, $2.65. She practically knew the whole catalog by heart. From the rayon bridal gown on page 30 priced at $50 to the do-it-yourself carpet tiles on page 1255 costing $5.90 for a package of ten.

Then a gentleman dressed in a navy blue suit stepped out from offstage. "That's Bob Barker!" Ruby shouted, not realizing at first it had been her that had said it, and then quickly covering her mouth with her hand, feeling terribly embarrassed. She wondered if folks would be thinking of her the way she thought of Imogene and her loud mouth. But hers wasn't the only voice shouting out Mr. Barker's introduction—everyone else was pointing and waving too.

"He just seems like the nicest man, don't you think so, Ruby?" Imogene asked, pulling on the skin of her arm.

"I don't know how nice he is, but he's just as good looking in person as he is on the TV," Loralva said. She waved to one of the producers. He wiggled his eyebrows up and down, like men did when Loralva had given them some sort of hope.

"I been thinking," Loralva said, turning to Ruby. "If I were to win a year's supply of Saran Wrap, I know exactly what I would do with it."

"Nothing like plastic wrap to keep the flies out of potato salad," Ruby said.

"I'm thinking more along the lines of wrapping it around my naked body. Heard that's what housewives do to get their husbands in the romantic mood. But I bet when we get back to Devine, if I use it on the new widower Ted Lewis, he'll forget that dead wife of his." She elbowed Ruby.

"Hope you don't get that *and* the depilatory cream," Imogene said.

She was interrupted by Rod Roddy coming on the microphone, "Welcome to . . . THE . . . PRICE . . . IS . . . RIGHT!" The audience jumped to their feet and waved their arms in the air again. Ruby flailed her arms around like Suddy on a particularly anxious, God-fearing day. The cameras up above swirled and spun. Across the aisle the handbell choir Ruby had stood in line with outside all twirled the Greek symbol for Jesus fish-on-a-stick above their heads. The man who'd built his own Big Spin wheel did jumping jacks two rows in front of them, practically knocking over his wife. Imogene looked up at the cameras and focused on one that was pointed toward her, foofing her hair, pulling the sideburn over her mole. Bells chimed, cash registers chinged, slot machines buzzed until Bob Barker's voice boomed through the microphone, "Who's our next contestant, Rod?"

Then the entire studio audience sucked in its breath. Loralva's Tequila Sunset fingernails clenched the edge of her armrest. From the handbell choir's direction Ruby heard a tiny, "My Father Who Art in Heaven, please let one of us be called down."

"Bob!" Rod spoke from his glass-enclosed box where he sat in his sapphire sequined blazer, "PAUL WESTLY is the next contestant on *The Price Is Right*! COME . . . ON . . . DOWN!"

Ruby let out her breath while everybody whooped and hollered. This Paul Westly sat a couple of rows in front of them. He and all his family had on blue T-shirts that said "Tuscaloosa loves PIR," with a heart in the middle to indicate the word *loves,* just like the ones Loralva had made for them. He high-fived everyone he passed as he made his way down to Contestants' Row. The audience was once again screaming and hollering. You couldn't help yourself. At the end of the aisle Paul took his place and now Bob Barker stood above him and the previous day's three remaining contestants.

"Tell us what we have for these folks today, Rod."

One set of orange and purple prize doors slid open. "How about a *STEAM CAPSULE AROMA SPA*!"

The whole place went, "Aaaaaah!"

Rod described the spa. "With its water jets, this spa will take you to the land of relaxation . . ."

The Steam Capsule Aroma Spa looked like an ordinary shower stall all spiffied up and rounded off like a spaceship or a giant Contac cold medicine capsule, with clear glass doors that anybody could see all your nakedness through, if they so desired.

While Rod Roddy told about it "making a person like new" with its "pulsating water jets," one of the Bob Barker's Beauties ran her hand up and down the edge of that spa like she was petting a cat. The Beauties wore chartreuse business suits, the blazers low cut with sequined lapels, and miniskirts shorter than short. All of them platinum blondes.

"That right there is Janice Pennington," Imogene whispered to Ruby, pointing toward the tallest one. More interested in the bidding and watching Bob Barker, Ruby paid no mind to Imogene.

"Paul, as the newest contestant, you get to bid first." Bob flashed a smile down on Contestants' Row. His dark suntanned face turned darker against his white teeth.

"Ooo-eee, I'd like to have me one of those spas in my house," Loralva said.

"Looks like a sinning capsule to me," Imogene said.

"What's your bid, Paul?" Bob Barker asked.

The audience started hollering out numbers. "One thousand two hundred!" "Eight hundred!"

All the prices swam in Ruby's head. She worried about Paul—what if he heard the wrong price? Ruby hadn't seen anything like this capsule in the catalogs they studied, so she kept her mouth shut. She didn't want to be responsible. Paul turned around to the studio audience and motioned for them to keep shouting out prices to him.

"Eight hundred!" The woman who must have been his momma hollered.

"Eight hundred dollars," Paul Westly said, turning back to Bob. He looked nervous as a calf in a branding stall.

"Lower, lower!" The rest of Paul's family shouted to him. Too late. Rod put the $800 bid down on the lighted numbers in front of him.

"Way over." Loralva shook her head.

Bob went on to the next contestant. A woman named Sheila, who had the name of some fella on her T-shirt—Stanford—said $500. Her face all lit up and happy.

"She's got it," Loralva told Ruby, very serious, "as long as those other two don't bid over her."

Ruby wanted Sheila to win, such a nice young lady.

A gray-haired woman who couldn't quit smiling bid $150.

"What a fool," Loralva smirked.

The last contestant couldn't make up her mind. "That would be me up there," Ruby said to Loralva. "Ain't never even heard of a Steam Capsule Aroma Spa. Sounds like something they would only have in California."

"Three . . . no . . . two thousand!" the contestant—EULALIA it read on her price-tag sticker—finally said.

Bob shook his head, but kept grinning. Loralva hooted, "Gotta pay attention. You overbid!"

"Don't, Loralva." Ruby elbowed her. "You'll make that lady feel bad."

The inside of the studio got quiet. The folks up on Contestants' Row all looked toward Bob onstage. Eulalia couldn't quit hopping up and down like she had to pee.

"Rod, tell us, what's the actual retail price for that lovely Steam Capsule Aroma Spa?" Bob rotated to face Rod.

"Steam Capsule Sinnin' Spa," Imogene corrected Bob under her breath.

"Oh yeah," Loralva said, "I could do some real fine sinnin' in that."

"The actual retail price is . . ." Rod announced and the studio audience swirled to look at him in his glass box. "Five hundred and fifty dollars, Bob!" He always said everything like it was just the most exciting news he'd ever heard in his life.

"Loralva, oh Lordy!" Ruby jumped up and down and hugged her sister as though she herself won that shower spaceship. "You knew the price!"

APPLAUSE—the sign above them flashed on and off. The audience screamed and danced around. Sheila, who won the bid by coming the closest to the price without going over, hugged all her friends, then ran toward the stairs to the stage, with a smile as big as a slice of cantaloupe.

The applause sign went off and the crowd quieted down. Then a Barker's Beauty rolled out what looked like a carnival booth. Twelve boxes, three rows of four, hung on the wall of the booth. The boxes on the top and bottom rows were covered in red cellophane. The row in the middle had the price $3,758, one number in each box. Along the top edge of the booth, in letters made to look like boxing gloves, it read PUNCH A BUNCH. Duke had told Loralva about this game—you had a better chance at betting against Satan himself. Poor Sheila, Ruby wished she'd gotten a different game.

"Do you know how this game is played, Sheila?" Bob always asked the contestants if they knew how to play the games and they always said they did, then he'd go right ahead and explain how it was played anyhow. "In a minute, Sheila, one of my Beauties is going to bring out the prize from behind that curtain." Bob pointed to the orange and bright pink curtain right beside them. "This price in the middle," he waved in front of the 3,758, "is not the correct price. Inside each of these red boxes is a number. What I want you to do, Sheila, is to punch through these paper blocks, either above or below this price in the middle. The boxes above the price will be one digit higher and the box below will be one number lower. It's up to you to decide which one is correct. You must punch out the actual retail price of . . ." Bob waved toward the curtain. Dian, show us that next prize *now*!"

The audience echoed, "Ooooooh!" One of the Beauties rolled out a sarcophagus.

"Is that a mummy coffin?" Ruby asked.

"Show us what's inside that box . . . Dian darlin'," Bob instructed the Beauty. Dian darlin' reached across the coffin with a seductive turn of the wrist and, careful not to break any of her lengthy nails, she lifted the lid on that Egyptian box. Then she flipped her long blond hair over her shoulder, smiling big at the audience as they all oohed and aahed over the coffin filled with books on Egypt. This was going be the prize Sheila had to punch out the right price for.

"That's boring," Imogene said. "Who'd want a bunch of books?"

"Haven't you watched this show enough times to know that ain't the actual prize?" Loralva said.

"Rod, fill us in . . ." Bob Barker said. Ruby thought for a

second he was faking and that he wasn't having as much fun as he let on.

"Well, Bob, this is an all-expense-paid trip to . . . *Egypt!* Two people will travel to Cairo, stay in the majestic Conrad International Hotel with rooms overlooking the Nile . . ."

"Nothing but ghosts and mummies," Imogene said with a snit.

"Are you ready to play Punch a Bunch?" Bob Barker asked, then stuck the microphone in Sheila's face.

Ruby crossed her fingers for Sheila.

She punched through the red shiny paper and got a four. Bob told her that was right, which caused the studio to dance around on their behinds. Then they cupped their hands around their mouths and began shouting out more advice. Next Sheila punched the box below the seven and got a six. Again, she was right. Ruby grabbed Loralva's arm and squeezed for good luck.

Bob said, "Sheila, if you get one of these two remaining numbers right, you are on your way to Egypt!"

She swung her fist through the red cellophane of the box above the five and that damn honking buzzer went off. This meant she'd guessed wrong. Ruby thought they should just mention it politely, instead of making a person feel foolish with that loud noise. The audience said, "Aaawww!" like they felt awful sorry for her.

Bob shook his head. "Come on, Sheila, pick the right one for this last number and you are as good as sitting on the Nile."

Sheila glared at those two remaining red-cellophaned boxes for darn near an eternity. The studio audience yelled and screamed numbers out, but Sheila didn't seem to hear. Then the old lady on the other side of Loralva belted out, "SEVEN—ON THE BOTTOM!" She bellowed louder than all the rest of the audience put together. Sheila swiveled halfway around like she couldn't quite place where the voice came from, then whacked her fist through the cellophane on the bottom box. A crimson seven flashed through.

The more pleasant-sounding whoop, whoop, whoop noise went off and all those friends of Stanford's went crazy, high-fiving and jumping around. Just being there made Ruby's heart race. It seemed the whole studio audience did cartwheels in their seats. Ruby's arms flailed all over the place as she spun in circles in front of her chair. This most definitely, without a question in her mind, was the most rip-roaring moment of her life. Even more soul-stirring than the weekend Loralva took her to the World Championship Chili Cook-off in Terlingua, Texas, where she won the jalapeño-pepper-eating contest.

"Boy howdy," Loralva said. "Sheila will get to be like that Cleopatra." Ruby pictured Elizabeth Taylor with Mark Antony in that movie, which then brought Violet's image to mind. Maybe when the cameras turned on them, Violet would catch a glimpse of Ruby and Imogene on the TV just as they'd seen Violet on the ButterMaid commercial. She waved at the cameras now with a bigger heart and a hopeful smile.

"We'll be back with more winners after these words." Bob Barker posed in front of a camera. Ruby wondered how he knew which of the big black TV cameras to look at with so many pivoting around. The Beauties slipped behind the curtains to get spiffied up, she reckoned. Stagehands in Levi's came running out and started rearranging things. They rolled a new game booth onto the stage. The plaque at the top of it read SHELL GAME, the two words spelled out in two-foot-tall block letters made out of shells, and there were neon lights strung up and down the edges of the booth. Ruby plopped down in her seat for a minute to catch her breath.

But before she knew it, the roar and rumblings had started up again. Two Beauties came out from behind the curtains and Mr. Barker strode across the stage. "Now, Rod! Fill us in on who our next contestant is!" The entire studio audience hollered.

Imogene grabbed Ruby's arm just above the elbow and squeezed tight. She whispered in all seriousness, "I can feel it in my bones. I'm going to get called down this time."

Loralva ran her fingernails through the feathers of her new Farrah Fawcett 'do. Ruby turned this way and that in her seat so she could see the person they called when they jumped up.

Then Rod Roddy's voice boomed out, "Let's have . . . LORALVA JEFFERSON . . . COME . . . ON . . . DOWN!"

Ruby spun in Loralva's direction but caught only her hips swirling as Loralva'd already leaped to her feet and was squeezing herself through their row. Spotlights spun around the room and the waves of light going over their heads made all the racket in the studio audience seem louder. Loralva tripped over her high-heeled sandals as she spilled out into the main aisle, but didn't fall and kept on running. Ruby wondered how she could swing her hips like that *and* run. Her sister had more talents than most.

Loralva danced around, all out of breath when she got down to the front. Bob laughed in that way he had that meant nothing. "Are you all right, Loralva? Am I saying that right? Low-ral-va?" His white teeth shimmering off that suntan.

"You got the name right, Bob honey." She threw her arms in the air and circled her hips with a "wooo!" The audience joined in. Her hip-huggers wiggled around way below her belly button as she turned to face them. While the whole audience roared at Loralva, Imogene sat rigid in her seat with her arms crossed and her mouth scrunched up like a pecan out of its shell.

Bob laughed, leaning over the front of the stage to talk to Loralva. Men always wanted to get closer to her. "You didn't think we'd call you down?"

"I'd hoped so, but you never know. My friend Imogene is just going to kill me." Loralva still jumped up and down a little from the thrill as she stole a glance back toward Ruby and Imogene. The audience had been instructed to sit down, so both ladies along with the rest of the audience sat in their seats, but Ruby waved big with both hands at her sister. She never believed Loralva would actually get called down.

"Where is your friend? Point her out to us." Bob scanned the audience.

The cameras zeroed in right where Imogene and Ruby sat. Ruby kept up the big waving and shouted to all the folks back in Devine, "Howdy, howdy!" She blew kisses, adding a few extra for Bunny and Bubbie. Imogene, she sat there with her eyes like a welder's torch, but when she realized the cameras were pointed directly at her, she put on a ladies' luncheon smile and foofed her black and white hair pulling the side piece over her mole.

The four people in Contestants' Row ogled up at Bob. As the new contestant down front, Loralva would give the first bid.

"Rod, tell us what we have for these folks now . . ." From a door in the floor of the stage rose a huge wooden egg-timer.

"AN ILLUMINATED GLOBE!" Mr. Roddy bellowed. "By Rand McNally, this world globe in its wooden stand lights up!" While Rod Roddy rambled on in his monotone describing voice, a Barker's Beauty leaned over to flick a switch on the side. Sure enough the whole world lit up. "Perfect for any den or library." Ruby'd never seen a globe light before—it sure would look sharp next to her new velour Barcalounger. She'd look like one of them intellectuals. But would Loralva know the price? Why couldn't they have given her something closer to normal like a Kenmore washer and dryer in harvest gold or that rototiller they'd just studied in the back of the Sears catalog in the yard tools section?

With a long-nailed finger the Beauty kept the globe spinning.

Ruby could have sworn Bob Barker winked at Loralva as he

asked, "What's your bid?" She started the bidding at $500 and Ruby thought for sure she had lost. Had to be worth a couple thousand, certainly.

Imogene commented, through her teeth, "Loralva obviously does not know about tasteful furnishings." Her eyes glared and her mouth was bunched up, but she kept one eye on the cameras, making certain to smile when they angled toward her.

A male contestant, who obviously didn't know diddly about shopping, bid $200. The rest came in below $500, except the last one at $1,000. That's what Ruby'd have bid.

"And the correct price . . . without going over is . . ." Bob pulled out a small card from an envelope. "Seven hundred and twenty dollars!" The place swelled with all the screaming. Ruby did a little jig in front of her seat. "Loralva, get yourself up here onstage." You could barely hear Bob over all the racket coming from the audience, but he appeared more than delighted to have her up there next to him. Ruby's heart burst with pride for Loralva and her bidding. Imogene stood up in front of her seat, but instead of watching she was pushing back her cuticles. Loralva took the three steps up to the stage and planted herself right next to that good-looking Bob Barker. She latched her arms around him, giving a big squeeze, then faced right at the camera saying, "Hey, Devine, Texas!" She was such a natural for the TV. Ruby thought that must be where Violet got it from.

The audience became rambunctious again as one of the Beauties wheeled out the Shell Game booth. "Do you know how to play the Shell Game, Loralva?" Bob asked.

"You betcha, Bob honey."

But Bob explained anyway, while Loralva stared right at the camera and blew a kiss home, then waved at the audience. Ruby waved back, big and wild.

At the signal, the audience sat down and Imogene leaned

over to Ruby's ear. "She'll lose this one for darn sure." If it wasn't for the TV cameras, Ruby would have slapped her. She should have last night. That made her think of the kids, but she steered her attention back to the game.

"Under each of these shells is the price of the item above it," Bob continued. A family-size box of Tide detergent sat on a stand with the price of $2.95 on a little white placard in front of it and a big conch shell leaning against it. Next to the Tide sat a jar of Peter Pan peanut butter and a price of $1.25. On the other side of the peanut butter sat a sack of Armstrong lawn mulch priced at $5.80. "I will be covering up the prices with the shells that are leaning next to them and then mixing them up." The Beauty exaggerated the movement of putting a shell on top of each price tag. "Then, Loralva"—Bob stopped to show his white smile for a moment—"you have to point to which shell belongs with which product. You with me so far?"

"I am *with* you, Bob honey." Loralva winked at the camera, then switched her weight on her hips a few times.

"*With* you," Imogene mimicked with a baby voice. Ruby put her finger to her lips to tell her to hush and scooted up to the edge of her seat.

"If you get the first one right, then you still have one more chance, but if you get the second one wrong you've lost the game." Bob patted Loralva on the lower back, maybe even a little too low, and led her to directly in front of the booth. Ruby wrung her hands.

Bob Barker shuffled the big conch shells around on the table. Loralva hesitated before choosing which one. "The one on the left!" the old lady on the other side of Loralva's seat hollered so loudly that Ruby nearly jumped higher than a jackrabbit. As the whole of the audience called out instructions, Ruby joined in with the old lady and shouted, "Left!"

Loralva got that one right. Now she had to get the next one.

The man behind Ruby belted out, "Take it baby!" The din had Ruby's ears ringing. Imogene cocked her head back, determining which camera focused on her. At the same time, Loralva searched the audience, motioning for Ruby to tell her what to do. Not that she really wanted Ruby's advice, but she just loved hamming it up, since it meant she'd have the cameras on her longer. Ruby asked the elderly lady next to her to help with the shouting because she had a set of lungs on her like a cow calving a breach. "In the middle!" they both screamed with their hands cupped around their mouths.

Bob Barker lifted the shell Loralva picked, the one in the middle, and sure enough, she won! The crowd clamored. The sides of that studio could have just burst right off. Now all Loralva had to do was win the Big Spin for a chance at the Showcase Showdown. Imogene went back to picking at her cuticles.

Bigger than the tire of a Caterpillar bulldozer, the Big Spin wheel had amounts in cents all along the outer edge. Each contestant got two chances at spinning, and they had to get as close to $1.00 as they could without going over. The two contestants who spun the best got to play the Showcase Showdown. There was just one exception to when a person's spins could surpass that $1.00 amount, and that was if you landed directly on the $1.00 itself, because then you'd get to spin a second time for more cash. And Loralva always had to be the exception.

Duke had told Loralva to spin easy. The wheel looked heavy because it was so big, but it wasn't really. She spun that wheel and it landed on the glittery $1.00. That meant she won an extra $1,000 right away. They let her spin a second time and she got that big wheel to land on that sparkly $1.00 again. Lights flashed and cash register noises echoed in the studio. She'd won $10,000! Ruby stuck her tongue out in the direction of the fella who bragged about having a Big Spin wheel in his garage. She felt a little embarrassed after doing it, but went quickly back to her whooping and applauding. The audience hooted and hollered and Loralva threw up high kicks in her hip-huggers. Bob Barker watched, gazing more at her behind than at the kicks themselves. Loralva put her arm around his shoulder and gave him a big smooch on the lips.

"You're pretty excited about this, Loralva," Bob Barker said with a cunning smile, then put the microphone up to her mouth.

"You ain't a-kidding. The bingo games we have back home ain't nothing compared to this." Loralva leaned over closer to the microphone, getting orange lipstick on it.

Now only Loralva and Sheila stood onstage with Bob. The Beauties who'd been demonstrating the prizes earlier disappeared behind the curtains. Ruby knew they'd make a grand appearance with each showcase. They looked so much alike, tall, skinny, in their chartreuse suits with sequined lapels and bleached blond hair, that Ruby had a hard time telling them apart, like the Doublemint Twins. Only it would be the Doublemint Triplets. She wondered if they might know Violet and wished she'd told Loralva to ask if she got up there. But she'd never considered they'd get this far.

Then it was time for the Showcase Showdown where the big-ticket prizes were all priced in one cluster. As a bigger winner than Sheila, Loralva got to decide whether to pass on the first showcase or bid on it. Rod Roddy told them what this first showcase included: "A greenhouse garden of Swedish quality. A grandfather clock. And a Prowler travel trailer!"

"Oooh," then "aaah," the audience gushed over each item, then they switched to screaming, "Pass, pass!"

"Pass?" Loralva mouthed out to Ruby.

"Yes!" Ruby nearly tore her lungs out. Ruby remembered Penny saying if they made it this far to always pass the first one so you could get a good look at both showcases, then not bid too high on the second.

"Well, Lo-ral-va," Bob Barker said, putting the microphone up to his mouth, "What's it gonna be?" Then switching the microphone to her.

Loralva remembered what she was told. "I'll pass, Bob honey."

Now the audience shouted bids out to Sheila. The old lady next to Ruby stuck a finger in her ribs, told her to holler out wrong bids so that Sheila'd lose. Ruby just couldn't do that, but she pretended to yell so as not to make the old lady feel bad. With the earsplitting ruckus going on she could just mumble nothings and no one could tell. The old lady yelled, "Three thousand!" which Ruby knew was way below the price. The Prowler travel trailer alone cost more than that. Sheila bid $8,500.

Then Rod showed them what the next showcase was. A bedroom suite by Broyhill sat behind a set of sliding fuchsia felt doors. A blond Beauty sat on the bed as it spun in a circle. This lazy Susan of a stage sat to the far right of Loralva, with everything situated for the audience and cameras to get the best view. Ruby never took her eyes off Loralva. If she'd been Suddy she'd have been praying, but she knew it was all Loralva's doing, not God's.

Then Rod turned their attention to . . . "A HIS-AND-HERS GOLF PACKAGE, WITH MATCHING HEAD COVERS." Which was rolled out by Dian, unzipping the zippers on the bag, and wearing a plaid tam that didn't quite go with her sequined suit.

The lady next to Ruby said, "I just bought a set of those matching golf clubs for me and my husband and then he had to go and drop dead."

"You know the price then?" Ruby wanted to hug her. They hadn't studied any golf equipment prices.

"Sure. Five hundred dollars."

Ruby started shouting out to Loralva. She would know the prices on the other items, but maybe not the golf clubs. "Five hundred!" Five fingers, then two circles with the fingers for zeros.

"For the golf set!" Loralva gave Ruby a puzzled look. She tried again.

"Wait! There's more!" Rod Roddy said. The curtain swayed open. "HOW ABOUT A NEW CAR!" A brand-spanking-new, Smokey and the Bandit Black Trans Am with the gold eagle painted on the hood twirled on the turntable stage to Loralva's right. "This 1977 Special Edition Trans Am comes with tinted glass T-tops." The front California license plate read PRIC RITE. In the driver's seat sat Janice Pennington waving out the window like a homecoming queen. The quaking of the crowd was more jarring than the weekend rodeo in Cicada over at Genie Rudman's corral.

Ruby held her hands up for Loralva to see. She tried again, this time with the price of the whole package. "FOURTEEN." One finger, four fingers. "THOUSAND!" she mouthed the word and made a circle with her thumb and fingers and stuck it out in the air three times—three zeros. The elderly lady shouted too, waving her hands in the air. Loralva held her hand up to her ear. Was she playacting or had she not heard? Ruby thought it sure looked like this time Loralva was having a hard time making a decision. Ruby kept fingering the price out to her.

"Ready to take a guess?" Bob Barker asked.

When Imogene pinched the loose skin on the back of Ruby's arm, Ruby swatted her away. She couldn't take her attention off Loralva, not now.

"Time's up," Bob said in his sunshine voice.

The bellowing audience just as quickly went quiet, and Loralva placed her bid. "Fourteen thousand two hundred, Bob honey." And she raised her arms over her head and jiggled her bosom for all the TV-watching world to see.

Bob Barker said, "Rod, tell us the actual retail price of the showcases we had for these folks today."

"Well, Bob . . ." The audience held its breath, as he announced that Sheila's bid was under by only two hundred dollars. That meant Loralva's bid had to be even closer without going over. Those golf clubs could make or break her. Ruby clenched her fists so tight her pinkie nails dug into her palms, but she didn't notice the pain because the game was just too close now.

Bob Barker hurried to Loralva's side. "And how well did *Miss* Loralva do, Rod?

"Well, Bob," Rod smiled and spoke slowly, but with no expression so Ruby couldn't tell whether or not to breathe. "The total price for showcase number two is . . . FOURTEEN THOUSAND ONE HUNDRED DOLLARS!" Loralva's bid was off by only $100, making her the Showcase Showdown winner. She raised one arm up in the air and put the other on her hip, then pranced around the stage moving in figure eights. It looked like she'd rehearsed it.

The studio audience went berserk. Lights flashing and pivoting around, the *Price Is Right* theme song playing. Ruby stammered for a second, then saw Janice Pennington motioning to her that the winner's friends and family got to join her onstage, and Ruby headed that way. Pushing and shoving through the crowd, slapping hands in the air. Ruby felt how she reckoned a movie star must feel—a thrill all her very own. As the cameras swung in her direction, she started to perspire a little under her bra and worried about wet spots showing when she got onstage. She found herself dancing through the aisle of people as she made her way along. The man they'd met outside with the Big Spin wheel replica built in his garage whistled at her as she passed. The Bible study group yelled, "Praise be your soul!" Ruby saw that Loralva still danced onstage. Now it was a fast-paced two-step linked arm in arm with Mr. Barker. They headed toward the left-hand stage where the shiny black and gold Trans Am sat spinning on another lazy Susan stage. Ruby'd lost sight of Imogene in the crowd.

"Loralva, the Grand Prize Winner!" kept going through Ruby's head. With all the folks pushing to the aisle to shake her hand she had a hard time getting through. Loralva waved big, gesturing for her to come on up. The stage couldn't have been more than eight feet away. The theme song with cash registers chinging and buzzers going off swirled in the studio air along with the blinking lights. One of the Beauties reached out toward her from the stage like someone would do to a man overboard off the side of a boat. Soon she headed up the steps to the stage.

At the top of the steps, Ruby looked around her and out toward the audience. So this was what it would be like to be Violet and be onstage. All these folks staring up at you. Ruby waved out to them. Janice Pennington came up and linked arms with Ruby and waved out too, making Ruby feel like she belonged to the gang. Just like a real movie actress. She tilted her head a little like she'd seen done. Altered her stance slightly so that one foot turned out and one hip protruded.

Ruby spotted Imogene over by the stage steps, about halfway between her and the Broyhill bedroom suite, primping and pulling that piece of hair in front of her ear, and instructing another of Barker's Beauties, Dian, on what her best camera angle was. Dian pointed toward Loralva and tried to head Imogene over there. Loralva swung by hollering, "Ruby honey!" Then swirled off in another big galloping circle toward the Trans Am.

Ruby turned. The one Beauty who had sat propped up on the bed in yellow baby-doll pajamas and high heels, one long and tan leg stretched out straight, one bent in a sexy pose, now twirled her legs off the side of the bed. Something was too familiar. Her eyes locked with Ruby's eyes. Somehow she conjured up Violet modeling on the edge of the Sealy Posturepedic.

"Wait!" Ruby screamed, hardly hearing herself over the din from the audience, and she took off like a roadrunner after a scorpion toward the bed and matching nightstands. Her arms extended out, opening her chest cavity, heart exposed for Violet to take. Before she could get to her, the curtain fell closed. She tried going around behind the back wall of the bedroom display, but Janice Pennington had a burly man's grip on her arm.

"That's my daughter!" she started to scream. She wiggled and pulled to get her arms free, but the pain in her twisted shoulders made her quit. "That's my daughter," she mumbled, recognizing it had been a wish, only a wish. A man in a fancy suit who'd come out of nowhere, looking like secret service, steered her body back toward the stage.

"This has been a Mark Goodson, Bill Todman production," Rod Roddy announced. It sounded so long ago.

Out on the center stage, Loralva lay on her stomach on the hood of the Smokey and the Bandit Trans Am, propped up on her elbows, kicking her high heels back and forth in the air.

Galloping Gala

The studio audience was ushered out the doors they had come in, while Ruby, Loralva and Imogene were escorted backstage. Ruby felt a little silly after realizing that the Barker's Beauty on the Broyhill bed was not her Violet after all, but any silliness was overridden by the strong drive she now had to get back to the motel and start making phone calls. She felt a sense of urgency that she didn't have before. All the uncertainty of whether Violet would want to see them and why Violet would have left in the first place didn't matter as much. Now Ruby knew that she had to get to Violet. That Ruby herself had to see and touch and talk to Violet one more time.

Backstage was not as dark as Ruby had thought. They walked in pairs down a hallway fiercely lit with fluorescents. A security guard had his arm looped through Ruby's, but not in as friendly a manner as Janice Pennington had onstage. Loralva pranced along in front with both her arms linked with the producer's who escorted her. Bob Barker and the Beauties had long since disappeared into a door right offstage. The walls along the hallway were crammed with photos of Bob Barker with Grand Prize winners. Ruby reckoned Loralva's photo would be up there soon.

"Did you see me handle that wheel during the Big Spin?" Loralva said.

"Like you had your own practice wheel at home," Ruby said.

"Could you tell I was calculating up the Egypt trip and the golf clubs in my head?" She twirled a lock of the producer's hair that dangled over his earlobe. He nodded, and even from behind, Ruby could see his big grin. He has designs on Loralva, Ruby thought. Most men do.

"Couldn't have made it all the way to *Grand Prize Winner!*"—she said the last three words like Bob Barker—"without you helping me study, Ruby honey!"

"Darn near got us disqualified is what she did," Imogene said from behind. A security guard escorted her as well, although he just walked along beside her, him with his arms at his sides, and Imogene with her arms crossed.

"Ruby had to go and nearly spoil it for all the rest of us. I was having a grand ole time of it and now I'm truly in a bad mood," Imogene said, tugging the piece of hair in front of her mole.

Ruby reckoned that was not true at all, and she said so. "Your bad mood, Imogene, is the same bad mood that started when Loralva got called down to Contestants' Row."

The hallway seemed to have no end, still white and bright.

"My bad mood did not drive me to attack that nice young Beauty sitting on the bed," Imogene said back.

"I told you. I thought it was Violet," Ruby replied. She wanted to get outside the CBS studios and start the Violet search. "I should have stayed back at the motel and kept on looking. I had no business being here when Violet's out there somewhere so close."

"You had to be here so I could win," Loralva said. "We'll start looking for Violet right now. We won't lose another second."

She turned to the producer next to her. "You know a ButterMaid named Violet Kincaid or Violet Davidson?"

"She's my daughter-in-law!" Imogene said over all their heads.

"If you run across her," Ruby said, leaning forward to try to talk to the producer that had latched on to Loralva, "we're staying here in Los Angeles, Hollywood even, until we locate her."

The producer fella looked at Loralva, then Ruby. "You're looking for an actress in Los Angeles?"

"She's one of them ButterMaids," Imogene said. Ruby knew they never should have let the skunk-headed mother-in-law come on this trip. She'd only be getting more and more in the way. "She's probably hanging out with movie stars and not game show folks."

The producer and the security guards all laughed together. "We'll let you know if we hear anything," the producer said. Ruby could tell from his tone that Imogene had insulted him and maybe lost them a chance. "We'll get all your information from Miss Loralva here"—he winked at her—"as we have plenty of paperwork for her to fill out." He stopped in front of a white door marked ADMINISTRATION—PERSONNEL AND ESCORTED CONTESTANTS ONLY.

They formed a semicircle around the doorway and he turned to all of them and said, "Loralva will be coming with me inside these offices to sign all the paperwork so the prizes can be delivered to Loralva's place in Texas." He turned to the security guards now. "Mrs. Kincaid and Mrs. Davidson will wait outside." With that he opened the door and waved Loralva in. As the door closed before they could say anything more, Loralva waggled her arms overhead in a last burst of excitement and screamed, "I'm the Grand Prize Winner!"

Ruby managed to get out "Woo-hoo!" before the door closed.

"Why are we not allowed?" Imogene asked her security guard. "We are her family." She reached to try the knob.

"Security risk," he answered.

"Security risk?!" Imogene's bad mood now went from bad to ugly. The guard took her by the elbow and they all began a swifter walk down to the end of the hall where there was a steel door with the words ALARM WILL SOUND painted in red across the handle.

Ruby wanted to stay with Loralva, and most definitely not be stuck with Imogene, but she also didn't want to cause any more trouble than she already had. At the end of the hall she watched as her security guard punched in a code and the steel door opened inward, letting in a blast of Southern California sunshine that competed with the fluorescent bulbs.

She wouldn't go so far as to say they were *heaved* out the back door—after all Ruby was feeling guilty and actually wanting to be outside instead of inside—but the guards did manage to get both of them out onto the asphalt parking lot despite Imogene grabbing the door's threshold and even telling one of the guards, "When you find out that I am a famous mother-in-law, you will regret ever handling me this way!"

They now found themselves facing the closed door to the studio, which was sealed tight with no handle on the outside. Imogene started to knock, but Ruby grabbed her wrist. "It won't do no good," she said to the red-in-the-face, not-so-famous mother-in-law.

"No good!" Imogene shouted at her, shaking Ruby's hand off her arm. "It's you who has done no good. It's your fault we don't get to be with Loralva in the offices with Bob Barker and Rod Roddy. We could be encountering folks who would know Violet. We could be making the acquaintance of other movie stars!"

Ruby stared at the skunk-headed lady with the chocolate chip mole revealed, and she felt all the moments that Imogene had said something bad about Violet in the past clash with all the moments that Imogene wouldn't be a grandma to the kids. With that gnawing at her along with the Violet search clambering in her head, there just wasn't enough room inside of her to contain it all any longer. So she hauled off and walloped the mother-in-law a short and fast one in the jaw. As Imogene started to fall back Ruby grabbed the sleeve of her I ♥ Bob Barker T-shirt, not to steady Imogene, but to bring her back into reach for another punch. She still wasn't thinking quite straight, at least that's what she said later to Warren and Loralva. But Imogene's shirt ripped at the shoulder revealing a dingy yellowed bra strap, and at the same time she dropped from Ruby's grasp. As Imogene toppled backward toward the asphalt, Ruby said, "*TV* star!"

Back in the motel room Ruby sat between Bunny and Bubbie with her arms wrapped around each, squeezing them in close to her, not caring that their wet bathing suits saturated the sofa cushions or her cherry skirt. All she knew was that she didn't ever want to lose these kids like she had Violet. That one instant of thinking Violet was within her reach had made her want to get out there and pound that filthy, hot Los Angeles pavement. She no longer felt afraid to step out and talk to all the longhairs and hippie freaks that had crossed her path when she walked across the street to the 7-Eleven to buy a fresh package of baloney to fry.

Bubbie tried to wiggle free.

"Why are we being punished, GranMomma," Bunny said. Those words made her let go, but reluctantly.

"Go play, but know that GranMomma is right here."

Bubbie gave her a moment and a look as if waiting for this person on the couch in the I ♥ Bob Barker T-shirt to turn back into his GranMomma. She shooed them out the door. Peeking out the curtain, she waited until they pushed open the pool gate, waving to Penny and Loralva on the chaise lounges, before she scurried back to the bedroom to get the piece of paper with the ButterMaid ad agency's phone number. She picked up the phone by the bed and dialed the numbers. But her rush soon dwindled.

Same old story, she thought as she hung up. They don't hire the actresses, the modeling agency they use does. She could try that agency, but the ad folks doubted the modeling agency would give out personal data. "Standard policy." In her head she heard her own voice reminding folks not to walk on the maple lanes in their cowboy boots. "Standard policy," she had to say to Buster Sheety every Friday night. "Every bowling alley will tell you the same thing."

When she called the modeling agency, she got as far as "We're sorry, but—" and she hung up. She laid back on the bed and stared at the popcorn ceiling, watching the little sparkles here and there. How could she think she could find Violet in this big city? Had she figured she'd just drive into town and somebody would have heard of her and known where Ruby could find her? This wasn't Devine, that was for darn sure. No, it worked the opposite here. First, you had to already know somebody in this town. How could you know a somebody when there were so many bodies all crammed in? She did know Penny and Warren and Barbi, but unless Violet had been stripping and hanging out in these less-than-desirable motels too, she didn't think these folks could help her. Loralva said she'd asked every producer and secretary and security guard that she met backstage at *The Price Is Right* if they'd ever run across a Violet Davidson or Violet Kincaid. "With purple eyes?" Ruby asked Loralva if she'd remembered to add. Her sister shook her head to indicate that she'd asked, but everyone had said no. Loralva had told her they'd find Violet even if she had to drive up and down every street in Los Angeles until they came across her. Ruby knew she'd have to figure out another way. But she didn't have a chance to think about it further when the whole gang came barreling in the motel room door at that moment, hollering out to her, "Ruby honey!" "GranMomma!" "Roooooby."

Didn't take them long to find her in the back room. "You tuckered out after the game show?" Imogene asked, still wearing her torn I ♥ Bob Barker shirt. Ruby felt a little twinge of guilt about what she'd done to her in the parking lot after the show, but not much of one.

"No time for rest, Ruby honey," Loralva said. "We're having a real live Hollywood party! Get up and put on some lipstick. Everyone's gonna be here and you'll still be in your game show wardrobe."

"I'm gonna go change into something swanky," Imogene said, heading off toward the connecting doors.

"Party?" Ruby asked.

"Yes." Loralva tore through her suitcase peeling away the layers of clothes. "I just called Duke from the motel office. I told you he'd given me the location of his next gig here in town, and so I contacted them and got his phone number because I wanted to share my *Price Is Right* news. In more ways than one, if you get my drift." She waggled her eyebrows and Ruby got her drift just fine. "Well, I also wanted to tell him thanks for his help in winning the Showcase Showdown. Wanted to see if I could show him my appreciation, you know." She held up an orange halter-top jumpsuit. "Does this go with these shoes?" Ruby nodded. "So I invited him and the rest of the band over for a pool party. And, they're on their way!"

How could Loralva make one lousy phone call and have Duke heading over for a party and Ruby'd been put on hold so many times she had all the Muzak recordings memorized? It didn't seem fair. Now there was this big stumper in front of her as well—she didn't have any idea what to do next. She certainly didn't feel up to a party.

"You know I'm excited for you, Loralva, but I can't—"

"You can't nothing," she replied. "You kids help your Gran-Momma pick out a party dress." And the two young ones went over to her suitcase at the end of the bed and picked out the beige blouse with shell buttons. "Something with some color," Loralva told them. "This is a party."

Ruby sat herself up. Loralva could bring out the last bit of energy anyone had left. She would participate, but only because this was the hugest day in her sister's life and she didn't want to spoil it for her.

She put on the Stars-and-Stripes outfit that Bunny and Bubbie picked out, smoothed her hair and applied some of Loralva's Cognac lipstick.

"Maybe they'll bring Willie Nelson with them," Loralva said as she headed back out the door.

Despite the fact she'd been up the entire night, then had both a thrilling and harrowing day, Ruby put on a perky face and went down to the pool.

"I love what you did with your lips, Ruby," Imogene said. "I must say it sure put some nice color in your face." She'd been cordial toward Ruby since the incident in the CBS studios parking lot. Ruby reckoned it was only because Imogene knew that to get to Violet she had to cooperate with Ruby. The mother-in-law was probably afraid that after whopping her good in the parking lot, Ruby might not let her participate in the search.

"You look mighty pretty yourself," Ruby told Imogene, but her compliment didn't have much oomph behind it.

Loralva adjusted the halter top on her sherbet-colored jumpsuit as they stood in silence waiting for the band. Ruby yawned, knowing she wouldn't be sleeping much that night. Nor any night until she found Violet.

Penny had made more margaritas. Barbi had lifted the back of her chaise lounge a few notches to more of a sitting position. It dawned on Ruby that she'd never seen the girl actually walk. At least when she sat up she'd tied her bathing suit straps. Bunny and Bubbie had long since passed the wrinkled stage of being in the water too long, but they swam until way past dark.

Duke and the band showed up not long after the sun went down. Loralva introduced Duke, Elmo, Paul and George to everyone. Each one wore a white cowboy hat and a plaid western shirt with pearl snap buttons. Duke clearly had the most years on them. Elmo couldn't have been more than twenty and Paul and George had only a couple of gray hairs each. They all gathered at one end of the pool, where the street lamp cast some light now that the sun had disappeared completely.

"Duke says you guys are here looking for someone," Elmo said when a short pause came in the conversation as margaritas were being poured.

"My daughter-in-law is a movie—" Imogene said, and then after a pause, "she's on a TV commercial." She pulled the short side hairs toward her black mole.

"He told us she's that new ButterMaid," Paul said. "Ooo-eee, hotcha mama."

"Do you know her?" Ruby asked, holding her breath.

"Nope, but she's damn good looking," Paul said, tipping his hat to Ruby.

"I must have mentioned it to the fellas, after Loralva telling me in Phoenix," Duke said. Ruby let out a sigh.

"Any luck so far?" Elmo asked. "I do a little acting, maybe I could ask around."

"Really?" Ruby thought this might be the chance. She knew she was going about it all wrong so far. But if Elmo could ask around, maybe he'd run into someone who knew her Violet. "I've called the ButterMaid folks and their advertising agency and nobody, not a soul, will give up her phone number. She's not listed in the regular phone book."

"Probably thinks she's too fancy for us now," Imogene said, then quickly shut up when Ruby turned to look at her.

"I'll ask," Elmo said. "Has she changed her name maybe?"

Ruby shrugged. She didn't like to consider that as it just made her chances even smaller.

"Did you call the union?" Duke asked.

"The union?" Ruby took a sip from her margarita, which she'd been afraid to drink because she was so exhausted and she thought adding tipsiness to that might make her pass out. "Why would the union want to help me find my Violet? They can't even find Jimmy Hoffa."

"No, AFTRA," Duke said. He smiled like a movie star, Ruby thought. No wonder Loralva was so smitten. "It's the television actors' union. If she's on a national TV spot then she's more than likely signed up with them. They'll at least know her agent."

Her agent, here we go again, Ruby thought, more dead-end phone calls. "Okay," she said, not wanting to offend. "I'll try them tomorrow."

After a few moments of silence that falls on a group when one member loses the party spirit, Duke asked, "Anybody up for some guitar picking?"

The burned hot dog odor that Ruby had decided was just what L.A. smelled like all the time sat heavy on them as the fellas played. Duke on the six string, George on the bass, Elmo picking a banjo and Paul with a mandolin. They started off with "When the Saints Come Marching In" and continued on for an hour or more. Ruby's spirits lifted and she snapped her fingers in time as Penny and Warren did some boot scooting around the pool. Loralva filled in as a backup singer real nice. Bunny and Bubbie sat cross-legged on towels, the boy bouncing a bit to the beat and Bunny clapping and singing along. For just an instant Ruby felt like she was back at the Bowl on a Saturday night when folks would bring their guitars and harmonicas and tap their feet along to the beat. Nights like that could keep a person happy forever if they never ended. They even sang Bill Lister's "RC Cola and a MoonPie." Bunny got a kick out of that. After Mark Williams's "I'm So Lonesome I Could Cry," they played "Tie a Yellow Ribbon 'Round the Old Oak Tree." Those words about "got to know what is and isn't mine," and "If you still want me," made Ruby tear up, so she stopped her finger snapping and stood up from her webbed pool chair and told them all it had come time to put herself to bed. The expressions on their faces read that they all knew as clearly as she did that she wouldn't actually be doing any sleeping. More than likely worrying instead.

Even before she made it out of the pool gate the band got to plucking again and Warren's tenor voice rumbled beneath everyone else's. Loralva had been kissing on Duke's neck and went back to it. As Ruby and the kids climbed the concrete stairs to the room, the clamor echoed and danced on the walls of the building with the street lamplight reflected off the water. Ruby ushered the kids inside, then turned around to give them all a wave. But they had already forgotten about her and started making it into the party they'd wanted to have all along.

Loralva stood at the pool edge, her jumpsuit lying on the ground across the way. Ruby had no idea her sister even knew how, but she raised her arms above her head, then did a swan dive into the deep end. The dazzle of the pink waves percolated on the motel wall as Ruby turned back and went inside their room.

Long Distance and Longhorns

The next day Ruby sat in front of the TV, hoping that Elmo would call anytime with word of someone that knew Violet. The television newscasts talked about nothing but how the rains had continued to pour in Texas. She'd called home once more. Tithes, Suddy said, had increased tenfold since having Sunday sermons at the Devine Bowl.

"What about the rains?" Ruby asked.

Suddy told Ruby about a leak in the pinsetter room. Bucket after bucket had to be emptied out the back door. Earl would be coming by, she said, to nail down a tarp until they could get the roof fixed after the rains. Earl. Always doing for her, Ruby thought. Always doing good.

"Maybe I should come back? Is it that bad?" Ruby asked. She wanted to go home, but she knew she wouldn't. She still had to find Violet. It was still pulling at her even through the big wall she felt slammed against.

"No, no," Suddy said, "we're all missing you, but we got it under control and Earl, sweet as he is on you, he'll take care of everything. But listen, dear, it's starting to lightning and thunder again, and I don't want to be on the phone in this weather. Makes me nervous with all that electricity in the air and a wire up close to my ear."

Ruby hung up and sat and watched the scenes from helicopters of the flooding in all of the states on the Gulf, but especially Texas. She sat by herself, though, because Imogene had left on the Tour of the Stars' Homes in hopes of running across Violet, and Loralva had taken off to sit in while Duke and the Skirt-Tailers practiced.

Earl sweet on her. No, that wasn't so. He was just real helpful, that was all. She liked that about him. She pictured him with his gray cowboy hat and his nice Wranglers that Señora Gonzalez who did his laundry kept ironed with a nice crease down the front of the legs. And that Lone Star belt buckle of his. He was mighty handsome, that was for darn sure.

The kids had been whining all morning. Bunny's Mrs. Beasley doll lay face down on the couch next to Ruby, completely ignored. They didn't want to watch what Ruby had on the TV and they didn't want to eat their toast with jelly and they didn't want anything but their momma and a MoonPie. But not one single MoonPie was left. After the breakfast dishes were cleared she'd walked over to the 7-Eleven, but they didn't have any. Then she'd stopped by the office and asked Penny where to go, but she told Ruby that the chocolate, marshmallow and graham cracker cookie, a mainstay in Texas, couldn't be found in these parts.

Then, when Bunny and Bubbie had started snapping and pushing and shoving over which cartoon they would watch, and Mrs. Beasley had gone flying across the room leaving behind some yellow yarn hair, Ruby had nothing to quiet them with except a spanking and forbidding them to watch TV. Right this moment, while she sat in the living room with a swelling shin from Bubbie's tantrum, which had included kicking his grandmomma with one solid little-boy boot-toe wallop, the kids had been banished to the back room where there was nothing much but the mirrored closet doors and the bed massager that didn't work without a quarter. Ruby could hear its trembling and quivering shudder, and knew Bubbie must have found one.

They still asked every day when they were going to get to see their momma. Or at least Bunny asked. Bubbie just perked his ears up to see what the answer would be. But she never had a complete response, or one that could even be considered satisfactory. Just "not today, maybe tomorrow."

According to the CBS News, it still rained buckets in Devine, Texas. Walter Cronkite didn't actually mention Devine, but he had said South Texas and Ruby knew that meant Devine or thereabouts, or Idyll County anyway. He had said it was raining like no other time on record. The cricket in the bowling alley had been right, and so had Ruby, it was an omen. Ruby knew she couldn't go home right yet, but she also wasn't so sure about going forward. She feared she'd be stuck here in the Pink 7 motel room with the coughing air conditioner for who knew how long.

She sat there rubbing the bruise on her shin from Bubbie's boot kick, then sat Mrs. Beasley upright. Earl came back to mind and what he had said to her on that day she found the cricket in the bowling alley. The part where he said she had to follow that trail until she couldn't no more. She should get up and make that one more phone call that Duke had suggested. A union for actors and actresses. Harley belonged to the firefighters' union, why not Violet her own.

She hauled out the fat yellow pages and looked under Unions. In between Uniforms and Upholsterers, there was nothing. She lugged the white pages out of the cabinet and plopped it down on the kitchen table. What had Duke said was the name of this union? AFTRA, she was pretty sure, because she remembered it sounded like the brand of razors that Rascal had used. But under

A in the white pages there was no AFTRA. She let out a big deep breath. Once again, going in circles. Soon she'd be dizzy. All those letters must stand for something, she figured. A, that almost always stood for Association or American. She'd try American because it came first in the alphabet.

She flipped the thin white pages. She was beginning to be irritated by phone books. They had not done her any good, and yet she'd been relying on them. She ran her finger down the page at American. *American Federation of Television and Radio Artists.* All the letters fit. She held her finger in place under the number and reached for the phone.

The connecting door rattled and she thought at first Imogene was coming through, but then she realized that Imogene had arrived in her own room, slamming the main door causing the connecting door to shake. Ruby dialed the phone number for AFTRA.

"Good afternoon, oops, sorry, not yet," the girl on the other end said. "Guess it's still morning." Then she giggled. She sounded no more than twelve, but Ruby figured that couldn't be since this was a union and there were laws against that now.

"Is this the actors' and actresses' union?" Ruby asked.

Another giggle, then, "Yes it is."

"I'm looking for someone," Ruby said, twirling the cord around her finger, wondering why she was still nervous when she'd said this same line to so many other people already and she knew what the answer would be.

"Talent?" the young receptionist asked.

"Excuse me?" Ruby said.

"Do you need talent?" Her gum popped into the receiver.

Ruby wasn't sure what this meant. She hadn't really thought about what her talents were. She supposed everyone had one, but she'd never really thought she needed any in particular. So she replied, "No, can't say that I need any."

"Okay," the girl said. "You already a member?"

"No," Ruby said, laughing a little at the thought that she could be an actress. "I'm looking for someone who is an actress though."

"Thought you didn't want talent?"

"It's not that I don't want talent," Ruby said. Now the phone cord had been stretched and recoiled itself into a big knot. "I am looking for my daughter." She hated having to say that one more time. It hurt more each time it came across her lips. "My daughter's an actress, a ButterMaid to be exact, and someone told me you all might could tell me where she's at."

The other end was quiet. Except the gum popping. "We have a standard policy," the girl started, and Ruby almost hung up straightaway, but she didn't see any need to be rude. The girl continued, "that we only give out the agent's phone number, not the artist's. What's your daughter's name?"

"Violet Davidson, or maybe Kincaid."

"Hold please."

Ruby pulled the cord taut and looked over at the TV to see more news on the floods. Now they were showing the devastation across the Guadalupe Valley. North of Idyll County, but still Texas.

"I have her file." The AFTRA receptionist was back. "Violet Kincaid." Somehow this felt a little closer. Finally, someone actually had a record of Violet existing. And she was using Kincaid! She still had something of Ruby left. She wanted to see inside that file. "Says here she's represented by the Carlyle Agency in Beverly Hills."

"Oh my," Ruby said. Wouldn't Imogene have a heyday knowing Violet's agent was in Beverly Hills, Ruby thought. "Any chance you can give me a little something more from that file? Maybe even just a street address? Maybe *her* phone number instead?" She'd tried all of this before, but she thought maybe this time it would work since this girl sounded so young.

"The actors take their privacy very seriously." The girl's tone had now changed. "How would Cher like it if we gave out her phone number willy-nilly?"

She had a point, Ruby thought. Although she still hoped she'd make an exception for her. "My daughter isn't exactly Cher," Ruby said.

"But she might be someday and then you could have tricked me into giving you her phone number. Please call her agent and he will direct you." Now her tone had really become quite snide. But Ruby liked thinking Violet might become Cher. Or maybe not.

"Will the agent give me her number?" Ruby asked, hoping that this could be the last stop.

Her tone softened a bit. "He won't give out any info unless it's regarding hiring his client. He's going to want to protect his client's privacy." She popped that dang gum again.

Another phone number to another agency. But Ruby didn't turn down the offer and she jotted the number on the pad she had put by the phone. She considered telling the young lady that she should take out her gum while talking on the phone, but instead just hung up after a short thank-you.

Ruby fixed herself a glass of iced tea. She knew the next call would be another dead end, but this dead end would be the last one. There wouldn't be anyone that this agency could pass her on to. So she decided to sit down for a minute and think about that feeling she had when the girl at AFTRA said she had a file on Violet. For just a moment she sensed she'd almost gotten somewhere. For now, she had the assurance that they were both in the same town. A helluva big town it was, too. She sat herself down on the couch to just think on it.

Imogene rattled around next door some more, causing Mrs. Beasley to slump over on the couch. Then the connecting door creaked and Imogene flew in the room.

"Suddy promised me before I left Devine that she'd keep an eye on Harley. Said she'd put the fear of God in him if he started seeing too much of that Becca Ann again." Imogene said the girl's name like it was a chewed-up, rancid pecan on her tongue. "Figured Suddy'd be happy to keep them separate, after all Becca Ann's momma is a Catholic and her daddy's a Presbyterian—one of them mixed marriages." She stood in the middle of the living room, facing the couch where Ruby sat.

"Imogene," Ruby could hear herself shouting, "almost all of Texas is under water."

Imogene blocked the TV screen with her middle and was in a bigger tizzy than Ida Mae Johnson when the skunk drowned in her above-ground pool.

"Can you scoot a little to the right?" Ruby said, motioning with her glass of iced tea, making the ice tinkle. She hadn't been watching, but she didn't want to have to deal with the mother-in-law at that moment when her own thoughts were on important things.

Imogene kept on. Her phone call to Devine had not gone well. "Harley was not at home when I called," Imogene told Ruby as though it was her fault.

Maybe he recognized your ring, Ruby thought, and instead said, "Maybe he got called out to a fire." The metal spring of the sofa poked her behind and made her want to get up.

"With all that rain? There's no fire except the one in my belly." Imogene stood with her feet planted like salt licks under mesquite trees. Her face stretched out smooth like it got when she wanted her way. "He should have been there. Long distance is expensive. So I called Judy Harper. Figured not only she'd know where he was, but I also wanted to tell her our good fortune at the game show." She paused, not for a response, but probably just for emphasis. "Judy told me some more news."

Ruby hoped it wasn't that someone had got washed away in their pickup truck trying to get through a crossing when the water ran too high and fast. Folks always did that. Drowned in no time.

"Turns out"—she talked right over Ruby's thoughts—"Harley"—she breathed in and out, like Penny on her cigarette holder—"my son, my one and only son who I raised to be an example to society." Ruby wanted to roll her eyes, but didn't dare. "He has gone off to Mexico with that"—her breath caught—"Becca Ann." She exhaled the name with disgust.

"To get married?" Ruby asked, shifting her weight on the couch and swaying as the broken springs gave in.

From the look on her face, Ruby was pretty darn certain that Imogene did not want to consider this. "They most certainly have *not,* they most certainly *better* not have!" Imogene's eyes flickered around the room looking at nothing. Must have been following her internal thoughts. "He's not marrying that girl and that's final!"

Ruby winced from the screaming bouncing off of her and the walls. "Sounds to me like you don't have much say in the matter."

"All this means is we have got to get to Violet even sooner. Ruby, you have got to get up off that couch and get out there and find her. She's here, we saw her on the TV!" She put her finger to the mole on the side of her head, and then turning her head to angle that side away from Ruby as if she had just remembered the defect was there, she began pulling the black strand of hair down to it.

Imogene continued as Ruby dug herself out of the couch and

got to her feet. "After all, it would be a darn shame for me to the be the mother-in-law to a TV star while Harley makes the mistake of marrying someone else."

"I'm doing just about all I can," Ruby said. "I want to find her as much as you do." Probably more, she reckoned.

"Where's Loralva?" Imogene said, stepping out of Ruby's way as she headed toward the kitchenette. "She can start driving us around in the 'bago."

"She's at Duke's. But, Imogene, how long do you think it would take to drive up and down every street in this big ole city?" Ruby made herself another glass of instant iced tea.

A key jangled in the front door and Loralva stepped in. "Ruby honey, guess what I got downstairs!"

"Did you bring another one of them band members home?" Imogene asked. "We have more important things to tend to. Harley is seeing Becca Ann again!"

"I got my Trans Am!" Loralva sideswiped Imogene heading toward Ruby. "Duke and me went down to the CBS studios where I did a little more sweet talkin' and Duke happened to know the prize manager. I'm just so thrilled. It drives like I imagine a man would if I had a key to his ignition."

The kids peeked around the corner, and Ruby motioned for them to come on out. They'd been punished long enough. She put Oreos on a saucer for them at the table. They acted disappointed. "We'll get more MoonPies when we get home," she told them.

"Ruby and I were just talking," Imogene said to Loralva, "about how important it is to get on the trail of Violet. See, my Harley is quite possibly marrying Becca Ann any day now." She put one hand to her chest, let out a big fake sigh and with the other hand tugged on her hair. Then she bit her bottom lip. "You see, with your new car—"

"I like Miss Becca Ann," Bunny interrupted. "She's like my

third momma." The little girl counted on Mrs. Beasley's fingers, "Momma, GranMomma and Miss Becca Ann."

"Oh now now," Imogene told the girl. "Don't go getting all confused. Your momma is your momma and that's all there is to it."

Ruby bristled. Then a loud honk came from outside.

"Come on down and see my car!" Loralva said. "Duke's waiting." She took off back downstairs. Ruby was on her tail.

In the parking lot they all gathered around the Special Edition Smokey and the Bandit Trans Am. The sleek black car sat in a parking space by the pool with the gold eagle painted on the hood upside down now that Duke and Warren had the hood up.

"Smells like formaldehyde," Imogene said.

"That's new car smell," Loralva said. "Reminds me of that cute car salesman with the tiny mustache over at the Chevrolet dealership in Cicada."

When she saw the look on Imogene's face, Ruby knew right away that Imogene wouldn't set foot in this car. It was too similar to the Camaro that the breakfast waitress at the Stuckey's on the I-10 outside of San Antonio drove, the same waitress that Harley's daddy left Imogene for.

Soon Loralva sat behind the wheel extending her arms out long and stiff as though headed down a lengthy stretch. Bubbie was kneeling on the bumper next to Warren and Duke, who stood staring into the engine, and Bunny and Penny were in the backseat opening and closing all the ashtrays and pushing the buttons for the electric windows. Ruby sat in the passenger seat, staring straight ahead at the giant upside-down golden eagle spread across the hood. Loralva had the motor running and the rumble had Ruby vibrating from her feet to her watery brain.

"Check it out," Loralva said. "Eight-track tape! The 'bago's only got cassette."

"Warren's got eight-tracks in the Gran Torino you can borrow," Penny said from the backseat no bigger than the motel towels.

"I'll get one of Duke's recordings," Loralva said, "play it as I drive around town." She hung her head out the window. "Duke honey, as soon as you got an album you gotta get me one on eight-track so I can play it in my car!"

"You betcha, cupcake!" Duke leaned around the side of the hood and winked at her.

Ruby watched Imogene rock on her heels under the awning of the motel, rolling the piece of hair in front of her mole. "I will be riding around town in a limousine soon as we find Violet," the mother-in-law said, "listening to Neil Diamond."

That's when Ruby started to cry. She didn't want to, not right then especially with Loralva so excited. But she was just so certain it wasn't going to happen. She wasn't ever going to find Violet. She told Loralva as much and she let her sister hold her while she sobbed.

With the gear shift between them she said, "Ruby honey, it's not so. We're gonna be out there tomorrow. I got a fun car to drive around in. Who cares how long it takes to find her when we're riding around in this beauty!"

Ruby cried harder at the thought of it taking forever. She couldn't do this much longer. Thing was, she didn't know what she was doing. "Loralva, I don't have any further I can go."

Bunny had quit flipping her ashtray lid back and forth and Penny was now trying to scramble out the back with the little girl in tow. Ruby had to scoot up on her bucket seat so they could crawl out.

Once they were alone in the car, Loralva zipped up all the windows tight.

"What are you talkin' about, Ruby honey?" Loralva said. "You been making headway all along."

"No," Ruby said, and she explained about all the calls and the "standard policy" and how she just couldn't bear to make this last call because it would mean the biggest dead end of all.

"Dead end?" Loralva said. "Well, I certainly don't believe that. Standard policy has never gotten in my way, now has it?"

Ruby agreed. Loralva's policy was no policy.

"I think we can figure out a way to get this next phone call to work for you. Tell me again what the AFTRA girl said—how 'only if they were hiring talent' would they give out the personal information?"

Ruby nodded, and sniffled. She hated ever crying in front of the grandkids.

"Then we'll just hire us some talent." Loralva sat back and nodded her head, so sure of her idea.

"Now you're talking crazy. We can't do that," Ruby said.

Imogene came over and tapped on Ruby's window. "Why do you all have the windows rolled up?" she asked, leaning her head down to get a good look inside.

Loralva ignored her. "I think I learned a few things at *The Price Is Right* yesterday and today. I know what you'll tell them when you call the agency."

"Just chatting," Ruby said through the glass to Imogene.

"You call them up and tell them you are wanting to hire an actress. An actress that looks like Violet." Loralva's voice gave away that she was getting more excited about her idea as she told it.

"How am I gonna tell them something like that?" Ruby said to Loralva, and then she shook her head at Imogene in response to her tapping some more on the glass and motioning for Ruby to roll down the window.

"It's easy," Loralva said, turning up the air conditioner and causing the big bulky engine to rev. "You just say you work for *The Price Is Right*. Yeah, that's it. That you need to hire . . ."

Imogene banged louder on the window. "You two have no business being locked up in there. Ruby is crying. I know this has to do with Violet. I've come all this way, you can't leave me out now!"

"She sounds desperate," Loralva said. "Good."

"Should I let her in?" Ruby asked, her finger on the electric window switch.

"No, we're almost done," Loralva said. She looked proud sitting in her new car. "You just call up and say you're Janice Pennington!"

"I'm what?" Ruby said. She pictured that swanky Miss Pennington in her chartreuse suit with sequined lapels and the short short miniskirt.

"You know when you had that pinsetter before you got the Brunswick automatics and he decided to go on the bowling tour, but before he quit working for the Devine Bowl he got his younger brother to come work for you so you weren't left empty handed?"

"He was a sweet fella," Ruby said with fond memories. "But what's that got to do with me being Janice Pennington?"

Imogene tapped harder on the window, which Ruby could tell irritated Loralva. She didn't want the mother-in-law's fingers touching her new car.

"You're going to say you're Janice and you are looking for a replacement while you go have a baby." With that she opened her car door. "Come on, let's go upstairs and call now."

"Janice Pennington is pregnant?" Ruby said. Imogene quit pounding on her window when Loralva got out of the car. "I didn't even know she was married."

"She's not married. It's just how you're going to get some kind of information on Violet."

"We don't have time for this crying and carrying on," Imogene shouted over the roof of the car at Loralva. The car doors were heavy and low hanging and Ruby had to open her door slow in order not to bump the mother-in-law with it.

"It'll be easy," Loralva said over her shoulder. Then, "Duke honey, I'll be back before you can even miss me."

"I already miss you," Duke hollered back.

"Are you still going on about *The Price Is Right*?" Imogene came around the Trans Am to walk with Ruby and Loralva to the room.

Ruby motioned to Penny that she'd only be a minute if she wouldn't mind keeping an eye on the kids.

"We need to be finding Violet!" Imogene said, pushing her way between the two sisters.

"We are," Loralva said to her. "Ruby's going to pretend she's Janice Pennington having a baby."

"Are you sure we should do Janice, Loralva? She doesn't even look anywhere near pregnant." Ruby concentrated on the asphalt, on her feet taking it one step at a time. It made her nervous to try to be a TV actress like Violet.

"What in the devil are you talking about?" Imogene said, pulling at her sideburn.

"Why don't you be Janice, not me?" Ruby said, looking across Imogene to Loralva. "You could have the voice and the sexiness, the whole bit."

"No, I'll be right there next to you, but you gotta be the one to do this. You'll know the questions to ask about Violet. Besides, you got sexy in you that you don't even know about."

That just threw Ruby into more of a nervous tizzy as they walked into their motel room.

Muzak and Pygmy Goats

Ruby didn't want to make one single phone call ever again. All these folks in California just battering her around, it weren't right. But she took in a deep, deep breath and dialed this one more number.

"Oh Loralva, I wish you'd do the talkin' for me," Ruby said. The sisters sat next to each other on the bed.

"If anyone should talk to them it should be me," Imogene said. "I'm the least likely to make a fool of herself. Loralva would just end up getting a dinner date. Ruby, you're just going to get scared." The skunk-headed mother-in-law shifted from foot to foot, her nerves practically tying themselves into knots. It didn't help that Imogene was now shoving her own nervousness onto Ruby.

"At least a dinner date would be an opportunity to get some answers. You'd just end up telling them about yourself," Loralva said.

"It's ringing!" Ruby said, waggling her hand to get them to be quiet.

"Find out what we should wear when we go to her house," Imogene said.

Imogene and Loralva had their own ways of thinking, but Ruby wondered if Mr. Carlyle would even give her the time of day. She doubted it, but she pushed her shoulders back as the phone rang once, twice and then a tiny voice said, "Good morning, Carlyle Agency, this is Ricki."

"Good morning to you too, Ricki." She decided it would be best to be friendly to them first. Kill them with kindness, a saying she believed in. "This is—" But she didn't get a chance to finish.

"I'd recognize your accent anywhere, Miss Kincaid," Ricki said. "Let me put you through. He's expecting your call."

Click, then more Muzak. She'd listened to more Muzak this week than all the fiddle playing in Texas. *He's expecting your call?*

"What'd they say?" Loralva and Imogene leaned in really close now.

Ruby knew she was wide eyed, not sure what to do next. "They think I'm Violet!" She held her hand over the mouthpiece, hoping she didn't give anything away. Her whole body stiffened and she thought she might cry. Her heart had most definitely come to a complete halt. In a small way, it felt special just being confused with Violet.

"Keep letting them think that!" Loralva whispered. "Go along with whatever they say. Tell them . . . tell them . . ." She searched her head for what was the exact perfect thing to say.

"Let me talk to them. I can be a better Violet than you." Imogene tried swiping the phone receiver from Ruby, but she shifted out of Imogene's reach.

"What do I say?" Ruby pleaded with Loralva.

"Flirt a little," Loralva said. "Tell him what a fine fella he is. Put a little pizzazz into—"

"That ain't gonna work," Imogene said. "You gotta be firm.

Tell him you won't take no for an answer. Tell him you'll find a better agent if he won't do what you want."

"Shhh! Someone's on the line." Ruby covered the mouthpiece and held the earpiece harder to her ear as though that would make it easier to hear. Loralva put her head next to Ruby's to listen in.

"Sorry to keep you holding, Lety," Ricki said. "He's on the other line. Do you want me to have him call you back?"

"NO!" Loralva mouthed, and shook her head wildly.

"Uh, no," Ruby said, not sure what her other option was. "I'll just wait. I don't have anything else to do."

"Thanks. It won't be long." Ricki clicked her back to the Musak.

"Don't have anything else to do!" Imogene mimicked Ruby. "You are a movie star. You have plenty to do!"

"TV star." Ruby gritted her teeth. "She called me Lety. Violet's using her name she made up in junior high." She smiled with the memory. Violet had wanted to be somebody else. Changed her name and told everyone to start calling her Lety, like most teenagers did. Nobody called her that, and it faded after a year or so. "What else don't I know about her?" Ruby got bug eyed again, wondering about the secrets beyond her reach. "How will I know how to get anything from them?"

"You're doing just fine, honey," Loralva said.

"I'll just tell him the truth," Ruby said. "That I'm Violet's momma and we want to get in touch with her. Who can turn that down?"

"Violet's agent, that's who," Loralva said. "They don't care none about nobody's momma in showbiz."

Ruby's pounding heart slowed down knowing that was the real truth. The future with Violet was getting dimmer.

Loralva must have noticed Ruby's slump in the shoulders

because she snatched the phone from her hand. "I'll take care of it. Don't you worry none."

"Hey!" Imogene said. "I am the better Violet imitator!"

At that same instant, Mr. Carlyle came on the line. A fast talker, his voice was deep and, Loralva would say later, the sexiest she'd ever heard, so sexy she could have just closed her eyes and listened to him talk all night long. It could be clearly heard through the phone receiver. "Lety! How's it going? Listen, I know why you're calling. I have your check from ButterMaid Corporation right here. Let me check to make sure we got the address right."

Loralva said, "Great," and nothing more, but waved at Ruby or Imogene or someone to hurry up and hand her the notepad and pencil on the nightstand. Ruby went to pick it up, but Imogene snatched it away and handed it to Loralva herself.

"Is it still Ocean Avenue?" he asked.

His voice made Loralva shudder as she wrote "Ocean Ave." on the pad she'd sat on her knee. "What number do you have on Ocean, honey?" Loralva asked.

"231A," he said, and Loralva wrote that down.

"Sounds like you got it," she said.

"Isn't the 90291 zip code Venice Beach?" he asked. "Thought you were moving to Hollywood Hills."

"Not yet," Loralva said, wavering her voice a bit, maybe trying to make it higher like Violet's.

"You're probably waiting for this check to make your down payment." He laughed. "It's going in tonight's mail. Should get it tomorrow or the next day. It's on its way, baby, just like you!"

Loralva laughed along with him, but Ruby pulled away from the phone receiver and looked at her sister. Hollywood Hills? Moving? They better hurry!

"Heh, heh," he laughed again, like Bob Barker, Ruby thought.

"Listen, gotta run, babe. But call me next week, I got another audition for a national spot coming up. Ban Roll-on. With your arms you're a shoo-in. More big money too. Call me."

"I most definitely will," Loralva said. " 'Preciate it, honey."

Ruby heard the phone click on the other end and she missed him already. She wanted to ask him how Violet was doing.

"Boy howdy! Woo-hoo! Hallejuah and all that Suddy crap! You are the Grand Prize Winner, Ruby honey! You got the Trans Am of information on Violet!" Loralva wrapped her arms around Ruby, almost causing her to fall over flat on the bed.

"We know where she's at!" Imogene got all flustered and straightened her skirt. "Hand me that address. I'm going over there right now." She talked all sappy sweet, making Ruby take notice because that meant she was scheming.

"How you planning on getting there?" Loralva said.

"I'll be the one," Ruby said, sitting up straight on the bed, "to visit Violet first."

"How are *you* planning on getting there?" Imogene imitated Loralva.

"I'll be driving her in the Trans Am. Ain't that right, Ruby honey?"

Ruby nodded. She realized she really did have to go now. There was no skirting around it. She wished she wouldn't have told them to be in the room with her when she called. No, that wasn't true. If they hadn't been, Ruby would have handled the call differently than Loralva and she'd be sitting here now staring at that big dead end she had anticipated. Instead, she had Violet's whereabouts on a piece of paper that Loralva tore off the pad and handed to her. She didn't want to ever let it go.

After they all three danced around the room, they went back down to the parking lot to share their news with the others.

While Duke twirled Loralva around, Bunny did the same with Mrs. Beasley. Bubbie and Warren stayed by the car, the little boy fascinated by the engine. Finally something he could poke at without causing too much harm, Ruby thought.

After a big hug, Penny told Ruby, "It's just all gonna be so easy from here."

Ruby just smiled, nodded, hoped she was right, but feared *easy* wasn't a word that applied to Violet. Or maybe she should be calling her Lety now.

Imogene straightened herself up prim and proper, no one to hug. She must have thought it would be easy from here as well. "We need to get on the road and head on out to that address." She put her hand on the glass of the T-top and patted it. "I don't think this will be very comfortable for all of us." She scrunched up her face. Ruby knew it was jealousy.

"Oh, I don't think you want to head out right now," Penny said, and Warren agreed. "It's nearly quitting time and the traffic between here and the West Side is not going to get you there before dark. You'll just be sitting and waiting."

"We'll manage fine in the 'bago," Imogene said, taking her hand off the car like it burned.

"You'd get around the city a lot easier in the smaller vehicle," Duke said. He squeezed Loralva's waist. Ruby knew he wanted Loralva to have her way and get to drive her new car.

"Penny and Duke both got a point," Loralva said. "I sat in two hours of traffic on my way to Duke's the other night. This is Los Angeles after all."

"It's a half-hour drive to Venice Beach from here on a good day," Duke said.

"Meaning no traffic," Penny said.

"It's all true," Warren's voice rumbled from behind the Trans Am's hood.

Bunny looped her arms around Ruby's legs, sensing the same thing—already roadblocks and they weren't even on the road. Bubbie banged a stick on the air filter, causing Loralva to quickly run over to his side and hug his little shoulders, then take the stick out of his hand.

As much as Ruby wanted to get on the road, she knew a new day would be the better time to start this next part of the journey. "I think a good night's sleep will be good for all of us. We can get up bright and early to start."

Bunny handed up her Mrs. Beasley doll to Ruby. "Can she go too?"

Something in the way that Imogene couldn't be happy for Loralva, and just the whole thing about her not taking her share of the responsibility with the grandkids, and now the opportunity to get to Violet the next day, all that made Ruby turn from Bunny's outstretched doll to the skunk-headed mother-in-law and say, "Loralva and me will go in the Trans Am tomorrow first thing. Imogene, you can stay with the kids."

Imogene's scrunched faced dropped into complete surprise instead. "I am not going to just sit by the wayside—"

"Someone has to stay here to call Devine every hour and make sure Harley don't marry Becca Ann," Loralva said.

Imogene couldn't decide which way to look. Loralva had brought up the most important point for her. She had to keep watch on Harley or this whole thing could fall apart for her. "Fine," she said. Then to Bubbie, "Guess you're gonna spend some time with your Mimaw Imogene starting tomorrow." He looked up at her and back over to Ruby and she knew he thought she'd double-crossed him. Imogene pursed her lips together and said to him, "You won't even kill so much as a cockroach while you're under my supervision."

Bunny took back the offer of her Mrs. Beasley doll.

★ ★ ★

Ruby lay in bed, thinking her skin would wiggle right off. Her left leg had the pricklies from not moving. She tried shaking it to get the blood flowing again.

"You still not sleeping?" Loralva grumbled from her side of the bed.

"Can't turn off the thinking part of my brain," Ruby said back, her voice sounding a little bit irritated, not at Loralva, but at Mr. Sandman. "Didn't mean to wake you." Although she was relieved to have the company.

"Try counting Earl Glidden's pygmy goats," Loralva said.

"Did that already, three hundred forty-two of them."

"Did you get that little hybrid spotted one even?"

"Got it," Ruby said. The feeling was coming back in her leg, so she quit shaking it.

"Always thought Earl should just have a barbecue and get that spotted goat out of his pasture before the whole herd becomes short and spotted," Loralva said.

Ruby turned her head on the pillow and looked toward her sister's silhouette, lit around the edges by the orange beam of the street lamp, which came in around the hems of the motel curtains. "I kinda like that spotted fella. Friendly as all get out. It'll come right up to your leg and rub on you like a cat."

Loralva turned her head toward Ruby. "You think," she half whispered, "that goat might be a cross with that black and white Tom that lives under Earl's house?"

Ruby laughed. Felt good to have a little tickle run through her. "No," she said.

"Reckon not." Loralva looked back up toward the ceiling. Ruby did the same and they continued a second or two of inside laughing over that half cat, half goat. Then Loralva said, "You know I keep telling you, Earl's got a hankering for you."

Ruby looked at her, not seeing much other than that orange

outline. "He's just as nice to me as he is to other folks in Devine. He takes Edna Luther twice as much goat milk as he does me."

"He knows you don't like to drink that barn-floor-tasting goat milk and that you don't make cheese. But how many meat goats has he brung over to your place?"

"Too many to count," Ruby said, "but that's only because he supplies the meat for the monthly Barbecue and Bowl."

Neither one said anything for a moment. Loralva always teased her about Earl. She reckoned her sister just wanted to take her mind off the Violet worries. "You really should consider him," Loralva said. Ruby recalled the way Earl hovered around the pineapple upside-down cake at their send-off. Kept staring at her. "Why don't you?"

Ruby's answer used to be, "I can't be doing that." But now, here in California with no idea what would happen next, she wondered about it. "I don't know," Ruby answered. And she didn't. She didn't know about anything anymore. "Maybe," she said aloud.

"Remember that time those cows got out of his back pasture and we had to help you herd them out of your parking lot?" Loralva continued. "He'd cut a piece out of his fence for them to pass through, just for you." Her sister was smiling, Ruby could tell even in the dark, from that crisp smacking sound that lips make when all's quiet. "It was obvious the fence had been cut—the wire cutters sat in the back of his pickup."

Ruby chuckled as it dawned on her that Earl's goats, cows and emus had all ended up in her parking lot on more than one occasion and all those times he'd been waiting by the phone, picked up on the first half of the ring when she called to tell him. Well, that old coot, she thought, then sighed.

"He does have that nice full head of hair," Loralva said.

"Yep." Ruby pictured Earl in her mind. Tall and slender in his Wranglers and Lone Star belt buckle. Maybe not as bowlegged as most. Some salt and pepper around the edges of his hair, sticking out from under that gray felt cowboy hat. Liked to wear red western shirts with mother-of-pearl snap buttons. "He always has on the snazziest boots," she said aloud.

"I'll say." Loralva whistled low between her teeth. "Saw him in a pair of ocelots with silver studs on the tips and I almost would have jumped into his lap but for I'd arrived with Sheriff Bartlett and he was carrying his gun."

Ruby didn't say anything and the dark room became even quieter. When she got back home she reckoned she'd start taking special note of Earl's attentions. But she couldn't be thinking about going home right now.

"If I could just have a sign," she said to Loralva. Her mind had gone back to Violet. "Something to let me know how things are going to go when we get to Violet's tomorrow."

"Signs, that's just Suddy feeding you God-on-high Bible-isms. Signs are just what you make them."

"I don't get you. How can I make a sign?"

"Oh, for Heaven's sake, Ruby, would you stop with what the sign's supposed to be telling you, and just tell it what you want."

She wanted Violet, and she wanted the slip of paper in her hand to be a sign she was closer to her. Ruby let her eyes focus on the dark. But the sign she saw rose bigger and scarier than the sign outside Lester's Burger Palace. That sign stood high on a narrow post and when a big wind came up it swayed and wove like a drunk high on tequila. Not a single pickup truck would park within a mile of that sign on a gusty night. The address still in Ruby's hand now felt just as wobbly as Lester's sign flashing BURGERS, BUNS & BEERS.

Gas, Leaky Valves and God

Slow down!" Ruby said, her voice jittery. "This ain't the Bandera race track." She clutched the armrest on one side and the cup holders in the console on the other.

"Can't help it," Loralva said. "Trans Ams just naturally go fast."

Ruby braced herself as the car whizzed down the highway off-ramp, moving in a big circle toward the city streets of Venice. It wasn't that Loralva drove too fast, although she did, it was more that Ruby wanted to slow down their getting there.

The air conditioner blew new-plastic scent on her face. Waylon Jennings and Willie Nelson sang "Mammas Don't Let Your Babies Grow Up to Be Cowboys" on the eight-track tape Loralva'd borrowed from Warren. Ruby wished she could be so lucky that Violet had grown up to be a cowgirl. But they didn't say nothing about Hollywood TV stars.

Headed toward Violet's home, Loralva driving like that Mario Andretti, discombobulation swirled both inside and outside her. She didn't know what to say to Violet, but she knew it'd be the truth. Trying to make her mind go to that place where she stood face-to-face with her daughter made her stomach circumambulate like a horse on its longe line. Of course she'd tell her about Bunny and Bubbie first thing: how Bunny'd started kindergarten, how Bubbie'd learned his multiplication tables, although he had trouble past the five times. She wouldn't tell her about the armadillo he'd pulled off the road or the dead coyote he found and poked at in the parking lot in Palm Springs, nor even about the baby sparrow caught by the motel pool.

She didn't want to urp on Loralva's new upholstery, so she tried concentrating on the fancy, filigreed gold eagle emblazoned on the Trans Am's glove compartment door. She paid no attention to Los Angeles whipping by outside her window, and she wouldn't even let her mind go to thinking about how the sky seemed to be getting grayer the closer they got to Violet's.

Waylon and Willie sang out from the speakers on four sides of her, and Loralva sang along. When the steel guitar twanged Loralva even sang a wha-wha-wha along with Waylon. Made Ruby homesick, longing for the Bowl, a Saturday night with the folks in Devine. They could never picture her here, riding in a black Trans Am, her legs stuck out in front of her in a car seat so low to the ground. This was nowhere near the Lone Star State filled with pickups she had to hoist herself into.

"There it is!" Loralva hollered, making Ruby jump and take her eyes off the gold eagle. "Ocean Avenue." The car whirled left down a smaller street.

Ocean Avenue didn't look like anything Ruby'd pictured. No mansions with big black wrought-iron gates sitting high on cliffs above the sea, no long, palm-tree-lined driveways. This first block looked like it could have been the corner of Washington and Cemetery Road in Devine. One house with white siding and blue shutters could have been Mrs. Duffy's house, only she had all those poodles in her yard.

"You certain this is the right street?" Ruby asked, one hand on her swirling stomach.

"Check the address." The car slowed down with the engine reverberating like an outboard.

Ruby ran her eyes over the tiny slip of smelly paper she held tightly in her hand. "231A Ocean Avenue."

"Four more blocks this way then."

Four more blocks. Four more blocks wasn't enough time to figure out what she was going to say or do. Four more blocks held hardly enough time to put on more lipstick. She stared out at all the houses packed snug together.

"Keep a lookout, Ruby honey. Violet might be walking down the sidewalk right past us." The engine growl caused Ruby to worry that it would announce their presence too soon. But she kept a lookout for her daughter.

"Lookee there!" Loralva said, causing Ruby to slide down in the low bucket seat. "That is one handsome fella. Think he's a movie star? If he ain't he oughta be." Loralva pushed the button for her electric window, put her fingers between her lips and whistled and waved.

The next block didn't have any houses, just a McDonald's on the corner. OVER 10 MILLION SERVED, it read under the yellow arches. Next to that was a Jack LaLanne's. Concrete discus throwers sat on either side of the door. Ruby'd seen those places advertised on the TV. Fellas pumping weights in their undershirts. In Devine, the men just lifted tire irons, bales of hay, occasionally shoved a cow over a few feet, or built a fence around forty acres to get those same muscles.

"Wrong way," Ruby said, "no houses this way. Don't feel right." A confusion of relief and disappointment swam around inside her belly.

"Only way," Loralva said. "Maybe the next block's different."

But it wasn't, and then they came to a dead end. As Loralva turned the car around, the Trans Am roared with each step on the gas and boomed in Ruby's ears as she tried to quit the thought that this piece of paper didn't have any value.

"Gotta be back that way," Loralva said as they reached the 200 block again. Ruby scoured the doorways for numbers. They passed a doughnut shop, a store with a sign that read Karma, Kandles and Krystals Discount Store and a place called Leather Togs by Bep where a tall skinny man wearing a shiny red leather jumpsuit leaned against the doorway.

"I'll ask," Loralva said, pulling into the Phillips 66 station across the street.

Ding-ding went the full-service bells as two fellas—one about sixteen, the other near Ruby's age, both dressed in charcoal gray coveralls with a name patch stitched in red over their hearts—came up to the car.

Paul, the one Ruby's age, stuck his head in Loralva's window, which she'd just lowered with the flick of a button. "Fill 'er up?" he asked.

Jay, the younger one, had already started cleaning the windshield with the squeegee and blue paper towels. Ruby smiled at him. Made her think of what Bubbie might be doing after school in a few years. Helping out at Jack's Gas-Up at the east end of Devine, or maybe right here in Los Angeles. That is, if he didn't get sent to prison for killing animals or worse.

"You can do more than just fill up my tank, honey," Loralva told Paul. "You can help me find this address." As Loralva snatched the piece of paper from her hand, Ruby worried that it might tear. Then Paul's grease-stained hands with the blackened fingernails took it and she had a strong urge to snatch it back.

Paul laughed a little and Ruby figured it meant they were

either a long way from where that address was or it didn't exist at all. She leaned over the console to get a good look at his face and to make sure she got the slip of paper back. "It's right around back," he said. "Just upstairs."

Just around back? Ruby turned toward the station building. Her heart stopped.

"What luck, Ruby honey," Loralva said, jabbing her shoulder.

"Yeah," Ruby said. She needed luck more than anything now. Luck was all she had left from this point forward.

"Jay," Paul said, "show them where the back stairs are."

Jay now reached across the span of the big back window with his squeegee.

"Right here, Ruby honey," Loralva said. "Just upstairs." She poked Ruby in the shoulder again, trying to get a reaction from her blank face. Her whole body trembled and her hands fumbled to snap her purse closed. She reached for the door handle, but now Jay stood next to her door squeegeeing her window. He smiled at her, but she didn't smile back.

"You go on," Loralva said, "I'll park the car and follow."

"Alone?" Ruby asked, not meaning to say it aloud, but she already had the car door open and one leg out.

Jay walked her around to the far side of the building, the squeegee dripping a trail of soapsuds beside them. Concrete steps and wrought iron banister like at the motel led up to a door on the second story of the gas station. "You interested in renting it?"

A sun-faded sign, barely readable, hung from the railing at the top of the stairs:

Mr. Bob's Bobs
Shampoo & Set $2.00
Cut & Style $3.00

Ruby stared up at it. It wasn't the sign she'd hoped for.

"It's not a hair place any longer. Dad just hasn't taken the sign down. He put a hot plate in and made it an apartment. It comes furnished. Pretty nice, actually. Are you looking for yourself?"

"Just visiting my daughter," Ruby said, hesitating on the first stair, looking at it, then at the door, almost calculating how far away she was.

"Oh, I thought you were here to see the rental. There's nobody that lives here now."

"The place is for rent?" Ruby held her wobbly stomach again.

"I don't understand," Jay shrugged. "Do you want to see the place or not?" He sounded more confused than irritated.

"I'm here," Ruby said, straightening her shoulders taking in a breath, not sure how to feel now. "I'm here to visit with a Miss Lety Kincaid."

"The one with the eyes." Jay nodded. "Ooo-eee. Wish she were still here, but she took off leaving behind half her stuff."

"She's gone then?" Ruby knew what to feel now and the disappointment came in a big wallop, but she stayed upright even though she swayed as though she could topple over. "But her things are there?"

"I can't let you in if you aren't here to look at the rental."

"Ain't that a shame." Loralva came around the corner toward them, her orange patent leather slides clicking on the asphalt. "Maybe you could help us out here." Loralva sashayed right past Ruby and up to Jay, and the young boy shrugged again. "You see, we've come all this way from Texas. Drove out here to see her daughter." She pointed at Ruby who still stood on the bottom stair.

"Texas?" Jay said, sounding anxious.

"That's right. Big state with big everything," Loralva told him. "Know the place?"

"Yes, ma'am."

Ruby wanted to hurry it up. She was feeling a bit woozy from what she figured was the gasoline fumes—that and Loralva's racetrack driving.

"Maybe"—Loralva got up real close to Jay—"Maybe you could help us get inside my niece's apartment. We've only come for a short visit." Loralva licked the tip of her finger and Ruby watched as Jay went all to shudders while Loralva pretended to wipe a little something off his face. It looked like she was wiping off a lipstick remnant after a big kiss.

"I can't let you in just to poke around," he said, his eyes following Loralva's fingertip. "Besides, it's a big mess, just heaps of trash she left behind."

"Thought you said it was nice," Ruby said.

"That was when I thought you might be a renter," Jay said, still ogling Loralva.

Ruby'd seen Loralva in action before. She knew she usually got what she was after, but this was Los Angeles and no one in the big city was particularly trusting of strangers. Loralva played with the zipper on his coveralls. "You could just pretend you're showing us the rental and then let us be alone for a while."

"I'll have to ask my dad. He's the owner of this station, and the landlord of the apartment."

"For me," Loralva said, her lips curling around the words. The lips she'd clearly painted a crimson red before she got out of the car. "Tell him I'll give him a ride in my new Trans Am."

Ruby couldn't see from where she stood, but she knew as well as she could smell premium Phillips gasoline at that moment that Loralva had winked and pursed her lips together in an almost kiss. A promise kiss.

He was gone like a shot, and back before Loralva and Ruby had even made it halfway up the stairs. "Here!" he said, a smile on his face bigger than the grille on the Mercedes-Benz that had just pulled up in full-serve. "Here are the keys. But Dad said you gotta give him that ride like you promised."

"You are the sweetest thing," Loralva told him as she took the key from him. "And you tell your daddy I'll be right back down."

He just shrugged, then ding-ding went the full-serve bells and he ran off again.

A pile of scraggly bougainvillea climbed up the side of the staircase. The raspberry-colored blooms gave off no scent. On the other side of the chain-link fence that separated the gas station from the property behind it stood the back of a two-story brick building and a parking lot filled with Dempsey Dumpsters emitting the sweet rancid odor of trash.

Loralva climbed on past Ruby and stood on the landing fiddling with the key in the lock. Ruby hurried to catch up to her, to be there when the door opened. Maybe she had a tiny hope that Violet might really be there after all, or maybe she just wanted to be where Loralva was so it wouldn't all seem so scary.

But once the door was opened, Ruby didn't venture much farther than the threshold at first. Loralva went straight in. Ruby thought that maybe if she just closed her eyes tight, her lids squished together, she could pretend it was all just a dream. That the room might swim around inside her head and become something else, do a switcheroo like what always happened in her dreams. But her eyes didn't close. They didn't even blink. They just stared at the piles of boxes and Glad bags of trash. The only furniture was a mattress across the room. The walls still had items thumbtacked to them. The whole place barely held more space than the truck bed of Jimmy Ray Johnson's two-ton dually.

Ruby took it all in from where she stood. Mostly took in the stink. At first she thought it could be a marijuana cigarette, but in seconds she recognized the odor as the same one around

Suddy when she got one of her tight and curly permanents. That stink and the two big, black porcelain sinks with a notch to fit a lady's narrow neck were all that was left of Bob's Bobs. The hot plate balanced between them on a shelf, and Ruby considered how convenient it would be to have two deep sinks like those. Without the white ring of soap scum around the edge, of course. Loralva sauntered around picking up what lay on the ground, then tossing it back down after she'd given it a good look or held it up to see if it might be her size.

Then Ruby's eyes caught on the photos tacked on the wall, all of her Violet staring back at her. She stepped in closer. There were lots of different poses—up close, the whole body, which was darn near naked in most cases, short, short minis, see-through gowns. Some pictures had her as a blonde, and in others she was a brunette. Must have been twenty or more photos of her Violet tacked on that wall drawing Ruby inside. Only one was framed, a black and white eight-by-ten of Violet in a sun hat bigger than one of Ida Mae Johnson's Easter hats, wearing a strapless sundress and lacy white stockings and a come-hither stare. There were bits of Violet all over the room. In one of the boxes by the sinks, Ruby found a whole stack of photos. One of them showed Violet as a blonde, and she'd autographed it *Lety Davis* in black magic marker.

"Lety Davis it says here," Ruby said, picking up the photo, letting the glossy finish stick to her fingers. "The agency called her Miss Kincaid on the phone."

"Probably her stage name," Loralva said.

Just like Barbi had said, Ruby thought.

Standing right up to the wall, Ruby looked at each photo, row after row, the edges of some curling. Loralva got up close to the one in particular that Ruby'd been trying to avoid. The almost naked one. Her breasts, bigger than Ruby'd remembered them, hung out of a skimpy torn T-shirt, hot pants cut almost to the crotch. Her hair was blown back, probably by a wind-blowing machine, Ruby reckoned. She was blond in that one. Didn't suit her, Ruby thought, that hair color made her look too washed out. She liked her the way she was, or rather had been.

"Bet this was the photograph that got her the job on the ButterMaid commercial, Ruby honey."

A white patch at the bottom of each photo read, Lety Davis, Carlyle Agency, 10121 Wilshire Blvd., Beverly Hills, CA 90210, (818) 795-5555. Ruby wasn't so sure she could get used to the new name. Lety. Figured she'd have to stick to calling her Violet. She tried saying it out loud, "Lety . . . Davis." Then quick-like, as though she was calling out to her, "Letee!" lilty on the ending.

"Don't sound right, do it?" Loralva said.

"Not so rounded like Violet. More modern, I suspect is why she done it." She stuck her nose up to the picture of Violet in the psychedelic minidress.

"If I became a movie star I'd keep my name. Bet there ain't a single Loralva in the history of movie making. Maybe I'd even go by just that, just Loralva. Like that Ann-Margret or Cher."

"Reckon I'd go by plain ole Ruby Kincaid. The last name because it's who I've been for the past thirty years, and the first name 'cause that's the name my momma gave me." She said this last part with a tinge of pissiness. She felt a prick of guilt remembering how years after she'd found Violet and taken her in somebody around town said they'd once heard Arlene call the little girl Paula. Maybe Violet felt it was her right to pick her own name for once, instead of everybody choosing higgledy-piggledy for her.

Ruby looked up and down, scanning the whole wall of pictures wondering if Violet had been on other TV programs and maybe she'd missed her. What if she'd been on *The Mary Tyler Moore Show*? It came on at the same time Ruby liked to watch *Hee Haw.* Violet could have been there and Ruby'd have missed her. Her heart raced thinking about how she could have known Violet was in Hollywood long before, and maybe already had this whole thing figured out.

Not every single picture in the room was of Violet, but pretty darn near. A poster hung on the wall to the right above a mattress. Ruby figured it must be a rock-and-roll star with that wild and crazy fluffed-out pink hair. He looked like when Imogene got carried away with the teasing comb and the rinse solution. It said FRAMPTON COMES ALIVE! across the top, and Ruby reckoned that had to be another way of saying he was about to have a conniption fit, because that's what he looked like. How much was Violet into that rock music? She recalled what Jimmy Ray Johnson had told her before she left Devine about drug fiends and rock and roll.

Below Mr. Frampton, the bed sat covered in a wide-striped orange and brown bedspread. It wasn't really covered as the bedspread was more wadded up than spread. The paisley sheets underneath were twisted and wadded as well.

"Know what this is, Ruby honey?" Then Loralva flopped down on the unmade bed and sank through.

Dear Lord, Ruby thought, she's going to disappear into the mattress. But Loralva bounced back up like she was riding a wave. They even heard the sloshing and slopping sound of water.

"A waterbed!" Loralva said, almost as happy as when she'd won the Big Spin on *The Price Is Right*. She bounced and jiggled up and down, kicked off her orange patent leather slides and slid out into the middle of the bed. Sloshing noises came from all around her. Ruby'd seen a waterbed before. Loralva's friend over in Cicada, Verdee Whitacre, had one. Almost all of Idyll County had gone over to her house one afternoon to get a good look at it. At least one half the county laid down on it and couldn't get back out. Ruby just admired it from a distance. She figured a regular mattress would do her just fine. Besides, how could a person sleep with all the worrying about leaks?

"Loralva, ain't right to mess with somebody else's things."

"Oh come on, Ruby. It's obvious she's gone."

Loralva was right. Why'd she keep having to be reminded of it? Even Jay had said the place was for rent.

"She's probably moved to her movie star mansion," Loralva said. "I think I should get me one of these. It's not like I couldn't find use for another bed. Maybe I could trade my Broyhill dining room suite for a bed like this one." She wiggled around some more, making the mattress slap against the sideboards. "Woo-hoo!" she carried on, riding the waterbed waves.

A box at the end of the bed had piles of paper stapled together into books, just thrown in like they were heading toward the trash. "These must be scripts," Ruby said, rifling through. Pulling a couple out of the pile, she handed a few to Loralva. The cover of one Ruby pulled out said *Starsky and Hutch.* She flipped through the pages looking for something, anything, that said what part Violet had played.

"Oh Lordy," Loralva said, as she flipped through one of hers. "*Only One Life,* Ruby. Violet tried out for our soap opera." She thumbed the pages and Ruby ran and sat on the wooden edge of the waterbed right next to Loralva. Looking over her shoulder they both saw it at the same time. Red ink underlining the part for a person named Cleo. Ruby read over Loralva's shoulder line by line. It didn't look good for Lina and Jason—their third marriage wouldn't work out after all.

"Well, I'll be jiggered," Loralva said, throwing the script back in the box.

"You don't suppose Violet got that part, do you?" Ruby asked, feeling panicky.

"No," Loralva said, digging through the box. "Didn't this Cleo woman already make one appearance, back when Jason was in the hospital for syphilis?"

Ruby didn't remember any Cleo from before, but she did remember the syphilis and figured that was why their relationship could never work. "Was this Cleo you remember blond-headed or brunette?"

"Think she was red-headed like me." She ran a long nail through her Farrah Fawcett feathered bangs. Ruby figured Loralva only said that to make her feel better and keep her from thinking Violet had played the part.

"You ain't a real redhead, and you don't know for sure about Violet not being this Cleo." She felt a lump climb up the whole of her esophagus and sit on the way back of her tongue. Felt like Violet was crossing them.

"Geez, Ruby honey." Loralva must have noticed the red hotness rise up from beneath Ruby's collar. "Get ahold of yourself. It's just a soap opera."

She swallowed hard and bit her lip to bring herself back around. A smelliness sat in the apartment. A stink of deceit worse than that perm smell.

Lying back on the lapping waterbed, Loralva continued, "Maybe when we do catch up to her she'll invite us to a Hollywood party." Then, pulling herself to her knees, and having to hold on to the wall in order to keep from toppling over with the waves, she said, "Hey, ain't this the man that plays on *Dukes of Hazzard*?"

Loralva stared at a photo sharing the bottom right-hand tack with the Mr. Frampton poster. Ruby stepped closer to take a look, but she'd gotten herself tangled in a Glad bag full of T-shirts and wigs. Agitated, she stepped out of the pile and got up close. What she saw gave her a twinge in her heart. Maybe a hopeful twinge, maybe a nostalgic twinge—she didn't know which.

Violet and the man had their arms looped around each other. In the picture she wore an organza floweredy robe and had forgotten all about wearing a slip underneath.

"She's pretty near buck naked," Ruby said. With her fingertip she touched Violet's smiling face, but it only felt glossy and slick. Like plastic.

"Reckon she's definitely hanging out with the likes of them now. Hope she takes a liking to us again so that maybe she can let me get close up to one of them Dukes. I've had pretty good luck with fellas who go by 'Duke.'"

"I don't want to be running around half naked, even if it means being with famous people." Ruby sensed the wall of Violet pictures staring at her.

"Aw, Ruby honey, come on."

Ruby shook her head, hearing the pitpat-pitpat of her heart. She turned to look at something else, something not so compromising. All she caught sight of was the photo of Violet in the hot pants beckoning.

"Don't nobody wear clothes in California!" leaped out of her throat.

Loralva stopped her rolling around on the bed to look up at her.

"Don't start with me," Ruby said, afraid Loralva'd have one of her smart-aleck remarks. Ruby mimicked Loralva, "It's natural. Never hurt me none. Nakedness has gotten me a long way." Then she slapped a hand over her mouth. Her heart was between her rib cage and skin, and it seemed it would soon burst out of her chest. "I'm sorry," she said. "It's like the devil hisself got inside me."

"You got twenty-five Violets all coming at you at one time. Just take it easy, Ruby honey."

"All this ain't right. It's got me more prickled than trying to take a rubber band off a barrel cactus."

"Maybe we oughta go. You're getting all twisted up."

Ruby didn't answer at first because while she was all wrought up, she did like that she was at least touching Violet's things, even if it weren't Violet herself. Still frustrated, she finally said, "There's nothing familiar of Violet here, not even these pictures." She looked around the four walls, taking them all in at once. "This is just another dead end." The ding-ding of the full-service bells down at the gas station rattled Ruby's nerves, making her want to hurry. Her breathing slowed and she thought she had control of her heart, which had almost jumped clean through her blouse. Loralva leaned back, the water's slap slowing down. Then she raised herself to the edge of the bed.

"Hey look." Loralva reached down to the floor to pick up a wooden box carved all over with pictures of camels and decorated with little ivory nuggets stuck here and there. When Ruby'd gotten tangled in the Glad trash bag more items had fallen out.

"Mmm, sandalwood." Loralva put the box to her nose. Looked foreign to Ruby. Then turning it over looking at it, jangling the contents, Loralva said, "Want me to open it?"

Ruby hadn't answered before Loralva was already poking around inside the box with a finger.

"Nothing much," Loralva said. "Just a couple of broken necklaces, stuff like that."

Then the gas station owner, Paul, appeared in the doorway. "When do I get that ride you promised me?" A cloud of gasoline fumes lingered around him. His sun-bleached hair was recently combed. He'd startled Ruby the way he just appeared. No announcement, no creaking of the stairs. What if Violet made it up those stairs just as quietly? What if she already had and had turned around without them knowing?

Loralva set the sandalwood box on the waterbed with a rattle. "Ruby honey, I'll be right back. Wait right here." As she climbed out of the bed the mattress rose and fell.

Ruby headed toward Paul as well. "You know anything about"—and she had to swallow first—"the girl who lived here?" A fear of knowing more than she really wanted slithered up her backbone.

"Just that she moved," he said, staring at Loralva as he talked to Ruby. Men did that. "Said this place stunk worse than a chicken coop. I've never heard anybody use that expression before. Have you?" He laughed, like he really didn't expect them to answer.

Ruby'd heard it before. Plenty of times. Told her that Violet was still Texan. "Do you have a forwarding address, at least?"

"Nope," he replied. "Like I said, she didn't leave the happiest person, but she lived here more than two years. Told me to keep the deposit, which I would have anyway with the way she left the place. Guess she moved up. She's making national commercials now, you know."

"Okay. Hurry it up then," Ruby told her sister, as Loralva took off out the door. It gave her the shudders to be left there all alone. Loralva and Paul took off down the stairs, and she heard the roar of the Trans Am engine. Ruby stood and gave a good hard look around the room. No pictures of Bunny and Bubbie, just Violet, Violet, Violet and that tiny picture of the *Dukes of Hazzard* fella, and the big one of the pink Mr. Frampton. She tried smiling at the Violet-covered wall, but since none of the photos had a happy smiling face in them she didn't get any response. Every last one of them staring back at her like it was Ruby that had done something wrong. Those strong, powerful amethyst eyes, saying, "I am the one."

She peeked inside the yellow tiled bathroom with its dinky shower stall, which wasn't any bigger than Ruby's front coat closet. Not even a school picture of Bubbie missing his front tooth like she'd kept on the mirror in her bathroom in Devine.

It was so quiet and still inside, just an occasional ding-ding from down at the gas station. Ruby listened for Violet in that room. The closest sound she heard was the tick-*tick,* tick-*tick,* of her own Timex with the bowling pins for hands that Rascal had bought her for their twenty-fifth wedding anniversary. She wound it, a little too tight.

She sat on the edge of the waterbed's wood frame, straightening the covers, pulling the sheet down and stuffing it into the corner where it had slid up and revealed the rubber mattress. She picked up the box Loralva had set on the bed and stuck her own finger through the junk. It was plumb full of loose beads rolling around on the bottom, with a corroded bobby pin stuck to the edge. A set of three pink plastic buttons and one big wooden one. A purple bauble earring with no mate. As she pushed aside a sliver of tarnished chain from among the beads, she found one last thing. A tiny silver ring. A ring so small that it wouldn't fit past the first knuckle on Ruby's pinkie. The ring that Violet had had on her finger the day Ruby'd found her on that front porch.

Her heart went pitpat-pitpat, then stopped mid-pit. She listened for somebody coming up the stairs. Nothing. It made the lump sitting in her throat double in size and ache to squeeze out. She wanted to put the lid on the box. She reached across the orange and brown striped bedspread for it, but it was too far out of her reach. She scooted over a bit, but when she went to put her hand onto the mattress to support herself, the water-filled rubber bladder sank under her. Her balance off, she tilted over and tried again to hold herself up with the bed, but then just toppled all the way over, sliding off the solid wood edge and plunking sideways into the mattress. Every time she tried putting weight on her arms she flopped up on the other side. She found herself wallowing around in the bed like a trout on the beach. The sandalwood box tumbled over spilling all of its contents. The plastic beads rolled off to new corners and hiding places. Baubles bounced into the sheets. Even the ring rolled out into the wad of bed linens. Grappling with the sheets and bedspread, Ruby reached for anything she could get her hands on that might help pull her up. She was drowning and she wasn't even underwater.

When she finally pulled herself from that bed and stood up, she was madder than a bluetick dog with a rattler in its pen. Ruby scrounged around the bed, keeping her feet firmly planted on the floor this time, gathering the lost beads into the box, searching for the ring. Even after reaching her hands down into the corners of the mattress, she couldn't find it. Oh, never mind, she thought, it was an ugly reminder of an ugly time. She should have thrown it away in the first place. Ruby had only kept it because it reminded her of the day she'd found her daughter. She sensed the eyes on the wall staring down at her. Yet it meant nothing to Violet. She'd left it behind in this apartment to be tossed out. She'd thrown away her last remnants of Devine. Of her past.

Finally, under a wad of paisley sheet and a purple bra that had gotten mixed in with the covers, the ring fell out and Ruby nabbed it. She looked at it for a second, rolling it between her fingers. It wasn't perfectly round but bent almost triangular, and bumped on her fingertips as she rolled it. Quickly, as if someone might be watching, she put it in the left breast pocket of her blouse. Then she resigned herself to waiting standing up.

Though the day was only nearing late afternoon, the apartment had already filled with darkness. A thin window above Mr. Frampton and the open front door allowed the only light to come in. Ruby had an urge to open a shutter or blind, but there were none, just half-naked Violets staring down at her. She didn't want to be there. This she knew for certain.

No photos of Bunny and Bubbie on the wall. This meant Violet had no worries about Bubbie and his acting up, no thoughts about telling Bunny where her momma had got off to. But for

Ruby, all she had to do was picture the kids' faces with MoonPie icing smeared in the corners of their mouths and she'd want them near. Violet, too, used to get chocolate smudges on her lips.

She went outside and onto the landing, pulling the door to behind her, shutting Violet in on one side, herself on the other. Now, standing on this landing, listening for the rumble of Loralva's Trans Am, Ruby looked around, taking in the rest of what Violet must have called home. That fire-red bougainvillea climbing the banister didn't grow in Devine with the frost in the winter, so Ruby'd never seen it up close. She wondered why something so beautiful would come without a scent. She'd take a little bundle of it back to the motel. A piece of Violet that wouldn't be too obvious, but would brighten up the dingy motel room. But as she reached inside the vine to break off a twig, what felt like a prickly pear spine slid up under her fingernail. She pulled her hand back quickly and stuck her finger in her mouth to soothe the pain. All that boiling heat eating away at her heart had caused her insides to melt, spilling out in tears. Never in her wildest dreams would she have figured a bougainvillea for having thorns. But there they were, on closer look, long spikes hidden in the twist of dark green limbs and leaves. She blew her nose on the Kleenex she kept tucked in her sleeve, but let the tears keep rolling like a salve. Ruby made her way down the stairs, sucking out tiny drops of blood from her sore finger. All the aches inside her came out with each drop tasting of wrought iron. The salt from her tears blended in as well. Her eyes clouded, and the sky, too, had started to get a fuzzy cloud cover coming from the direction of the ocean. Thick foggy clouds, not like the dark stormy clouds they'd get in Texas now and again. This was more of a wall.

She made her way down, and at the bottom of the steps she looked around for Loralva, the Trans Am, or even Paul. None were in sight. Maybe she should be worried something evil happened to Loralva, but she suspected Paul, who had some good-looking features, was the one in trouble. Poor Jay tended to all the windshields and gas tanks by his lonesome.

The red-leather-clad fella across the street at Leather Togs by Bep waved at Ruby. She didn't feel like being friendly right that moment, so she didn't wave back. Instead, she sat down on the second-to-the-last step and the cold concrete seeped through her culottes. June in Los Angeles and it was downright nippy. In Devine, you wouldn't hardly be able to make it halfway across the gravel parking lot in front of the Bowl before you'd start perspiring. A little shiver wound its way through her.

Her mind took to remembering a nip in the air on the day Violet was found, and it settled there. She'd had to use Crisco to work the tiny ring off Violet's finger. Maybe somewhere in the back of her mind Ruby'd wanted to keep a reminder of that bittersweet day. She'd never meant for Violet to have it. Violet must have found the ring herself at the bottom of the blue-velvet-lined jewelry box Ruby kept inside her panty drawer. What must Violet remember of that day? Did she remember it and maybe the awful days that came before it? Or did it wash from her memory like Ruby had always hoped?

She'd had no problem throwing away that soiled dress Violet had worn—swiss dot with puffy sleeves all deflated. Ruby didn't even put it in the wash. She dressed her in a pink frilly dress that Perlesta Clyde's daughter had outgrown and cleaned her up good before taking her to that nice doctor over in Del Agua.

Dr. Gibbons let Ruby listen to Violet's tiny three-year-old heart. When she'd put that stethoscope in her own earholes, she heard a heart beating, that was certain, loud and clear. But it didn't sound like the heartbeat she heard when she lay her head on Rascal's hairy chest in bed at night. No, this heart didn't beat so much as go: whoosh, click, whoosh, click, click, click, whoosh.

A heart whoosh, she supposed it would be called instead. Only thing the doctor said was wrong with her, only thing other than those bruises, was that she had a tiny hole in her heart.

"Does the blood leak out?" she'd asked that Dr. Gibbons with the red mustache. He'd shook his head and looked like he might even laugh, but then he said some other mumbo jumbo about how it was really a valve sticking or some such thing and Ruby thought it sounded like Rascal's diesel engine problems. Little Violet sat on the edge of the doctor's table, still as an owl, only her eyes moving, glancing toward them, then away.

"Will she"—Ruby had to whisper the next question so the little girl wouldn't hear—"will she live?" Little Violet pulled at the hem of Perlesta Clyde's daughter's dress and tugged on a thread with her knotted hands. The dark-haired girl with the narrow face, no baby fat at all, sat ridged and waiting. Shy, Ruby had figured. The doctor's red mustache twitched and he reassured Ruby that little Violet just wouldn't be up to running. Ruby breathed a sigh of more than relief because at the bowling alley where they'd be spending most of their time anyhow, no running was allowed, nor really even called for.

Now, sitting on those cold stairs, she remembered one more thing Dr. Gibbons had said. "She'll grow out of it." And Ruby felt her fingers go icy. Maybe Violet hadn't. Maybe instead the hole had grown bigger.

Taking the ring from her pocket she looked at the bent metal, tarnished to the color of charcoal grease. She slid it onto her pricked pointer finger even though it wouldn't go past the moon on her nail. It was snug there, and she imagined it on the little grubby hand of the three-year-old. Felt her own pulse throb against the tightness of the ring.

Jay walked up to her then, and stood almost directly in front of her. She saw his black and white high-top sneakers first, then the gray coveralls. "You aren't gonna get sick, are you?"

Ruby looked up, knowing she probably had mascara scars down her face. She'd let the tears roll on their own. Didn't feel like wiping them away. They felt warm and she felt cold, so it was a comfort in a way. "No, I'm fine," she said, thick and muddle-headed, not putting much effort into it.

"Because if you are, I can pull the water hose over here and clean it up."

"Just waiting for my sister to get back is all," she said, thinking he was a nice kid and some momma somewhere was probably proud.

"Oh yeah, huh." Jay shrugged. "Went off with my dad to the beach. My dad's divorced, you know. So it's okay, if that's what you're thinking."

Maybe Bubbie'd be a gentle boy like this when he grew up. "Bet your momma's proud of you. Working after school. Working hard, too."

"Who knows. She's married to somebody else. Lives in Nevada." He shifted his weight on the sneakers and kicked at a crack in the asphalt.

"Don't you see your momma no more?" Ruby felt the tears rise up in her all over again.

"Oh, she like, wanted me to go with her." He talked slow and casual like Ruby was realizing all Californians did. "But, man, there's no surf in Nevada."

"Did you know my daughter?" She pointed up the stairs. "Who lived up there?" She'd wanted to ask the question since he first walked up, but feared the answer. Scared he'd say yes and maybe tell her things she didn't want to hear. Awful things like Judy Harper and Jimmy Ray Johnson told her about dress-stealing transvestites.

"A little," Jay shrugged.

"What was she like?"

"She was all right. Kind of in a hurry all the time. I tried to be nice to her, but she never said anything back. Probably not interested in talking to a kid. Know what I mean?"

"Probably just all that hurrying, like you said," Ruby excused her daughter, wondering if Violet would give her the time of day.

"My dad says she's wanting the moon. The moon and the sky, but mostly what she's getting is—. Well, I can't repeat to you what he says she's getting. But she's got a TV spot now, so I guess it's working."

"Do you know where she's moved to?" She folded her hands together, trying to warm them.

"Nah. Better address probably." He looked at Ruby for a moment, like he was trying to figure out what to make of her. She twisted the ring once around her finger. The full-serve bells rang and he took off. She wanted to ask him if Violet ever mentioned her own children. That she was a momma. But she reckoned Violet hadn't. Something in the way he talked about her said he didn't think of her in that way. As a momma. But Ruby still did.

From across the street the red-leathered fella waved again. Ruby waved back, so as not to be impolite.

The sky got low and gray and thick. It did that a lot in California. In Devine, you knew what kind of day was sitting on top of you: hot and blazing, or wet and drenching. Loud cracking thunder with the sky lit up with lightning, or the whooshing of wind, or even the silent snapping of the heat. But not in California. The sky moved in and out like an accordion and never dropped an ounce of rain, just sat there goopy and dingy. To Ruby, that color sky had to weigh on folks' lives. It weighed on hers.

She wiped at the salty sticky stains on her face, hoping the tears would slow down for a bit. She wanted someone to talk to. Wanted Loralva to come back and make her laugh. Loralva never let bad moods slow down the fun for too long.

Maybe she should pray. Maybe if she said to that God in Heaven above that she wanted her Violet back, He'd hear her. He'd say, "Ruby honey" (she pictured him talking freely like Loralva), "you been so good and such a darling your whole darn" (because he wouldn't say damn) "life, that if you want your Violet back I'm gonna see to it that she comes back to you. And, as an extra bonus prize, I'll see to it that she's a bluebonnet of mommas to Bubbie and Bunny."

Thing was, Ruby didn't necessarily (this was the part she had to whisper, even in her head) believe there was a God, at least not one that acted like that. If there was a God, and she wasn't really saying there was or wasn't one, He'd be kinder than whoever she'd been dealing with so far. He'd see what needed to be done and she wouldn't have to ask. And she wasn't referring to requests for a new bowling ball or Imogene wanting a new Coupe de Ville with electric windows.

But Ruby was willing to figure for the sake of this moment that there was a God and she decided to pray, thinking it might be her last hope. She started composing her prayer. She wanted it to be the right words, the right request so it didn't get mixed up in the delivery. She didn't want Him to miss the importance of it.

She started with "Please bring us together again," and just thinking it made her heart go thumpy. That was too close to asking for a miracle, since Violet was now living all the way out in Hollywood. The Catholics were in charge of the miracles. The Protestants had hallelujah moments instead.

She tried "Give us back," no, not "back," because, thing was, that girl had some rottenness eating away at her long before she ran off. If He brought back *that* Violet it would just start all over again.

How about asking him to bring a new and improved family-size Violet like her box of Tide? Nope, because if she was new and improved, that is with none of those rotting spots on her heart, then it would be because she'd never been left on that front porch in the first place. In which case, she would have grown up with that Arlene Fowler woman instead of Ruby and Rascal. Ruby wasn't saying she appreciated what Arlene had done, no sirree. She wanted God to be clear on that point. But you can't pray to God to change the past, now can you?

Could she pray to Him to change the present?

Sitting on the bottom step of the long staircase to Violet's apartment, she waited for something to happen. Her will was strong enough. She'd come all this way. She asked Him right then to bring her a sign, a hint, a bit of her Violet that told her what she needed to do next to bring as much peace as was possible at this late date to the hearts of Bunny and Bubbie, and herself. She added herself considering she was the one doing the asking. Was that a good enough prayer? Did she need to say it in a church, someplace more powerful than the cold bottom step of Violet's apartment? Maybe she should call Suddy and ask her to put it out to the First Methodist congregation in Devine, which was now praying at the Bowl anyhow. Maybe they'd get the message to God, if there was one, that she needed a sign on what to do next. But no, she figured a true God would hear her all the way out here in California. With that, she stood up from the step. Waiting could make a person very hungry.

Across the pavement, Jay continued to clean windshields and pump gas as she went up to the soda pop machine that stood by the door of the station office. She put a quarter in and pulled on a bottle of Dr. Pepper from the holes on the side. But as she yanked she didn't pull hard enough and the quarter got swallowed. She yanked and pulled some more, but the Dr. Pepper wouldn't budge and the serrated edges of the bottle top started to cut into her hand. Jay noticed her struggle and hollered, "Go inside and wait, I'll get you another one. It jams all the time."

Once inside she scanned the boxes of candy bars and nuts and chips on the shelves in front of the cash register. And then, after having searched all the grocery and convenience stores near the Pink 7 Motel, Ruby spotted a box of MoonPies! She took the whole box. Bunny and Bubbie would be so pleased, especially after having to stay with Imogene. She'd give them one each as soon as she got back to the motel.

The full-serve bells rang and the roar of the engine made Ruby turn. The black and gold Trans Am vibrated in front of the doors. Jay came running in then and got the pop machine keys out of the drawer.

"You don't need to worry about the soda pop. I'll just take these," Ruby said.

That's when he noticed the mound of the cellophane-wrapped MoonPies in front of Ruby. "You like those too?" he said.

"It's a Texas treat," she said, as he rang her up. "Haven't been able to find MoonPies anywhere else in town."

"Yeah, that's what your daughter said too."

"She did often have a hankering for a MoonPie," Ruby said. Even Bunny knew that. She paid him for the pile of pies.

As she scooped them up and headed out the door to the Trans Am she almost ran into Paul as he came in.

"Whew, she's hot," he said, wiping his brow. And Ruby knew he didn't mean the car or the weather. She headed back to the vibrating black behemoth, wishing she had more than MoonPies from this visit.

That night she gave the kids MoonPies for dessert. They had also been treated to MoonPies for their snack when she got home. Now they watched the prime-time TV shows and Ruby counted how many MoonPies she had come away with. Sixteen. She'd left two in the carton at the station and remembered that it read "24/case" on the side. That meant they'd sold six, probably all to Violet.

She settled in to watch TV with the kids on the floor and Loralva on the couch beside her, the dinner dishes put away. Imogene had trotted off to her adjoining room saying she'd had *enough* for one day. She'd spent the day by the pool with the kids and had had too much sun, not to mention too much of the kids. She had a sunburn the color of a rhubarb pie.

Between sitcoms a newsbreak came on. Another report about the flooding in Texas. These hundred year floods were always the same. Ruby knew there'd be tremendous damage on her return and she didn't want to think about that along with what kind of damage she was facing right here in California.

The news station had helicopters buzzing the rooftops, showing all the cars sunk window deep and the hubcaps floating by. They flew over pastures that had turned into lakes and careened lower to get a shot of a homestead. Then Ruby saw the roof of Earl Glidden's ranch house. Someone came out the front doors waving up at the chopper. At first she thought he was in trouble and she bolted from her seat on the couch, pushed herself to a standing position.

"Hey, that's Earl Glidden!" Loralva said, as Ruby jumped from the couch.

But now, as Ruby saw him waving at those news cameras, she knew he wasn't waving because it was the TV station. He was waving at her. So she waved back. She'd be seeing him soon, she thought. *I'm following that trail, like you said,* she almost said to the TV. As the cameras moved on to more flood damage, she took her seat.

"Looked like he was doing okay," Loralva said. Ruby nodded. He made her homesick. She wanted to be back in Texas. She looked over at the pile of MoonPies on the kitchenette table.

You can't really ever get the Texas out of your blood, she reckoned. Then she screamed, "Loralva! I got it."

"What?" Loralva stood up too. "What is it?"

"Tomorrow," Ruby said, gulping, "tomorrow we go back to the filling station."

MoonPies and Mudflaps

I can't give you your money back," Paul said, standing behind the gas station counter staring at Ruby with the box of MoonPies she said she was returning. "I can't sell those things to anyone. No one likes them but your daughter. She asked me to order them in the first place."

"I don't want my money back." She set the box of MoonPies on the counter and scooted them across to Paul's side. "I just want you to put them back so that they'll be on the shelf when Violet comes back for one."

"What makes you so sure she'll be back?" he asked.

"She came back that one time after she moved out," Jay said, standing next to his father behind the cash register. "About a week after."

"She just came to get her mail," Paul said.

"Did she buy a MoonPie then?" Ruby wanted to know.

"I sold her three," Jay said.

Ruby was relieved to know her hunch had been right. Violet did come by to get MoonPies after she moved out. After all, this was the only place in town that sold them. They'd even ordered them special at Violet's request.

"She only came in that one time, about three weeks ago," Jay said, shrugging, and Paul nodded.

"Mind if I sit on the steps and wait for her?" Ruby asked. "I won't be a bother."

"We don't get that much mail for her anymore. Don't know how long it'll be till she picks it," Paul said. "She's rich now. May be she won't even come for it."

"You got MoonPies," Ruby answered. "She'll be back."

They couldn't think of any reason why she couldn't wait, so that's what she did.

That morning she had packed a lunch, and told Imogene what happened the day before. "You know how Violet loved her MoonPies. I just know she'll show up to that service station at least one more time for her MoonPies. I'm going be there every day until she does."

"Waste of time, if you ask me," Imogene had responded, eyeing the kids across the room. "Don't know why you'd want to sit at a dumpy gas station, just waiting. Tell those boys that work there to have her call when she shows up."

"She'd just run away again. Nope, I have to be there when she arrives." Ruby stuffed a tuna sandwich and a margarine tub of potato salad in a paper sack, then kissed the kids good-bye, telling them she was oh-so-close to finding their momma. She noticed Bunny didn't ask when they'd see her, and Bubbie didn't take his eyes off the TV screen. Even Loralva, when Ruby climbed in the car, wasn't so sure about this.

"You got Duke's number to call if you want to come home early, right?"

"I do," Ruby said, "but I'm determined to sit and wait."

And that's what she did. She'd brought along her plastic-covered foam stadium seat cushion that said HOOK 'EM HORNS in burnt orange and the remainder of the MoonPies that she'd bought the day before. If Violet did come back for a pie, she wanted them to be there for her. On the cold concrete steps she sat watching the cars pull into full-serve, soon knowing the timing of the bells. Ding-ding for the front set of tires, then she had enough time to say "Imogene eats crow" in her head before the back tires rolled over the tube a second time.

She ate her tuna sandwich at ten o'clock and then was hungry again by three. She bought a handful of Boston baked peanuts from the penny machine. Jay came over to her stoop now and again and chatted with her. He seemed to like her company as much as she liked his.

"Do you think she may be back this week?" she asked. "How often did she usually buy a MoonPie when she lived here?" She thought she could strategize about the time when Violet would arrive, because she was as certain Violet would be back as she was Loralva could get a man to swoon.

But Jay always just shrugged and said, "I didn't really get to know her all that well. Not that I didn't try."

Ruby knew what he meant, that Violet had a bit of a snobby attitude.

The day wore on and with each car that came into the station she craned her neck to see if it was Violet at the steering wheel. She had no doubt she'd recognize her daughter's slightest shadow. But not even so much as a whiff of Violet passed through that gas station all day. As it came closer to closing time at the station, when Loralva had promised to return, Ruby's butt bones ached so much from the concrete step that she decided she'd have to ask Penny if she could borrow a folding chair from the poolside for the following days.

She stood up and tried to stretch her body parts back into a straight position. Jay came over again. "We got mail for her today," he said. "It might be junk mail. It's one of those envelopes with the cellophane window, you know?"

Ruby rubbed the back of her hip where she'd gotten a good cramp right then. Jay dug his hands in his pockets. This didn't sound like anything all that important, just a piece of junk mail. Violet probably wouldn't even know it was missing. "Maybe it's a bill?" she asked, but she figured Jay or Paul would recognize a bill.

Jay kicked a crack in the asphalt with the toe of his high-top sneaker. "Dad said he thought it could be a check, but he doubted it."

"A check?" Ruby asked, her aches and pains disappearing. "Can I see it?"

"I guess," he said. She followed him to the office. A blue Pinto pulled up to the self-service pump. Ruby paused to see who was driving. It wasn't Violet, so she kept walking.

In the office, Paul slid the envelope across the counter and said, "I can't let you open it. It's probably just trash, but I have to hold on to it."

Ruby said that was okay. She didn't need to touch it because from where she stood on her side of the counter, right in front of the MoonPies, she could see that on the top right-hand corner of the envelope were the words *Carlyle Agency, LLC.* Through the clear plastic window she could see the checkered safety paper of a check. Her ButterMaid check, Ruby reckoned. Her heart whammed against her chest. They had tricked the agent into giving them Violet's old address, and in all the hullabaloo it hadn't dawned on her that the check would be arriving there too.

She looked up at Paul and Jay, and with her most serious of faces so they would know she meant it, she said, "She'll be back. Whatever you do, don't let on that I'm around."

* * *

When she walked into the apartment that night hell had split down the middle and Imogene held the ax. The skunk-headed mother-in-law had the phone up to her ear and she was yelling obviously at Suddy because she kept repeating, "I don't give a fig's patoot what you prayed for, you let Harley go and marry that girl! Now I'm ruined!" Bunny wailed, tugging on Imogene's skirt-tail to no avail, while Bubbie sat stiff as a gravestone, staring at the TV with news shots of the flood damage in South Texas.

"How could you let him run off to Mexico to marry that . . . that . . . simple cake baker!" Imogene screamed. "Don't matter! It ain't legal!" Her face scrunched so tight tears couldn't even eke out of her ducts. "You mean to tell me he took those divorce papers I'd thrown in the kitchen trash and filed them at the Idyll County Court House himself? He don't have the gumption." She paced the length of the phone cord would let her. "Going and having a mind of his own—what kind of ungrateful son is that? Seems everyone is turning against me. I won't be having none of that!"

Loralva had only dropped Ruby off then had gone off with Duke, who she was now seeing every day. Bunny hurried toward Ruby when she stepped in the door and Bubbie's face even seemed to soften a bit. "GranMomma!" Bunny cried, gobs of snot on her upper lip from crying for a long time.

"I will be there soon enough to set things back to my liking" were Imogene's last words as she hung up the phone with a slam. When she turned around and saw Ruby coming in the doorway she said, "Rooby! Everything is a bigger mess than a tornado path!"

"GranMomma!" Bunny wailed.

Ruby wanted to turn around and go back out and for the teensiest of seconds wondered if that's what made Violet leave, that same need for escape. Instead, she let Bunny wipe her smudgy face in the hem of her culottes and said, "No worries."

"Bubbie says—"

"Harley has gone completely against my wishes. It's like the devil has got into him." Imogene stood behind Bunny, her face red as a potted geranium.

"Momma told Bubbie—"

"When are you gonna get Violet? What you are doing isn't working! It could be too late already."

"Bubbie says she don't wanna be a momma!!" The liquid face buried itself in Ruby's skirt again.

"I've contacted the Hollywood police," Imogene said, still screaming her words, "and I'm going downtown tomorrow to file a missing persons report, or some such thing."

Ruby hoisted the little girl onto her hip, pushed past Imogene and went over to Bubbie. "Are you making up stories?"

"Ruby, are you listening to me!" Imogene had reached a decibel level equal to when she'd hollered into the phone at Suddy.

Bubbie wouldn't look at Ruby, and instead turned his eyes down to his grimy bare feet.

"The police will find her!" Imogene let out a huge angry sigh behind Ruby, then went to the connecting doors saying, "I'll just have that marriage to Becca Ann annulled, that's what I'll do." She now had a small smile on her face. Before she closed the door she yelled, "Ruby, you're wasting time at that filling station! I'm finding Violet and things are going to be different around here!"

That night Ruby slept fitfully and woke with a start several times. After one heart-thumping jolt she lay listening for something. She thought maybe she'd heard one of the kids call out, so she went down the short hall to the living room where the foldout couch took up the whole room. The air conditioning rumbled, so she listened hard for a small-voiced "GranMomma?" But Bunny lay on her back, pouty mouth open in a sleep gape. Bubbie lay curled up on his side, hands near his face, balled up in fists, but loosened from sleep. Neither kid showed any signs of what Ruby had rumbling around in her stomach. But hadn't their fits and fights gotten worse as the search got closer to its end? What if she actually got to Violet? Or what if they never got to Violet? She wasn't sure which was better anymore. The air conditioner conked off and Bubbie's fists tightened and his eyes fluttered. He stared at Ruby for a moment. She started to say "It's just me," but his lids dropped shut and his fists loosened, so she reckoned he figured it out or thought he was dreaming.

The next morning Imogene's hollering continued. "I'm going to that police station and you can stay here and mind those kids!"

"No," Ruby told her. "Violet's showing up today or tomorrow. I just know it." She combed Bunny's hair, yanking too hard on the tangles and making the little girl yelp.

"You are such a fool!" Imogene screamed so loud that Ruby knew Penny and Warren had to be hearing her all the way down in the motel office. "Those MoonPies are not going to lure her back! It's like you think they are lightning bugs and she's a striped bass. She won't bite!"

Ruby hadn't shared the news about the check with Imogene. She was afraid Imogene would take over, that she'd go to the gas station and scare Violet off. So she tried to ignore Imogene's rants and busied herself with getting the kids up, washed and dressed. Loralva hadn't returned from her night out with Duke and that was making her nervous already. They needed to get on the road. Ruby wanted to be at the gas station as soon as they opened.

"I called Suddy back last night and she said she would look into how legal a wedding in Mexico really is," Imogene said, still carrying on, her coffee cup splashing as she talked and waved her hands.

Bubbie sat in front of the TV in just his little-boy briefs, and wouldn't let Ruby put his clothes on. "Come on, Bub," she tried to coax.

"He said he ain't gonna get dressed for a momma that don't want him," Bunny said. The little girl squeezed her Mrs. Beasley doll tight as she stood between Ruby and Bubbie.

"We're gonna see. I'm going to find your momma today or tomorrow." Ruby tried to sound perky about it. Even Bunny had turned on her it seemed. "But only if I can get you dressed."

"You don't need to bother," Imogene said. "I'm going to take my shower now and then I'm heading to the police station. The kids don't need to be dressed to stay here."

Loralva walked in the door then and Ruby breathed a sigh of relief.

"We need to get back to the gas station," Ruby said. "I thought you were gonna be back last night!" Ruby's own voice started to rise. Bunny got teared up when that happened, so she tried to act calm again.

"That Duke!" Loralva said, smiling, oblivious to the fighting going on in the motel room right then. "He just wouldn't let me leave. Ooo-eee." She wiggled her hips.

"Loralva!" Ruby stood up. "We don't have time for this. We have to go!" Her hands sweaty, she dropped the hairbrush and it knocked Bunny's elbow on the way down. Already near tears, the girl let loose.

"You aren't leaving me here with those kids," Imogene said. "I'm going to get ready and then I'm leaving!" With that she stormed out the adjoining door.

"Things are a little uptight in here," Loralva said, looking at the three remaining faces.

"That's not the half of it," Ruby said. "Help me get the kids ready." She tried soothing Bunny by rubbing her sore elbow. "We have to get over there right away. I don't want to miss a single minute."

"Let me just tinkle," Loralva said.

"No! There's no time," Ruby said. Her throat had clenched and the words came out squeaky. She grabbed both the kids' hands. "Come on, let's take the kids down to Penny. She can watch them."

"I can't even pee?" Loralva said, setting her purse down.

"You go to the bathroom, I'll take the kids to Warren and Penny's and I'll meet you at the car."

"Okeydokey," Loralva said.

Couldn't she for once move a little faster, Ruby thought. She took the kids by their hands, Bunny still whining and Bubbie having to be half drug to the door, still in his briefs. Ruby wanted to get out the door before Imogene got back and she wanted to get to the gas station before they opened, but nothing was going her way. Was this a sign, she wondered as she made her way down the stairs with the kids.

Penny was more than happy to watch them. Ruby'd handed her the clothes she'd meant for Bubbie to wear and Penny'd told Ruby not to worry about them at all. She stood at the passenger door of the Trans Am now, trying the door handle again. It was locked. No one locked their cars in Devine. No need to. Hurry up, Loralva, she screamed in her head. Finally, she saw her sister come traipsing down the stairwell. She had combed her hair and put on lipstick too.

"We don't have time to dillydally!" Ruby yelled up to her sister, and wondered if it was possible to just completely burst out of her skin.

"We'll get there in plenty of time. What are you so worried about? They don't open for an hour," Loralva said.

"It's rush hour," Ruby said. "Penny said it will be a madhouse out there on those highways or freeways or whatever they call them."

Ruby looked out the side window of the Trans Am. It felt strange to be on a big five-lane freeway jam-packed with cars and be able to see the white painted line on the asphalt. She couldn't recall if she'd ever sat at a dead stop on a highway before.

Loralva tapped the horn. "We haven't moved in five minutes. They might as well call this the Interstate 10 parking lot." She pushed the down button on her electric window and hung her head out to see what was around the car in front of her. Just more traffic as far as she could see.

Ruby took a deep breath. She didn't want to say anything, but her nerves wouldn't let her keep her mouth shut. "Told you we needed to leave sooner. You should have gotten home when you said you would."

"Ruby honey, Duke is not the kind of man I can say no to. And you know there aren't very many men like that for me." She pulled her head back in the window and pushed the button that made the glass zip up.

Ruby reached over and turned up the air conditioner. She had been perspiring since she got in the car. It started when Imogene had yelled over the balcony as they drove off that she'd be getting the police and she'd find Violet first. "Surely, Loralva," Ruby said, trying to keep her cool and not doing very well, "you know this is the most important thing to me."

"Course I do!" Loralva said, pulling the car a few feet ahead as the traffic eked along. "But it's not going to make any difference what time you get there. Violet won't show up first thing. What are the chances of that?" She pulled ahead a few more feet.

"What am I going to say to her when I do see her?" Ruby

asked. The fella in the car next to them kept combing his hair with one of those wide combs that everyone in California carried in their back pockets.

"You're gonna tell her to come on home to Texas," Loralva said.

"She's not gonna want to come back to Texas when she's living out here now." Ruby stared at the gold eagle embossed on the floor mat.

"Reckon not," Loralva said, and the car fell silent underneath the roar of the idling engine.

"She's got two kids that she needs to consider," Ruby finally said. "I'll be sure to remind her of that." She looked out the side window as they slowly drove along an overpass. "All those cars down there on the side streets are moving regular speeds. How can that be? What are we doing up here at a near standstill when all those cars are moving?"

"The freeways are supposed to be faster," Loralva said.

"That don't make sense," Ruby said. "But nothing makes sense anymore." She leaned to the right and looked for the next big green sign. "Can you change lanes and get on over there?" Ruby asked. "I think our exit is coming up."

"I'll get over as soon as a space opens up," Loralva said, looking over her shoulder to the right.

"Turn your blinker on!" Ruby said, her voice getting skittery again. "How they gonna know you want over if you don't give them forewarning? Jack Griffith is always doing the same, never uses his blinker and when I get behind his pickup I fear for my life I'm going to rear-end him." Ruby's tongue had nerves fluttering and she couldn't keep quiet now.

The traffic started moving a bit more, actually getting up to speed, but Loralva still wasn't in the right lane to take the next exit. "You need to get over," Ruby reminded again, anxious that

Loralva would miss it and they'd be even later than they already were.

"I know, I know." Loralva turned her blinker on.

Finally! Ruby thought.

"Watch out for that car in front of you!" Ruby said. "You're following too close."

Loralva changed lanes and slowed down to take the exit. A brown Chrysler pulled in front of her and she had to hit the brakes.

"Oh Lordy," Ruby said, "we're not going to make it there at all."

"Would you hush up," Loralva said, "you sound like Imogene for damn sake."

"Imogene!" That just got Ruby going on more. She ranted all the way down the side street to the gas station about how Imogene wasn't doing her part and now she was going to ruin everything by calling the police.

"She can't even be a grandmother. You'd think she and Violet were blood relatives the way they don't own up to their responsibilities!" Ruby was saying as the car bounced over the driveway curb into the gas station. The bump in the road made her quiet down a bit. Paul stood beside a car in full-serve pumping gas. "They're already open," Ruby said. "Damn traffic jam." Then she noticed the fancy mudflaps on a yellow convertible Dodge Dart that sat at the full-serve pumps. "Would you get a load of those mudflaps," Ruby said to Loralva. Black leatherette rubber with a row of red reflectors along the bottom. The best part was the stainless steel studs that spelled out an initial.

"I gotta get me some of those for the Trans Am," Loralva said, as she pulled toward the parking area.

"Loralva"—Ruby turned her head toward her sister—"that's

a V on those mudflaps." Ruby looked over to see Jay working away in the office as Loralva drove across the asphalt.

"Loralva!" Ruby screamed.

"I see the puddle," Loralva said. "Now calm down." She veered the car over to the apartment staircase.

"No, over there in the office," Ruby said, pointing, and turning to look over her shoulder to see. "It's Violet! She's already here! Park the car. Oh my Lord! What do I do?"

"Violet?" Loralva said. "She's here?" She pulled the Trans Am up to the parking spaces by the far wall.

"Turn off the car!" Ruby said, crawling into her seat and onto her knees to look out the back window. *"Your loud engine will give away that we are here."*

"You don't want her to see you?" Loralva asked.

"Not until I'm ready!" Ruby saw the tall lanky back of Violet standing at the cash register. Jay was talking to her while Paul walked back in the door after pumping the gas out at the car.

"When are you going to be ready?" Loralva said. "She'll leave before you get up your nerve. Now go on."

Ruby watched her daughter's back for a few more seconds. She wore a sundress the same color yellow as her car, which was a convertible, of course. This was California.

"Get on over there," Loralva said. She reached across Ruby and opened the passenger door. "Go before she gets away again."

Ruby looked at Loralva, afraid of those last words. Then climbed out.

Her pace across the asphalt was fast, then slow, then fast. When she got up to the doorway she heard Jay saying, "Want me to ring up a MoonPie with that?"

Violet still had her back to Ruby and was laughing at Jay's question. Ruby put her finger to her lips to indicate to Paul a few feet away not to let on she was standing just outside the door. He shrugged, shook his head as if to say, whatever, it wasn't any of his business.

Ruby took in every part of Violet. She started with her long hair and wanted to reach out and touch it.

"Did Jay get you your check?" Paul asked her as he walked around the counter. Ruby's mind was scrambling around trying to think of the right way to enter, the right thing to say. Not too nice, but not too demanding. She wanted it to hit home.

"Got the check," Violet said. "Good thing I called my agent to ask for it. Never would have known it came here by mistake." Her yellow dress came to just the tops of her thighs. Her shoes were macramé ankle-strapped wedgies. High like Loralva would wear.

"Yeah, good thing," Jay said. Ruby could tell he had spotted her out the door and was trying not to look in her direction. Such a sweet kid. If only Bubbie could grow up to be like that.

"Hey, listen, do me a favor, okay?" Violet asked Paul and Jay. "Someone called my agent about this check and tricked him into giving them this address. Anyway, I think someone's looking for me and she may come by here."

Ruby's heart stopped. For the half a beat that it didn't move she thought Violet would say to tell this someone that she wanted to see her too. But that's not what Violet said at all and her heart went back to beating itself against her rib cage.

"Don't tell her anything about me, okay?" Violet put her money on the counter to pay the cost of the gas that Jay had just rung up.

The teenager took her cash and said, "Yeah, sure," and shrugged. Ruby thought he looked hurt and it wasn't even his own momma.

"How about you take these MoonPies off my hands," Paul said, reaching for the box.

"No thank you," Violet said, stepping back. "I've lost my taste for those things. Don't know who would eat them."

Ruby heard her cue. Knew that was when she needed to move in. She stepped inside the door and said, "I know two little ones who love them." She held her breath and felt her whole body tremble.

Violet turned around quickly. "Oh, man!" she said. Not the response Ruby had hoped for.

"We missed you, Violet," Ruby murmured, her hands quivering and her stomach feeling like it was on tumble dry with a crowbar.

Violet still stared, almost like she didn't quite recognize Ruby. "I guess I knew you'd find me someday." Her face went through a series of expressions.

"We saw you on the ButterMaid commercial," Ruby said, trying to fill in the puzzle for her. "You looked awful pretty." She smiled, forcing the edges of her mouth to tilt up a little further than they felt they had the right to go.

Jay and Paul scooted around them—Paul went out the back door to the garage and Jay passed them to fill up the cars that pulled in. After the "excuse me"s and changing of places Ruby was left not quite blocking Violet's way out the door.

"You doing all right out here?" Ruby asked.

Violet's mouth kept looking like it wanted to say something, but her jaw clenched it shut every time she opened it.

"Yeah sure," she finally said. "But look . . . I gotta run." She glanced at her watch to make the lie seem more real.

Ruby knew this was it—that Violet was about to make like a caged feral cat when the gate's opened. The shift in both their bodies gave it away too. Ruby moved forward as if to get a little closer, and Violet shifted to the side as though she hoped to slip away from Ruby's steady gaze. "Why'd you do it?" She stepped forward another step, and this time Violet stepped back and stiffened her shoulders.

"Do what?"

"Leave the kids. All of us. Without so much as a wave." She had wanted to sound calm, but her voice, unfortunately, had gone shaky.

"You have no business barging in on my life!" Violet threw her macramé purse that matched her shoes onto her shoulder.

"I ain't barging, I care." Ruby's warble faded some. All those pissy thoughts she'd been hoarding up inside her craw wanted to come out at the same time, but she let only one through. "I'm your momma. In the same way that you're a momma!"

"Look, leave me alone." She brushed past Ruby and out the door as she spoke. "You don't need to worry. I thought you would have forgotten all about me by now."

"That's silly. Why would I forget you?" Ruby stepped off the curb, trailing behind Violet. "Have you forgotten Bunny and Bubbie?"

At the mention of their names Violet stopped, then walked on a few more paces. "Forget?" She stopped again, turned to look at Ruby, then straightened her dress with her hands. She rolled her eyes, shook her head, then headed off again. "I really have to go. Really. I have important things to do." She went into a full trot.

Ruby speeded up her pace and tried to step in front of Violet. She wanted to block her way for once. Make her take notice. But it wasn't that easy to do. "Violet, we're all at a motel in Hollywood." She tried to find another sign. A sign that Violet had missed them. "We've come to see you."

"You went to way too much trouble," Violet said over her shoulder as she arrived at the Dodge Dart's driver's side door. "I'm not going back. My life is here." Her tone stayed still as the Perdenales waters in August.

Ruby hadn't said anything about going back, but because Violet had gone right on into the pit of things, she let more of what sat stuck in her craw climb out. "You have responsibilities! You're a momma!" She even whammed her foot on the asphalt as she yelled it.

This made Violet look at Ruby, then at the ground. Ruby stood across the car from her as though maybe she'd get in the passenger side of the Dart. With the convertible top down it seemed they were almost, but not quite, next to each other. She understands, Ruby thought. Then Violet looked up again and said, "You're that type. Not me." She waved as if to shoo off Ruby and opened her car door. "Your don't know what this is doing to me."

"I know what this *should* be doing to you!" Ruby yelled, her lips curling like a growling dog's.

Those violet eyes lifted to look at Ruby again. The stare said nothing to Ruby. The mouth turned down. She had been hurt by Ruby's words, but the wound wasn't the kind Ruby had intended. She wanted it to be a motivator. Instead, Violet caved inward. "I'm not capable," she said quietly. Her eyes now showed the hurt.

Ruby's ears rang from her own hollering, and her words now came out softer. "What do you want, Violet? What can we do to be—"

"Look, there's nothing you can do." She sighed long and deep. "Just let me be." She started to lower herself into the Dart but hesitated. "Thanks," she said, then climbed in.

Thanks? Ruby thought. That's all? "I don't want to be thanked!" she said as the car door closed. "I just want answers. We need to know." She opened the passenger side door of the convertible and slid in. "What about family? What about Texas?" She reached across the front seat to touch Violet's arm. She wanted to wrap her arms around her, but the electricity between them let her know she couldn't get that close. Violet's jaw was clenched.

"I gotta go." She wouldn't look at Ruby.

"You got two kids, Violet, two kids who wish they had a momma. And me, I miss you too." This last part came out with a quaver.

The words floated around Violet's ear. Then she shook her head a little like she was shaking off the images. She looked at Ruby's hand where it rested on the back of the seat. "It's Lety now." She started the Dart's engine.

"Lety, Violet, Paula. It doesn't matter. You're no different." She was, but she wasn't. She didn't have to be.

"Hey!" Jay hollered from the office. Ruby didn't hear him at first, didn't think he'd be calling to her. "You got a phone call."

Violet had closed her eyes in a wince. "I'm going to be late! Don't you get it?" She revved the motor and took the car out of park.

"You!" Jay said again, stepping out the door as Ruby turned around. "It's someone named Imogene. Says it's urgent."

Ruby didn't need this interruption now. Imogene couldn't stay out of anything, damn it. "Go tell Loralva over in the Trans Am," Ruby hollered back. She'd take care of it. She saw the boy shoot out across the asphalt to the black car.

"Violet! Listen to me!" Ruby couldn't stand it anymore. It was like talking to Imogene. "Bunny and Bubbie are *here*. In Hollywood. The least you can do is see them. Explain yourself!!" The last words a full-throttle scream. Paul's head peeked around the car he had come over to fill up at the next pump.

Violet shoved the car into drive, the engine going ca-chunk. Then, finally, she looked at Ruby. "I'm sure you went to a lot of trouble to find me." She let out a long breath. "But I don't have to do anything you tell me. I am not Violet Davidson from Devine, Texas, anymore!"

"Yes, you are," Ruby said. Then she just let it wail. "You are and always will be a momma. Ain't no way around that. Ever. You can leave, you can run away, you can do whatever little Violet Kincaid Davidson wants to do. You may not care how much stomping on hearts you do. You may even think your heart's been squashed so you got every right to do what you did. But you don't ever quit being a momma once you become one. Oh, you can become a *bad* momma. You can become a momma who doesn't care, who deserts her kids, but you are still a momma." Ruby's arms flailed. "I raised you differently. I know I did." She tried to catch her breath, but kept going through the tightness in her throat. "Despite what I did you turned out just like your real momma." Violet turned and looked at Ruby straight on when she mentioned Arlene. "It's true," she continued. "You went and left your own flesh and blood, always went after what would serve you best, never took anyone else into consideration and were always wild. Wild ain't so bad. Loralva's wild and she manages to not hurt anything except the occasional tender man's heart." Ruby sat up sideways on the edge of the seat and looked at Violet and saw who really sat there. "When it comes to little ones, it ain't right for a person to only think of themselves." She got a big choke holding the words in her throat after that. The words knotted around themselves, she reckoned.

Out of the corner of her eye Ruby could see Jay leaning in the window of the Trans Am. Then the driver's side door opened and Loralva got out.

"Violet," Ruby continued, because she still had more to say and she had to say it. She didn't want to, but she had to. Her daughter looked up at her like she still didn't give a damn, but Ruby could tell she was faking, so she went ahead and dealt her last card. "What if I hadn't cared what sat on that front porch twenty years ago? What if I'd just left you there because it hadn't been convenient for *me*? Where would you be now?" Ruby had never wanted to think about that. "Huh?" she asked, forcing the question on her. The girl would have never survived. She watched as Violet's eyes got bigger.

"I left Bunny and Bubbie with you," Violet said. "I knew they'd be fine. Better off even, because they'd have you instead of me."

Loralva ran across the pavement in her high heels and came panting up to the car. "Ruby, we gotta get back to the motel." She opened Ruby's door. "Bubbie tried to drown Bunny. They want you back there." She looked at Violet. Ruby was already standing on the asphalt before the words were all the way out of Loralva mouth.

"Bubbie did what?" Ruby said. She sounded hoarse now. She turned to Violet. "This is because of you!" Oh, she was madder than she had ever been in her whole life. Madder than if she'd sat in a pen of scorpions. "Are you coming with us? Are you coming to the motel to show the kids their momma does care? Because they don't think you do, you know."

Violet's purple eyes, wide as hubcaps how, wavered between Ruby's and Loralva's.

"Imogene said we need to hurry. An ambulance is on the way," Loralva said.

"An ambulance?" Ruby got the urgency now. She knew the seconds counted. No more time for Violet. "You coming?"

Violet opened her mouth to speak, then didn't. Ruby couldn't wait with the kids in trouble. That hesitation of Violet's gave everything away. She didn't have what Ruby had, that instinct to go now before it was too late. A real momma wouldn't hesitate. To Ruby, you didn't think about options.

Frog Legs

Penny and Warren's apartment in back of the motel office smelled of menthol cigarettes and coconut. Ruby hadn't even stepped all the way through the door from the registration desk before Bubbie was wrapped around her legs. He hiccuped. She could tell he'd been crying for a while. Bunny lay on the couch covered in a blanket. Ruby made her way toward her as well as she could with Bubbie not letting go.

"Let me go see Bunny," she told him.

Penny sat at the end of the couch by Bunny's feet. Her hair lay flat against her head and her velour pantsuit had crushed velvet crinkles to it. "She's been sleeping. All pooped out from breathing in all that water. The EMT fellas said she'd be fine."

During their drive back, Loralva had told Ruby what Imogene had said on the phone. When she walked in the door, Imogene tried explaining again, hysterically, not making much sense because she wouldn't place anybody anywhere, especially herself. But Ruby got the gist, that Imogene had come back from the police station and took charge of the kids again from

Penny, dropped them at the pool, then had gone to the motel room to use the bathroom. Barbi had witnessed the whole thing. Penny finally came out to pool to see what the ruckus was about and dove in and saved Bunny.

"That boy needs to be forbidden to ever be near his sister again," Imogene said, standing across the room switching feet incessantly, her arms crossed tightly on her chest.

Ruby put her hand on Bubbie's prickly crew-cut, looking down at him. His eyes gazed up at her pleading, like he didn't want his Mimaw Imogene to hear. "They were playing Frog Legs," Imogene snapped. Ruby'd seen them play this game before. Bubbie'd grab Bunny's legs and she'd try to pull him along as she swam away, or he'd swim and pull her. Usually the kid being pulled got their nose kicked or their jaw knocked, but something like this had never happened—a near drowning—not even close. If a kid got choked up the other just let go.

Ruby peeled the little boy off of her as she knelt on the ground to pat Bunny. "GranMomma," she said, "I almost drowneded." And reached for Ruby's neck.

"How you feeling, Bunny hon?"

"I saw the underside of the water like a mirror." Her nose stopped up, her pigtails matted.

"Did you? Well, I saw your momma today," Ruby said to both.

Imogene was at their side before either kid could even let it register. "You saw Violet? Why didn't you say so? Where is she now? What did she say? Should I—" She tugged on her sideburn trying to reach the mole.

"Is she coming to see me?" Bunny asked.

For the first time Bubbie looked scared instead of angry at the mention of his momma. The air to Ruby's brain was cut off by the lump in her throat, which grew as she realized what she should have told the kids a long time ago. She'd have to tell them what Bubbie already knew and what Bunny refused to accept. And that they'd all get by.

Later in their own motel room, they all sat in front of the TV and watched Bugs Bunny being chased off by Yosemite Sam firing his shotgun. Loralva sat between Ruby and Imogene, who kept complaining that the air conditioner blew on her face. Ruby would have traded places with her, but Bubbie had tucked his head under her arm and fallen asleep and she didn't want to wake him up. He'd cried for nearly two hours nonstop and she wanted him to sleep soundly for a while at least. Bunny sat between her great-aunt Loralva and Ruby.

"What I don't understand," Ruby said, "was why Barbi didn't do anything."

"Maybe she can't swim," Loralva said.

"Couldn't be that." Ruby shook her head. "She'd have at least gotten out of her chaise lounge and tried to reach for one of their hands."

"She said it never occurred to her," Imogene said, faking a shiver. She knew better than to be angry when she'd left the kids alone at the pool. Right now Imogene was sitting in the hot seat. Bubbie hadn't tried to drown Bunny at all. They'd been playing Frog Legs, but finished that game and started playing Blind Man—a game they made up on their own, where they walked around the pool deck with their eyes closed until someone fell in. Bunny had fallen into the deep end and couldn't get her bearings, panicked and started to drown. Bubbie had jumped in after her to save her, but the little girl was fighting so hard that he got kicked under. That was when Imogene walked through the pool gates and made her own assumptions. From Bunny and Bubbie's stories, Ruby had had to deduce the truth.

By the time Penny finally pulled them both out of the water, Bunny was in dire straits and Imogene started her ranting. Bubbie immediately believed he'd done more harm than good when Imogene accused him of trying to drown his little sister. When Warren yelled out the motel office door that the ambulance was on its way, it scared the boy into talking again, and he told everyone around him that he was sorry about everything, absolutely everything. Penny told Ruby the boy couldn't be consoled and kept saying, "And now GranMomma's gone too!"

Sitting in the motel room with everyone quieted down, Ruby knew that the skunk-headed lady wasn't feeling anything more than embarrassment about the whole thing.

Ruby's anger was fading. In the car on the way home, Loralva had said that she understood Violet. She had never wanted kids either. "But you never had them," Ruby said in response, her voice echoing around the beige interior of the sports car's low ceiling.

"I ain't saying what she done is right, leaving them and all. I'm just saying she wanted to follow her dream and she didn't want to be a momma living in a small town." Loralva careened through the cars on the freeway to get them back quickly.

"Yeah," Ruby said, calming down a little, but still worried about Bunny to no end. "Violet's first mistake may have been having them in the first place." She watched the freeway overpass go by through the T-top. "But I'm glad she did," she said.

Now, sitting on the couch, Ruby rehashed it all in her head. Violet may have been empty inside, but her kids weren't. Bubbie could be angry, but he caved at the end. Violet had never done that. She was like a heart that didn't beat, drained of blood. When Ruby had returned Bubbie whispered in her ear, "I'm sorry, GranMomma." Then he cried and cried, saying, "I didn't mean to—I won't never ever—" His little tightened body trembled with what must have been a boiling-over point, because Ruby said to him, "You're just so mad at your momma, ain't you?" and he bawled without stopping, a wail like his daddy's fire engine.

"Maybe I should go back to that Phillips 66 station myself and wait for her to come back." Imogene turned and looked at Loralva and Ruby on the couch. "Did you get her license plate number? I would have at least thought of that." Imogene got rigid as she tried so hard to hold back her natural impulse to harp on things.

Loralva looked her up and down so that Ruby didn't have to. "What's the point? Harley's already married to somebody else now." Imogene had finally gotten hold of Harley and sure enough he and Becca Ann had run off to Mexico to marry. Said the floods had them running scared and they didn't want to wait any longer. Turned out it was considered a completely legal union in the United States as well.

"We're heading back to Devine tomorrow, Imogene. No point in waiting around," Ruby said.

"Tomorrow?" Loralva asked. And Bunny turned her head up to Ruby too, along with Mrs. Beasley.

"We got what we came for," Ruby said.

"Actually we didn't," Imogene said.

Loralva stood up. "Then I better be saying good-bye to Duke."

Ruby could tell her sister was flustered, which she didn't usually get over a man. "Sorry, Loralva, it just seems important to get us all back to Devine as soon as we can. Texas is home."

"Never should have made this trip," Imogene said under her breath and Ruby could tell the true Imogene was coming back to the surface. She had felt guilty longer than usual. She'd be back to ranting and raving by morning.

Bubbie snuggled deeper under Ruby's arm, his mange spot all but gone. Bunny went over and lay on a pillow by the television set, picking her little nose and sucking on Mrs. Beasley's cotton arm. She'd asked several times if her momma would come by anyway, maybe if she were good, or if she prayed to God, but Ruby told her none of those things would work. That it would take time, but eventually she would come to accept it. She hoped she was telling the truth. Ruby shifted her grandson to the side a bit, but made sure he still leaned against her.

The Devine Bowl

The Devine Bowl smelled a little moldy from all the rain and having been closed up for so long. The Methodist Church had quit holding Sunday services there when the parking lot flooded, and Suddy just closed up altogether. Ruby propped all the doors open that first day back. She even left them open while she ran the air conditioner. Big waste of money, she knew, but right then she had to get the bowling alley as spiffy as she could in time for league night, which was in just a few hours.

She surveyed the whole place after she propped open the last door. The dark saloon just to her left. Loralva would be arriving any minute to get the Idyll-On-Up up and running for the night. Straight ahead of her Ruby admired the six lanes of maple. Suddy had let Lane Two's pinsetter go ungreased, so it hung lop-sided. She'd have to go in the back and fix that before the games started. To her right was the Lustre King 300 ball polisher and the shoe rental counter. When it rained as bad as it had while they'd been gone, the shoes always got a little riper. She'd have to spray deodorizer in each pair. She wondered if she'd have enough time to get everything done before the league bowlers started arriving. Better hurry, she told herself, but didn't budge. It's just nice to be home, she thought.

The kids were outside playing. She could hear Bunny squealing and Bubbie laughing. He'd probably stuck a stinkbug in her face or made her touch a tarantula. Those damn spiders were such a nuisance around there. Harmless, but Bunny didn't know better yet.

With the door propped open, she hadn't heard the cowbell on the door jingle announcing him coming in, so when she turned around to begin deodorizing the shoes she found Earl leaning against the Food Alley counter. He startled her at first, but she was glad to see him. Surprised herself at just how glad. He'd been watching her, she could tell by the way his eyes didn't flicker when she turned around.

"Heard you were back," he said.

"We are, and without you know who," Ruby said. She hoped she didn't have to explain too much.

"You did all you could," he said. "You always do."

"Does it stink in here to you?" she asked, wanting to change the subject.

"Smells just like it always does, but even sweeter now that you're back." He tipped his hat and stood a little straighter. His Lone Star belt buckle caught a flash of fluorescent light.

Ruby smiled. She had that all-over good feeling like she got in Hollywood when Loralva told her Earl had a hankering for her. She had to get to work though. She wasn't Loralva and couldn't take time off to flirt. The bowling alley never would have become the place in all of Idyll County to be if she'd been a flirt. "Don't have time for small talk," she told him.

"That's okay," he replied. "I'll help."

Ruby started to say no, that it was okay, she could do it

herself. But she stopped herself. "Would you mind coming in back with me then?" she said instead. "I need help fixing the pinsetter on Lane Two."

They'd started to head back to the engine room when the phone rang. Ruby reached across the shoe rental counter for the receiver. "Hope that's my beer guy. The kegs have all run dry."

"Ruby honey!" It was Loralva instead. "I'm gonna be late!"

Of course, Ruby thought. Things are back to normal.

"But I got a good excuse," Loralva said.

As usual, Ruby figured. She nodded at Earl that she'd just be a second longer.

"Duke called from California. He wants me to come out and be on another game show! This time it's *The Match Game!*"

"The Match Game?" Ruby said.

"Yeah! Ain't it fabulous! That Gene Rayburn can sure make me laugh. And you gotta help me practice, Ruby honey!"